A Texas Romance

Book Eight, 1885-86

Praying my story gives God glory!

All of Caryl's Books

Historical Christian Texas Romances
Vow Unbroken – 1832 / *Hearts Stolen – 1839-1844*
Hope Reborn – 1850-51 / *Sins of the Mothers – 1851-53* /
Daughters of the Heart – 1853-54 / *Just Kin – 1861-65* / *At Liberty to Love – 1865-66* / *Covering Love – 1885-86*

Contemporary Christian
Red River Romances - *The Preacher's Faith* / *Sing a New Song* / *One and Done*
Apple Orchard Romances - *Lady Luck's a Loser*

Biblical Fiction
The Generations - *A Little Lower Than the Angels* / *Then the Deluge Comes* / *Replenish the Earth* / *Children of Eber*

Mid-Grade / Young Adult
River Bottom Ranch Stories - *The Adventures of Sergeant Socks: The Journey Home, bk 1* / *The Bravest Heart, bk 2* / *Amazing Graci, Guardian of the River Bottom Goats, bk 3*
Days of Dread Trilogy - *The King's Highway, bk 1*

Miscellaneous Novels
The Thief of Dreams >>> **Warning: not written for the Christian market!** / *The Price Paid (based on WWII true story)* / *Absolute Pi* (audio; mystery) / *Apple Orchard B&B* (now re-released as Lady Luck's a Loser)

Non-fiction
Great Firehouse Cooks of Texas / *Antiquing in North Texas* / *Story & Style, The Craft of Writing Creative Fiction*

5-Star reviews of Covering Love

…beautifully, cleverly written, almost a two in one [with] themes of family, forgiveness, trust and guidance. Another cracking novel in the Texas Romance epic. I am looking forward to the next instalment.

--Julia Wilson, Reader in the United Kingdom

I loved reading an amazing story filled with all the extended Buckmeyer's family members with younger ones' love story being shared. Great plots for each character…that brought laughter and tears throughout this great historical romance. McAdoo's books *must* be read by those who enjoy historical romance that are filled with clean, heartfelt romance and the Gospel!!

--Marilyn Ridgway, reader in Illinois

I so enjoyed the sweet, charming, and thrilling romance stories intertwined within Covering Love. Faced with life-threatening circumstances, love covers all. The love between our characters takes root and blossoms against all odds of parental expectations, an undesired betrothal, age differences, and more—love truly covers all. You will laugh, cry, and feel so good while reading Covering Love!

--Katie Fowler, blogger at A Reader's Brain

The author really doesn't hold back and she lets her faith shine through in the writing. This book has love, forgiveness, second chances, and a lot more. There are tasks put to characters that make you wonder if they can handle it or how the situation will turn out and the book doesn't disappoint.

--Ashley Winters, blogger at Ashley's Bookshelf

Texas Romance Characters in Covering Love ... *alphabetically*

in this story—fuller profiles of all the families after 'The End'

~ **Baylor, LEVI Bartholomew** – born November 2, 1817 orphaned at age five; was reared by Aunt Sue Baylor until fourteen, then Uncle Henry Buckmeyer, too, after he married Aunt Sue. Levi became husband to Rosaleen 'Sassy' or 'Rose' Fogelsong Nightingale Baylor and step-father to Charley Nightingale and Bart Baylor (Comanche Chief Bold Eagle's son); then Pa to Stephen Austin, Daniel Boone, Wallace Rusk, and Rachel Rose.

~ **Buckmeyer, Meri Charlotte** – born December 2, 1851 to Henry and May

~ **Buckmeyer, David Crockett** – born October 4, 1851 firstborn of Henry and May.

~ **Buckmeyer, Millicent MAY Meriwether** born August 23, 1808. Married Henry Buckmeyer in 1850 and gave birth to David Crockett in 1851 and Charlotte in 1854. MayMee is her grandmother name

~ **Buckmeyer, Patrick HENRY** - born March 6, 1798; married Susannah 'Sue' Baylor in 1832, and became a widower in Dec '44 at his son Houston's birth. Finding love again, he married May Meriwether in 1850 and fathered Crockett and Charlotte. And he's a PawPaw now.

~ **Buckmeyer, Sam HOUSTON** – born December 11, 1844. Henry and Sue's fifth child, first son. His mother passed at his birth, so was motherless until he was six years old.

~ **Eversole, CECELIA Carol 'CeCe' Buckmeyer** – born April 10, 1836. Henry and Sue's third child. Marries Elijah Eversole in 1854. Mother to Evelyn May born September 14, 1879

~ **Eversole, ELIJAH** – born January 2, 1826, moved to California in the gold rush days where his parents abandoned him as a teen. He followed in his father's blacksmith trade and loves inventing and building new helpful machines. Jethro Risen and Moses Jones make him a partner in a gold mine. He marries Cecelia Buckmeyer in 1854. Father to Evelyn May born September 14, 1879

~ **Eversole, EVELYN "EVIE" May** – born June 28, 1878 to Elijah and Cecelia Eversole

~ **Graves, BECCA Joy Risen** – born to Mary Rachel Buckmeyer Risen and Jethro (blood daughter of Clinton) April 10, 1853, ran off in 1869? And went North, met and married Randal Ramsey Graves

~ **Graves, DIEDRA** – born in September 29, 1868, orphaned at the age of eight and reared by her brother Randal

~ **Graves, RANDAL Ramsey**

~ **Graves, Zacharias 'ZACH' or 'BUBBA' Randal** – born to Randal and Becca Risen Graves March 6, 1884

~ **Moran, NASH** – New York business partner of Crockett Buckmeyer

~ **Nightingale, Charles 'CHARLEY' Nathaniel -** born son to a Comanche chief Feb 27 '40 to the captive third wife Rosaleen, but Charles Nightingale was his mother's husband and his blood father. Rescued in 1844 with his mother by Texas Rangers Levi Baylor and Wallace Rusk, he killed a man at ten when Comancheros came to steal him and his mother to return them to Bold Eagle. He marries Lacey Rose Langley in November, 1865. Father to ??Nathaniel (blood son of ?), ? (with Marah), and Nathaniel born June 28, 1870.

~ **Nightingale, NATHANIEL** – born June 28, 1870 to Charley and Lacey Rose

~ **Risen, JETHRO** – born September 22, 1830 partner of Moses Jones in a gold mine. Married Mary Rachel Buckmeyer Wheeler in 1853 and later that year, reconnected with his estranged father, Boaz. Founds the Mercy House Orphanage and Miners' Bank in San Francisco.

~ **Risen, MARY RACHEL Buckmeyer Wheeler** – born August 3, 1833. Henry and Sue's firstborn eloped with Caleb Wheeler in 1951 without Daddy's blessing and moved to San Francisco where she took over the renamed Lone Star Mercantile. Her husband soon murdered, she becomes the widowed mother of Susannah "SUSIE" Wheeler. Remarries Jethro Risen in 1853, adopted an orphan, Francine "FRANCY" and birthed baby girl Rebecca "BECCA" in April, 1853 (blood daughter of Edward Clinton) and Boaz Reuel, Jethro's firstborn son, in December, 1854.

Covering Love

Caryl McAdoo

© 2017 by Caryl McAdoo

First Edition January 27, 2017

Printed and bound in the United States of America

ISBN-13 : 978-1540-7044-67

ISBN-10 : 1540-7044-67

For contact with the author or speaking engagements, please visit www.CarylMcAdoo.com
or write Post Office Box 622, Clarksville, Texas 75426

Dedication

I dedicate this story to my *Father in Heaven*. His Word is a light unto the path He guides me along, and I love it more than any other book in the world. I'm so grateful to Him for giving me stories to share and pray that He gives me opportunities to be a blessing every day.

My beloved husband certainly deserves it to be dedicated to him. He doesn't only *tell* me that he loves me almost every day, he *shows* me in so many ways. Like Christ, *Ron* knows me best and loves me still and always puts me first over himself—even though I call him a turkey buzzard sometimes. He is always reminding me that Love covers a multitude of sin and encouraging me.

I've probably said it a hundred times, but I think I know how Mary, the mother of Yeshua, felt when she told Gabriel, "Blessed am I among women" because I am so blessed having him as my husband. God could have chosen so many wonderful women, but He chose me to be Ron's wife, evidence of His overwhelming love for me . . . little ol' me!

And I'll dedicate it also to the lady in my life who's heard all of my grumbles through the years, known my sins and loved me through them all, prayed for me—I'm pretty sure on a daily basis—stood by my side through thick and thin, never judging, always only loving, supported me in all the crazy things I've done since the age of twenty-five when we first met and became 'sister-friends', *Elaine Vincent.*

Her love has certainly covered a multitude of sins!

Hatred stirreth up strifes:
but love covereth all sins.

Proverbs 10:12

Acknowledgements

You've given me a vision of amazing things to come. You've called me into service to advance Your Kingdom. All I want to do is sing Your praise and glorify You all my days! Father draw me ever closer . . . while I wait.

While I wait, make me a blessing to everyone I know. While I wait keep hope alive, Lord. I long to please You so. While I wait, I'll trust You deeper, knowing You are on the throne. I will wait. I will wait on You alone. (lyrics of a new song He gave me) I love You, Abba!

And I love you, husband of mine. You are such a gift to me. Thank you for giving yourself to care for me and our babies, your faithfulness, your patience, kindness, and gentleness! I've enjoyed growing old with you, my Ron, and look forward to many more years together in service of the King. Thank you for loving God so much and guiding me and the children to love and trust Him.

I want to thank Ruthie Madison for helping me with this cover and finding the perfect lady to be May's daughter. You stayed with me through all my persnickety changes to get it just perfect!

So thankful am I for Lenda Selph, my proofreader! And Louise Koiner, Cassandra Wessel, and Marilyn Ridgway for editing help on this one, too. Y'all's sharp eyes on my manuscripts are such a blessing to me. Thank you for your thoroughness and love.

Acknowledging my readers is always necessary because you are the ones who read my stories and enjoy them and tell your friends! I appreciate your time and your financial support and hope you will pray for me to always stay focused on giving God glory in all I do! Hugs for leaving all those wonderful reviews, clicking 'Share' and 'Like' on Facebook, and your tweeting, too. May God bless you and give you favor for blessing me so big.

A new commandment I give unto you, That ye love one another; as I have loved you, that ye also love one another. By this shall all men know that ye are my disciples, if ye have love one to another.   John 13:34-35

Be kindly affectioned one to another with brotherly love; in honour preferring one another;   Romans 12:10

Beloved, let us love one another: for love is of God; and every one that loveth is born of God, and knoweth God. He that loveth not knoweth not God; for God is love.

1 John 4:7-8

Chapter One

A sob sounded; something akin to a kitten crying for its mama. Evie cocked her head and closed one eye just like the captain, but she still couldn't tell what made the noise. She returned to her story.

How she loved this part! It would always be her favorite adventure of Red Rooster, the Gentleman Pirate.

Someone rapped lightly on her door, then it creaked open. "Baby doll?"

"Up here, Daddy." She closed her book then hurried to the slide and slid into his waiting arms. As always, he caught her, and twirled her around three times. She kissed his cheek. "I'm so glad that you're home early. I missed you."

"Well, I've got some sad news. Your grandfather got bucked off a new horse, so we're going to Texas."

"No! That couldn't be!" She pushed out of his arms and wiggled to the floor. "Why, everyone says PawPaw is the best horseman ever. And Mama said there's not a horse he can't ride. You've heard her say it a million times. Are you teasing me? Because if you are, this isn't very funny."

"Not this time, baby. I wouldn't tease about this. He did get thrown and hurt himself bad. I've come to assist you getting packed." He bowed. "I'm at your service, young miss. We leave for the train in two hours."

Wow, to Texas! And she'd get to ride the train! She'd not been to the Lone Star State in two years and could only remember bits and pieces of that trip.

In her prayers, she told God she couldn't wait until next year to meet her new pony that PawPaw bought especially for her. But she never meant for him to get hurt.

That made her so sad.

"He'll get better right, Daddy? Him and MayMee are still coming for Thanksgiving. Isn't that right? Because in her letter, she promised she'd bring me her new Red Rooster book. And we're still going back to Texas after the new year, right? Just like we already planned?"

"We'll have to see, Evie."

"You know how much I really love the whales in this story, but I'm not finished reading it again yet. It's his . . ." She closed the book and held out the front cover. "See? *The San Juan Islands Adventure* story, and he's been seeing killer whales! Those are the huge black and white ones."

"That's great. Now we need to pack your bag. Where is it? You can bring your book along to read on the train. Bring two or three."

"Well, I think we should wait and go tomorrow after Sally's birthday party. Because I don't want to miss it at all, and besides, I have a wonderful present for her. Do you want to know what it is? Do you, Daddy?"

"Not now, Evelyn." He opened her closet door. "Where is your carpetbag? We're running out of time."

What was wrong with him? She glared. He never hardly ever called her by her proper name, and he wasn't listening. That just wasn't right. How could she leave in two hours when the party wasn't until tomorrow? "But Daddy."

"No buts."

"Still, we can't leave now! Mama knows how bad I want to go Sally's party." Tears welled. "PawPaw can't be hurt that bad. He'll understand if we're one day later. And . . . and . . ."

Another sob silenced her. She raced toward her parents' room, riding the banister to the bottom, then flung open their door without bothering to knock—one of her daddy's strictest rules—but she didn't care that day.

Being upstairs, he wouldn't know anyway. He couldn't beat her there because he never ran in the house or slid down the banister.

Her mother stood beside the bed, staring at her open steamer trunk, crying.

"Mama?"

She turned toward Evie and held her arms out. Her eyes were all red, and tears wet her cheeks. It was true. PawPaw must be hurt really bad. It broke her heart to see her mother so sad. She forgot all about Sally and the party.

What kind of monster horse could buck PawPaw off?

Like trying to pour backstrap molasses on a cold day, getting ready for the train seemed horribly slow, but Daddy got it all done.

Holding Mama's hand tight, Evie climbed aboard the huge metal car then watched out the window for Aunt Mary Rachel and Uncle Jethro. They finally got there, but no one else boarded. Where were all her cousins?

Weren't they coming? Would she have anyone at all to play with?

Whoosh. Chug. Then another whoosh sounded, followed by faster chugs.

The station moved behind her. The whistle blew loud two times. How could that be? Evie pressed her nose to the glass. The few folks who still stood on the boardwalk waved.

White smoke from the train filled the late afternoon sky, blocking out the sun's brightness.

Her cousins must not love PawPaw or want to see him get better. She watched for a bit longer, then sat back down next to her mother, leaning in tight against her. The whole car must be just for them. That part seemed fun, but still . . . no one to play with . . .

Only she hardly ever had playmates except when she went to school . . . or Mama went visiting.

But knowing that a bad horse hurt PawPaw was worse than not having anyone to play with, and her mother being so sad, the very worst.

Was he crying like Mama?

A nice man with white gloves came with a cart full of food. She chose the roast beef and took some of the carrots, but no potatoes—and never any smelly onions. Oooo, she hated those. Even thinking about them made her want to spit. She got a little bowl of green beans, too.

None of it tasted good as what Cookie served, but then no one else's food ever did.

After eating almost all of it, she set her napkin on her plate and smiled at her father. "Daddy, once PawPaw teaches me to ride, can we bring my Twinkle Toes back to California? He's all mine you know. He bought him just for me, so I don't have to share him with my Texas cousins, and he can surely come to California."

"We'll see, but he might be sad to leave his home there."

"But he'd have me instead of all his horse friends, and . . . PawPaw called Twink the perfect horse for me. I'm for sure and for certain he'll love me as much as I already love him." She turned toward her mother. "Remember, Mama? MayMee put it in her letter."

"Yes, baby, I remember. But your grandfather may not . . ." She looked away, holding her bottom lip with her top teeth like maybe she was trying not to cry again.

Evie hated it whenever Mama cried. If they lined up all the mothers in the whole world, she'd choose hers every time. "Don't worry, Mama. He'll be better by the time we get there, right?"

"I hope so, baby girl."

That evening, she read some while the grownups talked, but she listened, too. Aunt Mary Rachel said something about him being eighty-seven. Evie never knew anyone that old.

PawPaw must have lived a long time . . . almost forever. Then Uncle Jethro talked about what a good life the great man had lived.

Why was he saying that? Did he think PawPaw might die? She never thought about that. How could he? What about him teaching her to ride?

Every time she glanced up, out of the corner of her eye, she'd catch one of them looking at the other with worried, sad faces. Daddy's and Uncle Jethro's weren't as gloomy as her aunt's and mother's.

Sometimes, the adults used code words and moved their lips without making any sounds. Did they think she was a baby or something? That they couldn't talk about the truth around her? Well, she could fix that.

Way before she even got sleepy, she started bobbing her head on purpose. Then after a while, she slumped over next to her mama and play-acted asleep. Exactly as she figured, real quick the big people started talking like she couldn't hear every word.

Mostly stuff she already knew.

They told lots of good stories about PawPaw though.

How he'd fought in three wars and been stabbed with an Arkansas toothpick and got shot in the shoulder; about the time the Indians came to steal back Aunt Rose, how he saved Miss Jewel and Mister Jean Paul—plus lots of their relatives—from being slaves, and many more.

Then they started talking about his accident.

Uncle Jethro piped up and told them what he'd heard. "Right after we got the telegram, I walked over to Doctor Theleman's and told him what happened to Henry. He made it sound like a miracle that a man his age even survived."

Of course, her pawpaw would live! No fall off a horse could do him in. He could sir vive anything because she loved him too much. And so did Mama.

Besides, everyone always said he was one tough old bird.

She sat straight up and glared at her uncle. "He's going to be fine. I know it. Doctor Theleman doesn't know everything. God can heal PawPaw. Can't He, Mama?"

Tears erupted. Maybe her grandfather might go to Heaven.

Her mama wrapped her up tight with her arms. "I'm with you, Evie. God and your PawPaw can do anything."

Henry stepped to the shore's edge. His mother and his beautiful Susannah waved. Blue Dog, at his wife's side, wagged his tail. Was that Wallace standing next to him on the other side? Mercy.

How many years had it been? Where was May?

"PawPaw."

He turned around. His favorite granddaughter held her arms out. He glanced back across the water. Everyone smiled and waved for him to come over, but he turned back and took a step toward the six-year-old.

Intense pain radiated from his side. Someone moaned. A hand touched his.

"Sweetheart, do you want more laudanum?"

Opening his eyes, he found May standing next to him. There she was. "Anyone here yet?"

"No, darling. They haven't had time, but they're on their way. They left Thursday, and today's Friday, so they should be here sometime tomorrow."

"So soon?" He coughed, and the pain worsened.

"They're coming by train."

"It is, my love. Yes, to that painkiller. And a whiskey chaser. That stuff tastes terrible."

"A please-ma'am would be nice, you old goat." With everything ready, she elevated his head and poured the medicine down his gullet.

Soon enough, the barking agony quieted some. "I dreamed of Evelyn. I really want to see her one more time."

"Tomorrow dear . . . maybe sometime late today, but . . ."
He nodded toward the bottle of opium. "I know. Give me
another sip, please. Maybe I can doze off again."

The iron wheels squealed. Evie pressed her nose to the cool
window glass. Sparks flew as the train slowed. "They must be
stopping to get more water. That's what makes the locomotive's
steam engine run. Right, Daddy?"

"Yes, baby girl." He didn't look up from his stupid newspaper.
Why he wanted to read all that boring stuff, she didn't know.
She offered a smile, though he probably wouldn't even see it, and
she didn't really much want to anyway.

"Well, it is. The nice man told me all about it, and it runs on
steam from hot water. "

"That's good." He nodded, but still didn't bother looking over
at her.

She exhaled through her mouth, but that didn't work either.

Maybe she'd read, too. She reached for her book, but right
before her fingers touched the binding, she changed her mind and
retrieved her cigar box with all the letters from PawPaw and
MayMee. She especially liked the ones he wrote all by himself.

Easy to tell them apart, too, because her grandmother spelled
better and had a prettier penmanship, but she didn't . . . well, she
loved Evie . . . but she probably wasn't her maymee's favorite—
not like her pawpaw. He didn't mind telling anyone who would
listen that she was his favorite granddaughter in the whole wide
world.

She loved him best of all.

And like the big clock in the hall bonged right on time every
day, every hour, his letters arrived once a week, no matter what.
She read the one where he first told her about Twinkle Toes—one
of her favorites, and she'd finally get to meet her pony.

Would Mama and Daddy stay long enough for PawPaw to get
healed so he could teach her how to ride?

Folding it nicely and returning it to her box, she looked up and started to ask her daddy again. Oh, well, still reading.

And besides, she'd already rubbed him red asking so many questions about when her pawpaw would be well. She hoped the doctors got him all fixed up fine and fancy and everything.

Sounding the letters out, she figured the sign on the train station said Austin, Texas. Her grandparents didn't live in the capital though. They lived in Llano, but the train didn't go there. Austin was the closest place it stopped.

That's what the nice man told her.

Her parents and Aunt Mary Rachel talked about it only took thirty-three hours to get from California to the Lone Star State's capital. Sure seemed way longer than that though. Maybe more like a week.

Thinking of her friend, she regretted missing the party again, but hoped she liked the Red Rooster book MayMee signed especially for her and the special pink satchel Evie begged Mama to get so Sally would have a bag to keep all her books in. Cookie promised to see to it that she got it on time for her party.

Right there at the station, a fancy carriage waited for them. A team of six beautiful horses—that all matched no less—would take them to PawPaw's. Two men loaded all the bags and trunks then climbed up in the high top seat.

"Why are there two mister drivers, Mama?"

"One will drive, and the other is his helper who makes sure no highway men try to stop us. They say the second man rides shotgun."

"Like pirates! Except I didn't see any shotgun. He only had those two big six-shooters—one on each hip like that terrible, mean ol' Black Bull. 'Member him? The villain Red Rooster had to fight to save Madam Merciful. Do you remember?" She turned to her father. "Daddy, are there pirates here about in Texas?"

"No, but sometimes they have desperadoes."

"What is a desperado?"

"A bad man who steals."

"I never heard of one, but MayMee ought to have Red Rooster fight one of those guys, too. Do you suppose Black Bull was a desperado?"

"Could be."

Why wouldn't he listen well to her?

He might only be pulling her leg though because he teased her all the time, so she kept an eye out for the truth. She'd really hate getting waylaid or shipwrecked or anything bad. She needed to get to Llano to kiss her pawpaw's hurts away, just like her mama made hers vanish.

"Evie, wake up. We're here."

She sat up, rubbed her eyes, and looked around. Here where? Then she saw the house. Oh, yes, she remembered. "We're at PawPaw's already?"

"Yes, dear."

She waited for her daddy to climb out of the carriage first then leapt off into his arms. He didn't twirl her. Just set her down. Where's the fun in that? She backed up a couple of steps then turned and ran up onto the porch, flying to her pawpaw's room.

A tall boy, one she didn't know, stood in front of the door. He looked all dressed up in his church clothes like maybe he'd come from a funeral, since it wasn't Sunday.

"Move, please. You're in my way."

"You can't come in right now. My father and grandfather are tending to the General."

"Who?" Then she remembered a lot of folks called her grandfather the General on account of he ran the war once. But for a long time, he'd only been PawPaw. "Never you mind. He's my pawpaw, and I've come all the way from San Francisco. That's in California. So you need to get out of my way."

The boy shook his head. "No, not yet. They'll let us know. Who are you anyway?"

"I'm Evelyn May Eversole, but most everyone calls me Evie. Who are you?"

"Nathaniel Nightingale."

"Who's your daddy? And your granddaddy? Do I know them? Are you one of my cousins? I have a lot of them."

"Charley Nightingale's my pa, and Levi Baylor's my grandpa. Who's yours?"

"Oh! Then you probably are my cousin! You see, I know Uncle Charley and Aunt Lacey—she's your mother."

"I know."

"And Levi Baylor? Humph. Everyone knows him, sure enough. He's the greatest Texas Ranger who ever lived."

"I know."

"But how come I don't you? How old are you, Nathan? I'm six."

"Not Nathan, Nathaniel. And I'm fifteen. I have no idea why you don't know me. Maybe because you've never been to Clarksville. That's where we live. Is Aunt CeCe your mama? Or Aunt Mary Rachel?"

"Cecelia Eversole, and Elijah is my father. Now would you please get out of my way? I'm PawPaw's favorite granddaughter, and I've come to kiss him well."

Nathaniel laughed then shook his head as if he didn't believe her. She balled both fists, pursed her lips, and glared. But he still didn't move.

"Evie? Is that my baby girl? Let her in."

The door opened, and she shot past Mister Nightingale, giving him an elbow and a smirk on her way by. She ran to PawPaw's bed.

Chapter Two

Henry bit back the pain and forced his lips to smile. "My favorite baby girl. I'm so glad to see you."

She took his hand into hers then bent over and kissed it. "There, PawPaw. Now you can get all better."

If only it were that easy. "I'm afraid not, Evie." He looked past the little one to her mother, standing right behind her. Mary Rachel stood next to her, then half a room of folks. "Where's Crockett?"

"Not here yet, Daddy, but he's on his way."

He nodded. "Alright then. Everyone get out now, I'm not going anywhere yet."

"But PawPaw, you can't go anywhere! Remember? You promised to teach me how to ride Twinkle Toes. Why, I haven't even met my pony yet because I came straight to see you first. I needed to kiss your hurt away."

"That's right, I did promise. Nathaniel? You in here, Son?"

The boy stepped forward past his father and grandfather and stood ramrod straight. "Yes, sir, General. Right here, sir."

"A boon, Son?"

"Yes, sir, of course. Anything."

"Teach my favorite granddaughter here how to ride."

"Yes, sir."

"Good. Now I need the room. Please, everyone but Levi and May can go do something else."

In mere seconds, they vacated his abode. He faced the man who couldn't be more son if Buckmeyer blood ran through his veins, which it did not. "You finally going to stand for governor?"

Levi laughed, then shook his head. "Wouldn't be any fun without Rose at my side. And if you'll remember, I just turned sixty-seven. No one wants an old man like me in Austin."

"Same argument you used last time about you running."

"Yes, sir. Guess I'm a lot like my favorite uncle. He never ran for any office either, though he should have been President."

"You flatter me." His hip barked louder than he could stand. "Oh, Lord, get my boy home soon. May, where's that laudanum?"

"Right here, my love." She slipped her hand under his head and lifted him enough to get a double slug down. "Whiskey?"

"Please."

"Here, sir." Levi held the bottle to his lips.

"I love you both."

The drug worked, but his wife and nephew vanished, and he stood once more on the shore of the glass-like sea. But no one waved from the other side.

A mist rolled in, and Sue suddenly stood next to him. He'd forgotten how beautiful she was, the tilt of her chin and the twinkles in her eyes.

But she didn't look a day older than when he first saw her on the porch of that trading post, her hair blowing in the wind of that storm coming in. He loved her from that moment on.

Had she come to carry him home?

Where was his mother? And Wallace and . . .

"Not yet, my dearest Henry. The Lord has granted your request, and you may stay until Crockett gets home."

"Praise His name." He intertwined his fingers into his first wife's as he'd done a thousand times. Unlike Jacob, he didn't know which of his two brides he loved most. "Have you seen Evie?"

"No."

"Oh, Sue, she's exactly like your daddy described you at her age." He chuckled. "CeCe and Elijah brought her from California the first time a couple of years ago, think she was four. Exactly like you, though, already reading."

"I so look forward to meeting her."

"We've been writing letters back and forth, one a week. I found her a pony, and she named him Twinkle Toes."

She touched his cheek. "I'll see you again soon, Husband. Tell all my babies I love them."

The minute she laid eyes on the beautiful spotted pony, little bumps came all over her arms and legs. Evie fell head over hills in love.

His almost-white silvery mane hung down longer than his neck, and his beautiful tail hung almost to the ground. They shone like a golden light, and the sun lit up their silver strands.

His shiny coat was the color of her daddy's Winchester barrel right after he'd polish it to a sheen, and Twinkle Toes had round silver spots, on his hips mostly, some lighter ones all over.

Oh, how she wanted to go right in there and hug him . . . but knowing how bad a horse hurt PawPaw—and him being a great horseman—she decided not to take any chances. Twinkle Toes was pretty big compared to her, so she stood outside the gate and talked to him, told him how beautiful he was and how much she loved him.

He walked right over and let her rub his nose then tossed his head.

The barn's little door opened.

Would she be in trouble for coming by herself? She ducked under the gate. Twink didn't even flinch. She peeked under the bottom board.

Only Nathaniel. But he'd taken off his church clothes and wore jeans with a blue shirt, a big hat, and some old scuffed boots. He looked like a real cowboy. She slumped back down.

"Evelyn? You in here? Your mama said she saw you come this way."

"What if I am?"

"Where are you? The General asked me to teach you to ride."

She crawled under the stall's gate into the barn's big middle part. "I want my pawpaw to teach me. He promised."

The boy neared then lowered to one knee, looking her square in the eye. "I'm sure you do, Evie, but he can't walk with a broken hip. No telling what else is messed up. Your pawpaw's in no shape to teach you anything. Much less how to ride."

"He still could! I know he could."

"But he asked me to do it as a special favor so here I am. Now . . . do you want to learn to ride or not?"

She liked Nathaniel's soft tone.

And that he didn't tower over her, but came down to her level. Plus, he was rather handsome. She hadn't noticed before the intense color of his eyes; like the summer sky's deepest blue on a cloudless day over the Pacific.

All of a sudden she got those same little bumps all over her arms and legs.

"Fine then. You can teach me because I do want to learn to ride properly."

"Good."

"But only for today. PawPaw will be better tomorrow . . . or the day after. You can give me lessons until then."

Standing, he extended his hand. "Come on, let's get to it."

"His name is Twinkle Toes. Like Merrylegs in Black Beauty. Sometimes, I call him Twink for short. Like Evie—that's my nickname everyone calls me. How did you know my real name?"

"Guess I heard it somewhere."

"Well, I like you calling me by it. You say it very pretty."

He laughed. "Pretty name for a pretty young lady."

"Thank you."

After brushing her pony really good all over then feeling all four legs for hot spots and looking at all his hooves for rocks just like Nathaniel showed her, she had to smell of each frog to make sure there weren't any problems.

Her new teacher finally pronounced Twinkle Toes ready to saddle. He didn't seem to mind that she asked so many questions.

She really wanted to know why he did—or had her do— everything concerning the pony PawPaw bought especially for her.

The boy acted so nice and polite, too, for taking the time to explain it all. PawPaw would do that, so it was almost like him teaching her. He answered all her questions and really listened. She loved that about Nathaniel as well.

After putting the bit in Twink's mouth very gently and buckling the bridle's leather straps that went behind his ears, he picked up a square of heavy wool. "Blanket first then the saddle. Always from the left side."

"Why? Do horses know right from left?"

One shoulder hiked a bit, and he glanced down, smiling. "Never thought to ask anyone the why of it. Guess on account of it's . . . just . . . how it's done. Maybe because most folks are right handed?"

"That sounds like a good reason." She liked that. Asking a question he didn't know the answer to and him admitting it instead of lying or making up something. She could always tell when someone lied.

Holding out the reins toward her, he grinned. "Here you go, little miss. He's all ready. Now lead him on out."

Her breath caught. Flutterbyes swarmed her tummy, but Twinkle Toes was her pony, and PawPaw said in his letter that he acted very well-behaved. He wrote that the silver-dappled gray had been trained by the best.

To be certain, he'd be very good and gentle pony. He'd told her she'd be an excellent horselady, too.

So, she couldn't act the baby, especially not with Nathaniel standing right there watching. She filled her lungs and took the leather straps then clucked a couple of times like she'd seen him do.

"Come on, Twinkle Toes. Time for a ride!" She strolled out of the stall, and he followed along perfectly as though she'd been leading her horse around all her life.

The pen at the back of the barn—Nathaniel called it a corral— was big, but not too huge. She stopped once inside, then he followed, closing the gate behind himself. He held his hands out. "Want me to lift you up?"

She tried to say yes, but could only manage a nod. Hands so strong, but very gentle, lifted her high and into the saddle, almost as if she weighed no more than a seagull's feather. The saddle felt good and made her almost as tall as him.

Well, the ground was a long way down there.

Unaware of what to expect, she definitely didn't anticipate the pony would do nothing. But that's exactly what her Twink did. He didn't buck or run or rear or act a fool in any way. He just stood there.

Exactly like PawPaw said. He was great, a perfect pretty spotted pony.

"Very softly, squeeze with your knees and touch your heels to his flanks. His flanks are right behind your feet where his rear legs join his body."

She did as told. "Like this?"

"Yes, ma'am."

Her steed moved. "I did it!" She was riding! "Yippee, cousin! Look at me! I'm riding. This is so much fun!"

He walked beside her as Twink carried her around the corral. "You do know we're not blood kin, don't you?"

She glanced over. She'd been so wrong about him in so many ways. "We're not?"

"No, ma'am. My father, Charles Nathaniel Nightingale was . . . well, his blood father was also a Charles, except my grandmother, Rosaleen Fogelsong didn't put junior on him, seeing as how . . ."

"It's alright. I know what Uncle Charley's real father did. Mama says he's a big . . . uh . . . mist. So Sassy is your mother.

You see, I've read *The Ranger* and *The Granger* and all of MayMee's pirate books. Did you know PawPaw is really Red Rooster, the Gentleman Pirate? Well, I mean, she made the gentleman to act just like PawPaw."

"I think you mean bigamist. Yes, he married two women at the same time." He laughed. "And for sure we all know about MayMee's books, and . . ." He turned toward the house. "Uh oh, looks like they want us to come in."

"Aww, do we have to? I barely got to ride any time at all." Her bottom lip pouted.

"It's getting late, and they probably want us to wash up for supper. You can ride some more tomorrow, but we still have to unsaddle him and brush him down."

"There's so much to do before and after. Promise I can ride again tomorrow?"

"Sure. Lord willing, and the creek don't rise."

"So you're a Christian? I am, too! I only got baptized a month ago, but I've been saved longer than that."

"Well, good for you. I'll open the gate, and you can ride him all the way back to his stall."

She did as told. Hmmm. Why didn't he tell her when he was saved? How could he not be? He surely knew Jesus. She needed to think on that.

In reverse order, Nathaniel got Twinkle Toes all nice and comfy in his stall with more help from her that time. She fetched a scoop of oats and put it in his feeder then threw him three pitchforks full of hay all by herself.

His water bucket was almost full, so she didn't need to haul any more right then.

Before she left, she wrapped her arms around his neck and squeezed as hard as she could. She loved her pony and loved that, no matter how hard she squeezed, it didn't hurt him because he was so strong and wonderful. PawPaw sure knew his stuff.

Twink was the perfect pony.

He nuzzled his nose against her.

"Would you look at that. He's loving you right back."

"He is?"

"Well, sure enough. But then you're probably the prettiest little cowgirl he ever saw."

"Well, thank you very much, but I'm not a cowgirl because Twink isn't a cow. I'm more of a horselady."

"I stand corrected. The prettiest horselady Twinkle Toes has ever seen."

She skipped all the way back to the big house, ran up the porch's steps and into the parlor where her parents and all her aunts and uncles sat around and visited.

Running straight to her daddy, she crawled into his lap. She couldn't wait to tell him, but Aunt Mary Rachel was talking about some boring art gallery in San Francisco, and Evie couldn't interrupt.

She either finished the story or took too long of a breath. Either way, Evie saw it as her opportunity.

"Did you see me riding Twinkle Toes, Daddy?"

"Yes, I did, baby."

She smiled then looked right at her Uncle Charley. "Do you suppose Nathaniel could come live with us in California? He could stay in my room with me."

Chapter Three

His father's jaw muscles tightened. Nathaniel had seen it so many times before; the old man trying not to laugh at someone. He bit his bottom lip, but still, it erupted.

A big roaring hoot that captured the whole room, passing around, first, giggles, then full-blown, belly-bending laughter. At least all but two—him and poor little Evelyn who obviously had no idea why what she said prompted the uproar.

Her eyes grew bigger and puddled.

Sliding out of her daddy's lap, she turned a slow three-sixty, wavering between glaring and about to burst into tears.

A few of the ladies seemed to try to stifle themselves, but most boomed, as though unable to stop their part in the merriment, like what the six-year-old had said was the funniest thing ever. She balled both fists then ran from the room.

Aunt Mary Rachel stuck out her hand. "Baby, come back! We're only . . ." More giggles trumped whatever she intended to say.

Nathaniel eased out and cold-trailed Evelyn to the barn. Found her right where he figured, in the stall with her pony. He leaned over the gate. "The General told me once about our Uncles Houston and Bart almost laughing themselves sick after a cavalry charge, during the Civil War."

She looked up. Red eyes and wet cheeks told the tale. "Go away, Nathaniel! I'm going to live here now with Twinkle Toes. He loves me. He'll never laugh at me."

"Anyway, wanted you to know your PawPaw told me after periods of high stress, the least little thing that's humorous can trigger an exaggerated emotional release. I figure that's what happened. Everyone is on edge about . . . ."

Him and his stupid mouth.

She stared, like waiting for the rest . . . or as if she needed the time for her boiler to heat up because then a bit of steam seeped out of her ears. "On edge about what?"

"The General."

"What? Because he got hurt?"

He'd done it now, but wouldn't lie to her. He shook his head.

"Then what? Tell me now why they were laughing so hard."

"You see . . . it's on account of . . . they're all so upset because . . . he's dying, sweet Evelyn. I'm sorry to have to tell you, but your grandfather is dying."

"He is not." She got to her feet and dared him with both fists on her hips. "That's a lie! Say it again, and I'll . . . I'll . . . ."

"I'd never lie to you, Evelyn. Especially about something like that. Pa says he's only hanging on because of Uncle Crockett not being here yet."

"No!" She flung the gate open. The hinges squealed, then it banged against the stall wall boards. "That can't be true!"

He held out his arms toward her, and she ran to them. He lifted her and hugged her tight as the girl's waterworks opened in earnest.

Evie buried her face in his shoulder. He smelled strong and clean. But what he said . . . it wasn't fair. Her pawpaw was one tough old bird. Everyone said it, and then, just because some stupid horse bucked him off, he had to die?

What would she ever do without his letters?

She loved hearing from him and looked forward to each one so much.

Plus, whom could she write to?

And what about the Red Rooster books? Would MayMee ever write another without her inspiration? PawPaw was almost always beside her.

She leaned out. "It isn't fair."

"I know. I love him, too. I don't know what I would have done without him and Mama May."

What? MayMee was his mother? Evie wiped her cheeks. He held her so gently, but his arms were so strong. "Why'd you call her that? Is she your mama? And why do you call PawPaw the General?"

"Oh, when I came here with Pap that time. Well . . . it's what he called them, and I liked it. It shows respect, don't you think?"

"I guess so." She pondered the confusing family relationships. "Who's your pap again?"

"Levi Baylor is my grandfather, and sometimes he calls yours the General . . . or Uncle Henry, but most times he seems to prefer using his old military rank. If we're around other men, Pa and I call my Pappy, Colonel. That was his rank, both in the war and with the Texas Rangers."

"But he was only a captain when he rescued Sassy . . . your daddy's mother. What do you call your grandmother again?"

"Gran."

She liked Nathaniel, liked him holding her. "Why do you suppose they were all laughing at me?"

His lips thinned, and he looked over her head.

"You promised not ever to lie to me. Now tell me and tell me true."

"Oh, I won't lie, but . . . well, it's . . . kind of hard if you're not grown up like me." He smiled. "Do you know about . . . uh . . .

hmmm . . . uh . . ." He studied the ceiling like looking for something.

"About grownups?"

"Well, yes. You know." He only met her eyes for a few seconds, then seemed to be looking all over that barn for something. "They get married and everything—after they fall in love. Only married couples—a man and woman—share a bedroom."

"But you don't have to be married. Sisters and brothers do, too."

"True. But we aren't . . . you know . . . siblings. Besides, that's girls with girls and boys with boys. Only after marriage do a male and a female share a bedroom."

"Oh." That made sense. "So they laughed because I said you could share my room?"

"Yes, that was pretty much it."

"Well, if your pa says yes, then when you come, we can go ahead and get married, then you can stay in my room with me. I've got the best room ever. Sally—she's my best friend—she loves visiting. We have high tea and play dolls, and . . ." She chuckled. "My daddy built me a slide for my reading nook."

"You have a nook just for reading?"

"Oh, yes. It used to be the attic, but he had some men come and help him turn it into my special place."

"Is that right?"

"Of course it is. I'll never lie to you either, Nathaniel. Anyway, you'll really love my special place. And Mama said she would make arrangements for Twinkle Toes to come to California and live at a farm only a few miles out of town. She said that I can go see him at least twice a week. I'll need you there if—"

"Whoa, girl. Slow down and take a breath. I can't come to San Francisco."

"Why not? You could teach me how to be the best horselady ever, just like the General asked you to. Remember? I like calling him that. Don't you think you need to keep your promise,

Nathaniel? Do you think just because he dies, you don't have to? Because I think—"

"I said, breathe."

She did as he told her. Actually took two good deep breaths.

The sorrow of her pawpaw having to die still saddened her heart, but the pain wasn't so sharp, not with thinking about Nathaniel coming home with her and getting married.

After all, he was about the most handsome boy she ever knew, and she loved him holding her tight. He never talked down to her like she was a baby, and he told her the truth.

It was so funny how red-faced he got, explaining why the grownups laughed. She still didn't think it was all that amusing. Mama always said time was aplenty for discussing all that stuff later.

But maybe with Nathaniel coming . . .

"There you two are."

She looked over his shoulder. Daddy hurried toward her.

"Evie, baby, we were not laughing at you."

"I know, Daddy. My cousin here—except that he's not really any blood kin at all—explained it all to me. Kind of like after a big battle, and . . ."

Wiggling free, she slid to the ground, slipped her hand into Nathaniel's, and tugged.

With her other, she grabbed her father's hand then pulled them both toward the patch of sunlight that had rays coming down from Heaven through the hayloft door upstairs. Lots of little particles danced in them.

"What's for supper?"

The drug-induced fog cleared. Henry didn't care much for reality, except it truly wasn't bad; a man knowing he was about to meet his Maker. He licked his lips then whistled two notes, the same ones he'd taught all his children.

Levi appeared at his bedside. "What can I get you, Uncle?"

"Where's May?"

"Sleeping I hope. I relieved her about an hour ago."

"Good. Fetch Rebecca, Mary Rachel, Gwendolyn, Cecelia and Bonnie Claire, then when I'm done." His voice cracked. He swallowed hard then obviously tried clearing his throat with a weak cough. "After them, I want Houston then you."

"Yes, sir." He turned.

"Son, before you go, get me a slug of laudanum and that whiskey bottle."

"Yes, sir."

Like always since he was fourteen years old, the man followed his orders. Before the drug wore off any at all, his and Sue's girls stood around his bed. Tears welled, but he blinked them back.

"I am so blessed." He smiled at his oldest. "You stole my heart from the first."

"I know, Daddy." Withholding none, tears streamed down her cheeks. "You were the answer to my prayer, and I loved you from the start—even if you couldn't sing." She laughed, and her sisters joined in.

"Poor Daddy." More giggles followed.

"Ladies, I've seen your mother twice now. She said to tell her babies that she loved you all, and that I could stay until Crockett arrives." He looked at each in turn then let his eyes rest on his oldest and true favorite. "Sweetheart, give me a slug of that medicine there. And Mary Rachel, get the whiskey bottle. I'll need a drink of that to chase the taste."

They obliged their father as usual.

He closed his eyes until the drug quieted the pain's bark, allowing him to manage a smile. "You girls kiss me goodbye then send in Houston on your way out."

Tears flowed aplenty—theirs and his—but they didn't linger. Such good daughters. If not for Mary Rachel running off with that Wheeler boy . . . and then . . . he put that thought away. Jethro Risen's love had covered that sin.

Such a God-fearing man, he'd been a real blessing. How many years had they been the picture of marital bliss?

His firstborn son—the promised one that Susannah died having—stepped in then closed the door. "CeCe said you wanted me."

"Are we good, Son? Is there anything left to be said between us?"

"Not a thing, sir. I love you."

"I know that, but—"

"No, Pa, really, it all worked for the best." The boy laughed. "If you hadn't done what you did, and I hadn't of done what I did, then . . ." He stepped closer. "She's the true love of my life, exactly like you and mama. God worked everything for the good."

He'd planned on telling him about seeing his real mother and her sending love, but May had been the only mama he'd known. "Good, has she accepted the Lord yet?"

"No, but I'll never give up on her."

"I'm not sure about everything where I'm headed, but if allowed, I'll keep on praying to that end. Come kiss me goodbye, Son, then send in Levi."

"Yes, sir."

The Colonel marched in like so many times before, but instead of anticipation of what new adventure awaited, only a stern resolution registered in his eyes, marred by bloodshot trickles, and old tears tracked his cheeks.

"I didn't tell Rebecca, and you don't need to either, but I saw Wallace standing on the far shore next to my mother and your Aunt Sue."

"Yes, sir. I expect to be reunited with Auntie and my old partner soon enough myself."

"I'll tell them as much." Henry blinked away more tears. "Son, you're the best man I've known . . . bar none. I couldn't love you more if you'd been my flesh and blood."

Levi wiped his cheeks. "I know, sir, and I love you, too. You've been a fine example to follow. I'd be proud to be blood kin, but blessed by what I got."

He smiled. "There's something I want you to do."

"Anything, sir."

"Take me home. Plant me next to Sue."

"Yes, sir. What if May objects?"

"She won't. We buried Chester and Miss Jewel where there'd be room for me next to your auntie and May on my other side next to her brother."

"Yes, sir."

"And Levi, there's one more thing."

Chapter Four

Levi didn't like the General's tone. The man sounded as though he had something up his sleeve. Exactly like him though. Even on his death bed, he'd hatched some scheme. "Whatever you need, sir." How could he not honor a last request?

"I want you to find Becca."

"I see. I give you my word that I will if I can, sir. Any idea where I should start?"

"The Pinkerton's tracked her to Seattle, Washington. She boarded a steamer heading north. I can't remember the name, but it's in their report. I called off the search after that, but I want you to take Crockett with you and go find her."

"Then what? Take her back to San Francisco?"

"No, bring her here. To May."

"Mercy, sir. It's been years. What if she doesn't want to come back?"

"Tell her it was her pawpaw's dying request, and that there's a right nice inheritance waiting for her. But she's got to come to Texas to get it."

"Have you talked to May about this?"

"No, but she'll understand. And . . ." He winced then nodded toward his medicine. "My hip. And back . . ."

"Yes, sir." Levi held the laudanum until the only father he'd ever known drained the bottle, then grabbed the whiskey for him. He gulped at least a third of the remaining liquor.

The old man had already consumed enough of the drug to kill most folks, but whatever he wanted and as much of it, he'd have. Levi would fight anyone who said different.

"What if Crockett refuses to go? I hear he's having a gay old time in New York."

"If he refuses, you and Charley hogtie him and put him on the train."

"Yes, sir."

Henry's eyes glazed, then his lids slipped to half-mast. His breathing slowed but held steady. He claimed the Lord had said he could stay until his youngest arrived. Hopefully, that was a true vision the man had seen and not wishful thinking.

"Levi."

"Yes, sir."

"Have Jethro and Mary Rachel tell you the whole story about why Becca ran off."

"Yes, sir."

His eyes closed completely, and he took to making little puffing noises. Levi settled into his straight-backed chair. He'd always figured there was more to the girl's story. The Pacific Northwest.

No telling where Becca had gone from Seattle, or even if she was still up there. And dragging Crockett to the far ends of the earth . . .

But then maybe that's what Henry had in mind. Getting him away from his mother. Without May to protect and pamper her baby boy, Levi might be able to knock off some of the dandy he'd become.

He leaned his head back and closed his eyes. If only Blue Dog or Wallace were here to help him stand watch.

Evie stared at her MayMee, hoping she'd open her eyes, but Mama had made her promise not to wake her grandmother. What if . . .

"Come snuggle with me, baby girl." Her almost-only grandparent lifted her sheet and quilt, inviting her in.

She was awake!

Evie crawled in next to MayMee, her favorite old lady. Not that she'd ever met her daddy's mother to compare the two.

For a bit, she relaxed then decided the time to ask seemed right. She wasn't sleepy, and lying in bed when there were books to read or a pony to ride and good-looking boys about was not her idea of fun.

"Where's my new pirate book, MayMee? The one you said I could read when you came for Thanksgiving."

"Oh, I see. And here all along I thought you wanted to cuddle with me."

"Uh . . . yes, ma'am. Sure I do, but . . . I . . . I mean . . ." Oh, no. She'd hurt the dear lady's feelings.

Then MayMee laughed. "Relax, baby girl. I'm only teasing. Can you read cursive?"

"Yes, ma'am. Mama taught me how, so I could read yours and PawPaw's letters all by myself. I like to read each one several times, you know."

"Aww. That's so sweet. You are a very dear child, Evie. Your PawPaw and I love you very much."

"I know. I'm his favorite."

The lady laughed again and that time tickled Evie's ribs, so she joined in the merriment.

"Indeed you are! So, you have got to be the smartest six-year-old I've ever known! It's great you can read cursive, because that's how I write my stories before they're books. It's called a manuscript. Matter of fact, I would love for you to read it and let me know if you think there are any changes that need to be made."

"That would be wonderful."

"You think so?"

"Oh, yes, ma'am. I can write down the page numbers and tell you what I think might make the story better. Just a little better, I should've said, because you always write the best stories."

"Excellent. Your critique will be priceless, young lady. I'll certainly treasure it."

"So can I read it now? I'm ready to start. Mama said PawPaw's sleeping, and that you need to be resting, too. I didn't want to wake you, but I do certainly love your books. And thank you, too, for your compliment about me being smart. I try not to act like a know-it-all. Sally—she's my best friend—says I do sometimes."

"I'd say you are a very humble little girl. You don't act at all prideful, in my opinion."

"Thank you again, MayMee." She scrunched her shoulders and smiled until her eyes were squinty. "I'm so excited to read your manuscript. Sally will be so jealous. I know I'm going to love it."

"But you won't gloat, because you are so gracious. I would be honored for you to edit the new story. That's what it's called."

"So I'm going to be the great May Meriwether's edit girl?"

Her eyes twinkled, and MayMee laughed some more. "Yes, ma'am. You are going to be my editor-in-chief. It's in the top drawer of the desk in the library upstairs. On the left. Do you need me to get it for you?"

"Oh, no. You don't have to get up. I'm sure I can find it. Remember PawPaw sent me that drawing of the whole house." She rolled away then rolled back and kissed MayMee's big soft lips. "Thank you! I love you, Captain!" She saluted just like the first mate did when Red Rooster gave him an order. "Or should I say aye-aye?"

Her little joke and probably her big grin, too, made her MayMee smile, and Evie loved making her smile.

"Either is good. Go on now, and maybe I can catch forty more winks before PawPaw needs me."

Later that selfsame day, after Nathaniel finished all the chores he'd been given, he went looking for Evelyn. He'd promised to give her another lesson and for sure didn't want her accusing him of lying.

The thought brought a smile. After only two inquiries, he found her upstairs in the General's library, sitting the man's chair, staring at a piece of paper.

But the small fry turned into a beautiful woman before his eyes. She looked up and smiled. His heart reveled in the love shining from her beautiful blue eyes. Something so sweet passed between them . . . almost holy.

He shook his head, and the six-year-old in the General's chair grinned. "Hey, Nathaniel. What are you doing?"

"Hey. Looking for you. Want another lesson?" What had happened? The grown Evelyn had loved him . . . and he loved her. Was he seeing the future?

She lowered the top of the page. "Yes, of course, but first . . . Do you know about *The Gray Lady* and Uncle Houston and Aunt Leilani?"

"Sure. What about them?"

"I never did, and I don't know why. I wonder why Mama wouldn't tell me about it. After all, he is her brother. But I'll tell you now and tell you true! This *Gray Lady Down* is a great story that I've never read. Do you have a copy?"

"Nope. Didn't know Mama May had written one about Uncle Houston. Where'd you get it?"

"Maybe it's still only just a manuscript. That means it isn't a book yet. It was in the drawer."

If the General caught her rummaging—except he would never climb the stairs again. "Are you supposed to be in here? Reading those pages?"

The little lady patted the tall stack. "Well, MayMee sent me to read the next pirate book for her, and she said it was in the top left drawer, but . . . uh . . . well . . ."

"Then why is the right-hand side drawer open?"

"Uh-oh. My other left is what Daddy would call it. I'm always confusing left and right. That is so funny, too, since I am so smart. Not that I'm bragging though; Daddy said if it's a fact, it isn't blowing your own horn. And I am smart, but I don't go around telling everybody because I don't want them thinking I'm . . ."

"Too big for your britches? Stricken with a swollen head?"

She grinned. "Either would do. But I can tell you, only you, because you won't think ill of me, would you, Nathaniel?"

"Hey, truth is truth."

"Yes, sir. And I figure I can tell you anything."

"Of course you can. And you being so smart . . . that's one of the things I like about you—why I agreed to teach you to ride. So then . . . Mama May didn't give you permission to read . . . What did you say the name of that one was?"

"*Gray Lady Down*. What do you think that means?"

"I'm not sure, but you ought to put it away exactly like you found it. She might not want you to see it yet."

"Well, she wanted me to read the new pirate story for her, but then I saw the other one, and . . . after all, she didn't tell me the name of Red Rooster's new adventure, so . . . well . . . this one is so good, and . . . Do you suppose I could have my lesson in about an hour? Will that be alright?"

"Sure, if you want." He slipped into the desk's right hand wingback, the same one he sat so many times listening to the General tell a story or explain something . . . that would never happen again. "How about you read to me? I love Mama May's pirate books, too."

"You do?"

"Sure. Did you know she started writing them because Uncle Houston and Aunt Bonnie asked her to tell them bedtime stories when she first came to Texas?"

"Yes, silly. Everyone knows that story. And that the Rooster is fashioned after PawPaw." She opened the drawer and pulled out a shorter stack of pages than the *Gray Lady Down* pile and picked up the first page. "*Princess Louisa Bay, a Red Rooster, the Gentleman Pirate Adventure* by May Meriwether. Chapter One."

"How do you suppose she describes all those exotic places she writes about so well?"

"Didn't you hear? Before she came to Texas, she sailed around the whole world!"

"No, I hadn't heard that."

"Oh, yes. On her first book tour."

"I knew she'd been to Europe." Nathaniel raised his eyebrows and tucked his chin. "Anyway, read on, little miss."

"Hoist the main sail, mates. Had a red sky last night and fair weather this morn. I be thanking the Lord for the day I was born." She looked at him. "Don't you love it that she starts every one the same way? Good that only the start is the same though."

"I do. Now read, or we'll never make it to the barn."

Scrunching her nose, for a minute she acted like she would stick her tongue out, but went back to the page and the story instead. She read so easily and didn't stumble over any of the words.

Before she turned the second page, she had him right there on the Jervis Straight heading toward the hidden bay with the General . . . or rather the Captain, in hot pursuit of the notorious sea hag Isadora.

Twice, in the first couple of chapters, she stopped to make notes. Seemed Mama May had forgotten exactly how many men the Rooster sent to their reward in his famous career—not that a one of them bettered the world one iota.

Then the little eagle eye spotted that Madam Merciful's earrings were wrong.

"I think MayMee might be having a little trouble remembering everything in all the other books." She tisked then sighed. "But it'll be alright now that she's got me to help her. It's my job, and I love doing it."

It seemed odd, being drawn into the imaginary world of the seafaring captain, and even more so into the sway of the little reader. How had she affected him so? He'd be fine to sit there and listen to her the rest of the afternoon.

Odd though, finding the precocious six-year-old's company as enjoyable as he did. Sure made him understand why she was the General's favorite . . . seemed everyone loved the little cotton top, and now he knew why.

Then right before dark, she set the page down and looked toward the window. "What's that?"

He jumped to his feet and pulled the curtain back, as if her every minor desire was his to do or die. The setting sun shone through what looked like a golden fog. Only a dust cloud though. "Appears Uncle Crockett finally made it."

"What? No, it can't be!" She bolted out of the chair and raced to the door, screaming at the top of her lungs. "Daddy!"

Chapter Five

Evie flew down the stairs two at a time, racing to the front door. "Daddy, come quick! Make him go away."

Her father reached the vestibule two steps before her, but instead of doing her bidding, he snatched her up. "What is it, baby doll? Who should I send away?"

"Uncle Crockett! He's here, and . . . and . . ." Tears welled until she could hardly see through them. He couldn't come. She didn't want him there! He climbed the steps onto the porch! "No! Go away! Tell him, Daddy!"

The door opened and the new arrival wore a puzzled expression.

Her daddy shuffled her to his other hip. "Baby, its Uncle Crockett. What's the matter? Don't you remember him?"

"No! He can't come in! PawPaw will die now, and I don't want him to!" She glared at her uncle. "Please, go away. Go back to New York and spend the rest of MayMee's money!" Looking him straight in the eye and begging in her mind, she willed him to do her bidding.

But he only shook his head. "Evie." Crockett looked at her daddy. "Right?"

"That's correct. Evelyn May Eversole." Her father turned to her. "This is your mother's youngest brother, baby girl."

The intruder brought death with him. "You should have stayed away, my pawpaw will only die now!"

"Sweetheart, I don't want him to die either, but he's my father. I need to see him. Talk with him." He looked to her daddy. "I came as quickly as I could. How's he doing?"

Her father shook his head "If not for the laudanum . . ."

"Where is he?"

She wiggled free and stood in front of the man that looked more like her pawpaw than all of her relatives, though younger. "No, you can't, please go away."

"Please, Evie, step aside."

She balled both fists. "No! Now go away! You can't be here!"

Henry pulled his hand back. Blue Dog shot his tongue out, getting in one more lick before realization dawned. "Oh, Blue, where you been, boy? What are you warning me about?"

A little girl screamed. The dog nudged his arm with his nose. Henry forced his eyes open. Was that his Evie? "Why's my baby girl carrying on like that?"

Levi stood beside his bed. "Crockett's here, and she doesn't want him to see you."

His sweet wife sat beside him and brushed the hair from his forehead.

Of course. "Because she's a smart one, that girl. Give me a shot of my medicine then fetch her. Would you, please, Son?"

"Sure, sir." Levi complied. Such a good man that one. If he'd had a dozen more like him, he could have made Texas a Republic again like he and old Sam talked about so many times. But what did it matter now? He was about to go to a far better place.

"Oh, my dearest husband. What am I going to do without you?" May wiped a tear from her eye.

"It'll be hard, darling, and I'm sorry for that. Part of what you get for marrying an old man." He coughed then held her hand to his cheek. "But it'll get better. And it will be fine. We'll see each other again."

"You promise?"

"I do."

"I love you more than life, Henry Buckmeyer. You're a great man, and I've been so blessed to be your wife."

"I love you, too, sweetheart."

The door opened, and his favorite little granddaughter ran to his bedside. "PawPaw, tell them! Make him go away. I don't want you to die."

Poor thing. Tears ran down her cheeks, and her button nose dripped. So much like his Sue.

None of his girls looked as much like her as this little gal. So passionate, pigheaded, and that same sparkle in her eyes that he loved so much when her dander rose up. "Sweetheart, I can't stay. I've got to go home."

"But you are home! This is your home! And we all love you! I'll miss you, PawPaw!"

"Well, I'll miss you, too. But . . . we'll see each other again in Heaven one day. Baby girl, I'm hurting so bad . . ." His hip yelped extra loud. "The drug . . . it isn't working much anymore. Kiss me goodbye, doll, then let my boy come see me."

Poor little girl, she just didn't understand. Nathaniel pressed against the far wall as the six-year-old buried her face in the crook of the General's arm and wept.

Anyone with eyes could see it was breaking the old man's heart, but who in their right mind would ask him to stay in his condition? Other than Evie?

"That's enough, baby girl." Her pawpaw reached over, and with his other hand, touched her forehead. "I'm ordering you to buck up."

She nodded, whimpered several times, then raised her pretty little face. She wiped her cheeks with her fingers and her nose with her forearm.

"But . . . but . . . Who's going to write me every week now? And tell me stuff like I'm all grown up and not a baby?" She grinned. "Except I love it when you call me baby girl. And I know I'm your favorite, but . . . Oh, PawPaw!" More tears rolled down her cheeks, but she wiped them right away. "I love you so much."

"I love you, too, Evelyn. But to everything there is a time and a season. Says so in the Good Book and now it's my time. So kiss me big, then let me go. I need to see my youngest son."

She stood on her tiptoes and kissed his cheek. The General looked her in the eyes a long time. "Bye, baby girl."

"Bye, PawPaw." She patted his cheek. Mama May wiped her own cheeks. He glanced over the girl's head and caught Nathaniel's eye. The look brought him over to the bedside. "Take her to her mother, please."

"Yes, sir." He lifted Evelyn, who reached out to the General, but made no attempt to stay or cause any more fuss. Once in the hall, she turned, buried her face in his shoulder, and wept. He reached the parlor.

Aunt CeCe participated in a clutch of ladies, chatting quietly in the far corner next to the window.

He put his mouth close to the girl's ear. "I'll write to you."

Bringing her sobs to an abrupt end, she pushed back and looked him in the eye. "You promise?"

"Yes, ma'am, I do. Every week if I can, but for sure, once a month."

"I'd like that. And I'll write you back letter for letter. You'll like getting mail. It's fun." She hung her head then looked back up. "If you miss though, I'll have to sic my Blue Dog on you."

"You have a Blue Dog pup?"

"Not yet, but Mama said I could have one."

"That's swell."

"PawPaw was supposed to find me one, and I was going to bring her home with me after the New Year. Him and MayMee are . . . They were coming to California for Thanksgiving." Her eyes filled with tears again. "Now he won't, can't."

"Don't cry. Know what? I've got two Blue pups, and if you want, you can have the bit . . . uh . . . female. You wanted a girl, right?" Him and his big mouth. Wouldn't do for her to be knowing that word for a few more years.

She giggled. "I know what you were going say, silly. I'm not really a baby, even if everyone calls me that." He sat down with her, and her giggles turned into rolling laughter. Then the waterworks returned.

Poor baby girl. Her mother must have heard and came running over then took her.

Not that he wouldn't have held her for as long as she wanted. She was so sweet, and his heart hurt for her sake.

Crockett waited while the room cleared—all but Charlotte. It smelled stale, like sickness . . . or was it death? Ma should open the windows, let some fresh air in. He hated being there, but he had to come. Couldn't not say goodbye. He stepped beside the bed and slipped his hand into his sister's.

"I'm so . . . sorry, baby."

Charlotte squeezed, but didn't take her eyes off her pa. "Don't be silly. You don't have to apologize."

"Still, my biggest regret is not being there to give you away. For that, I'm so sorry."

A single chuckle escaped Charlotte, but it threatened to turn into a sob. Pulling her hand from his, she bent over him and kissed his cheek then wore a hole in it, rubbing, petting, stroking him incessantly. Always was such a daddy's girl.

"I love you so much. I don't want you to go." Then the waterworks burst forth in earnest.

Tears streamed down his mother's cheeks, too.

Pa patted her hand then looked at Crockett and mouthed, take her out.

"I love you more, and . . . Don't want to leave either, but . . . to everything there is a season, and it's my time under Heaven. Choose your husband well, baby, and listen . . . to your mother." His breath came hard, and he labored so to speak. "Now say goodbye, sweet girl, and leave me with your brother. I love you, Charlotte, and I'm so proud of you."

Crockett placed his hands on her shoulders and pulled gently. "Come on, Sis." She stood, filled her lungs, then wiped her cheeks and managed a broken whisper. "I love you."

"I love you, too, baby. I . . . need to talk with your brother."

Crockett wrapped his arm around his baby sister and escorted her to the door, closed it behind her, then returned to his father's bed.

Never in his whole life had his father looked old or weak, but he seemed so . . . so . . . helpless and vulnerable. His own fault though. Who at his age goes hunting strays? And on a green-broke stud colt. Only Patrick Henry Buckmeyer. That's who.

"Pa?"

Opening his eyes, he grinned. Nothing weak in those eyes, still as hard as ever.

"Son, I've been waiting for you."

"Yes, sir. Got here fast as I could. Sorry it took so long."

"How's New York?"

"Oh, about the same, I guess."

"Something I want you to do for me."

He looked across the bed. His mother shook her head then hiked one shoulder. He lowered his gaze. "If I can, sir."

His father grimaced, filled his lungs, then bore into him with his steely baby blues, except they'd faded some. "Oh, you can—if you will."

"Yes, sir. Nothing I can't do if I put my mind to it. Isn't that what you've told me all my life?" Why was he letting him bait him? "So. What is it you want me to do, Pa?"

"Go with Levi and find Becca. Bring her home to your mother."

"How in the world? The girl ran off . . . like what? Four or five years ago? She could be anywhere. That'd be nothing but a wild goose chase."

"No, not anywhere. The Pinkertons tracked her to Seattle and found out she sailed North from there on the *Desolation Queen*. I intended to go myself, but . . ." He closed his eyes and clamped his mouth shut.

"Henry, do you need more medicine?"

"No." His eyes opened. "Levi's already agreed. Now either you will or you won't. Which is it?"

"Why, Pa? Why are you asking this?"

Henry stared at his youngest. The waves of pain came stronger and harder, but he ignored them best he could. Hadn't had a good breath in . . . how long? Couldn't have much time left.

"Son, I have my reasons, and you know I hate explaining myself. She's my granddaughter. Now tell me your mind. Will you do this for me? Go find her. Or not?"

The boy's gazed shifted between him and his mother like she'd supply his answer or give him leave to lie. Henry wanted to say more, but the time had come to stop talking and let the young man make up his mind.

So much like him, yet unlike him, too, in that his mother had spoiled him near rotten.

Hopefully, a year or two on the trail with Levi would fix some of that.

After too long a wait, Crockett exhaled then nodded. "Alright. Fine. I'll go. For yours and Becca's sakes, I'll go with Levi. We'll find her and bring her back."

"Good . . .to your mother. Here." With great effort, as if the world had stopped turning, he faced May. "Love her through . . . reconcile her . . . with Mary Rachel."

"If I can, my love, but you're sure asking a lot of Levi and Crockett."

He sucked a breath, and held it until the barking eased some. "I know, but it needs doing . . . besides her parents, she loved our boy the best."

Sensed she might want to argue, but thank God, must have decided against it. Instead, she blessed him with one of those beautiful smiles.

"I love you."

"I know."

"Love you, too, Son."

"And I love you, Pa."

"I know. I'll be expecting to see you again one day. So, we good? Anything else need saying?"

"No, sir. Nothing."

Another waved crashed in on him, but he found his voice. "Give your old man a kiss, then go get everyone in here so I can tell them all I'll see them again. On the other side."

A room full of faces he loved. He never dreamed so many of his friends and family had gathered. The cookstoves must be staying red hot. Did he have any lauder left? Not that he'd be needing it. Would May have plenty?

He nodded toward Levi. "Sit me up, Son."

He came closer then looked toward the dark bottle of pain killer, his eyes questioning. Henry shook his head then braced himself for the wave of searing, white hot daggers the movement would bring.

Once up high enough to see the whole room, he spent a few heartbeats on each face. When finished, he waited for an ebb.

None came so he bucked up, reached down, and found his voice. "I love you all, and it's been a pleasure . . ." He sniffed then blinked back tears. "Thank you for coming . . . being here. Now, if you would, I need you all to leave, so I can have a few moments with my May."

Almost like they couldn't get out fast enough, the room emptied. All but Evie and Nathaniel, tears streamed down the girl's cheeks while the boy hovered over the child, appearing ready to haul her out if need be. He sure liked that one.

Shame he didn't have more time with him . . . especially after the . . .

Oh, well, never mind that. He caught the boy's eye and nodded toward the girl. She held both hands out toward him as Nathaniel carried her out.

Henry summoned what strength he had left and pushed himself down a bit before meeting May's eyes. "Come lay on my arm one last time."

She did, then the pain vanished. He and she were one.

Chapter Six

May lay her head on his shoulder.

Her breath caught.

How could she bear it? There was no way. She hated goodbyes. Didn't want to hear any more—not ever! Henry had saved her, given her a life worth living.

By his side, she'd blossomed. In his strong arms, flourished. But never to feel them around her again, never to hear his voice, know his wisdom . . .

She could never say goodbye . . . not to her Henry.

Dear Lord . . .

Her chest ached. Her every breath pierced her soul.

How? How?

Oh, that she could crawl closer beside him, into him, and make that last journey with him. If only her heart would stop its foul beating. How could she be without him? She never wanted to be separated from him . . . ever . . .

But she had no choice.

No options.

It was coming, and she couldn't stop it.

Oh, God, how can I stand it? Take me, too. Please, Father, take me, too.

Then he was gone.

And she was left.

Tears welled. Everything vanished. She stood on the shore of a crystal clear sea. On the opposite side, two winged men lowered her Henry to the shore.

A gathering double or triple the size of the one that filled her parlor at that very moment crowded around him, cheering and patting him on the back as though he'd gotten himself elected President.

Was Sue amongst them?

Surely, she must be.

He gazed toward May, waved, then blew her a kiss as he had so many times. She stepped toward the water, but he turned and walked into a bright light that shone even greater in the distance, surrounded by all those who loved him and had been waiting.

"You can't go now. Your time will come soon enough."

Startled, she turned toward the voice.

An old man—strange looking, exactly like the one Henry had described giving him directions at the Cuthand Trading Post when she'd written *The Granger*—and the same old prophet guy who'd spoken over Charley as a boy when Levi was bringing Rose home to the Red River Valley...at that camp meeting.

Could the old man have been the same one Charley and Lacey had seen, too? Or that wild-haired prophet man who never died back in New York. What was his name then? Dempsey . . . or . . .

Might even be that dapper old boy Houston said warned him in China.

"Why can't I go now? I want to go with him. I don't want to be alone."

"Too many souls need you." The gentleman smiled then vanished.

When she looked around for him, she discovered herself back in her room, lying next to her husband's lifeless, cooling body. The odor drove her from the bed. She marched out, wiping her cheeks as she went.

The room before her quieted. "He's with the Lord now."

Somehow, the words brought strength. She was the matriarch, heading a family that looked to her, depended on her. Especially with Levi going after Becca.

Her husband's right-hand man stood next to her with Crockett, Charley, and Houston on the other side.

"If you and the boys would clean him up one last time, Levi, and put that pair of wool longjohns on him, then the girls and I will get him dressed. Being Henry, he's already ordered a coffin from Mister Wallace in Annona. Came in last week. It's out in the barn. We can take him up to Clarksville in that."

They jumped to it as if it had been the General himself who issued the order. She spotted little Evie with her faced buried in her daddy's shoulder and went to her. May sat down beside Elijah. "Sweetheart?"

The six-year-old turned toward her; the baby's eyes red and swollen, filled with tears. "Yes, ma'am."

"Didn't your PawPaw tell you to buck up?"

She bit her bottom lip and nodded. "Yes, ma'am."

"I know it's hard. And so sad to think we won't see him again on this earth. We've all cried plenty of tears, too. But really, we're only crying for ourselves, you know. PawPaw's in such a much better place now. Did you know he isn't hurting anymore?"

"He isn't? How do you know?"

She lifted the girl's hand and squeezed. "I saw him there—in Heaven. Just for a moment, but he was happy and smiling. So we've got to stop all our tears." She stood. "That goes for all of you. Let's buck it up, and be happy for Henry instead of sad for ourselves. How many times have we heard him say, 'The Lord gives, and the Lord takes away, blessed be the name of the Lord'?"

Baby girl slipped from her daddy's lap and stood beside her, taking her hand again and squeezing it. "That sounds just like my pawpaw. He'd like us to be happy."

Deep into that night, after they had her pawpaw laid out in the dining hall, Evie listened to her parents, aunts, and uncles tell stories.

Some she'd heard or had read about in one of MayMee's books, but most told little pieces of his life. She loved Aunt Rebecca's story when she'd made him sing. That happened before he married her mother.

She stared and stared at the casket, listening to all the family's tales. It didn't seem real that he was gone. His body lay inside the box, but he wasn't there. Was he hot in there?

It was a hot day.

Texas was a very hot place.

Hearing about Uncle Houston and Uncle Bart getting soaked one night during the war, then having to face Levi Baylor the next day, tickled her to giggles. She stifled them though because she didn't want the grownups to send her to bed.

She'd certainly never want to have to dance to that tune.

Uncle Levi was too much like PawPaw. She never wanted him upset with her.

The very best were the stories about his Blue Dog.

Those made her want one of his pups even more. She could see herself galloping across the prairie, her and Twinkle Toes' manes flying in the wind with Her Royal Blueness running point, sniffing out the pirates' trails.

Ahoy, ye maties! We'll uncover the buried treasure or perish in the effort!

Twice she pinched herself to chase away the sandman, but in the end, he shoveled too much, too fast.

She found herself in a grand adventure aboard the *Lone Star Maid* with Captain Rooster at the helm, gallivanting through the San Juan Islands then north into the Gulf Islands with MayMee's new storyline woven into the dream.

The next day, the sun beat her up by two hands worth, but no one seemed to mind or call her sleepyhead or a lay-about.

They were all busy getting ready to take the General home. She liked him being her pawpaw and her being his favorite, too, but she still liked using his old rank sometimes.

That swelled her heart, knowing he'd been in charge of a whole army.

That dumb ol' Jefferson Davis should have made Henry Buckmeyer his ranking General—that's what Nathaniel said, and she wholly agreed—then he might not have lost the war.

Except, her grandfather never cottoned to owning a human being. And the South wanted to keep their slaves . . . she still didn't understand why he fought on the wrong side.

That next morning, she beat the sun up. Figured that would balance things out.

Soon as she dressed, she ran out to the barn, wanted to make sure Twink was grained plenty early and his halter and lead rope hung where they belonged. He'd be leaving out with the first group of wagons, heading east by southeast soon as breakfast was over.

Everyone agreed that would be best, seeing as how the carriage and wagon carrying PawPaw would come last, after dinner, and travel faster than a pony would want to go.

Plus, MayMee figured some of the folks along the way would want to pay their respects, seeing how the great man touched so many lives.

And behind his hearse—Evie didn't much like that word—they'd have a riderless stallion, one of the famous Black's great-grandsons that had never been ridden. She liked all the pomp and ceremony when a great man died.

PawPaw certainly deserved every bit of it. Could he see from Heaven?

Did he know how much everyone loved him?

Those questions and so many more swirled as the journey back to Clarksville began. In the old days it would have taken over a month to get there, but with the trains, going from the Llano

Ranch to Austin took longer than getting from the capital to Red
River County.

Had there ever been a bigger funeral? Her uncles and aunties
seemed to know everyone.

All her cousins were there and lots of new friends to play with,
too. She loved Uncle Levi's house, but why wouldn't she? They
said PawPaw built it, and she'd read so much about it in
MayMee's books.

They planted him good and deep next to the grandmother
she'd never known, but with plenty of room on his other side for
MayMee when she joined him in Heaven. Then everyone went to
one big last meal together, before they had to leave.

Evie pulled Uncle Charley aside. "Can Nathaniel stay here
until we go home? He hasn't finished teaching me how to ride."

"Have you asked him? Does he want to?"

"Yes, sir, I did. He said it was up to you."

"What about his mother? Have you asked her?"

"Oh, yes, sir. Aunt Lacey said the same thing. That it's up to
you. So can he?"

"Your PawPaw did ask him to teach you, so I guess we can
handle his chores for a while if he wants to stay."

Those happened to be the best three days ever. After he
convinced her she could hang on with her legs and didn't need to
keep one hand on the saddle's horn, the rest came easy. Not that
she was ready to trail out with the herd or anything silly like that.

Sally would be so jealous. She'd probably beg and plead until
her daddy got her a pony, too. And he surely would. Then Evelyn
could teach her to ride, and the two of them could be horseladies
together. It'd be so much fun.

Maybe Uncle Jethro could talk the board at the Mercy House
to get ponies for the orphans, too. She and Sally could teach them
all to ride.

That last afternoon, while she and her own personal wrangler
brushed out Twink, she made her mind up. She'd been turning the
idea over and over, looking at it from all the angles just like
PawPaw said he did when he had a major decision.

After thinking of everything she could, she'd convinced herself and was iron clad sure.

She followed Nathaniel out of the stall. "I want a boon, kind sir." She liked that word PawPaw had used. And calling him a kind sir might soften him up to agree to her favor.

He grinned as though she played some game. "Your wish is my command if it is in my power, fair maiden."

"No. Let's start over."

He grabbed the hay fork. "Fine. What game are we playing?"

"That's why I want to start over, This isn't any game. It's serious."

He tossed a forkful of hay into Twink's stall. "A favor then . . . again, if I can."

"Oh, you can. I want you to promise that you'll wait for me."

Nathaniel eyed her hard. Exactly what was she talking about? "Explain yourself."

"What don't you understand? It's like . . ." She spread her hands wide. "You know, not doing something until something else happens."

"So what is it I'm not doing? Or waiting for?"

"Me, silly."

Her?

If the little girl was talking about what he hoped, how ironic would that be?

But he still wanted her to spell it out. "Now who's being silly? Wait for you to do what? Tell me what you're talking about, Evelyn."

"Well, Mama was seventeen when she told my father she was worth waiting for. She crawled through the attic to tell him, too. And she's said a zillion times she was old enough then, but PawPaw played pigheaded on account of Aunt Mary Rachel running off with Susie's daddy."

"I've heard that story."

"Anyway, I've decided you're the one I want to marry. But I obviously have some growing up to do. So I want you to wait for me until I do. You've got to say yes. It's only ten more years. I'll be seven soon. Not so long, and you'll only be twenty-five. That's about the perfect age for a man, don't you agree? Then we'll get married in the spring of 1897—I want lots of flowers at my wedding."

"What if, during all this growing up you've got to do, you fall in love with someone else out in California, and you don't love me then?"

"No chance. You see, I love you now, and I'll love you then. Because I love you with my whole heart! Will you wait, Nathaniel?"

Should he drop to one knee? That might seem a bit much, especially if someone walked into the barn. She was worth it though, and she'd like that. Should he save that for when she was seventeen? "Yes, Evelyn, I'll wait for you. I pledge my heart to you, to love only you. I'll wait. I promise."

"Yay! Hallelujah!" She stuck out her hand. "Shake on it."

He took it, and she shook real big as if they'd traded horses.

"Good, I'm so excited and very glad that's settled."

No one could know how it about broke his heart when she boarded the train, but he had chores to keep him busy. No way was he doing anything stupid. Just like the General said, it didn't have to be like father, like son.

His pa had done enough stupid stuff with the female of the species to last both their lifetimes.

Crockett sat his father's rocker, though it somehow belonged to Levi instead of Houston—the natural born son—and watched the sunlight slide down the far tree line.

When it reached the first row of cotton, he put his empty coffee cup down and turned. "I've looked at it from all sides, Ma, and I can't be gone three months. Much less a year."

She shook her head. "You know. Maybe he was right all these years, but you, young man, gave my dead husband—your father—your word, and if you . . ." Tears welled, and she looked away.

"If I what?"

She looked back. "No. I could never bring myself to cut you off. But your father's right about Becca. Short of her daddy, you've got the best chance of bringing her back."

"Do you know what the big fight was all about?"

"I do, but I gave my word to keep it to myself, and I'll not break it. Henry told Levi to talk with Jethro and Mary Rachel for the whole story, and he has, but . . ." She hiked one shoulder. "I suppose they're mulling it over. He's planning on going from here to San Francisco then on to Seattle."

"I know. He's already told me that part, gave me a list of stuff I need to bring with me. Made it sound like we're going on some fishing trip or something."

The screen door opened. Crockett jumped to his feet. "Here, sir. I believe this is yours now."

The man smiled. "No, it will always be the General's. Guess he's loaned it to me for the duration."

Crockett had always liked Levi Baylor well enough, even if he never fully understood his father's relationship with the man. Almost like the interloper was some kind of hero out of Greek mythology. Could he really stand him for a year? He was almost as hard-nosed as the old man. "Yes, sir. Guess we'll all be living beneath Henry Buckmeyer's shadow for years to come." Why had he used that tone? The man was barely cold.

His mother glared, but didn't respond.

The Texas Ranger—who might've been easier to take if he was ten feet tall and older than dirt—shook his head.

"He wasn't my blood, but the closest thing to a father I knew. Now, if you disrespect his memory again in my presence, I'll put you on the floor and stomp you until you learn some manners."

Not many men would be able, but the old coot probably was one who could. "Yes, sir. I'm sorry, sir." He turned to his mother. "Sorry, Ma. That'll never happen again."

That time he used a different tone, but it had the same effect.

"That's good, boy. You can talk to me anyway you want, but . . ." His honorary brother let his words drift in the wind. Crockett got the message.

"Still. In my opinion, my father has sent us on a wild goose chase."

"No, he has not. Wallace and I ran Bold Eagle to ground across the Rio Bravo then brought him back to swing. You and I will find Becca. She's left too many tracks."

"*Desolation Queen*, right? A grand name for a vessel to disappear on, don't you agree?" Crockett took his mother's coffee cup. "Hope you're right."

Chapter Seven

Evie pulled the pup in tight against her leg, Her Royal Blueness proved to be such a good dog, exactly like her great-grand sire. She loved it that Queenie and Twink had made fast friends, especially since the stupid conductor said she had to stay in the stall with him in the livestock car.

Positioning her writing table on her lap just right, she opened the secret compartment, unplugged the ink, dipped her quill, then started her letter. She liked writing in Twink's stall.

> *Dearest MayMee,*
> *We're not home yet, still in Texas. I love you so much and miss you already. I truly hope you'll still go ahead and come for Thanksgiving this year and stay with us just like we planned.*

Evie set the quill pen down and rubbed Queenie's head. Should she mention PawPaw? Or not? She turned that over several times then decided not. MayMee probably thought about him every minute already, so no reason to bring him up and make her sadder.

With the feather's end, she tickled her chin just like the great May Meriwether.

Every time, she did it right before she put pen to ink then returned to her missive. Had anyone else noticed? Evie wanted to be a great writer, too, so she could tell all the stories of their family, like MayMee.

Making up some new Red Rooster ones would be fun, too. Maybe where he gave up his pirating ways and settled down to taking visitors to see all the awesome sights he'd been privy to—an honest job.

He'd be so good at that, and lots of landlubbers would thoroughly enjoy all the islands he'd been visiting in all his adventures.

She'd have to talk with MayMee about that.

> *I don't know if you noticed, but I sort of accidently on purpose read some of Gray Lady Down, I really liked—no, I loved it! It would be my pleasure to be your editor on that book, too.*
>
> *If you would send me the manuscript, I can read the rest. So much was happening then, but I can't get that story out of my head.*
>
> *I asked, and mama only knows some of it. And oh, I forgot to finish your new Red Rooster book. I hope you found my notes helpful. I'm so sorry. I just now remembered, but you could send that one, too, and I could edit them both.*

She dipped the quill again should she ask for that one as well?

> *That is, if you have an extra copy lying around. If I could, I'd love to read it.*
>
> *Again I love you so much and miss you. If you come, you could stay even longer if you want to. And it would be great if you could bring Nathaniel with you when you do come to do your favors when you travel. I'm sure he'd be a big help to you.*

He probably has chores, but surely you could talk his parents into it. Did you know he met us in Clarksville to give me Her Royal Blueness? That's what I named my new Blue Dog pup. She's a dilly, such a good dog!

I call her Queenie. The train conductor is making her ride in Twink's stall.

Daddy says I can't sleep with them, but he lets me stay in here a lot during the days. It's where I am right now, writing this letter! Twinkle Toes and Queenie just love each other. I'm so glad they're best friends!

Well, I guess I'm going to stop now. I need to get a missive—I'm so glad you taught me that new word. I think it's so pretty.

Anyway, I need to get one written to Nathaniel. I probably won't get to post them until we get all the way to California. I hope he has one there, waiting on me. Did you know he promised to write?

Should she take MayMee into her confidence? Could she tell her about the special deal she and Nathaniel shook on? Maybe . . . but only when she could talk to her face to face, not in a letter because someone might read it. But she couldn't wait to tell Sally.

He promised to write me a letter once a week—or for sure at least once a month—and every time he sends me one, I promised to write him back. One for one, don't you think that's fair?

We'll be pen-pals then. But he has to start. I think it would be forward of me to write first, don't you?

I'm not sure exactly what 'forward' means, but Aunt Charlotte was telling Mama about one of her lady friends who was so forward, it made her sick. If I'm using it wrong, let me know just like P

She pulled back the pen, why had she? Oh well, wasn't like she could scratch it out.

> *PawPaw used to. I hope it doesn't make you sad I brought him up.*
>
> *Love Evie,*
>
> *P.S. If I write more before I post this, I'll just start over and leave him out. Love and kisses and hugs to my favoritest grandest grandmother, MayMee.*

Reading it back over three times, she corrected her spelling errors as neatly as possible then put it away. She gave Queenie the piece of ham she'd saved from her dinner, scratched her ears real good, stuck the little table tray under her arm, then jumped up.

With a hard, tight hug of Twink's neck, she admonished her pup to stay.

It seemed awful that he had to have his halter on the whole way and be doubled tied, but everyone said it was for his own good, and that he'd be fine. Her pony could reach his hay and water, so . . .

Not much she could do about it. She patted Queenie one last time then slid the stall door open enough to slip out, careful not to scratch her table.

The pup whined, but not too much before she went to howling.

She hurried to the boxcar's door. Queenie's lament spurred her on faster. She found her parents and some strangers visiting over what looked like tea.

It didn't smell like coffee. She liked tea with ice and lots of honey or cane syrup, but not hot, no matter how sweet. They rarely let her make anything really sweet enough.

Slipping in next to Daddy, she leaned into him. A little nap might be nice. She closed her eyes and opened her ears real wide. No telling what grownups would say once they thought their baby girl was asleep.

Crockett tapped on the door. How many times over the years had he knocked on the same one? Better question, how many girls and ladies had called it their own?

"Go away."

He knuckled it harder. "Come on, Sis. It's me. Open up."

She cracked the portal. "Crockett, what are you doing up here?"

"I need a favor."

"Too bad. The answer is no." She rubbed her eyes. "I am not lending you any more money, so go back to bed!"

"Let me in."

The force of the door swung wide and moved her back. "Fine, Brother. Come on in." She exhaled audibly. "Why can't we discuss this tomorrow? Why do you always . . . grrrr . . . you see, Mother! He's incorrigible!"

Ma sat on the bed. He smiled. "Sorry, didn't know I was interrupting you ladies, but if you don't mind, I need a word in private with Charlotte."

"If you can't say whatever it is in front of her, then you don't need to be saying it at all. Just get out of here. You cannot come into my room and chase Mother out!"

"Fine, if you insist. I need you to go to New York."

"What for?"

"It's like this. My partner is a whiz at sniffing out great deals, but he needs someone to keep a firm grip on him. He wants to gallop when he should trot, if you get my drift. If I'm expected to gallivant all over the Northwest, I need someone I can trust in New York, watching over things. You're it."

"Son. You're wanting your sister to take over your business while you're gone? That's asking too much."

"Oh, but requesting me to traipse up to the Oregon Territory is fine by you? Sure seems like some fancy double standards." He smiled at his baby sister. "Besides, you do have a pretty hefty stake in my success . . . and . . . last I heard, you are between suitors. What do you say? Come on and help your big brother out?"

"I'll consider it. If . . . you'll answer one question."

"How about you agree, then I'll tell you whatever you want."

"In that case, I get three questions. And if . . . you answer truthfully . . . and only if, then I'll go." She looked to Ma. "That is if I can stay in the brownstone."

"You two are so much like your father, God rest his soul. Of course you can."

He couldn't argue that point, especially with his sister. And his half-sister Mary Rachel—if only a third of the stories he heard about her business dealings were true, she might be a better horsetrader than them all.

But he'd match Charlotte with about anyone else. "Fine."

She jumped to her feet and stuck out her hand. "Deal."

He stifled a laugh then grabbed his little sister's hand. "What's your first question?"

She squeezed. "Shake on it first."

"Pa said a man's word was his bond. Are you implying I'd welch?"

"No. But why aren't you shaking on it?"

"Fine, then." He did as she wanted, pumped her hand twice, then pulled his free. "Ask away."

"Why'd you agree to go?"

"Pa asked me, that's why. And the fact that I love Becca. Couldn't think of a way out. It's hard to turn down you dear old father's dying request."

She stared into his eyes. He gazed right back into hers. "Any other reasons?"

He filled his lungs, exhaled, then hiked his far shoulder. "Uncle Levi and our mother—basically the whole clan . . . how could I face any of them if I denied Pa's last request?"

"I'll take that one."

"Have you made any money yet in your business dealings?"

The little snot.

"No, not yet. You knew that. Why are you wasting questions?"

"So, if when you get back, and I've got a stack of gold coins the Black couldn't jump over, then I'm best, right?"

"What? Hogwash! After I've done all the work and got everything at the precipice? Ready to make it big? I don't think so. We all know well enough how much like Pa you are when it comes to trading, but no way does you watching my ship come in make you better, little girl." He smiled. "What's your last question?"

"Forget it. If you're not willing to admit I bested you."

"That wasn't the deal. I agreed to answer three questions with the truth. Sometimes the truth hurts, baby sister. Am I right, Ma?"

What could she do but agree?

"Sorry, sweetheart, but . . . that was the agreement."

"Ha! Now come on with that last question, and we can get this over with."

"Fine, chowderhead!" She rolled her eyes, looking like she was thinking up a tough one. "Why didn't you propose to Alice?"

"Meri Charlotte Buckmeyer! What business of yours is that?"

"You said you'd answer three questions."

With a look, he appealed to his mother.

"Sorry, Son. I'd like to know the answer to that myself. I always thought she would make a splendid mother for my grandchildren."

"I see how you both are. Well, here it is. I caught her making eyes at Dennis Parker, and it didn't cause me any grief. Not even a twinge, so I knew then and there it wasn't true love."

He stepped in behind her and whispered. "I hope you're happy."

She spun back around. "Not really! You're answer certainly surprised me though. Sad, but rather gallant."

He nodded. "Henry Buckmeyer's youngest son could do no less."

While they all said their greetings, Evie hid behind her mother. Queenie stood right beside her, striking her leg with every wag. She hated it that he came, but she had to face the music. He'd always be her uncle.

Plus, he looked more like PawPaw than any of them.

"Evie, don't you have something to say?"

Stepping out, she glanced up then studied the floor. The stones in the vestibule in shades of blues and greens resembled the ocean. At least that's what they reminded her of, and she loved them. She really liked that word, vestibule.

She filled her lungs then bucked it up and looked Uncle Crockett right in the eye. "I'm sorry I was so mean to you, but—"

"No buts, young lady." Her father's tone said it all.

"Yes, sir. I'm sorry, Uncle, will you please forgive me for my rude behavior?" She forced herself to hold his eyes and not look at the stones again, though that's what her brain wanted to do.

He knelt onto one knee and grinned. "Yes, of course I'll forgive you . . . on one condition."

"What is it?"

"If you promise to give me pick from that blue pup's first litter."

That was not what she expected. Why, Her Royal Blueness might never have pups. But . . . if she didn't then there'd be no pick and she still kept her end of the bargain. She looked up at her Daddy. He only shrugged, and Mama only stood there smiling.

"Oh, alright. Pick of the first litter is yours."

"And so you know, Evie, I totally understand the reasons behind your actions. Believe me, if staying away would have helped, I never would've showed, but . . . ." He held an arm, and she scooted over and sat on his knee bench with his arm around her. "Pa was eighty-seven years old and shouldn't have been riding that green-broke stud colt."

"But he's the best horseman in Texas!"

"Maybe, but I heard old men need to stick with old horses."

"Is that true?" She searched Uncle's eyes for any tell of him lying then glanced at her mother.

"Sounds logical to me, sweetheart."

"And so it is." He tousled her curls. "I love you, Evelyn."

She kissed his cheek. There. That wasn't hard at all. "I love you too, Uncle." She wrapped her arms around his neck and squeezed.

"Hey. I almost forgot. I've got something for you."

"You do?" She leaned back. "What is it?"

"Your MayMee sent you a box." He motioned her up then walked outside.

Her breath caught. Was it? Could it be?" She looked to her Uncle Levi, hoping for information, a hint or something. But he only shrugged.

Real quick, her uncle returned, holding a hat box. Why had MayMee sent her a hat?

"Here, baby girl." He held her surprise out.

She took it, set it on the flagstone floor, and pulled the lid off. Someone squealed. Had that come out of her? Must have because the great May Meriwether had sent her *Gray Lady Down*! And under that, the new Red Rooster adventure story. And under that! A thick folded letter! Oh, how wonderful! She loved MayMee!

All the adults grinned like on her birthday when she opened presents. And those had been lovely gifts, but MayMee's took the brass ring!

"Thank you so much, Uncle! This is wonderful!" She ran and hugged his leg.

"Don't thank me. I only lugged it halfway across the country. It was Ma who sent it. Thank her."

"Oh, I surely will, but you still brought it, so I'm grateful for that, too."

"Well, you're welcome."

"Are we good now, Uncle Crockett?" She backed away and grinned. "Because if we are, may I ask for a boon?"

"We're leaving tomorrow, but if I can, I will."

"I want you to write to me. I want to know all about it—you and Uncle finding Becca and all. You see, there's something I want to do, so I'll need to know everything that happens. MayMee said I have the gift."

"I'm sure you do."

And she's going to teach me how to write stories, and it would be so wonderful if I could follow in her footsteps. I hope to pen novels that people all over the world can read if they want to. And love mine like they love hers."

His lips spread wide. "No promises, but I will if I can."

"Oh, thank you! Do you know our address?"

"Yes, ma'am. I surely do."

"That's wonderful. I can't wait to hear from you!"

"Evie, how about you taking your hat box and going upstairs, please. We grownups need to talk."

Without a word, she scooped up her treasure and raced to her reading loft.

Not that he cared for tea much, but Crockett sipped it while he studied the photograph of Becca.

Seemed to him his sister and brother-in-law needed the formality, or was their own laced with courage to fortify them in saying whatever they intended to allow.

Finally, Elijah cleared his throat. "Mary Rachel, well, she and Jethro prayed about it, and what they decided is that love covers."

Levi leaned out and looked past Crockett. "What's that supposed to mean?"

"That whatever it was they fought about..." CeCe put her hands in her lap and stiffened her back, like it pained her to say what she was about to say. "Whatever got Becca so riled up that she ran off. Well, it isn't something they care to discuss. If Becca wants to tell you then it's fine with them, but they are not discussing it—with anyone."

"Ma said she knew. I mean if it's something that will help us find her, then what's the big secret all about?" Crockett hated not knowing a thing when someone else knew it. Becca would tell him. Of that he was sure.

Levi stood. "So that's that. We've got the photograph. Give Mary Rachel and Jethro our love, and tell them we'll let them know when we find her."

"But you're bringing her back here, right?"

Crockett set the tea cup down and joined Levi. "No, Sis. Pa said bring her to Ma. Guess he figured she had the best chance at reconciliation."

"Forget guessing and figuring. Unless the girl specifically asks to come to San Francisco on the way to Texas, we're heading straight there with her. I promised the General I'd bring her to May, and that's that—even if we do come back through here."

CeCe rose so ladylike and genteel, nothing like the young girl from the stories his father told. Guess that's what high society and vast wealth did to some folks.

"Why would Daddy do that? Perhaps he was right, but . . . this is her home, and . . . Well, I guess MayMee might have a better chance, especially if there's still hard feelings."

Evie finished her letter first, but resisted finding the place where she'd stop reading the *Gray Lady Down* and started over on the missive. This time through, she'd go slower and check for any hidden messages buried between the lines of MayMee's neat flowing script. She loved how the great May Meriwether wrote.

Dearest Evie,

I love you, too, and thank you so much for writing. It pleased me, and I'm sure it would thrill your PawPaw that you love Twinkle Toes so much. It was so kind of Nathaniel to bring you Queenie, and I'm glad she's being such a good puppy.

Yes, I did see where you read some of Lady's manuscript, and I also found your notes on the Red

Rooster book. Great catches! I'm still considering some of your suggested changes. Sweetheart, be aware that Gray Lady is not finished, and perhaps, may never be. I gave Houston my word that until he gives his permission, I'll not publish it, and . . .

Queenie whined and nudged her hand with her nose. "Do you need to go out, baby girl?"

Chapter Eight

Evie opened the door. "Come on, girl. I'll race you to the back door."

Beating the pup to end of her hall, she jumped onto the banister and slid to the first landing. Queenie reached it just as she started on the polished rail that would take her to the bottom. The dog beat her, but then she was running on four feet.

Outside, the sight of her parents and Aunt Mary Rachel and Uncle Jethro talking in the solarium halted her in her tracks. She looked away but eased that direction.

If someone was saying something she could hear, then . . . not like she'd planned to snoop. She stopped short and stayed behind the three fir trees that shaded the glass house.

Queenie still hadn't found just the right spot to do her business, so Evie really needed to be out here with her, right?

"Did Levi seem upset?"

"Some, but not really."

What would the old Texas Ranger have to be mad about? Evie opened her ears even wider.

"What about Crockett?"

"Curious, but not irritated."

"Well, thank you for talking with them for us. Levi Baylor is a hard man to tell no."

"Yes, he's almost as bad as Daddy."

Wetness startled her. She looked down. Queenie was licking her hand. She swallowed, putting her heart back where it belonged. "Good girl." She skipped back to the house. Maybe Nathaniel knew what was afoot. He'd tell her if he knew.

Right that minute, back in Texas, Charlotte and her mother were having a confab of their own.

"Mother, why are you being so pigheaded? Just because Pa is gone to Heaven doesn't mean you have to be so stubborn."

"I'll have you know, young lady, that I am not being stubborn or hardheaded or obstinate. It's called practical and logical. And you, my darling daughter, do most certainly need a traveling companion and help, once you get to New York."

"Mother, I'm thirty years old, and I can take care of myself. I've got my Derringer and I know how to use it. I've got my ankle holster, and I may not have told you, but I found the most adorable wee purse gun. You've got to know, I am my father's own daughter when it comes to firearms."

"I don't care if you strap six shooters on each hip. You are not traveling alone, and that's final. It's entirely improper."

"Oh, Mother, you are hopelessly old-fashioned. Fine, then you come with me. A trip to the city will do you good."

"No, no, no, a thousand times no. I have no desire to ever set foot in New York City again. I'm going back to Llano. That's my home. I've got to finish my pirate book, and I've decided to kill off the Rooster."

"What? You can't do that! What's wrong with you? Little kids the world over will be too sad! Just because Daddy's gone doesn't mean you have to kill one of the most famous gentleman pirates ever."

Her mother put on her May Meriwether famous author face. "No, he needs to die. And that's that. Now who are you going to get to go with you?"

She thought about continuing, but when the woman got her dander up, only Crockett or Daddy could sweet talk her out of it. And with her number one ally dead and buried, Charlotte didn't have much hope.

"I don't know, Ma. But if you insist . . . Tell you what. Promise me to ask Evelyn what she thinks about killing off the Red Rooster, and I'll find someone. Deal?"

"I'll think about it."

Later that night, waiting for sleep, Charlotte compiled two lists.

One with possible traveling companions, and the other of young ladies of Red River County she considered to be suitable mates for her brother. She couldn't have him marrying a Yankee girl and set up housekeeping way up north, only coming back for holidays.

Only one name made both, Honey Blanton.

Last she heard, she was between suitors as well . . . if that's what her circle called it nowadays. Perhaps a trip to town would solve her dilemma, or rather her mother's.

While Honey had never come out and claimed a crush on Crockett, she'd most assuredly implied it a time or two, and though a few years younger . . .

Maybe the trip would uncover the truth that she'd secretly hoped he'd come courting. The young lady did like to visit, and might prove somewhat entertaining. She worked the lists a bit more, but no other name shone as brightly as Miss Blanton's.

And best of all, while she wasn't hard on the eyes, neither was she in Charlotte's class looks-wise.

Who in their right mind wanted an employee that turned heads?

The next morning, she enlisted her cousin—well, by marriage on her mother's side—to take her to Clarksville.

Unlike her big brother, who whenever he got good and ready to go somewhere, he saddled his horse or walked out the door without a 'by your leave' to anyone if he didn't want, she had to arrange a driver and someone to harness a wagon or carriage.

Not a bit equitable. Why Mother thought it improper for a young woman to ride to town on a steed, she'd never understand. The concept was so old-fashioned, and so was Ma.

New York would be different. Especially with her prude parent safely back in Llano. Why had she ever insinuated that her mother be her traveling companion?

What had she been thinking?

Without the woman there, no one would be saying anything about her comings and goings. Her time would be her own, and her whereabouts no one's business.

Doing as she pleased certainly had its appeal.

The city should also supply a whole new pool of suitors. All the young men in Red River County seemed related by blood or marriage, and the Llano house . . . it was just too far. Besides, that region also remained too sparsely populated.

The gentleman callers who'd come a courting thus far, she considered less than refined.

A smart, handsome New Yorker might be just the ticket. But he'd have to agree to live in Texas. Hmmm. What would Mother have to say about that?

Jean Paul stopped the wagon in front of the house Pa had bought his mother and him when he'd given them both their freedom. Been a freeman since back in the early 1840s. She couldn't ask for better company.

Did they still call themselves that? Or just Negro now? The times they were a changing, but for the better. All the slaves had been freed since the war.

Men. They proved so stupid sometimes . . . thinking one should own another. And they might as well wake up and make suffrage universal.

A woman's opinion should be as important as a man's. And she should have the right to express it, especially when it came to voting for elected officials.

The silvery-haired man jumped down and held his hand out as she descended the porch steps. "You ready, Miss Charlotte?"

"Yes, sir." She let the old man help her up into the wagon.

The screen door opened then slammed. She turned. Her mother hurried toward her. "Post these letters for me, sweetheart. Would you?"

"Of course."

"Do you need money for stamps?"

She shot her the incredulous look, she hoped a good imitation of the one that had been infuriating her and Crockett for over twenty years, then smiled rather demurely. "No, Ma. I have hard cold cash. Pa would roll over in his grave if I was to leave the house without money or my pistols."

"I love you."

She gave her a real smile. "I love you, too."

Twice in the two-hour ride to town, she almost opened both letters.

Whom she wrote to in New York intrigued her, and she wondered if she'd asked Evelyn about killing off the Rooster. But, she didn't want anyone opening her mail, so she didn't let her curiosity infringe on her mother's right to privacy.

However, if she had the audacity to enlist some old crone friend of hers to keep an eye out on her and report back . . . then there'd be all Billy h. . . No, she would not even think that curse word or its substitution.

Such language didn't fit her genteel and ladylike persona. Vulgarity or swearing was only crude and . . . Who was she joshing?

If not for Ma washing hers and Crockett's mouths out with lye soap, they'd both probably swear like saloon flies.

The Blanton home lay two blocks south of the square, a rather nice saw-board, two-story that could use a coat of white wash. Still though, one of the better houses in Clarksville.

After pleasantries had been exchanged, she got right to the point. "Honey, I have to go to New York as a favor to my brother, and Mother insists that I have a travel companion and then someone to help me once I arrive. Of course, I will pay all your expenses and a stipend if you might consider the arrangements. Are you interested? You were my first choice."

"Why, Charlotte, I never knew you even . . . that is . . . I'm quite honored by your invitation. How long do you plan on being gone?"

"That's entirely in the air, I'm afraid. Crockett's on some wild goose adventure to bring home a wayward cousin of ours, and until he is able to return to New York, I'm needed there. I'm sorry, but the length of the trip remains undetermined. No doubt it will probably be after the New Year at the least."

"I see."

"It'll be great fun should you decide to go. No telling what mischief we might get into! We'll have my mother's brownstone residence, so no seedy hotels."

The girl giggled with her, then stood. "May I offer you a glass of cool lemonade, friend?"

"I'd love one, but Jean Paul—did you ever know him?"

The girl nodded. "Oh, yes. Mammy's son."

"That's who she used to be. We've all called her Miss Jewel ever since Ma gave her a proper name before I was ever born."

"Oh. I do apologize . . . it's what Mama always called her. Wonderful how your poppa bought them then freed them. He always was such a generous man. I'm so sorry that . . . I mean, I haven't had the opportunity to properly offer my condolences to you."

"Well, thank you. Anyway, Jean Paul's gathering supplies, and I promised him I wouldn't be long. Perhaps you need a little time to discuss the trip with your parents." She wanted to say more, but according to her father, in any negotiation, less usually meant more.

And he enjoyed the reputation of being the best horsetrader in the valley.

"How much of a stipend, Charlotte? If I may ask."

"Of course you may. How much do you want?"

"A dollar a day."

"Soldiers during the war only got fifteen a month. Negros twelve."

"I'm neither, plus, that was twenty years ago."

"True." The money wasn't an issue, but she hated taking the hindmost . . . oh, well . . . What was a few dollars between friends? Besides, it would come straight out of Crockett's share. "If I say yes, do you suppose you could be ready by tomorrow?"

"To leave? So soon?"

"Indeed. The quicker the better."

The girl beamed. "I'll discuss my plans with Mama. I'm sure even if Poppa has objections, she can sway him." She extended her hand. "I'll be waiting at the station with bells on."

"Let's make it thirty a month." Charlotte took her hand and shook.

"Deal. Paid in advance."

Charlotte snickered. "Greenback or gold coin?"

"Either, but could someone here possibly put half in my parents' account each month?"

"No problem."

"Excellent. Oh, I'm so excited. Thank you so much for asking me."

"Me, too." That certainly went easy enough, and for thirty a month, Honey could do all the heavy lifting.

While the men traveled north, and the ladies chugged their way east, Evie got a plethora of correspondence all in one day. She loved mail . . . almost as much as she loved Twinkle Toes and Her Royal Blueness.

All the way home from that morning's ride, she'd pondered which one she should read first. For sure and for certain,

Nathaniel's would be saved for last. Perhaps Crockett's should be first then MayMee's.

Both had penned a missive. Oh, she loved using words that Sally didn't know, except she had to keep looking for new ones all the time.

That girl seemed almost as smart as Evie and caught on quickly, too. Shame her friend could only visit the stable twice a week. She hadn't progressed to the no-holding-onto-the-saddle horn point, but then, her steed Dolly couldn't compare to Twink.

Who named a horse Dolly? The mare was a pretty pony, but had a rough stride.

Twinkle Toes' gait was smooth as glass, like riding on air, especially when she posted.

Right before the carriage stopped in front of the house, she decided to go with MayMee's first, then Crockett's, then her betrothed's. She hadn't dared use that word on her best friend yet.

The girl could not keep a secret, but she came by that naturally, so Evie couldn't hold it against her. Mis'ess Vincent had the flappiest tongue in the bay.

Once Sally told her mama, it would only take minutes—or less—for her own dear mother to know and be up in her room wanting an explanation. Grownups just wouldn't understand. Wasn't like she was running off next week. She had ten more years to go before her seventeenth birthday.

And besides, she liked it being hers and Nathaniel's private agreement.

She waited outside, but the pup didn't seem interested in relieving herself. "You can't expect me to stand out here all day, Queenie. Are you sure? I don't want to have to come down for a while. I have three letters to read, in case you don't know."

On that note, as if Her Royal Blueness understood every word, she squatted and tinkled. Tinkled sounded a lot like twinkled, only a 'W' added made it more of a glorious word. After all, stars twinkled. Queenie barked and bounced around, obviously ready to go inside.

Racing upstairs—she never stood a chance of beating the puppy—Evie took the risers two at time. Good thing her mother wasn't watching. With her riding attire hung neatly back in the closet, she slipped into that day's dress with only one petticoat.

More than that made her too hot.

After only a few minutes of reading her first letter and MayMee talking about the *Gray Lady*, she resolved to start over on the manuscript after her missives. She might even save Nathaniel's until her bedtime prayers—after Mama left, of course.

Dearest Evelyn,

She read down to the heart of the matter, skimming a lot of goings on in Clarksville, but not the why of MayMee putting pen to ink. She could read it more carefully later.

I have a question.

Ah! The heart of the matter. She read on.

Since PawPaw passed, I've been toying with the idea of killing off Red Rouster. You know I fashioned the character after my beloved. It seems right to me. But I wanted to know your opinion first before I made a finel determination.

Oooo, that might not be a new word, but it certainly was a long one. Determination. Would Sally be able to spell it? MayMee did, so maybe those others misspelled were just typos, and really didn't count.

Letting the piece of paper sink slowly into her lap, she stared at the wall-planks Daddy had salvaged from a real clipper—one of the many abandoned in the bay when its crew jumped ship, hunting the mother lode.

Quite poetic that her father, who unlike his parents, had never caught the gold fever, ended up being given a stake in one of the richest mines in all of California. He'd purchased several derelicts that he'd made even more money off of, selling the parts.

Of course, as he would always say when telling the story, I kept the best wood and brass for this little house we built.

Guess compared to the mansions on Knob Hill, their home would be considered small, but then their knoll lay much closer to everything, and like her mama said, you can only be in one room at a time.

One place at a time. Was it right for PawPaw to be in Heaven and in the Red Rooster's stories at the same time?

How would she answer MayMee? She returned to the letter and finished reading it all, then without even thinking of going straight to Uncle Crockett's, she retrieved her lap desk, ink, quill, and paper.

The feather tickled her chin, and she went to work, scratching out her reply, careful to use her very best penmanship.

> *Dearest MayMee,*
>
> *Thank you for writing. I love every letter!*
>
> *This one made me a bit sad though. Even the mention of killing Red Rooster off stabbed my heart. My first thought was, 'No! Don't do it!' Then I got to thinking.*
>
> *As the author, it must make you very sad to write about the Captain having new adventures when your inspiration for him won't.*
>
> *I don't want you to be any sadder than you must already be, so I must say, I would think it would be only fair to share some of the sadness around . . . then perhaps, you won't have as much.*
>
> *After all, PawPaw's in Heaven now, so shouldn't the Gentleman Pirate go there, too?*
>
> *MayMee, maybe you could write that he quit his thieving ways and found God. But I have to ask this: Who's going to get the Lone Star Maid? It has to be Madam Merciful, right? I mean since that's you.*
>
> *And how about the crew insisting that she rescue the Cricket out of the northernmost Gulf Islands?*

That pirate is Uncle Crockett, right? Maybe she could save him from that island dungeon he's been imprisoned on up in the Jervis Straight, where Chatterbox Falls is?

And then he'd be free to grab the treasure his father buried on Quadra Island and go save the Princess Carlatta.

In the end of it all, however you decide, yes. It will be sad. I already mentioned that, I know . . . how extremely sad it would be. But wonderful, too, if he can get saved then turned from his wicked ways.

No matter how much a gentleman he was, thou shall not steal is one of the Ten Commandments.

So I say yes. Kill him off. But how about if he dies saving some poor seal pup? Or oh, MayMee! My head is spinning with so many ideas.

If you ever need an imagination girl, just come get me. We can write stories all day long, then in the evening ride horses across the countryside looking for adventures to write about the next day.

She lifted her quill. Yes, one day she would be a famous author just like her May Meriwether . . . follow in her grandmother's footsteps, even though she wasn't of her blood, she had a writer's heart. She laid the paper aside for the ink to dry, then without rereading MayMee's letter, she tore open the one from her grandmother's son.

"Oh, my."

Chapter Nine

This idiot tried to rob us.

Evie set the missive down and closed her eyes. A shipwrecked pirate perhaps? Looking for a grub stake? No, swashbucklers only got marooned on deserted islands. Then maybe a down-and-out miner? He'd need money for supplies.

Sure . . . that would fly. A poor man with gold fever. She picked up her Uncle's letter again and read on.

Upon arrival in Seattle, a quaint little seaport, we secured lodging then decided to visit an eatery highly recommended by one of our shipmates on the voyage. We came up the coast on what they call the inner passage.

Just as we passed one building a mere block from our destination, this hooligan jumped out, brandishing a flaying knife. Its blade looked
   perfectly wicked. I guess about eight inches in length.

He jabbed it toward Levi's chest and says in his gravelly voice, "Give me all your money."

Evie dear, I never have seen anything like it. Now mind you, our uncle is old! Sixty-seven. I wouldn't have believed it, but I saw it with my own eyes. I tell you no lies.

Apparently, all the stories about him are true. Not that I ever doubted, but you didn't know Uncle Wallace.

I barely can remember him myself, but I remember his stories, always bragging on his best friend. And you've read Ma's The Ranger, right? How Wallace loved embellishing his and Uncle's adventures.

But now I'm thinking perhaps not so much after all.

Oh my goodness! For pity's sake! Would he ever get to the story? He needed to lose all that introspection. She loved her new word. She'd just read it in MayMee's letter. He needed to get to the good part! And Evie could certainly see what her grandmother had been telling her about too much of that internal thinking ruining an otherwise perfect, action-packed story!

Finding her place again, she continued reading.

With his left arm, Uncle knocked the knife away. At the same time, he pulled his hideaway pistol. He's taken to wearing a shoulder holster. If I'd blinked, I would have missed it!

One second, the guy's trying to rob us, the next, he's hightailing it down the alley.

Well, baby girl, figured I best write it down for you— not that I would ever forget Uncle Levi saving our bacon. I probably would have given the man my walking around money.

Your PawPaw taught me to have a few dollars in my trousers' pocket, but keep my wallet inside my coat, so he wouldn't have gotten much.

Anyway, we're here, and tomorrow, we'll leave for San Juan Island. The ship Becca sailed out on would most likely have stopped in Roche to load lime and lumber, so we'll start there.

Then on into British Territory and probably Vancouver's Island. The area is exceptionally beautiful.

Always thought East Texas Pines were magnificent, but I must say, they cannot hold a candle to the evergreens of the Northwest Territories.

Love, Uncle Crockett

P.S. Write me your news, but post it to Llano. I can read it when I get back.

Oh, to have been there! Evie reread the good part, but if there, she would probably have missed the whole scene because of hiding behind the most famous Texas Ranger of them all. She couldn't wait to tell Sally . . . and her parents!

Or should she rethink that and let them read it for the first time in . . .

What would she name her new book? *Multitude of Sin and Love.*

Her father had told Uncle Crockett and Uncle Levi that was why Aunt Mary Rachel and Uncle Jethro declined telling them the whole story about Becca . . . because it said in the Bible that love covers a multitude of sin.

Maybe Auntie sinned a whole lot before she ran off. Is that why they wouldn't tell?

Since MayMee planned on killing off the Red Rooster, instead of pirate books, Evie could write about the Rangers . . . well, Uncle Crockett wasn't really a Ranger, but she loved the idea.

Maybe Uncle Levi could swear him in as an under-deputy or something. The younger could be a Ranger . . .

Or what about bears? Like Berry! She loved the stuffed brown bear MayMee gave her; the very one she'd played with when she was a little girl. *Berry and Burl, A Bear's Tale.* That might make a good title, and she would have so much fun writing the story. Maybe she would have to talk about that with the best author in the world.

But Uncle Crockett . . . would he make a good Ranger? Probably too soft in real life from spending all of MayMee's money and wasting time doing nothing worthwhile in the big city. That's what everyone said.

Had he ever thought about making an honest living? Being brave and hauling in bad guys?

That should harden him up a lot if living the high life in New York didn't. What exactly was the high life? She'd have to ask Mama. She and Aunt Gwen had talked about it sometimes.

Setting his missive aside, retrieved her lap table, got everything ready, then after the mandatory tickle, put pen to paper.

To my new favorite Uncle,
Thank you so much for writing, I'll post this to Llano like you requested, but it's truly a shame I can't send it to you up north somewhere. However, I understand.

She closed one eye so she could see better what to write, but before she decided on what to tell next, Her Royal Blueness went to licking her off hand.

That's what PawPaw always called the one she wasn't using at the time. She loved remembering the things he used to say. He was the smartest man she ever knew . . . well, maybe after Daddy.

"What is it, Queenie?"

Someone calling a faint 'Evie' drifted across her ear.

"Oh, thanks, girl. You hear Mama before she hollers."

She jumped up. "Coming."

What new adventure awaited?

Charlotte stuck her hand out and stopped her traveling companion from grabbing the trunks. The girl looked at her, and she mouthed, let him, nodding toward the footman.

The man unloaded her two steamers and Honey's carpet bag onto the stoop then extended his hand. Charlotte paid him his hire plus four bits extra. Daddy taught her excellent service deserved a reward.

The tip won her a 'good day, miss' and a lift of his cap. She returned his gesture with a smile and slight nod.

Wouldn't want Pa rolling over in his grave for any impoliteness toward the help.

The door swung open.

"Miss Charlotte, you're here! It is so grand to see your face again. My, my, just look at you. Why, you get prettier every time I see you, baby girl! Twice as beautiful as I remember, too. Looking so much like your mother, you are. She wired, so I've been expecting you for the better part of two days now. And who's this lovely vision you've brought along?"

"Honey Blanton, meet Beatrice Ammi. We all call her Bammie. She's been with us for years and takes care of the brownstone—and us—as though we were her own."

The housekeeper grinned big, wiped her hands on her apron, then grabbed the biggest trunk. "Good to meet you, Honey."

"Oh, the pleasure is all mine, ma'am."

She glanced back to Charlotte. "I've got your room all ready and the guest room . . . well, it stays ready. I'll get Miss Honey settled in. And tell me now, where has Mister Crockett gotten himself off to?

Why didn't he accompany you two young ladies? You shouldn't be traveling alone."

"Oh, Bammie, you're as bad as Mother. From his deathbed, Daddy sent my brother on a wild goose chase up into the Oregon Territory—and who knows how far beyond—to find an errant cousin and bring her home." She turned to her traveling companion. "You'll love the room. It has a great view of the park."

"And sweet child, I was so very sorry to hear the sad news about your father. I sent my condolences."

"Yes, ma'am, thank you. I knew you had, and your note meant a lot to Ma."

After sending word to her brother's partner, Charlotte opened the smaller trunk, hung the dresses in the closet, and put away her lingerie. The gown she'd planned on wearing that night for dinner, she draped over the mannequin.

A tear tried to escape, but she blinked it back.

The extravagant tailors' dummy, a gift from her father the last time he'd come to the city, made her suddenly sad. Why was she being so sentimental?

How she wished he hadn't done it. Riding a green broke stud colt at his age . . . simply ludicrous. She still missed him every day, as if a part of her thought he'd live forever . . . or at least long enough to walk her down the aisle.

Not that she planned on that happening any time soon, but . . . Perhaps Uncle Levi would be a sufficient substitute.

Uncle Chester would have been first in line for the duty. She missed him, too. How did people do it? Those who had no assurance of a reunion in eternity with their deceased loved ones? A light tap sounded on her door and brought her out of her morbid musings.

"Come in."

Having the live-in proved such a blessing. From the hall, she poked her head in. "Mister Nash Moran sent word that he would be pleased to dine with us tonight. Is there anything special I should fix?"

"All your meals are plenty special. Anything you have will be wonderful."

The old lady grinned. "Miss Charlotte, you have always been too kind."

Nash made an extra effort to time his arrival to the minute, but ended up two minutes late. Hopefully, Crockett's sister wouldn't be too much a stickler on punctuality. Once inside, the young lady's smirk said otherwise, but he ignored it.

"I've heard so much about you, Miss Buckmeyer, and am so pleased to finally make your acquaintance. Your brother said you were cute, but he must have a blind spot. That word certainly does not do you justice. Why, you're—"

She cut him off before he could finish. "Crockett has spoken of you as well, Mister Moran." The vision of loveliness extended her hand toward the dining hall. "Shall we? The food was hot. Hopefully, it hasn't got too cold."

He smiled then stopped at the open double doorway. My, my. Another young lady, pretty in her own right, but cute would suffice for her. She missed being in Charlotte's class by a red dog mile.

His partner's sister stopped at the head of the table and waited, standing beside her seat. Catching on, he hurried to help with her chair then sat to her left across from . . .

"Mister Moran, I'd like to introduce Honey Blanton, my good friend and traveling companion."

He nodded. "Is Honey your given name or does it only designate how sweet you are?"

The lady smiled. "No, I hate to say, that's what my mother named me. Daddy never should have let her, so I blame him as much."

"No, you shouldn't dislike it. Honey is very memorable."

"Well, I've never known a Nash before." The lovely young woman tucked her chin demurely. "Is there a story that goes along with such an unusual name, sir?"

"As a matter of fact . . ." Before he could say more, the first course arrived. A delicious salad, though he normally didn't care for rabbit food. It had raisins and little nuts—the kind of which, he couldn't place, not walnuts or pecans. With each course, he got only snippets of conversation from either, but way more batting eyelashes from the Miss Honey.

Not so many though from his partner's little sister. The warm blackberry cobbler smothered with cold cream finished the meal to perfection. Indeed, his full belly was well satisfied. He loved Bammie's cooking and would enjoy nothing more than a steady diet of it. Well, perhaps not more than a certain . . .

Charlotte stood.

He jumped to his feet. "A sherry in my mother's office? It's already laid out and decantered."

"Oooo, so sassy," barely escaped under his breath.

"Excuse me, sir? I didn't hear what you said."

"Isn't that where your famous mother wrote *The Ranger*?"

"No, earlier titles perhaps, but she penned that novel at our old house in Clarksville—the one our Uncle Levi now owns. Actually, he is the Ranger. The man who rescued Aunt Rose—her family still refers to her as Sassy. Have you read it? Men enjoy it as much as the ladies." One lip raised slightly.

Might she smile? He nodded, but didn't say more.

Without further ado, she twirled and marched out then through the office door and sat herself at a rather empty desk, save for the wine tray and two glasses. Apparently, Honey wasn't invited.

The lady poured—something he would have expected her to ask him to do—then set a glass in front of a wingback guard chair, one he'd sat many times. He refrained from tasting the brew until she took a sip of her own. "Excellent." He doffed his crystal goblet. "Thank you for suggesting it."

Batting her lashes slowly, she offered one slight nod. "Crockett said he was posting a letter to you. Have you received it?"

"Indeed. I was sad to hear about your father and also upset about your brother's absence for such an extended time."

"Well, I'm here now. And as you may or may not know, I was a silent partner to this venture. But no more. From this point forward, all decisions involving money must have my approval."

"Fair enough. The Golden Rule certainly applies: he—or she—who has the gold, sets the rules. Anything else, boss?" Hopefully, he didn't put too much sarcasm in his voice.

"Definitely. Don't ever call me boss again. I'll expect you here every morning at seven sharp, six days a week. What you do on Sundays is your business."

"Seven." The 'that late' didn't make it out, instead he only smiled like he beat the sun up every single day.

"Sharp, as my father before me, I hate waiting on anyone."

"Yes, ma'am."

Chapter Ten

Charlotte turned slowly in front of the full length, free-standing mirror. "Not bad."

Mercy! Had she said that out loud? Better watch it. Pride comes before a fall, except her father had always misquoted that scripture. It was actually worse. Pride was followed by destruction in the Biblical version, a haughty spirit before a fall.

Sixteenth chapter of Proverbs, eighteenth verse; though she never told him that. Bless his heart. He knew all things in Heaven.

A light tap on her door garnered her attention.

Honey peeked around. "Breakfast is almost ready."

"Perfect." She followed her friend to the kitchen. She'd always loved eating at the brownstone, especially the few times she'd had the privilege of doing so with her parents.

Once Bammie had cleared the dishes and while she sipped her last cup of coffee, Charlotte decided on Honey's role in this new venture. She set her cup down a bit hard, then looked across the table.

"While Nash is here, I would like for you to take notes of what is said whenever the conversation is related to business."

The lady nodded and appeared to be rather thrilled with herself. "Yes, ma'am. I'll be pleased to, and any other chore that's needed."

"Good." Charlotte liked her attitude. The grandfather clock in the hall struck its first chime of the new hour. "Would you escort Mister Moran to my mother's office? I'll be there shortly." She smiled at her lady-in-waiting.

The next chime of seven sounded as the man knuckled the door.

Honey grinned then hurried to do as she'd been told.

With her players in place, Charlotte promenaded onto her new stage. She loved the part she'd crafted for herself. What an ill-starred shame he had called her boss. Had she thought of it, it would be a perfect title. As it was, she would insist on . . . What?

"Good morning."

Honey silently followed on his heels and took the straight-backed chair against the back wall.

Nodding as she slipped into the chair that fit her so well— good?—she had trouble with those adverbs sometimes. Well must be correct because it sounded more snooty.

"And a good morning to you, sir. I want to spend some time this morning to go over exactly where the business stands. Why don't you start by telling me the state of our affairs as you see them?"

"Where should I begin?" He looked from her to Honey, as though the girl might have an answer, then back. "You know about our building?"

Wow, that came from out of the blue. Her brother had bought a building? The twit. Why hadn't he bothered to tell her? "Actually, I do not. When did that happen and where is it?"

"Six months, three days . . ." He closed one eye and looked over her head with the other one. "And approximately five hours ago. We signed the papers at noon that day." He grinned like he'd just proven she shouldn't be in charge.

"Mister Moran, no one—especially me—likes sarcasm. Now, please sir, tell me about our building."

"Three stories above ground, two under. I found it, and your brother came up with the cash for its purchase."

"Oh yes, I'm well aware of that."

"I've rented out the top floor. That income covers my draw and how we pay for the remodel expenses of the ground floor. We've had offers on it, but as yet, no one has agreed to our terms."

Dare she ask? But she'd been the one to invite Honey into this meeting. She looked to her helper. "Could you please fetch me another cup of coffee?"

"Certainly, ma'am." The girl jumped up and left the room.

"How much are you . . . did you call it a draw?"

"Yes, ma'am. I get fifty a month against my thirty percent, plus I keep a suite off our office on the second floor for living quarters."

"I see."

"The monies I draw will be repaid at the final reckoning. The lodging is a perk as are all transportation expenses. I'm on my own for meals."

The man had the same percentage as she? That was no good, but at least she controlled her brother's majority while he traipsed around the Oregon Territory with Uncle Levi.

Good thing she'd sent Honey out; wouldn't want her having any inclinations of asking for more. Of course, her duties required so much less time and experience as well.

Might be Mister Moran who'd be asking for more if he knew her salary.

So much she didn't know. But then her father hadn't known a thing about flatboats before he traded for the first one. She loved that story and how it'd worked out so notably as that business led directly to purchasing his first stagecoach.

Though trains had taken over the transportation industry of late, the coaches still served a purpose.

"And the location of the building?"

"Not far from here. Three streets over on Second."

"You said the ground floor was being remodeled. Why? If we have no tenant, wouldn't it be prudent to wait? Adapt our upgrades according to their specific needs?"

"It had been a bank, but they sold out. The next owner got caught up in the crash of '82. The place sat vacant for almost thirty months, so, we were thinking of shops and restaurants off a very pleasant main hall. Your brother wants plenty of plants and maybe a fountain."

"Very interesting. An intriguing idea. Has it been done in other locations? Is that where you and Crockett got the idea?" Sounded great. That all sounded like so much fun. Why hadn't her idiot brother told her about the building? Or his intentions with it? After all, her money had been invested, too.

The door opened, and Honey reappeared carrying a steaming cup which she set on her desk. "Thank you. We're discussing the building's first floor and its remodel." She turned to Nash. "What kind of offers have you gotten?"

"Straight rent. We've been asking for rent plus a percentage."

Wow. An even better deal. Could her brother have been such an innovator, or were all the great ideas coming from his partner? She'd never seen Crockett as much of a visionary . . . "This is all very interesting. I want to see the plans; better yet, see the property itself. Does the building have a name?"

"A name? Hmmm, hadn't thought of giving it a name. You mean like a pet?" He turned toward Honey and smiled as if he thought her question amusing. "We can go anytime. Did your brother tell you about the orchard?"

"Well, it's apparent he didn't keep me informed at all. So, fill me in on it." She would have a piece of her big brother's hide the next time she saw him.

Her new partner nodded. "Apples. Three hundred acres upstate. Crockett must not have told you why he needed more funds the last time he asked for money. That's when we acquired it. At least I assumed he got it from you."

She shook her head. "Mother and I . . . well . . . I suppose we assumed the worse. Our father may have known. He always claimed Ma spoiled my brother rotten, but in my humble opinion, he was just as bad. Where is it, and is it making any money?"

"Ever heard of Poughkeepsie?"

"No, so is it profitable?"

"Not yet, the previous owner overextended himself planting trees and building a press house. We should break even this year and show a little next, but the year after is when we should recoup all of our investment. By then, fewer than half the trees will have started bearing. After that, should be a gold mine once it's in full production."

"I want to see that, too. Make the arrangements." She bit her tongue to keep from saying please. He needed to know she was in charge now. "Anything else?"

"Yes, ma'am. Is tomorrow soon enough?"

"It is." She lifted her brow, a practiced expression. "Anything else?"

"How about the Blue Moon? Are you aware of her?"

"No. My brother bought a tavern?"

He smiled. "Not a bar, and we didn't buy it outright, only shares in the clipper ship—leaves out laden with whatever cargo the owners believe will bring the best return. The boat's publicly financed."

"Very interesting,"

"While she's gone, the shares are traded. A rumor circulated awhile back that the Moon had run aground in Jamaica, but I traced that particular lie back to the bunch who'd spread the false report. Same thing happened the year before."

"They purposely lied? Why?"

"To bring the share price down." His tone made it clear he couldn't believe she'd asked. As though she should have figured it out.

The brute.

"Your brother and I beat them at their own game though. Bought a thousand shares at half their original price before the scoundrels could make their move that time."

"I see." Her tone, she hoped, implied she didn't appreciate his insinuation, but she refrained from defending herself. Pa drilled it into her that strength never defended itself. "When is she due back in port?"

"No one knows. That's the rub. She could be here today or next month or three years from now. If the owners know, they never let on. But no extra shares are sold after she sails."

Why in the world had she been lollygagging all these years back in Texas? "That seems a bit odd. One would think investors would want to know such a pertinent piece of information."

"Return on the dollar has always been so high, guess they're happy to take their profits whenever she comes in."

"So . . . real estate, fruit, and cargo. What other pies have we got our fingers in?"

"Just one more. We've secured east-of-the-Mississippi manufacturing rights to the Eversole four-row planter. Crockett found that deal. Right now, we're hiring it out, but I've been keeping my eye peeled for the right forge to buy."

"Really." She never would have thought . . .

"Oh yes, and there are several more irons in the fire, but nothing that's firmed up yet."

Ah, so. Her brother hadn't told Mister Moran everything either. He'd have no way of knowing Elijah Eversole was a half-brother by marriage. She stood. "Unless there's something else that needs tending, I'm ready to see our building."

"Yes, ma'am." He jumped to his feet.

Levi signed the registry as L.B. Baylor right below Crockett's D.C. Buckmeyer. For sure, did not need anyone putting two and two together into a fight or fawn. He hated both. Second biggest mistake of his life, letting May write his and Rose's story.

Ladies the world over acted like they knew him personally and always wanted a catch-up on Rose and the children. Men sought to try on the famous Texas Ranger for size. See if he really ate railroad ties and spit iron spikes.

The clerk swung the book back, looked at the names, then held out two keys. "Room sixteen, gents. Check out is at noon."

Levi took his key and slid it into his vest pocket. "Where's Front Street?"

The man nodded toward the west. "Two blocks over. What you be looking for?"

"Thanks. You just told me." Levi tipped his hat then turned to his companion. He didn't live sixty-seven years by running his mouth. "Want to come with me?"

Crockett nodded. "Let's stow our grips first."

"Sure." He'd almost forgot about his luggage.

Wasn't used to traveling so encumbered. He and Wallace might have only a saddlebag and be on the trail for weeks, but then, young Crockett probably never lived off the land in his life.

Right that minute, his love for Henry and will to accomplish his favor grew a bit thin.

While Crockett put away his clothes all nice and neat, like they couldn't possibly live in the carpet bag one more minute, Levi surveyed the street below, checked the view from both of the room's windows, then stood by the door.

"Come on. We're burning daylight."

The boy shot him a look. Same one he'd been getting from Henry's youngest for years. Wasn't sure exactly what he meant by it, but Levi took it as insolence or worse.

"Yes, sir."

Tone wasn't much better. He found the place easy enough, but no sight of the woman he hoped to see. The boy took a corner table and slipped into the far chair. At least he knew something. Levi bellied up to the bar. "Sophia still work here?"

"Yes, sir, sure does." The barkeep wiped the wood directly in front of Levi. "What can I pour you?"

"Two beers. When do you expect her?"

"She's here. In the back, cooking."

Levi put a silver dollar on the bar. "Be so kind and let her know an old friend is here."

The man reached under the counter and slipped over a half dollar. "The beers are two bits apiece."

"The sign says a dime."

"That's Canadian. US coin is more."

Levi picked up the mugs then nodded to his change. "Tell Sophie I'm here."

The man slid the coins off the bar into his hand. "My pleasure, sir."

The boy took a big gulp then set the drink down. "Rather bitter."

Trying his own, he found something he could agree on. But he didn't buy the brew only to drink. The man returned with an older lady. At first glance, he didn't see the girl he remembered. Then once in the light, there she was.

Her beauty had matured, and her hair silvered. Still, pretty much the same girl who'd sought refuge from Bull Glover and his no-count son.

Levi stood.

She spied him, squealed, then ran toward him. "Levi Baylor! What in this world?" She slowed, and he caught her, and swung her around. "Good to see you, girl. Been too long."

"Yes, it has. I was so sad to hear about Rose, Levi. Are the children all fine? How's Charley and Bart? That old softie Henry still with us?"

"Kids are all good. Henry passed awhile back. That's why we're here."

She shook her head. "Oh, no. Guess I figured he'd live forever. What happened? Your wire didn't say anything about him."

She sat down, and he told her the story.

Before he could ask about Becca, a balding man with a big belly came through the kitchen door.

"Sophia, get your black hide back in here. We've got dinner to cook."

Levi stood and stepped in front of her.

She touched his arm, and he faced her. "He's my boss. I need this job."

"How about working for me?"

"I'd love that, but . . ."

Levi stepped toward fat man. "She quits. Find someone else to boss around."

"She can't quit." He glared like he hoped Levi would say something else.

Chapter Eleven

Fat man's eyes flared, and his hand went to his pocket.

Crockett jumped to his feet. "Hold on." He stepped around the table. "Sir." The cook looked at him. "Before anyone does anything rash, perhaps you are unaware of exactly who my big brother is."

"Don't matter one little bit who this old man claims to be. He can't come in here and take my help, especially when the wench owes me money."

Ah, filthy lucre, an easy fix. "Perhaps financial compensation is in order?"

The man snorted and pulled his hand out of his pocket. His chubby fingers wrapped around cold steel.

Sophia gasped.

Crockett's pulse quickened. He reached for his own weapon. Movement faster than his eyes could follow blurred on his left. In less than a blink, Levi's left hand wrapped around fat man's wrist. The other held his thirty-eight in the guy's face.

"No call to die today. Now, my brother was trying to solve our dilemma here. You said the lady owed you money."

"Forty-two dollars, Canadian."

"That so Sophia?"

"Yes, sir, but less today's wages."

"You ain't finished your shift, so you got nothing coming."

Crockett couldn't believe the man's tone, especially looking down the barrel of his brother's pistol.

"Forty and two it is." He retrieved his wallet from his inside coat pocket and counted out the money. Good thing he'd exchanged some of his greenbacks.

Releasing his left hand, Levi kept the pistol's barrel pointed at the man's nose. "There's your money. We're leaving. Don't do anything stupid."

The proprietor sneered, but returned his gun to his pocket and gathered up the cash.

Sophia held up her hand. "Will you wait? I need my things."

"Go ahead and get them. We'll all stand right here until you . . . Barkeep. You best come up empty-handed."

The man raised up slowly then placed both hands in the air.

Not one time had Crockett bothered to check out the guy behind the bar.

Wow, all the stories about the Ranger must be true, and he'd bet Wallace Rusk hadn't embellished on a one of them after all. No telling what the barkeep had planned, but him not protesting—and throwing his hands in the air like he did?

Told it all.

Evie put the letter down. Mercy! Trouble just followed Uncle Levi around! When she fictionalized their adventures, she'd have him wing the barkeep as he brought his shotgun up because shotguns are so much more impressive than pistols. After all, like MayMee said, in the front pages of a book, it declared the story a work of fiction.

That meant a writer could embellish all she wanted. Not that May Meriwether did much of that. The truth alone of those long ago days was really exciting all by itself.

Shame she hadn't been born back then. And that she never got to ride the seven seas like Uncle Houston. She glanced at her stack of pages.

One day, they'd be a novel. A whole book with her name on the cover, except she wasn't sure about keeping the title. *Gray Lady Down* might give away too much of the story. She shook off the thought. It'd be a long time before she would have to decide on that.

Plus, if her uncle didn't agree while he was alive . . . and if MayMee left the manuscript in her care after she went to Heaven to be with PawPaw . . . then Evie could finish the story and call it whatever she wanted. Right?

What if MayMee didn't say it in her will? Evie would have to write and ask her to for sure and for certain. And ask if she wanted to see her first draft of her uncle's adventure up North or wait until she had it just right.

Hey, that could be a good title. *Up North*. She leaned over and said it out loud. "*Up North*."

Queenie thumped her tail against Evie's leg.

"Good. It's settled then. That's what we'll call it."

She grabbed her lap table, got everything ready, then almost put pen to paper before she remembered to tickle her chin.

Dear MayMee,

How are you? I hope you're well and having fun every day.

As you can see from your copy he asked me to scribe for you, I received another letter from Uncle Crockett today. I'm confused. How does Uncle Levi know a lady named Sophia? I kind of, sort of remember her from one of your books. Was it The Novelist or The Ranger? Or maybe just from the stories told when we came?

But Aunt Rose was always the love of Uncle's life, so how come the Sophia lady is running to him now? And why would Uncle Crockett be willing to pay that mean man who was her boss forty-two dollars?

Even though it's Canadian money, isn't that still an awful lot? Or is it more? So I figured they must both know her pretty well. I figure she must have been a minor character since I can't seem to remember her very well.

Queenie whined, stood, then slid down and ran to the bedroom door.

"Mercy, you just went."

Her mother's voice reached her ear. "Evie!"

"Why didn't you say so, girl? A woof would have been nice." She put her writing material away, set the table to the side then jumped up. Thirty-six steps and two really fast slides down the banister got her there quick.

Maybe even record time! She needed one of those watches with a sweep hand to mark the seconds. Or better yet, she could get Sally to count to see how fast she could make it.

Whew! Her mother came out of the sewing room just as Evie got her dress smoothed out all ladylike. Of course, Queenie had found her first and sat beside her mother's feet as though she'd won the race.

Except that it didn't count because she had four feet. Or more precisely, paws.

"Did you call me, Mama?"

"I did. Dinner is ready."

Food. She liked eating well enough—especially her favorite, baked potatoes with English peas—but sometimes, the opportunity for a chance to ask the old folks a question was even better. And with just a few words she had her mother talking a blue streak.

Back in her loft she resumed her missive.

Mama told me about Bull and Braxton, and poor Sophia being a slave over our noon repast. I like that word, don't you? So what happened to Bull's gold?

Was that the treasure in book three? And, Mama thinks she was going to have a baby when she headed north. Was she? Did she? Do you know what happened to the baby? Do you know?

She also thinks she and Aunt Rose used to write back and forth. Is that how Uncle knew she was in Victoria? I think it's wonderful to have a city named after you. Do you suppose the Queen of England does?

Anyway, I've decided to call my novel about my uncles' adventure Up North. What do you think of that for a title?

And I love it that now I know the real story about Black Bull and Red Rooster's fight over Madam Merciful. You are so clever! Oh, and in my barroom fight, I'm thinking of having Uncle Levi wing the barman as he gets his shotgun up.

More drama, am I right? Or should I stick to the facts?

As you will see, you are reading my letter first, right? But either way, my uncles are making progress. I must say, I'm wondering why Sophia would leave her home and go with them.

Does she know Becca, too? Sure would be nice if I could ask Uncle Crockett questions, but I guess I'll keep a list since I have to wait for him to get home.

Oh, what if you came, and you and I were to go find them Up North? I surely am liking that title better and better, but if you don't, you truly can tell me. Then maybe we could think of a better one, except . . .

The grandfather clock struck twice. She blew on her last page, capped the ink, and carefully set her writing table aside.

"Come on, girl. We can finish this tonight. We're going to the stables to meet Sally this afternoon. You'll sure be happy to see Twinkle Toes, won't you?"

A double bark sounded right on cue. Evie truly believed the dog understood everything she said, after all she was an exceptional great-great-great-grandpup of the famous Blue Dog or was it more greats? She wasn't sure.

Could he have been as smart as Her Royal Blueness? She pondered the thought, sliding down the banister again.

"Evelyn May Eversole! What do you think you're doing, young lady? Or should I say young hooligan?"

Uh oh.

When it rained, it poured. May chided herself for even thinking that old cliché, but it did fit. She toyed with her three letters—well, to be more precise, two—and a missive from Evie. She smiled, picturing the baby girl search the dictionary for new words.

Then she decided on Crockett's first.

The two other senders weren't traipsing across the frozen north country. She retrieved the letter opener from the middle drawer. For too many heartbeats, she looked at the sliver of gold topped with a nugget from Jethro's and Elijah's mine.

What a gift! One of her and Henry's more prized possessions.

Hardheaded old goat. He'd still be kicking if . . . She tucked that thought away. He wasn't, and she needed to be about living. She slipped the opener in and pulled it across the seal.

Dear Ma,

Hope this finds you in good spirits and not missing Pa too bad. Levi told me about a hog hunt you went on before you two got married. If I had heard that story, I didn't remember it.

Have you used it in one of the pirate books? I'm a couple behind. Anyway, we talk about him a lot now that Sophia is traveling with us. Oh, you didn't even know we found her. We did.

I wrote to Evie, so she should be sending you another letter soon. No need to write everything twice. She almost begged me, and how can anyone tell that baby girl no?

If I am blessed with a daughter one day, I hope she's just like her. I asked her to be my scribe and send you a copy.

You'll know then how we came about having the ex-slave traveling with us. I'll tell you, Ma, my 'big brother' is some kind of man. I'm convinced all the tall tales told about the Ranger—I almost used ex, but he has informed me there's no such thing.

He is and will always be one—anyway, I now believe all those stories are true.

After seeing the man in two perilous situations . . . even though he's old, he's still lightning quick. In a flash, he had his pistol out and at the ready, while I stood motionless, trying to decide on what to do.

He insisted on us taking turns at standing watch. As though someone was going to bust into our hotel room. Mercy! He claims he has so many enemies, that even up north, he can't let his guard down.

So far, it's been a waste of good sleep. But then I'd hate waking up dead or being robbed.

Now I might be talking out of school, but it appears to me that the man is in love or perhaps infatuated is a more appropriate term. He's acting real protective of Miss Sophia, and they sure seem to exchange a lot of looks and sly smiles. Might be some private joke they have.

Who knows? He offered to send her back to Texas, but she wanted to come with us and Levi agreed—quite readily if you ask me. Seems her son took off at an early age not wanting to live under her rules.

What half-grown kid does? So she's trying to find him before she comes back.

She remembered the beautiful young pregnant girl and how Henry had looked at her. His excuse of her being a spitting image of her mother . . . then his admission of loving that woman even before Sue.

It would be easy to understand how Levi might fall for her. He'd been alone so many years.

Such a terrible loss. Rose being alive and vibrant, in her prime, then gone in a moment, impaled by a straw shot at her by that twister.

How she hated Texas for its tornadoes, but figured they were better to deal with than the East Coast hurricanes. She'd lived through too many of those as a child.

> *Oh. Almost forgot. We found out where Becca worked for a while. Levi tracked down a steamboat captain who remembered taking her to Juneau. So that's our next destination if you want to try to post a letter to general delivery there.*
>
> *Anyway, the man remembered her traveling with another lady and two men.*
>
> *More later, Ma. It's almost time to wake Levi. Guess that's one good thing about guard duty, gives me time to write. Have you heard from Charlotte?*
>
> *Hopefully, she'll not mess things up too bad before I get home.*
>
> > *Love you more than you'll ever know.*
> > *David Crockett Buckmeyer.*
>
> *P.S. I still haven't forgiven you two for hanging that name on me. After all, how can someone live up to a legend?*
>
> *Houston on the other hand loves it that he's named after old Sam.*
>
> *I love you, Ma. Take care of yourself.*

May read the letter again, pressed it flat with her hands, then put it away in the desk's bottom right drawer with all the others. Did Henry know all the goings on, or was he too busy praising the Lord?

She blinked back a tear then opened the envelope from Charlotte. Best see if her baby needed anything before she read Evie's.

At the missive's end, she let it fall to her lap. "Oh my."

Chapter Twelve

Charlotte signed the three places indicated, accepted her copy of the documents, then nodded at the banker. "Thank you, sir, for handling our transaction swiftly and with such decorum." She stood.

The man rose to his feet and almost bowed. "You're most welcome, Miss Buckmeyer. Please, anytime I may be of assistance."

She turned. The junior officer who'd been keeping Honey occupied hurried toward her.

"Bentley will see you and your companion out and arrange whatever transportation you require."

"No need, sir. Mother's brownstone is only a few blocks down. Thank you again."

Once outside and free of the bank's flunky, Charlotte kept her face like stone. Pa would be so proud. Why, she was a genius! The deal would prove impeccable.

Apparently, Honey could not contain herself. "Well? What happened?"

Finally, she allowed herself a grin and spun toward her new partner.

"Exactly what I said! After all, it was my cash Ma sent. Just a matter of transferring it from my account in Llano to this bank. Folks wire money all the time these days. With me such a substantial new account holder, and being willing to put up half the funds, he couldn't say no. We got the loan."

"Really? So it's true? I'm . . . uh . . . we're going to have a New York dress shop?"

"No, my friend. You had it right the first time. It will be your shop. We're partners, but past sewing a button back on . . ." She smiled even bigger. "I've never wanted to work retail."

"Oh, Charlotte! I never dreamed! Having a fancy ladies shop is simply beyond my wildest imaginations. What am I saying? I would never have begun to imagine such a thing . . . not even in Clarksville!"

"Good, glad you like the notion."

"Like it? I love it! Why . . . I'll be a New York City proprietor! And the space is . . . perfect, divine! That huge front window so folks can see in, and . . ."

"And of course, it will pay rent to Buckmeyer & Moran—so it feathers that nest—and I can't wait to see Crockett's face when I tell him. But . . . we negotiated a very reasonable amount, don't you think? Especially considering the prime location."

Honey's shoulders scrunched as though she was six again, hands grasped in the center of her chest. "Oh, yes! And no rent until the third tenant moved in! It . . . it was . . . simply genius."

"Well, I'm glad you're so excited. You do have an eye for fashion and decorating, and you make friends so easily. You'll be a natural. And your boutique will draw other retail shops, as well. I'm certain . . . so don't get too excited about the no rent part."

The recipient of the unexpected windfall put her hands to her cheeks. Maybe to keep her face from splitting in two, she smiled so big. "A boutique! I love calling it that. Honey's Dress Boutique. Is that too . . . too . . .?"

"No, of course it is not. Why, it's perfect! Umm, unless . . ." Charlotte gave her a wink. "You wanted to add millinery and sell some hats as well."

"I love it! Honey's Boutique and Millinery it is." The young lady fluttered her lashes, looking suddenly so concerned. Tears welled and flooded over. "How can I ever thank you enough?"

Charlotte wiped the girl's cheeks. "Make us both lots of money. Once the bank loan and my investment capital is repaid, with interest, then our shares reverse. I'll be the minority partner, and you'll have the option of buying me out . . .or not."

"No, no. I'll love having you as a partner."

"Either way, the space is leased, and we'll both make a pile of money."

"Oh, yes! That part's so exciting, too!"

She held a finger up. "If you sell enough dresses, hats . . . Why not shoes, too?"

"Of course! Shoes! And clutches to match!"

"And all the other things ladies love to spend their husbands' money on!" Charlotte giggled. "I guess all that could fall under just boutique if you wanted to shorten it. Honey's Boutique."

"Great idea. Short and simple is more memorable. Oh, I know I can make a go of it. I feel it in my bones."

"Good. Come on, we're meeting Nash for dinner. He's got a new deal he wants us to look into." She picked up the pace. Didn't want to make Mister Moran wait.

With the boutique now a go, Honey would stay plenty busy and keep out of Charlotte's hair. Double blessings with the first ground floor tenant in her building signed.

Interior remodeling could begin post haste.

Splitting up the space for multiple businesses instead of waiting forever for one huge company to come along . . . what could she say? Nothing but a pure, unadulterated stroke of commercial savvy that surprised even herself.

And best of all, she only had to finance half. For that, she had the last say in any and all decisions until the shop retired the loan.

But she didn't have to do any of the work!

She loved it, loved this town. She put a little extra in her stride. New York did that to a girl, especially with the little nip in the air and the leaves changing hues. Her favorite season blew just around the corner.

All night the early fall storm had iced the edges of the Knik River, but its gale force winds had let up some, and hadn't dumped a lot of new snow overnight. Only the big room's timepiece told him a new day broke.

Darkness shrouded the bay. Nary a mast to be seen. As much as Levi wanted to sail south, the possibilities seemed bleak. Only a fool or greenhorn refused to adjust to the circumstances. He was neither.

Stomping and scraping the last of the snow and ice off his boots, he opened the door, entered, then closed it behind him, careful not to drop his armload of wood.

Sophia greeted him with a steaming mug then waited until he offloaded the half dozen split sticks and sat beside the furs before handing him his coffee. She took the chair across from him.

Not her usual spot.

She smiled then shook her head. "Becca said the Russian thinks this will be a bad one. Claims the first big storm always is."

What did he know about weather up there? Seemed logical that if anyone knew, the old boy would. He shrugged and stuck his free hand toward the fire, taking a sip of joe. "Maybe. Guess he'd know. Weather can surprise you though. Why, it's so unpredictable in Texas, you only counted on it when you look out the window."

She glanced back toward the bedroom hall. "Before they all get up, there's something I want to ask you." She dropped her gaze and studied the fire.

After too long of her not saying anything else, he leaned forward and lowered his voice. Did she have bad news? Had something happened? "What is it, girl?"

She looked up and shot him a quizzical look. "I'm hardly a girl, Levi Baylor. I'm not exactly sure how old I am, but somewhere between forty-seven and fifty is my best guess."

"Spring chicken compared to me. But I get your point. Now what is it? Before that baby decides it's time for him to eat."

"Fine. I'll just spit it out if that's how you want it. So . . . I've been thinking . . ."

"Thought you were spitting it out."

"I'm trying! I believe we should arrange a marriage."

"What? Crockett and Deidra? You sure about that? What about Randal's partner?"

"Not them. I'm talking about us."

"Me and you?"

"Yes, is that so unimaginable? Is it wrong to think we should get married? If what that trapper says proves right, and we're stuck here until spring, I can't believe there's anywhere I'd rather spend the time than at your side." She smiled a tempting little grin. "Or in your bed."

"All the sudden, you want to get hitched? With the likes of me? Sophia, I'm old enough to be your pa."

"No, you are not. Crockett said you were only sixty-seven, but you look more like fifty-seven if you're a day! And I can guarantee to bring enough love into the union for both of us. I've come to love you like no other. Actually, I loved you from the first time I ever saw you. I think Rose sensed it."

"She did? How do you suppose—"

"I know how much you loved her, Levi, and . . . well . . . There's been a lot of boots under my bed over the years, but I've not loved any of them. They never compared to you. Never been legally married either. Not a one of them was half the man you are . . ."

"I'm afraid you've built me up in your head to be something I'm not. I'm only a man, an ordinary man who lives life day by day."

"Ordinary you are not. You don't have to love me. Just being yours will be plenty enough, and I swear I'll make you a good wife."

A tear rolled down her cheek, glistening with the fire's reflection. She searched his eyes as he looked deeply into hers. She was serious. "Say something, please. Before that baby wakes."

"I'm mulling it over. Sounds like a fair idea, long as you know I'll never stop loving Rose. I've been real comfortable with you, and . . ." He couldn't bring himself to say it aloud. He leaned in further and motioned her closer, then put his mouth to her ear and whispered.

She leaned back and grinned. "Don't matter. Either way, we'll be happy together, I promise you. I'll see to it. Please, my dear sir, make my dreams come true."

What could he say but . . . "Well then, will you marry me, Sophia?"

She smiled. "Yes, I will. I'll marry you, Levi Baylor."

Two warm, miniature hands on Crockett's cheeks drew his eyes open. "Morning, Bubba."

"No."

"Is that the only word you know?"

"No." The boy grinned and his eyes sparkled. He looked toward the door.

The boy's partner in this crime stood just inside his room, holding a steaming mug. "Get it together, Uncle. We're in a hurry."

"You're such a nuisance." He sat up some. The boy fell on his chest, pushing him back flat. He grabbed him and counted his ribs in a gust of giggles. "So the little man's daddy finally get back?"

"No, not yet. Now come on, Davy. The snow's let up some, and we need to go."

"You know you're the only who calls me that."

"So?"

"What's the rush?"

She returned his smile. "You'll see. Come on, Bubba. Roll off and let him up."

The boy shook his head. "No."

"What did you say, Zacharias Randal Graves? You best mind your mother right now, little boy."

The child rolled to the far side then peeked over Crockett's chest. "No. No, no, no!" He burst into giggles again.

Glaring, she started after him.

"He's fine. Go on and give us guys some privacy."

Stepping next to the bed, she set his coffee on the little side table, shook her finger at him and her son, then hurried out.

He rubbed his chin. Too cold to shave. Would Deidra like it if he raised a beard?

If only half the one his old man came home with from war, it'd be awesome. Shame Ma insisted he shave it. Might as well see. Hopefully, his facial hair had thickened some since the last time he stopped scraping his hide.

Once dressed and ready to face whatever, he hoisted the boy onto his shoulders, ducked under the jam, and headed down the hall to the big room.

The sight of his niece's sister-in-law decked out in her hooded fur coat took his breath. She held her arms out, and the boy wiggled and squirmed. Crockett put him down. He ran to his aunt fast as his pudgy little legs could get him there. She swooped him up and buried her face in his neck. If only she'd do that to him . . .

A squeal split the air and his ears. Zach leaned back, gasping for breath. "No!"

Deidra did twice more then put him on the floor and glanced up. "We best go while we can."

"No."

Becca pulled him free from her sister-in-law's legs then went to putting his heavy coat on. "Be good, Bubba." Apparently, she put enough steel in her tone that the boy did the unexpected and complied.

Levi stood by the door with his arm around Sophia. A bemused expression plastered his face, while the lady seemed . . . downright giddy. "What's going on? Where are we going in such a hurry?"

His big brother threw him a little nod. "To the church. Sophia and I have decided to get married."

"Married? What?" He studied the two of them for a moment. They acted like a couple of twenty-year-olds who'd just found each other and discovered true love or something.

Except . . . well . . . Who was he to pass judgment? "Kind of sudden, but you're both old enough to know what you're doing I guess." He emphasized the word old.

"Watch it, boy."

"Oh, yeah?" He grinned at Levi. "Sounds like congratulations are in order. Anyone told the priest?"

"It's all arranged. Now grab your coat." Becca pulled Zach's hood up and stood. "Hurry. We want to get this done while there's a break in the weather."

The pause didn't last long, and only a few folks in the village made it on such short notice, but it was a wedding. His brother was blessed.

The whole time the old Russian-Orthodox priest droned on in broken English, Crockett's gaze kept wandering to Deidra. Sure would be fine having someone to cuddle with.

His mind's eye pictured her dressed in white walking the aisle toward him.

What? Such a crazy thought. Or was it?

Maybe if he did get hitched, Becca would let him have Bubba. He almost laughed out loud on that one. Not likely, but a pleasant thought. With a wife, better still would be having a little guy of his own.

Then the time came for the groom to kiss his bride.

Like it waited for that precise moment, the storm's roar increased by double.

The clapboard church rattled in the wind.

The front door opened.

A man stumbled in. "I need help."

Chapter Thirteen

From where he stood, Crockett didn't have a prayer of reaching the man ahead of the three guys in the back of the church. Evidence suggested this might be the partner. He cold-trailed the group back to the trading post then took the hindmost while Becca and her sister-in-law saw to Randal.

Before long, Deidra showed, clutching a sleeping Bubba. How could babies fall asleep in such uncomfortable . . . What was he thinking?

Lying on his aunt's bosom had to be one of the softest, most pleasing and comfortable places in the world. No wonder the little guy gave it up, especially it being his usual morning nap time.

And from what Becca had told him, the boy hadn't been around his father all that much. In his eighteen months, his pa had been traipsing the frozen north. Traveling and trapping, and negotiating with all the natives he could convince to trade with him.

Crockett took a seat across from his . . . What? Was he related in any way to the young lady? "If your arms get tired of Bubba's dead weight, I'll take a turn."

She shook her head. "He's fine. I'd hate for him to wake up. Lately, he's been missing a lot of morning naps. The last thing Becca needs today is a grumpy baby."

"How's your brother? Someone said he'd taken a fever?"

"Joel said he slipped and fell into a creek two days ago. Once he got his clothes changed and warmed up, he appeared to be fine, but this morning, he couldn't wake him up."

"Oh no."

"That's when he decided it best to bring him on in. He put him under the furs, hitched their sleds and teams together, and brought him here fast as he could."

"Joel. That's Captain Johnston, Randal's partner?"

She nodded. "They served in the army together then both came up here in '80 for the Juneau strike. Found some gold, but the fur trade seemed like the true mother lode to them."

Crockett nodded. He'd heard some of the story, but hadn't paid much attention. Before the storm struck, all he wanted was to get his niece's husband home, so they could all go south. But it sure seemed he and Levi were stuck until the breakup.

What a silly name for spring. At least, he'd have plenty of time to write Evie.

The front door opened then closed as quickly. An old native woman looked directly at Deidra. "Where is he?"

"Third door down on the left."

The lady extracted a bag from her pocket then shrugged off her heavy fur coat. She pointed her chin toward the hall. "Boil some water."

Crockett figured he best get to it since Deidra had Bubba, and Levi and Sophia had disappeared right after the wedding party made their way to the trading post.

Filling the soup pot a third of the way full from the water barrel, he put it on the iron hook and swung it in over the fire. Figured it needed a bit more wood, so he fetched that then sat back down across from the woman with whom he shared his nephew.

She smiled. "I like a man who can boil water."

Before he could think of a reply, the captain strolled into the room.

The man looked around then took the chair beside the lady then faced Crockett. "You Rebecca's uncle?"

"One of them. The other one just got married this morning, so I don't suspect you'll see him for a while."

"You must be Crockett."

He stuck out his hand. "Yes, sir. Crockett Buckmeyer, and you're Joel Johnston?"

The man grabbed hold then attempted to crush Crockett's paw. After what had to be called a draw, he let go. "That's me."

"Did your mother like alliteration? Or was it your old man who hung that double jay on you?" Why did he say that? The guy could be the nicest person in the world. Just because he shook hands too hard, didn't make him a bad man worthy of sarcasm.

"You're the New York dandy. The one who's been burning through his mother's money I heard about. Right?"

Wrong. Crockett nodded. "Yes, sir. That'd be me."

Flashing a big smile his way, Deidra glanced down at Bubba, then mouthed no fighting.

"At least you admit it, know what you are." Double J grinned like he'd won the argument.

A biting response died on Crockett's tongue. Keeping the lady happy more paramount than being a smart mouth, he let the captain have the last word.

Besides, there'd be plenty of time to knock Joel down a peg or two if they really were going to be snowed in there until the breakup.

And if his old man taught him anything . . .

the last laugh was always the best.

While the storm raged over the Knik River, the weather in New York only hinted at the cold and snow sure to come. But not that fine Saturday. Nash willed it so.

His partner's little spitfire sister had agreed to a picnic in Central Park, unchaperoned no less.

At the spot she insisted he spread his blanket, directly across from her mother's brownstone, no doubt the housekeep would be on the roof with a spyglass . . . and probably a carbine at the ready to shoot him dead first sign of any impropriety.

While she'd left work early, he arrived at the appointed time and claimed the perfect place under a giant chestnut.

Once clear of sticks, twigs, and larger pebbles he put one of his favorite quilts his mother had made over the old army blanket he spread first. She'd probably have a spell if she knew how he was using it. Especially the little surprise he hid under one corner.

But then if the desires of his heart were granted, he could give her the one thing she desired the most.

At the appointed time, Meri Charlotte Buckmeyer stepped out of the brownstone, carrying a basket.

Decked out in her Sunday best, she grinned then waited at the curb for a carriage to pass before almost skipping across the vacant lot between the brownstone and the park. He jumped to his feet and took her burden, then helped her ease down.

Why did women do it? She needed plenty of help amidst all those petticoats.

"What did Bammie send us?"

"Fried chicken, of course. Isn't that what you absolutely must eat on a picnic?"

"Apparently this one anyway. But who could protest? Hers cannot be bested." He reached under the far corner of his quilt. "Care for a glass?" He held the bottle out. "They tapped the first barrel from last year's crop."

"Really?" She examined the label. "This apple cider is from our orchard?" Her smile grew, and her eyes twinkled. "How wonderful!"

"Yes, ma'am. They sent us a case. Came in late yesterday evening after you and Honey called it a day."

She spread out the different dishes the housekeeper had sent then retrieved two glasses from her basket. "Only since it's from our press, and so special, being the first barrel and all, yes, sir, I'll have one. Had I known, I could've asked Bammie to pack goblets. As it is . . ."

He filled hers half full, splashed a good swallow's worth in his, then held it up in the air. "Cheers."

Clinking the kitchen crystal to his, she touched the edge to her lips and raised it tentatively. "Wow, that's very good. Delicious as a matter of fact. Nothing at all like I expected."

"Isn't it?"

She took a bigger gulp then blew out her breath. "Why, it's simply exceptional! I do believe we'll make a fortune." She heaped a plate with a breast, wing, and all the trimmings.

Accepting her offering, he nodded agreement. "Thank you, ma'am." While she took the pulley bone and served herself minute portions of the baked beans and coleslaw, he dug in. "I have a proposition. How about we trade?"

"Trade what?"

"You live in the building, and I'll bunk in the brownstone. Lay around all day eating Bammie's cooking."

Her back stiffened. "Are you insinuating all I do is lie around all day? You don't think I pull my weight?"

What had he done? "No, not at all, I only . . . I mean, I never intended to . . ."

She grinned a wicked little smirk. "As if you could stand not scouting out the next big deal. Can't you tell when a girl is only teasing, Mister Moran?"

"Please." He reached for and covered her hand. "Nash. Aren't first names fitting?"

"Perhaps."

"But, listen. I'm serious. I could always have the clients come to me there, it'd seem more casual, personal. Feeding my prospects her cooking would be the finishing touch. We'd be rich before spring."

She sipped her cider. "You're hopeless, Nash Moran."

"So . . . is that a no? You aren't up for a swap?"

"That is correct." She extended her glass. "I'd have a splash more."

After four pieces of yard bird and a goodly second portion of beans and potato salad, he nibbled the oatmeal cookie, rich with plump raisins and watched her. She wasn't perfect, but close.

Her being Crockett's sister might prove troublesome, but apparently, her mother hadn't been stingy with either of her children.

No telling how much money the lady's books generated each year. Had to be in the thousands . . . if not more.

"Tomorrow morning, would you care to take a short trip with me? Honey can come, too, if you deem it necessary."

She set her chicken down, wiped her hands as if thinking over his proposal. Was it the going at all? Or whether a traveling companion would be needed? "How short?"

"Just an hour or so north. I'd like for you to meet my mother."

Charlotte glanced at the brownstone. Was that Bammie watching from the office window? The dear. What would she think? Looking back to her business partner, she pondered.

Could he be wanting to change his role? He definitely was husband material—she heard that almost daily from her new partner—but acknowledging him as a suitor might stifle all the fun she was having.

Would Honey's heart be broken? She had hinted more than once she'd like for the man to court her.

"Truly? Interesting indeed, but to what end, Nash?"

The question seemed to pain him some, but he recovered quickly and smiled. "I've told her so much about you, and well, she's requested the visit. I suppose she's anxious to put a face to your name."

"Oh. So I am to audition. And if your mother approves of little ol' me, then what? You'll go down on one knee?"

"No one said anything about proposing." He looked up at the chestnut. Its leaves were gorgeous hues. "But . . . I mean if you're interested, I guess I could . . . you know . . ." His face reddened, and he glanced at the brownstone. Had he seen Bammie?

"Why! Are you blushing, Mister Moran?"

He grinned. "Was I?"

She gave him her best smirk—the one that never failed to infuriate Crockett or make her father chuckle. "Yes, sir. About three shades of red. Maybe with a teeny bit of green around those gills of yours."

"Oh? Now I've grown gills? Are you sure about all this, any of it?"

"I'd guess many a lady's gotten lost in those dimples of yours."

"Possibly."

"Oh, I'm quite sure. But fine. I will go with you. Auditioning for Mother Moran should prove interesting. You've never mentioned your father. Do you have one?" She seemed to remember her brother mentioning something about the man dying in the war.

"He's gone."

"Oh, I'm sorry. What happened?"

"Battle of Bull Run. We don't know for certain. Captured or killed? The army only listed him as missing. Mother tracked down the only man from his squad who survived, and he didn't know anything. Life goes on. We got along."

"How old were you then?"

"Nine the last time I saw him."

The desire to wrap her arms around him and comfort the little boy in him almost overwhelmed her. But that wouldn't be proper, and he'd probably misunderstand.

"That horrible war. I remember Pa and all the men leaving, but they all came home, even Wallace Rusk, but he . . ." Tears welled. Even after all these years.

"The one who wouldn't let them cut off his leg?"

Blinking back the wetness, she nodded and cleared her throat. "Well, I'd say we've burned enough daylight. You said this was a working picnic, shouldn't we be getting to it?"

"Excellent idea." He grinned and pulled a piece of paper from his inside coat pocket, unfolded it, then held it toward her. "A friend of a friend is in need of funds."

She studied the annotated drawing for a few moments then handed it back. "Exactly what is it?"

"A copy of the patent application, it's been granted."

"I can see that. But of what?"

From his inside pocket, he retrieved a fancy-looking mechanical pen. She hated the nasty things. "This." He extended it, but she didn't take it. Liable to get ink all over her new dress.

"Ink pens have been around for years. I prefer quills, and that's all I use."

"I know, but this one is different. The ink is stored." He moved his finger along the middle section of the contraption. "Inside the barrel. Look again; it's right there in the drawing."

"Really? There's ink inside the thing? That sounds messy. My mother taught me how to write without making a mess, so . . ."

"Ah, but how many words can you write before you have to dip your quill?"

"Three, maybe four. Depends. But that gives me time to think . . . and tickle my chin with the feather." She smiled, but he remained dead serious.

"I've seen you do that. Still . . . consider . . . with this writing instrument . . . you can write." He stuck out his bottom lip. "Three pages—maybe even more—before you have to refill the barrel. And that little chore doesn't take long at all." He handed the patent paper back. "See right there? The separate picture."

"What? It sucks up the ink on its own? And your friend's friend invented this pen." That sounded harsher than she intended.

"No. He bought an option to manufacture them, along with an exclusive marketing agreement for the East Coast."

She nodded. "And he's short of cash?"

"The option runs out at the end of the year, along with the marketing agreement."

"How much does he need?"

"Five thousand."

"What's he offering?"

Chapter Fourteen

The autumn sun shone down, but the slight breeze kept the temperature comfortable. Charlotte listened to Nash explain the deal offered but made no comment. Instead, she nodded toward the pen. "Is that thing ready to write?"

"Yes, ma'am."

"What about when it runs out of ink? Show me exactly what I would need to do."

"It will work with any ink bottle." He jabbed the pen's metal tip into a phantom bottle then put his fingernail under the miniature leaver. "Pull here three times, and you're ready to go again."

"Help me up, please, sir." She held her hand out. The big galoot jumped to his feet then took her hand into his.

As though but a child, he didn't even have to brace himself as she rose to her feet. Then he didn't let go of her hand, and she failed to pull it away for several frantic beats of her heart. She finally managed at least to speak. "Thank you, sir."

"My pleasure."

Why was she still holding his hand?

"I'll want to try the implement before I draw any conclusion." She looked around at all the people obviously enjoying the beautiful day. "I don't think my mother would like it one whit if I traveled to . . ." She questioned him with her eyes.

"New Rochelle?"

"Is that where you grew up?"

He nodded. "Yes, ma'am. Mother still lives in the farmhouse I was born in, but other than a small garden, she lets a neighbor sharecrop the land."

"So, what I've been trying to say . . ." She applied at least a demure attempt to remove her hand, but he held fast, and she relaxed it again into the strength of his as though she never tried.

Instead, she squeezed. "I'll get Honey to come with us. Are we hiring a carriage, or . . ." Again her question hung.

"Certainly. Mother has inquired about her as well." Leading her hand under his, he caught it with his other then set it on his forearm.

The bulge of muscle quite apparent beneath his shirtsleeve and coat caused her to swallow. He picked her hanging inquiry out of the air. "We'll take the train."

The basket still rested on the quilt. "Do you know the train's schedule then?"

A genuine ease about him calmed her. That, she appreciated. He covered her hand on his arm with his other, and smiled. "Of course, I do, Charlotte. I'll call for you—and your companion—at half past eight."

And oh, so polite! She returned the grin. "We will be ready."

"Good. We should arrive there in plenty of time to attend services at Mother's church."

"I'd like that. Now, if you'll kindly unhand me and fetch my basket and your quilt, we can go and actually try out this new invention of yours. I'm overdue to write my mother. At the least, I can use the mechanical contraption for the first draft."

Waiting quietly in the kitchen, he chatted with Bammie while the cook worked on supper. The rogue would no doubt be staying for another meal. She hated that Honey laughed and giggled in there with them, but had nothing for her to do at the moment . . . and it was Saturday afternoon.

The boutique hadn't opened yet. Soon enough, the young lady wouldn't have any lay-about time.

The pen's clean flow surprised Charlotte. Nothing like she'd expected, although if asked, she couldn't have said exactly what that was. But its point carried the ink evenly and smoothly across the paper.

And indeed, she wrote three whole pages without having to reload the thing.

Amazing.

The next night, long after the moon shone above, she lingered, putting off bed and sleep. Reading over the three pages she'd written yesterday after the picnic, she twirled the new pen in her fingers.

Then she pulled out a new sheet of white paper, loving the feel and look of the twenty-eight pound page. After all, what was money for if not getting what you wanted?

And she always wanted the best.

Why, without even knowing prices, she invariably chose the most expensive of the choices, no matter what the purchase.

It appeared to be an uncanny sixth sense Ma had passed on. She smiled thinking how Pa always liked the best as well. He just hated paying full value—for anything.

Pulling the cap from her new favorite writing instrument, she touched the barrel's end to her chin—that part wasn't the same— then began with a time notation.

Sunday Evening
My dearest Mother,

I'm so conflicted. We've just returned from New Rochelle to the brownstone. If only you had come with me instead of Honey. She's been wonderful in almost every way, but the one exception has proved so frustrating.

Perhaps even downright irritating if I am to be perfectly honest.

I hate putting my thoughts about Nash Moran on paper, but . . . well, I don't have anyone to talk to about him, especially since my only real friend—at least here in New York—is smitten with the man.

Bammie confided that Honey uses her as a sounding board on the evening prior to finalizing our business agreement.

The visit today proved enjoyable. His mother was lovely and quite amiable. And the quaint farmhouse he grew up in was homey and neat as a pin.

Its exterior could've used a good coat of white wash, but Mis'ess Moran's gardens and the yard plantings were so beautiful. She definitely has a green thumb.

Oh, Ma, I fear a love triangle is brewing. What am I to do?

Honey is so infatuated with the man. Though he's all but gotten down on one knee with me! I oft wonder if it's my financial security that makes me more appealing. I don't know how to think.

Is there any possible way you might come for a visit?

Anyway, I can't talk to Bammie either. Not about Honey and Nash. It seems if I allow Mister Moran to court me, the boutique's success might be jeopardized, and I'm convinced that it will be a big money maker.

Is that reason enough to tell Nash I prefer to keep our relationship on a professional, business partners-only basis?

Please, Ma. I miss you so. Come help me, and If you do, and you like this new pen as much as I do—and if I can get the rights at a good price . . .

That's certainly a lot of ifs, I know, but think about a half page ad with you gushing over the ??? I haven't decided what to call it. Modern writing implement? Smooth Writing?

And of course, if you used it at a big book signing for your new pirate book . . . When is it going to release again?

Anyway, the pen—Dip Saver? Ink drink? Fountain pen?—could be a nice addition to our portfolio. Crockett would be so jealous.

Speaking of my wayward brother, I haven't heard a word from him since the letter he posted from Victoria. Have you? It must be terrifying to have someone pull a pistol on you. Praise the Lord that Levi was with him.

Guess Pa knew he needed our big brother along to watch his hairy back.

Pretty please! Come to New York. I need my mother. Plus I want you to meet Nash. I really like him . . . but love??? How soon after you met Pa did you know you loved him? It was pretty quick, right?

But how soon exactly? See? You need to be here. You know the fall colors alone are worth your trip. And your favorite daughter is begging.

You could be here in a week.

I'm going to bed now. I might add more in the morning, but for sure and for certain, I'll post this tomorrow. It's a pure shame that Western Union is so expensive and not private in any way.

Hopefully, this will reach you in the normal time, and you'll decide to pack and come straightaway to help your baby girl in her time of need. ha!

Joking aside. Please, please, pretty please. I really need you and love you and . . .

Forever your daughter and biggest fan!
Love.
Meri Charlotte

Crockett bounced Bubba on his knee for the million and one hundredth time. He gasped extra loud and slumped over, feigning death.

"No, no, no!" The boy rocked and kicked like urging his mount to climb the last few feet up the creek's bank.

"Bubba, you're killing Uncle."

"No!" He giggled and kicked harder.

A swishing blur came to his rescue. "Zachery Graves." Deidra snatched the boy up and nuzzled his neck. "Don't want to wear out your horse now, do you?"

The boy grinned, and his eyes twinkled like he might like that. "No." He hugged her tight then slobbered her cheek with a kiss. Made Crockett want to trade places with his nephew . . . or was the boy really a cousin? No, sister's child's son . . . his great-nephew.

Guess it didn't matter. Kin is all that counted, and the boy's paternal aunt lady was not.

She kissed the baby on the cheek then leaned over and whispered. "Becca would like a word."

Hmmm. Why the intrigue? Wasn't like he hadn't seen her half an hour ago when he volunteered to watch the boy.

He mouthed 'where'?

Deidra nodded down the hall then moved her luscious lips to form wash house. He waited while the lady waltzed the boy toward her room singing a lullaby as she went.

What a mother that one would make. Like all of the sudden, he needed to visit the outhouse, he headed to the front door.

The north wind reminded him he didn't have on anything but a flannel shirt and trousers; too late to remedy that oversight. He hurried to the outbuilding where Becca and Deidra usually boiled the wash together.

Knocking off that wind made a big difference and made him thankful for the warmth of the shed.

His niece, who was almost his age, lifted the wooden paddle then set it aside and faced him. "I need a favor."

"Sure. What can I do for you?"

"This evening when Randal announces he's going with Joel, I want you to insist that you take his place."

The chuckle almost made it out, but her eyes said she was serious. "Where is your husband's partner planning on going? And why would Randal even consider accompanying him? He's barely off his death bed."

"Exactly, but Joel is insisting that he go, and I . . ." She shrugged. "Never mind what I think. There's two more posts where furs need to be picked up, but it's grueling travel with the sled dogs, and I really need for you to insist. Randal is so stubborn, and I know he feels obligated to do his share. If you love me, volunteer for his part."

"A boon you desire, fair maid." He grinned like they were children again playing Red Rooster and Madam Merciful.

"Yes, sir. I'm in such a tither."

"Of course. I am happy to set you at peace and will volunteer post haste for this most hazardous of missions, I'll not a minute waste."

She giggled. "You could always make up good poems like MayMee."

"But a boon for a boon I'll require. Though yours won't be as hard."

She smiled at his poor attempt at melodrama. "Up to half my kingdom, Sir Rooster. And all the roses in my yard."

"I'd settle for Bubba. I'd make a wonderful father."

"You would indeed, but . . . no." She smirked. "Not a chance."

"Well, if I can't have what I really want, then how about telling me what the big fight was about that ignited my quest to find you and bring you home?"

The mirth instantly died. "Please, Davey, don't." Tears welled.

"Becca, don't cry. Forgive me for asking. It's only that curiosity killed the uncle. Oh man, there's nothing to rhyme with that. Killed the mountain lion? Fine, mion, hion, pie in . . .?"

A bit of a smile returned to her lips, but her eyes still glistened. "Thank you."

Her youngest uncle had always held a special place in Becca's heart, but that evening when he would not take no for an answer on replacing her husband, he became her most favorite non-kissing relative of all.

Truth be known, there was that one time. But she'd sworn him to secrecy. After all, he'd been ten and her only eight, so it really didn't count.

She'd told him Red Rooster and Madam Merciful never kissed in any of MayMee's stories, but he still convinced her.

That night, after the baby finally gave up and snuggled in, Randal made a half-hearted attempt at being angry with her. She refused to take the bait and instead, changed the subject. "Joel's jealous."

"What's Crockett done? Has he said something to my sister?"

"Not that I'm aware. And I'm certain Deidra would have told me if he had. But I was talking about our inheritance, not my uncle."

"I think you're misreading him. He sees it as an advantage— an influx of capital for our business."

She didn't say more, but if the amount of money waiting for them in Texas was anywhere as much as she figured, there'd be no way she was coming back to the frozen north or staying in business with Mister Johnston.

How could anyone be so blind to the man's shortcomings?

Just because he saved him again, except they shouldn't have been out before the creeks froze over good and hard. And the way the man thought Deidra belonged to him.

How could Randal believe he had the right to bestow his sister as a favor to his friend?

From the first she'd not liked him or seen why anyone would want to be the galoot's partner.

Long after Randal rolled over and his breaths hit a rhythm, Becca lay still, staring into the cold darkness. She hated herself for forcing Crockett to spend time with Joel, but if the shadow hanging over her heart was a true harbinger of the evil her husband's partner planned . . .

Better for Crockett to go than her weakened and trusting husband.

She definitely needed to warn her uncle.

If only she were wrong. Or that Levi would insist on going, too. Darkness obscured her smile. She'd never thought of someone so old being amorous, but evidently . . .

Sure seemed the old boy only had eyes for Sophia and had become pretty much oblivious to the goings on around him. Must be love, or at least a powerful case of . . . What? Senility?

Sleep finally found her, but it was not blessed. The years melted away, and she stood in her mother's sitting room.

"Why, Mother? Why all of the sudden are you acting like this?"

"I said no, and that's final. You need to accept my decision and stop badgering me."

"But you're being pigheaded! Just like you claimed PawPaw was! So you've become your father?"

"Young lady, you do not need to bring up Henry Buckmeyer. I'm not him."

"Well, you're acting like him. I don't see why I have to be the only one in all of San Francisco to miss the grandest party of the whole year!"

"If I were going to be like anyone, your grandfather would be the best possible person in all the world to imitate. If he were here, he'd tell you the same thing. You have no business traipsing up on Nob Hill to any social that any of those snobs are having. Mercy, Rebecca Rose."

"You're the snob! There's nothing wrong with those people, and I know you aren't jealous. What is it? Why are you so adamant? I'm a grown woman! What's so wrong with Adam Clinton and his family?"

"Everything. Now drop it."

"No, I won't. I'll not drop it. I'm going, and there's nothing you can do about it." She turned away. A hand grabbed her arm. She whirled. "Unhand me, Mother. Adam's asked me, and I'm going. That's that."

"Rebellion is as the sin of witchcraft, Becca. You simply cannot, and that, my darling daughter, is that. Trust me."

Never in all of Becca's born days had she seen the great Mary Rachel Buckmeyer Risen's eyes spit such fire. Was that hate seeping out of her nose? Or only plain old snot?

Becca jerked her arm free. "Unless you tell me why I shouldn't, I'm going. I told Adam that I'd love to be on his arm come Saturday, so I'm going."

"You can't. I'll have your daddy hogtie you if I need to."

"You wouldn't!"

"Try me, young lady! I will never allow you to step foot into that house or be courted by Adam Clinton. Period!"

"You're being so unreasonable! That isn't like you at all. What did the Clintons do to make you hate them so much?"

A hand on her shoulder shook. "Wake up, Becca."

"What?" Her eyes popped open, but to blackness.

"You were having the dream again."

"I was? What did I say?"

"Just hollering at your mother is what woke me. Something about Clinton."

"I'm sorry."

"Don't be. It's your mother who should be sorry."

She snugged in tight. For sure and for certain, Randal Graves had saved her, and she would do whatever it took to keep him safe and sound.

Hopefully, her efforts would not cost her favorite uncle's life. Her husband's lips found that special spot on her neck. Once the chill lessened, she pressed in even tighter.

Crockett racked his memory, but the only Clinton he came up with was the ex-Governor of New York, and Becca grew up in San Francisco. Nob Hill. Hmmm, where all the really rich folks lived.

Not that Jethro Risen wasn't well-heeled, but according to Becca, he gave away too much of his wealth to be considered filthy rich.

One's pockets had to be overflowing with mounds of lucre to rub elbows with the Nob Hill crowd.

He rolled over, fluffed his pillow, but doubted if he could get back to sleep. Something lurked just beyond his mind's grasp. Something important. Foreboding, like if he didn't figure out what the Lord was trying to show him, it could cost him dearly.

Sweet slumber beckoned. About to succumb, he got hit like a brick with realization, and his eyes popped open. He rolled out of bed, struck a match, and lit the oil lamp on the bedside table.

Instead of chasing the thought away, the light confirmed his suspicion.

"That has to be it."

Chapter Fifteen

After two days of preparation and twice going out on short runs of ten miles each—which almost killed him, but he'd never show it—his niece's husband pronounced Crockett ready. Not that mushing seemed that hard.

The dogs were well trained and eager to run. Appeared all he had to do was hang on and remember the commands.

Nothing to it.

Except . . . his observations had confirmed his suspicions.

The third morning, he woke early, but of course, he didn't beat his brother up. Did Levi Baylor ever sleep?

Then on the other hand, he hadn't had to boil any coffee since forever. He grabbed a mug then took the seat cross from Levi next to the fire.

"You ready?"

"Yes, sir. I think so. Randal's a good teacher, and the dogs are . . ." He shrugged. "They seem excellent. Guess I'm not much of a judge."

The man stuck his hand in his coat pocket and handed over a small pistol and holster. "Never hurts to have a third weapon. The little guy fits right nice in the small of your back."

"Thank you."

"You're welcome. You remember the story of Nick Ward?"

Crockett chuckled. "Yes, sir. I've even told it a time or two."

"You ever hear what got him going bad?"

"No, sir."

"We usually didn't tell that part, let it stay under the blood. But I see a lot of Nick in Joel Johnson."

Crockett nodded. Seemed the Lord had been warning his brother, too. "So what happened?"

"Fell in love with a sporting lady who thought Wallace Rusk hung the moon."

"I've seen it, too. Joel wants Becca." He looked over his shoulder at the empty room. "Why didn't he let Randal die out on the trail?"

"My guess is he figured he'd be the hero bringing him back. Probably figured he'd die here. Might have, too, except for that old woman's herbs and such. Well, that and I don't know about you, but I was praying hard for the boy. To God be the glory."

Indeed he had been seeking the Lord on the man's behalf. A slight grin fell on his lips. To his brother, anyone younger than fifty-five qualified as a boy.

"So you figure he wanted another chance with Randal? That's why he insisted they make this last run before the pass got snowed in?"

"I do, but now he might be figuring to settle for the sister. I'd sleep with a pistol in each hand and one eye open."

"You could go with us. We could take turns standing watch."

The old man smiled. "I hate being cold. Besides, I've got a new wife to see to. I've warned you and lent you my hideaway gun. What more do you want?"

He held his hands out and shrugged.

"Oh, and I did tell Mister Johnson not to come back without you, dead or alive. And if there was any mark on you, I'd put a slug behind his ear."

A mental picture flashed across his mind's eye that initiated a chuckle. "That's comforting." He took a sip, his coffee almost cool enough to enjoy. "Tell me and me tell true. What do you think of Deidra?"

"Pretty enough. Too young for you."

"She's seventeen."

"And you're what, forty?"

"Thirty-two, you old geezer."

"You sweet on her?"

"Think she'd make a great mother. You seen her with Bubba?"

"Sure. But playing with someone else's child is not the same as mothering one of your own."

"Or raising up two you didn't father?"

"Those boys were more mine than anyone's." Levi stared into the fire. "Don't love my own blood any more."

"So her age is the only thing?"

One shoulder flicked. "If you love her, nothing else matters."

Crockett leaned back and studied the glowing embers feeding the fire. For sure and for certain, he loved his mother and sisters . . . and his brothers. But none of that could compare to the desire to have and hold the young lady.

The need to make her his own got downright overpowering at times.

But he also wanted the boy or one like him almost as bad.

Could it be his desire to be a father blinded him?

Had his Pa's death flamed a craving for a son? Someone to bury him when his time came. He didn't want to perish out on that cold journey. Of that, he was positive.

His mother had campaigned with both him and Charlotte for more grandbabies. She never said it, but one of her own blood, he figured.

Not that she didn't love the others.

His new traveling companion woke next. Then shortly, the whole house was abuzz. The women served a big breakfast. Lots of hugs and glad hands followed.

Then, like she'd waited on purpose, Becca grabbed him and pulled him into a bear hug right before the big send-off.

"Thank you, again." She squeezed harder, and put her lips next to his ear. "Watch your back, Davey. I don't trust Joel."

He held her out, nodded, then mouthed, neither do I.

Up trail, the wind stinging his face, it seemed the team ran even faster, as if they couldn't stand being behind Joel's dogs. Being out in the silent landscape invigorated his senses though.

And the mountains . . . he'd seen plenty of ranges in his lifetime, but the majesty of the Alaska one with their white-capped peaks climbing toward heaven . . . definitely a beautiful place.

Remembering the scripture on how God heaved up the mountains where He stepped brought a smile to his lips.

Even there, in the middle of nowhere, the Creator was with him.

He could almost feel His presence and the prayers of his family.

The first day on the trail ended quicker than Crockett figured, but then the real work began. While he'd known Joel and Randal cooked for the dogs, he'd not given it much thought as to what that entailed.

With the ice brake secured, and the two teams resting, he gathered dead fall while Captain Johnston filled the big pot with snow.

Build a fire. Chop the fish. Add more snow. Chop more fish. Feed the fire. Set out the bowls. The whole time, the dogs watched the goings on. He could almost hear them saying faster, faster. We're starving over here.

It surprised Crockett that none of the dogs tried to fight or even growl at its mate, but then as instructed, he started serving— the lead dog first, then he worked his way backwards, filling their bowls with the gruel mixture.

Their water was the snow in the gruel.

Joel explained each animal needed a gallon per twenty-four hours, so the process would be repeated three times every day. The sleds moved on the dogs' bellies—or rather—what was in them.

Once the animals were seen to, a dinner of hard tack and jerky sufficed for him and Joel, followed by coffee.

"You surprised me today."

Crockett shrugged. Was the man trying to lull him into thinking he didn't have any nefarious intentions? "How so?"

"Didn't shirk or whine once. I liked that. You ain't half bad for a flatlander."

"Weren't you born in Ohio?"

"True, but I got up here quick as I could. Can't think of anywhere else I'd want to live."

"Not me. Ever been to New York?"

"Nope, and from what I've heard, I don't care to go, even for a visit."

"Of all the places I've been across the world—Europe, India, Australia, and all over the United States—it's my favorite city. But I do appreciate Alaska's beauty."

"You can have the big city." The man pitched his dregs. "Might want to catch some shut eye. We have to feed the dogs again two hours before we head out, and tomorrow will be worse than today."

"You want the first or second watch?"

"No need, Crank will warn me if man or beast gets within a hundred yards."

"That's your lead dog, right?"

The man nodded then laid it down in the spot he'd cleared of snow when he'd filled the dog's pot. Crockett eased out his thirty-eight, tucked it under his arm, then leaned against the tree he'd been sitting in front of. He allowed himself a smile.

Being Henry Buckmeyer's son did have its advantages.

Learning how to sleep sitting up with one eye peeled and both ears wide open was only one of the few things his old man had drummed in him.

Like he figured, Joel didn't try anything that first night. And as the man predicted, getting to Rainy Pass proved no easy task, but at least his muscles weren't barking too loud.

Apparently, all the hard work he'd hated so much growing up hadn't been in vain after all. Bless Pa's heart.

The next day attested to the harshness of the land he traveled. Worse, once reaching the highest point at the far end of the Alaska Range—though nowhere near the mountain's tops—Joel stopped, started a fire, and went to cooking the dog's gruel.

After the mandatory two hours of rest after the team ate, the man threw his chin north.

The white valley below stretched out ribboned with crooked fingers of wooded rivers between vast stretches of tundra. Rocky crags rose on all sides.

"Some kind of sight. You can almost see tomorrow."

"Almost." Crockett had to admit, the scenery could surely take his breath away. Or was it the freezing cold or the howling wind that robbed him?

"About a quarter mile or so, we'll drop about a thousand yards in a couple of miles. Best ride your claw brake the whole way. If it looks like you're going to pass me, throw out your snow hook. Don't dally about it either. If the dogs think the sled is catching up, they'll run faster or veer off the trail."

Crockett nodded. "Anything else?"

"Ain't that enough? You're liable to break your fool neck. Hope the team and sled don't get broke up too bad."

He didn't respond, but apparently this little downhill jaunt was what Joel was counting on to do him in.

"Mush, Crank. Take us on down."

The man's lead dog strained against his harness, barking and pulling the team into action. The sled's iron-rimmed runners cut through the snow.

Crockett's team sprang up and pulled without a word. He grabbed the handles, ran a few steps, then jumped on top of the foot boards. He loved the takeoffs.

The first hundred yards or so, Joel's team pulled ahead, then the man's off foot pressed down on his claw break just as the sled slipped over an edge, carrying him out of sight.

Had to be the beginning to what he figured was the descent Joel spoke of. Crockett waited until he reached the same spot then mashed on the birch rod between his feet.

His own sled slowed a bit then broke over the edge.

In spite of the brake, his speed increased. As though suddenly freed from all the extra weight, the dogs sped up like they wanted to show what they could do.

The distance between him and Joel closed rapidly to only twenty paces or less. His lead dog veered to the gee side like he hankered to pass the other sled.

Crockett's heart pounded. Should he throw out the hook that early? Joel looked back and hollered something, but his words blew by, lost to the wind. The man shook his head then turned his attention back to the trail.

Pressing all his weight onto the brake, his heart pressed hard against his throat.

If someone offered a million bucks, he couldn't spit.

Nothing he did slowed the animals. His team still gained on Joel's.

The man looked back again and swung his arm wide. Was he pitching his own hook? Crockett slung off his right mitten, reached over and grabbed the thing, but his gloved fingers refused to grasp the hook.

Were they frozen stiff? Was this to be his end?

Almost on top of the lead sled, he stuck his hand back in the mitten, praising the Lord for the neck strings.

He couldn't stop the dogs.

On the trail not too far ahead, the path narrowed as it cut through a right nice stand of Spruce. He released his foot off the claw brake.

"On by," he hollered with all his breath.

His team shot alongside of Joel's on the inside. The man's eyes screamed and shot fire.

His lead dog passed Crank, and as if a swarm of hornets stung the whole team, they surged ahead. His sled overtook Joel's lead dog only a few yards before the trail narrowed. He leaned left, his rig flew by a spruce, missing it by only inches.

For a half mile or so, he let the dogs run before he remembered to breathe.

As the grade became less severe, he pumped the brake again hollering, "Easy" each time his boot mashed the pole. The trail broke through the forest onto a vast frozen tundra.

"Whoa. Whoa now."

Took three stop commands, each louder than the last, and him throwing out the snow hook with both feet standing on the claw brake, but he got the dogs stopped. He looked over his shoulder. Joel's team eased in next to his, halting the sled right beside him.

"You're a bigger fool than I thought."

Crockett shrugged. "Where to now?"

Chapter Sixteen

Becca twirled into his arms. A hand touched her shoulder, but she didn't take her eyes off her partner. Fingers gripped tighter. She opened her eyes. A shadow loomed over her.

"Where did you go last night?"

In a flash, she was wide awake.

"If you must know, I went to the party. It was wonderful, too. The most elegant event you could ever imagine. Not that you would know or care about a social life. You and Daddy could have gone. Adam would have been happy to extend an invitation."

The woman's eyes spit fire. "I cannot believe you, Rebecca Rose! I told you in no uncertain terms not to go, then you lied to me and went anyway."

Becca rolled out of bed and extended her chin toward her tormentor. "So what? I'm sixteen years old, for goodness sake! I'm not a baby anymore, Mother, and you can't tell me what to do! I can come and go as I please!"

"Do not talk to me in that tone, young lady, and don't raise your voice to your mother either! As long as you live under our roof, you will show me and your daddy respect and obey our rules. Do you hear me?"

Her father suddenly stood behind her unreasonable mother. "Now what is all this yelling about?"

She glared at her father. "Daddy, would you please do something with your wife?"

A blur approached, then a sharp pop stung her cheek and knocked her head to the side. Mother slapped her. She slapped her! Tears blinded her, and both hands went to the spot, covering and protecting the burning skin.

Blinking until her sight returned, she spit some fire of her own through hot tears. "How dare you!"

"How dare you go to Knob Hill!"

She rubbed the throbbing spot and stepped out of swinging reach. "You are so stubborn and mean! There's nothing wrong with the Clintons."

"Oh, if you only knew." The woman's words dripped hate, and she visibly shook with anger. "You think you're all grown, and that you can do what you want, but you don't know anything! You haven't got the sense God gave a goose!"

She steeled herself and found a slow and easy tone. The Bible said a soft answer turned away wrath, and she'd never seen her mother so angry. "Do you know what, Mother? You best tell me now."

"Tell. You. What?"

"I don't know!" Her voice got louder without her meaning for it to, but she could not believe her mother. "Whatever it is that's caused you to hate the Clintons so much! You're being completely irrational. They are wonderful people. Tell her, Daddy!"

"Becca, you do not know what you're talking about. Your mother has her reasons." He placed a hand around his wife's waist and tugged. "Honey, let's address this later. Give yourself time to calm down."

"Calm down? You want me to calm down!" She whirled out of his half hug. "Don't you turn on me, Jethro Risen!"

"Sweetheart, I'm doing no such thing. Tempers are too high right now, and I think it wise to let things cool down a little."

His last sentence had some tone of his own.

He took her hand. "Come on. Let's go downstairs and have another cup of coffee." He turned toward Becca. "You calm down, too, young lady. I will not have you speaking to your mother that way."

"She started it, Daddy. I was sound asleep and she came in here yelling. She's so mean, and she makes me so angry sometimes!"

"Becca." His voice carried a warning as he pulled Mother toward the door. "Get some clothes on then come on down and we'll talk about it."

Blood roiled inside, and her head pounded. He was going to take her side! The slap still stung. Her mother had no reason! From the depths of her gut it rumbled up like hot lava from a volcano.

Just before they disappeared out the door, a guttural scream erupted. "You might as well know!"

Her mother jerked her hand from Daddy's and whirled away from him, charging back toward her, screaming. "Know. What."

"That Adam and I are getting married! He's coming this afternoon to talk to Daddy, ask for his blessing. But we are getting married whether you and Daddy like it or not!" Tears streamed down her cheeks, and she sobbed, but she couldn't back down.

Not then.

"Why do you hate his family, Mother? What did they ever do to you?"

Something new filled her mother's eyes. Was that terror? What was she afraid of?

"What did they do? You want to know what Edward Clinton did to me?"

"Mary Rachel. Now is not the time."

She spun to him. "Did you hear what she said? Now is definitely the time, Jethro!"

"Then tell me. This is your last chance. Adam and I love each other, and we are getting married."

Grabbing the chair from her desk, he set it near the bed. "Sit down, Mary Rachel." He pointed to the bed. "Sit, Becca."

She did as told. Now maybe at last she could get the truth.

"Tell her, sweetheart. This secret has loomed over this family long enough. She needs to know." He faced Becca. "And you will keep your mouth shut and listen to your mother. Do you understand me?"

"Yes, sir, but—"

"No buts. Sit. And listen."

Pulling the quilt up over her sheets, she sat as told. What in the world could their secret be? The pain in his eyes cut her to the heart. "I'm listening." He turned away, so she faced her mother. "What's he talking about?"

Tears filled her mother's eyes. She looked beaten and quite pitiful. "Adam."

"What, Mother?" Her voice came out calm and carried her concern. "What about Adam? Did he—?"

"He's your . . ."

"Becca, sweetheart, wake up!"

Mercy!

She came awake for real. "What? What is it?"

"Baby, you were having the dream again."

"Yes, I know. Thank you, Randal." She rolled toward him and cuddled up tight.

"You were getting loud. I didn't want you to wake Bubba."

"Thank you for that, too. I love you so much, Husband. It's everything you've done that I'm grateful for."

He kissed her forehead. One of the few things he did that irritated her, but very few. "It's the other way around, bunny bear. I bless the Lord each day for you."

"Where do you think Crockett and Joel are by now?"

"I figure they should reach Halfway Trading Post some time the day after tomorrow."

"That's the first one, right?"

"Yes, ma'am."

"He asked me."

"Who asked you what?"

"Crockett. He wanted to know what Mother and I fought about that caused me to run off."

"What did you tell him?"

"Nothing. I requested he not ask."

"It's your decision. Tell him or not. I'll stand by you either way."

"I love you."

He kissed her for real that time then put his lips next to her ear. "Not as much as I love you."

She rolled onto her side and stole some of his body heat. "Is that so, Mister Graves? Well, I don't think so." She quieted him with a kiss of her own.

Later that day, up in her reading nook, Evie laid out her cigar box and the *Gray Lady Down* manuscript. "Queenie, you decide which one you want to listen to. Letters or the story?"

The pup sat on her haunches, glanced at the box, then the stack of papers, but didn't nose either.

"I know we've read them both. I sort of wanted to read Nathaniel's letter again, but I'm sick Mama won't take us to Kansas City to meet up with him and Uncle Charley at the end of their cattle drive. So I know it will only make me sad. That's why you should decide."

With an oh-well-I-don't-care expression, Queenie laid down with one paw on the manuscript.

"Good choice. I've been hankering to read it from the start again. Been dreaming about the *Gray Lady*. Don't you think it's a wonderful adventure?"

Lifting the first page, she smiled. MayMee had added her name as a co-author: *Gray Lady Down* by May Meriwether and Evelyn Eversole. She closed one eye, but the future didn't appear on the horizon.

Would she be a Nightingale by then? Or should she keep Eversole like MayMee kept her maiden name for her pseudonym?

That word that meant you had another name for your writing other than your real name leapt ahead to become one her new favorites. She would ask Nathaniel the next time she saw him if she should have a pseudonym.

Wouldn't do to put something like that in a letter. No telling who might see it then laugh at her.

Oh, how she hated to be made fun of. That was worst of all. She shook off that thought and let her eyes feast on the flowing letters she loved so. MayMee wrote so pretty.

San Francisco Harbor
1866

Houston stood on the dock and studied the clipper ship, admiring her sleek lines and thick, straight masts.

"Are you sure about this?"

Tearing his gaze away from the Lady, he grinned at the man who was closer than a brother. "Just as sure as you were about marrying Francy."

"Now what does my marital bliss have to do with anything? You need to come on back to Texas."

"No, thank you. Pa cost us the war. Never figured him for a coward but turned out he had a yellow streak and I have no desire to be around him."

"You don't know that for sure and for certain. Uncle Henry only wanted to keep us safe and protect Texas. Least you could do is talk with him about it."

"No need. Think about it, Bart. If we'd won the Civil War, Texas would be a Republic again, and we wouldn't have those carpetbaggers and scalawags all over the place."

A huff designated Bart's displeasure. "I'm done arguing. Come home."

Pointing to the ship, Houston finalized his decision. "You're looking at my home."

"Mercy, Sam Houston Buckmeyer! Listen to some logic. You're going to get out there in the middle of the Pacific, and a giant squid or a killer whale will eat you. I'll never see you again."

"Won't have to mourn me though on account you'll never know."

"Oh, I will. Come home with us. We'll raise cattle together, drive them north, get rich like we've talked about forever."

"Nope. My mind's made up. I'm going to sea. Put as much distance between me and Henry Buckmeyer as I can."

Though he claimed he was done arguing, Bart kept after it. Talked a blue streak right up until time to get aboard the steamer with his new wife and head south. That night it hit Houston like an axe handle to his back.

One thing Bartholomew said that could hold some truth. He might never see his boon buddy again.

One more strike against his father.

But exactly like when Caesar crossed the Rubicon, the die was cast. His fate rode right out there on the waters of the San Francisco Bay.

It took a full month for all the repairs to be completed, a crew secured, provision laid in, and his thirty days crash course that might qualify him as a seaman third class.

On that long- awaited morning, with the men at the ready to weigh anchor and the tug hooked up to tow the Lady to open waters, the captain brought him and the first-mate into his cabin.

"Mister Savage, if you have not ascertained as much, Mister Buckmeyer here needs all the help you can give."

The mate shot him a glance then turned back to the captain. "Aye, sir. I'll keep an eye peeled for the boy."

"Savage . . . he's a man nigh to your own age, I'd guess. Let's be respectful."

"Aye, sir."

"I'll be twenty-two in December."

The mate looked down his nose and laughed. "Only a dozen years older, nothing to brag about."

"Glad you see that way. He is, after all, my wife's nephew, and we wouldn't want anything bad to happen to him, now would we?"

"No need for concern on my account, Captain. The men now . . ." He shrugged.

"I can take care of myself." Houston squared his shoulders and jutted his chin out a bit. He didn't care for the man before. His arrogance wore thin.

The Captain patted his shoulder. "I'm sure you can, Son. They're a good lot for a bunch of drunken sots, but I have faith. And Savage here has your back. Am I right?"

He looked to the shorter man.

"Aye, sir. I've locked down the rum and have the only key, so once we're under sail, them blokes'll do their duty."

"Good. Dismissed, Savage."

"Aye aye, sir."

Though he figured on following the first mate out, the captain nodded. "A word, Son."

"Yes, sir." He stepped aside and let the first mate by.

The captain followed him to the hall then closed the door and stepped back into the room.

"Forgive me my little lie, but Savage doesn't need to know about our true intentions. Not yet anyway." The older man smiled. "Best see to what we need to get underway."

Before she could pick up the next page, Queenie sat up and whined.

"It's time, baby doll." The faint echo tickled Evie's ears. "Come on, girl. We go to the stable today, don't want to keep Twinkle Toes waiting.

In a room with three other men beside his traveling companion, Crockett allowed himself to sleep for real. But he did keep his hand on the thirty-eight.

Would he ever be without it again? Joel beat him awake and had coffee boiling. The big pot, filled with water already, had a bit of steam rising, too.

No one could call the man a shirker. A murderer, maybe, but a hard working one. He smiled at his silent, inside joke and took the offered mug of steaming brew.

At what they charged for a pouch of coffee, the cup was worth a fair-sized rabbit skin, but to hear Joel tell it, hare fur didn't bring much.

The two trappers and merchant—except, according to his stories, he trapped almost as much as the other two—didn't rouse until well after the dogs ate their breakfast and all the trade hides were loaded onto the sleds.

As Joel had said he hoped, the man he wanted to see woke on his own before the two hours of waiting on the dogs to get their food digested. The trapper poured himself a cup, rubbed his bloodshot eyes, then took a seat next to the fire.

"I've been thinking, Tuck. I'll up my offer for that coat. That five-dollar gold piece I showed you yesterday, and another three silver. Plus, my good man, I'm willing to throw in two more bottles of that fine sipping whiskey you boys enjoyed last night."

The man cursed then spit into the fire. "Joel, you're a thief. That coat took better than forty white mink pelts, and the hood alone, three fox. I can get forty gold for it in Juneau, and you know it."

"We ain't in Juneau. I'll throw in a pound of coffee."

"No, sir. Add a double eagle, and I might consider it."

Crockett listened as the two men bartered, but Tuck never budged. Finally, Joel took the Lord's name in vain, and that did it. Crockett threw the man a nod. "I'll give you thirty gold, right now. Weighed out and proved."

"Let me see your color, son. Dust or nugget?"

Retrieving his pouch, he opened the double flap then fished out the double eagle and two five-dollar gold pieces then returned the leather to its resting place. He put the coins on the table and smiled. "U.S. coin good enough?"

The man's eyes lit up. "Yes, sir, plenty. And to think I was about to sell it to that thief over there."

While the man handed over the coat, Joel eased toward his backside. Crockett set the fur on the table, stuck his hand in his coat, and whirled. The man's knife slashed air, but only because he dodged.

The thirty-eight immediately appeared at nose level.

"Now what are you thinking, partner? That it's a good day to die?"

Joel pointed the knife, a rather large hog sticker, at him. "You should stay out of my business."

"Free country." He waved the pistol toward the door. "Get yourself to wherever you're going. I'm heading back to the Knik River."

"Fine by me. You'll die on the trail without me." He headed for the door. "Good luck, idiot."

He waved the gun again. "Never believed in luck. Now get gone."

Joel snorted, looked around the room, then marched out. "This ain't over."

Crockett followed the man, stepping out onto the porch. Wouldn't do for him to mess with his sled or dogs.

The trapper called Tuck joined him as Joel took off. Shaft stood, but lay back at Crockett's command. Once the real idiot disappeared over the first hill, Tuck nudged Crockett's shoulder.

"You got any more of that gold?"

Chapter Seventeen

Becca opened her eyes, and looked over toward Randal, still sawing logs. A delicious aroma rode the air. Not the first one up. She eased back the covers, slipped quietly out of bed, then used the bedpan. She padded down the hall toward the kitchen.

The closer she got, the warmer her welcome.

Betting her Uncle Levi would be the early riser, she pulled her housecoat tighter. She rounded the corner with a grin. "Morning, Uncle." She poured her favorite mug full of the black gold then sat the chair across from him, relishing the fire's warmth.

"Becca." Other than his initial greeting, he sat silent until she emptied her first cup.

She stood. "Need a refill?"

"Sure, thanks."

When she returned, guess he'd decided on a conversation after all. "Your mother had nightmares after my Aunt Sue died."

"Yes, sir. I've heard that. Had to be hard seeing her mother bleeding out. The new baby to wash up and care for."

"Don't ever remember her being as loud as you've been the last few nights."

"Oh? I'm truly sorry if I woke you."

"Don't be. My old bones won't lay in any rack for long. Especially not that granite slab you've got us on." He let a wry chuckle escape.

She wanted to ask, but dared not. Hopefully, he'd drop it.

"You know the Good Book says, blessed is the peacemaker."

"Yes, sir, I do. It surely does." She glanced over her shoulder, but as much as she wanted someone—anyone—to be waltzing in, no one showed.

"I got it pretty well figured out, sweetheart. Sure would like to help you and your parents to reconcile."

Her and her big mouth. Why did she have to relive what had gone from the best night of her life to the worst day ever just because Crockett asked about it?

"So what do you think you know, Uncle?"

"Way back when, I heard tell your mama was sweet on Edward Clinton. That was right before she showed up in Texas with Jethro Risen, unmarried and obviously expecting, seeing as how you came along five months later."

"Ah."

"At that time and since, they let us all believe your daddy was your daddy, but I'm figuring maybe he wasn't."

Studying the floor, she gathered her thoughts. Jethro Risen was the best father a girl could ever ask for. He just wasn't hers, not blood anyways. She made herself look into his eyes.

"She would never have told me. If I hadn't disobeyed and gone to the Clinton's big party . . . with Adam no less . . . He and I had even been talking marriage."

"For a fact, she should have told you sooner. Mary Rachel was dead wrong in that, but you're wrong, too. Running away never solves anything."

She filled her lungs and looked away.

"I asked them about it."

She nodded, but refused to tear her eyes away from the fire. "What did they say?"

"Well, actually they sent your Aunt CeCe and Uncle Elijah to tell me they didn't want to talk about it. Love covered a multitude of sins. That's the word they sent."

Becca pondered that one.

Were they trying to cover their own immorality? Or were they claiming she was the big sinner? Sure, she had lied and disobeyed, but . . . She looked at him. She loved him so much, had forever.

"That morning, she slapped my face so hard I saw stars. Guess she didn't want to have to mention that. But you know what was worse? What just tore my heart in two?"

His eyes held so much compassion. He shook his head. "What, baby?"

"Jethro Risen took her side."

He held out his arm, and she scooted her chair over and let him wrap her up tight to his side. After a bit, he kissed her cheek then put his mouth close to her ear. "Sounds like Bubba's wanting his breakfast."

Other than one crying jag, the city didn't pain her anywhere near as much as May expected. Oh, how she loved walking the streets of New York on Henry's arm.

Everywhere she looked, memories of showing him the sights choked her up. But . . . she had other business at hand and couldn't live in the past—as wonderful as it had been.

Her baby girl needed her.

Those first two nights in the brownstone proved almost overwhelming in the company of Honey and Nash, seeing the young people interact, and getting caught up with Bammie.

By the time the house went quiet, she put Charlotte off. Mercy, she'd traveled better than fifteen hundred miles and claimed worn-out when her daughter wanted to talk.

Never mentioned that she wanted to size up the players before doling out any advice.

The third night over a nice cup of tea in the parlor, her youngest practically demanded an answer . . . with a rather coy and demure mask plastered on her face, of course. "Well, Ma, what do you think?"

"That this tea is a little sweet. Next time, I'll have only one sugar." She stirred the golden liquid, tinkling the silver spoon on the bone china. "It's still enjoyable though."

Her answer drew a rather pensive expression. "Please." The whine wasn't demanding, but almost.

She sighed. "Well, Nash Moran is hard driven. Appears to me, he craves success above all else, save one thing. Honey, now, I believe you've made an excellent choice in partnering with that young lady."

"Me, too. Glad you agree."

"If the boutique doesn't make it, then I don't know how to write a book." She smiled, but Charlotte didn't. "The pen has merit, but—"

An outstretched hand called for a pause. "Wait! Before we get off on that, I want to know about Nash? What's that 'save one thing' all about?"

"Oh, well that's obvious, darling. Other than success, he only seeks your approval. More than his next breath, I might add."

"Really? You can tell that after only being around him for two days?"

"Sweetheart, besides bringing fictional characters to life, I'm a card player of note. Consequently, I'm a quick study and excellent judge of character."

"So, you think he's in love with me?"

She laughed. "That my dear is only for you and him to figure out over a lifetime. Who loves the other most . . . if at all. I thought I loved your father."

"Mother! Are you saying you didn't love Pa?"

"Let me finish. Of course I loved him. To some extent in the beginning, but with each passing year, my love grew and deepened. Sometimes passion blinds a body. Once we agreed, I did not want to wait another minute to say, I do."

"What do you think about Honey and Nash? You've seen how they make eyes at each other, haven't you?"

"My love, Honey is jealous of you. She's seen the way the young man looks at you and can't stand it that he doesn't look at her the same way."

"So what should I do?"

"I'll tell you more after this coming Saturday afternoon."

"What happens Saturday?"

"He casually asked if I played Whist. He next inquired as to my capability, was I any good at it. I said, of course, and asked why. Next thing I knew, we're partnering at this club he hopes to invade for business purposes."

"Well, I never. Why didn't he ask me? I play! Pa and I used to whip you and Crockett all the time."

May shook her head. If only she could have more of those carefree days, playing cards with Henry and her babies . . . She looked at her daughter. Was that a tinge of jealousy marring her beautiful mug?

"Well, I think it's entirely inappropriate for you and Nash to run off to some club together. Playing cards, no less!"

Late into the night, Charlotte steamed and stewed over Nash's betrayal.

The next morning in the kitchen, her mother never asked about her well-being. Good thing, too. After all, she'd almost begged her to come, then had to pry out any thoughts, only to find out she was making dates with the man Charlotte thought she might love!

Never had she dreamed Ma and Nash would conspire to make her life miserable!

Whist, my left toe!

Even one cup of coffee sat heavy. For sure and for certain, she wanted no sweet bread. Nothing else Bammie offered enticed her either.

With a plastered smile and a curt see-you-at-dinner, she marched out the very minute Honey proclaimed herself ready for the day.

In icy silence, she marched the three blocks to her building. A part of her nagged that Crockett and Mister Moran were her partners, but possession was nine-tenths of the law, wasn't it?

Besides, she'd put way more time and effort into the brick and mortar structure. Crockett had no real investment in it at all.

Once she set her mind to a thing, her big brother couldn't tell her no anymore than Pa could.

Her shoulders did a little ha-ha-ha dance.

Yes, it would be hers alone.

And as such, she might have to evict that wastrel who squatted on the second floor.

Once her female partner entwined herself in the boutique's final interior touches and first merchandise orders, Charlotte found Mister Moran sitting her brother's chair, studying her building's blueprint. The profligate looked up. "Good morning."

"Is it now?"

He shot her his crooked little boy grin that reminded her of her Pa's smile. Most days, it would brighten her soul, but not this one. Maybe never again.

"Trouble?"

"Why, no. What in the whole wide world would give you such a notion? Aren't the birds singing in the trees? Everything's all peaches and cream, Mister Moran."

His lips thinned, obviously stifling whatever ill-humored rebuttal about to come out of his no-account mouth.

"Sarcasm does not become you, my dear lady. What is it? Tell me plain and simple, won't you please? I've obviously done something that's offended you."

Not the least bit fair that he knew her so well after such a short time. She hated that. But then how long had her big-mouthed brother been telling tales about her, too? "You! That's what's wrong! How dare you!"

"How dare me what? I can't think of a thing I've done. Still, whatever it was, forgive me, please."

"No. I won't. You've gone and done it already, and without a thought . . . of me, as to . . ." She shook her head, twirled, and marched toward the door.

A blur approached then stood between her and the exit. "Charlotte Buckmeyer! What is it? What have I done? Really, tell me. I deserve at the least to know what's got you so riled."

She hated it even more that he didn't know or care. "Get out of my way, Nash. I'm going home."

He backed up. "Fine. I'll come with you."

"Texas is a long way away, and you'd be bored to tears there."

"Texas? Why? Have you heard something? It surely isn't true! I've not even looked at another woman since I set eyes on you. I swear it. Not the whole time you've been here."

"Oh, now I know personally that's nothing but a big old lie! Liar! I've seen you making eyes at Honey! And you couldn't wait to invite my mother to play cards at your new club either, could you? Didn't you even think that maybe I might enjoy an afternoon of Whist?"

He held both hands up. "So all this is about my asking your mother to play cards this Saturday? Good gravy, Charlotte. How unreasonable can you be? Your mother? Really? You're jealous of your own mother?" He huffed. "And Honey? How could she begin to compare with you?"

Her intent to deny his accusations turned straightaway into agreement when she shook her head, then of its own accord, swiveled into a nod.

"I suppose, yes. Somewhat. But it isn't really her as much as it's you! Not even thinking to ask me to play as your partner! And no matter what you say, I don't like how you and Honey make eyes at each other every time you're in the same room. It's thoroughly disgusting."

His lips spread into a broad grin.

Oh! He was so infuriating!

"I like it when you're jealous. Brings out the green in your eyes, but sweet Charlotte, I happened to come by the information that William Vanderbilt is a huge fan of your mother's work. Once she arrived in New York, I dropped her name, hoping to wrangle an invitation to his card club—not mine. You can't imagine the business deals that happen there."

"Didn't I read that Mister Vanderbilt is sick?"

"Yes, that's true. William Henry, the old man, is in pretty bad shape, actually. But his son, William Kissam Vanderbilt, is our age. Once your mother and I have bested him and his partner, I'm hoping we can arrange a rematch at the brownstone for him to meet you."

She peered into the windows of his soul. He never flinched the slightest bit or looked away. Instead, he stared right back at her like proving every word he'd spoken was the Lord's own truth. "Well . . . What about Honey? You, sir, have for sure and for certain been looking at her! I've seen it with my own eyes because neither of you seem to care one bit it's right in front of me!"

He glanced around, closed the door, then stepped to her, taking her shoulders in his grasp. "Charlotte. Sweetheart. Honey cannot hold a candle to you. I admit, she appears to be somewhat smitten—and well, it's flattering—and I also admit to . . . I've . . ." He grimaced then shrugged. "Maybe I have—"

Almost able to feel the sting on her palm, she slapped him on her mind's stage. But other than Crockett when she was only six, she'd never hit another human being in her whole life.

"You've what! Encouraged her? How evil is that if you have no interest in the girl?"

He grinned then bounced his eyebrows. "Evil, am I?"

Ha! She might just have to reconsider her position on administering a bit of physical pain upon his fun-making self.

"What'd I say?"

"Well, I wouldn't go so far as evil, but I'd admit to unthoughtful."

"Way too kind! It's . . . it's . . . downright mean!"

"Alright then, but I do love it when you're jealous."

"Awhile back, you liked, now you're saying you love. Tell me, Mister Moran, for once and for all! Which is it?"

He unhanded her, bent at the waist, and moved closer. "Can I kiss you?"

"No! You may certainly not! Now tell me. Like or love?"

"It's love. The truth is I love—"

Staring into his eyes, she raised up on her tiptoes and pressed her lips to his, hushing him. His hands touched her back and pressed, she jerked back. "Mind your manners, Mister Moran."

"Yes, ma'am. Truth is, I love it when you're jealous."

"Ha! Is that all?"

Chapter Eighteen

Charlotte glared, but he didn't answer her question. The cad! "Well? What is it, Mister Moran? Do you just love teasing me and making me jealous? Do you enjoy playing with my heart the way a cat toys with its prey? Is there more, or not?"

"May I kiss you again?"

"No!" She whirled out of his embrace. "Now answer my questions."

He put his hands behind his back. "How about you kissing me then?"

Did she dare? Just the night before—as if the Lord was warning her—her mother spoke of passion sometimes clouding the issue.

But still . . . her lips longed for . . . they wouldn't be denied. She loved his big soft lips and everything in her wanted to kiss them again. She shouldn't give in though. "Keep those hands right where they are."

"Yes, ma'am. I promise." He closed his eyes and leaned toward her.

With her eyes wide open, she moved in and pressed her lips against his again. The minute they touched hers, she closed her eyes and lost herself. Fire burned hot from his mouth to her heart, and she could not get enough.

The silly thing about beat out of her chest. Her throat tightened with the need for breath. It all . . . almost . . . overwhelmed . . .

A breath might end it. She couldn't make herself pull away and breathe. He backed away. Her hands reached for him, desiring to pull him back, but he dropped to one knee."

"Marry me. I love you more than life. Please say you'll marry me, Charlotte. I'll—"

"What? No! Maybe. Get up this minute. You're such a josher! Why would you ask me such a question?"

"I told you. I love you. I want you to be mine and mine alone for the rest of my life. I'm not joking. I'm dead serious, Charlotte. I want you to be my wife." His eyes watered. Were they going to overflow? Was he going to cry? Was he truly serious? Could he be?

"Nash, please get up and go back to doing whatever it was you were doing with the blueprint. I need to . . . Never you mind what I need to do. Be at the brownstone tonight at seven sharp. I'll give you my answer then."

He stood and stared into her eyes. He had to stop that or her eyes would tear and give her away! "Seven sharp."

"Go on then." For several booms of her heart, he didn't move. Not a muscle. What was he thinking? What was he going to do? Cry? Grab her and hold her hostage until she said yes?

Would that be a bad thing? He could read her so easily . . . like one of her mother's novels, but . . .

Finally! He cleared his throat and stepped toward the desk. "I almost forgot. Yesterday afternoon, an offer came in."

"An offer on what?" He sounded as if nothing had happened between them . . . like she hadn't given him her heart in the kiss . . . as if he hadn't proposed. "Why didn't you tell me first thing?"

He grinned, that crooked little smile that reminded her of Pa, the one she loved. "Well, I intended to, but became a bit preoccupied. After all, the love of my life came in all angry in the most foul mood, then she—"

"You really believe that I'm the love of your life? How can you know?"

"Yes, ma'am, I definitely do. From the first moment I laid eyes on you, I knew it. You're so intelligent and intriguing. The more I'm around you, my desire only deepens. I want you to be mine forever. That's love, pure and simple. Why do you think I took you to meet my mother?"

Could it be true? Her desire had only grown stronger, too. Did that mean love? It didn't feel so pure and simple as he put it. She'd thought maybe, but this deal with . . . "I'm sorry. I really have got to go, but first . . . tell me about the offer."

He laid it all out. Exactly what he'd hoped for, except for the few changes they requested.

And a fancy restaurant would be a boon to all the shops, especially the boutique. He motioned her to the desk to show her, but instead of standing next to him, she stayed on the far side. Couldn't risk being so close to him.

Finally, he looked up. "What do you think?"

"That they'll be the perfect tenants, and their deposit will get us going on the second floor. We'll be able to finish it much sooner than anticipated."

"They want the changes post haste, before they move in, and we're presently short of funds."

"Humph. Some of us are not. Draw up the papers. Once I've met the principals, I'll sign off if you're ready to."

"Of course!" He flashed his biggest smile. "Yes, ma'am."

Backing toward the door, while he jabbered on, she let her eyes feast on him, from the top of his head to the tip of polished shoes then back to his face. Yes, indeed, she wanted him plenty, but . . . "I've got to go. Seven sharp."

"I'll be there. You can count on it."

She marched from the office straight to Honey's Boutique. She found the proprietor dressing a mannequin in a darling dress. A big floppy hat sat on a stool next to it.

Maybe she'd have to buy the outfit? But first things first. Not knowing any other way to say it, she just blurted it out. "Nash just asked me to marry him."

"Oh!" The exclamation was also a gasp. Honey's hand flew to her mouth. "Well! Oh? When, just now?"

"Yes, ma'am."

"What did you tell him?"

A part of her wanted to leave that part off, but why avoid the truth? "At first, I thought he was being a tease. I told him no and to get up off his knee."

"He went down on his knee? How romantic . . ."

"Then I told him maybe. I told him to be at the brownstone at seven sharp, and I'd give him my answer then."

The girl nodded, closed her eyes as though trying to work it all out in her head, then finally offered a weak smile. "Why the maybe, Charlotte? He's like . . ."

"Honey. I know you're smitten with him. And that the cad has been flirting with you to make me jealous."

"What? He told you that?"

"Not in so many words, but he said that he loved to make me jealous, so I figured."

"So I guess he's not interested in me at all."

"I'm sorry, friend, but apparently not." Charlotte filled her lungs. Skating on thin ice had never been her forte. She needed to tread very lightly. "I don't want this or anything else to come between us. But especially not Nash."

Honey picked up the hat, put it on the dummy, cocked it to the other side then turned and faced her. "You'd not marry him because of me? Charlotte, I—"

"Whoa. I didn't say that, not exactly. What I need to know before I give him my answer is how it will affect us? We are partners after all."

The girl's head bobbed as she studied the walls. Her eyes glistened, and she kept blinking, obviously trying not to let any tear fall.

After too many head nods to count, she looked Charlotte in the eye. "Yes, I was smitten with the man, but if he's such a cad as to only make eyes at me to provoke you, then he is not the man I thought he was."

"So . . . if I tell him yes, then there will not be any bad blood between us?"

The girl laughed. "May I slap his face?"

Charlotte returned the mirth. "He deserves it, but no."

Honey opened her arms. "Congratulations, dear friend. I hope you'll be happy."

Were the hug and congratulations premature?

"Say, where again was that hairdresser you were telling me about? I need a trim."

With a name, directions, and a tilt of her head, she added, "Not too much, though. Your tresses are beautiful, almost perfect. Especially if there's a wedding on the horizon."

Right that minute, one thousand one hundred and eighty-nine miles west of New York City, in one of Kansas City's more notorious houses not far from the stockyards, Nathaniel Nightingale awoke with a dull ache in both legs.

Never in his fifteen years could he remember waking with such a pain. He pried one eye open.

Where was he?

He rose onto an elbow. The throb behind his eyes drove him back to the feather pillow.

How'd he get there? Wherever there was.

The door opened. A lady at least his mother's age wearing a thin ruffled housecoat sashayed in, carrying a stack of clothes. "Morning, sweetheart, but barely. It'll be high noon soon enough."

Nathaniel pulled the sheet up to his neck, covering his nakedness. He looked around. Where were his trousers? "Who are you? And where am I?"

"You don't remember?" She put the pile on the bed's edge.

He recognized his shirt in the stack. "No, ma'am." He peeked under the sheet at his bare self again. "Those my clothes? And if they are, what are you doing with them?"

"Yours alright. Got torn a little. Soaked, too, in the fight, so we mended and washed them. Just now took them off the line. Your pa is ready to get, said to wake you up since you could get dressed again."

He shook his head, but no memory of anything past the supper meal and that second beer showed through the mental fog banging his head like some of those Chinese cymbals. "Where am I again?"

"Kansas City, and this here's my private room." She laughed. "Mind telling me who Evelyn is?"

"My cousin, except we're not blood kin. Why you asking?"

She grinned. "Ah, kissing cousins. That explains it. Anytime one of my girls got fresh you claimed Evelyn wouldn't like it one little bit."

Oh . . . his head throbbed . . . it was starting to come back. "So, we . . . uh . . . didn't . . . uh . . ."

"That's right, sweetheart. After you got really drunk, I brought you on up here to sleep it off."

Nathaniel touched his sore jaw. "Did I hit that man?"

"You were so sweet, but darling, I don't have much honor to defend anymore."

The whole night came back like a blue Northern, blowing across his soul. "No, ma'am. No matter your past, no need for anyone to be talking to you like that cowpoke was."

Once dressed and on his way out of town, he purposed in his heart to do three things.

One, never ever tell his mother about what he and Pa did in Kansas City. Two, never drink another drop of liquor, and three, never let Evie know he spent the night in the bed of a sporting lady.

His little lady would never understand.

 The hall clock struck the seventh note. Late, and Charlotte had said clearly seven sharp. He'd repeated her and promised to be there. Maybe he regretted his proposal.

One thing for certain is that he knew full well how she hated not being on time. If it were true, if he lamented asking for her hand, the least he could do was be on time to tell her so.

"He'll be along, friend. Something's held him up."

She looked across the table. Was that a tinge of hope on Honey's mug? What was she thinking? That Nash running late could possibly mean he'd changed his mind? Well, why wouldn't she?

Charlotte pondered the same rationale.

The rogue. If he didn't have a broken bone or cut that might bleed out so quickly that he couldn't walk the three blocks from her building to the brownstone...

"Perhaps. But as soon as Mother's down, we're eating. With or without Mister Moran."

"Has she seen—?"

"No! And don't you say a word."

The girl clamped her lips shut into a stupid grin then shook her head. "Why, you know I'd never do such a thing, Charlotte Buckmeyer."

Descending footfalls sounded. Exactly like her mother to wait until what she figured to be the last second to make her grand entrance. Why did she always have to be so dramatic? Humph. Must not have been paying close attention.

Or had she decided not to wait on Mister Moran, too?

"Meri Charlotte Buckmeyer! Have mercy on my soul, child. What have you gone and done?"

Immediately, she touched the side of her head. It felt quite bald. "Well certainly, Ma, you can see. Do you hate it?"

Hand over her heart, her mother—who'd stopped dead in her tracks barely inside the room—found her feet and moved toward her seat at the head of the table.

"Dear, why in the world? Oh, I am so sorry. We'll sue the hairdresser who did this to you! How dare she whack off your beautiful long hair!"

"We'll do no such thing. It's the latest fashion if you didn't know. Of course, you don't though. What would a seventy-five-year-old woman know about the latest trends?"

"Do you mean to tell me this . . . this . . . style . . . was your idea?" She gasped. "Are you saying that you did it on purpose?"

"Actually . . . yes." Charlotte sat a little taller, her face warming by the minute. "I was ready for a change. It looked absolutely fabulous in the photographs, so chic and stylish."

Had she made a mistake? A huge horrible mistake? She couldn't back down though. Hopefully, once Nash graced them with his presence, his reaction would be more positive.

Or would it? He might hate it, too.

"It is the latest trend." Honey emphasized the word 'is' then cleared her throat, obviously avoiding looking Ma in the eyes.

At least she took Charlotte's side though. Could the girl want her to look ugly, masculine, like a man? Maybe counting the haircut a giant boon to help take Nash away? Honey's shimmering blonde curls hung almost to her waist.

Arrguuhh! Oh, how that very minute, she regretted cutting off so much.

"I think it's stunning, very becoming. It'll only take some getting used to. Don't you agree, MayMee?"

A part of Charlotte hated it that her friend used Ma's grandmother name, but it's what she'd insisted her boutique partner call Mother rather than the too formal Mis'ess Buckmeyer mouthful. Still, she wasn't family, and it sounded so . . . so . . .

What was wrong with her? What did it matter?

That scoundrel had asked her to marry him then thought twice about it and was standing her up. He'd probably hate her hair, too. If he ever arrived to see her surprise. Why had she done it? Her mother certainly could have been much more gracious. It didn't look that bad.

"Honey, if you would be so kind as to help Bammie serve, we should really go ahead with supper. Apparently, Mister Moran has decided to dine elsewhere."

Resentment and disappointment hung heavy between offered theories of the man's whereabouts. Even though each and every course was as excellent as ever, Charlotte only picked at her plate.

How could he do that to her? Stand her up on the date that she promised to give her answer as to being his wife. His wife!

Would that be what she could expect her whole life if she agreed? He'd said it was love, pure and simple.

But what appeared most pure and simple was that he didn't love her at all. If he had, he would have been there on time. She glanced at the clock for the hundredth time as it began its hourly litany.

A full hour late. He definitely changed his mind.

Her heart, once so full of anticipation and what she thought was love for Nash Moran, ached in her chest. She'd been duped. She'd make him vacate her building post haste and for evermore, he'd be a silent partner she never had to lay eyes on again.

Over dessert, her steam cooled to concern with each tick of the hall clock. Had something dire happened to keep him away? She replayed Lacey's story of being mugged on the streets of New York.

Right outside the theatre. Her first husband being stabbed and . . . dying. Her throat choked, and an overwhelming fear rose from her gut to torment her heart.

Though the conversation had long since left the subject of where Nash might be, she had to ask. "Do you suppose he's been mugged?"

Their ill-intended excuses did nothing to quell the anxiety. At the meal's end with the table cleared, for her there was nothing left to do but retire. Nash wasn't coming at all.

No matter how badly she hoped he'd rush through the door filled with a perfectly good reason... She sat at her dressing table and stared at her reflection, trying to pull her hair out to be a little longer.

She never should have . . . It was just as well, though. It made little difference now what Nash thought. But he'd called her the love of his life.

Why hadn't he come? Why had she decided to let that woman cut her hair so short? She threw the brush across the room! She sure didn't need it! Her hair would never be tangled again. That was for sure and for certain!

A light tap on her door drew her away from her remorse. Had he finally arrived? She swung around. "Yes?"

The door opened part way. "Care for a nightcap?"

"Why not? I'm not the least bit sleepy."

Her mother swished in, tapped the door shut with her foot, and put the silver tray on the little table between her two Queen Anne chairs.

Charlotte joined her. "Can you believe the man? He asked me to marry him, Ma. He said I was the love of his life. I was to give him my answer tonight."

The grand old lady took a sip then sighed. "Think he got cold feet?"

"I don't know what to think." She rubbed her hands over her head. She kept forgetting how bald it felt. Why had she done it? And of all days . . . "I kissed him this afternoon. It was before he asked."

"Baby, why? You aren't engaged yet."

"I know, but then he asked and . . ."

"What did you tell him?"

"At first, I said no then . . ." She shrugged. "It was like I couldn't stand it, Ma. His lips were so soft and kissable. That's when he told me love was all pure and simple and why he'd taken me to meet his mother. I actually kissed him twice."

"Charlotte."

Her eyes closed and she couldn't help a little grin. In that moment it had seemed so easy to believe him. She relived the kiss. "I made him put his hands behind his back and kissed him again."

"You're glowing, you know." Her mother grinned. "Do you love him, my precious?"

"I don't know. I mean, a part of me wants him so badly that it literally hurts. I think I was going to say yes. But right this minute, I want to . . ." She bowed and rubbed her face with both hands. "I don't know what I want to do. What if he's lying in a hospital . . . somewhere bleeding or . . . If he were able, wouldn't he have at least . . ."

"Don't borrow trouble, darling. I'm sure he has a perfectly good excuse, and even if it is cold feet, then all you're out is two—is that right? You've only kissed him twice? Nothing else happened after?"

"Mother! How could you ask such a thing? Of course, nothing else. Well, except he told me this up-and-coming chef had made an offer for the first floor space. He had a few concessions—which we'll be glad to do—for a new restaurant. It'll be perfect. "

"Well, good . . . for the new tenant and that nothing more happened. It isn't unheard of, dear. And there is always . . ."

"What are you talking about, Ma?"

"Generational curses."

She'd heard the stories, but she'd never make the same mistake as her parents' mothers had made. "I promised both you and Pa to keep myself pure, and I've kept that promise. I would never, ever . . ." She smiled. "Do I need to go on?"

"No, of course not, but . . . I don't ever want there to be anything that we can't talk about. I've lived a long, wonderful life, my sweet, and you do acquire more than a little wisdom along the way. I want to help you avoid as much pain and heartache as possible."

"I know, Ma. Of course you do." She held up her glass. Her mother touched the rim of hers to it then drained the brandy. "One more, then bed?"

After tossing and turning, she awoke with a start too many times to count. Where was he? What had happened to him?

Way before the sun, with only a few carriage horses clomping the city streets to life, she gave up hunting for any real sleep. First thing, she would check at the hospital.

She found her mother and Bammie sitting the kitchen table, swilling coffee.

"You're up early."

"I couldn't get Nash off my mind." Charlotte filled her favorite cup then slipped in next to the cook. "Don't suppose either of you have any new ideas."

"Well, dear, I was telling your mama that the man is a fool. He should have moved Heaven and earth to be here early with his hat in hand." The old dear grinned. "You are the catch of all catches, not to mention that meal I slaved over. He missed it, his loss. I'd made all his favorites, too."

"You're too sweet, Bammie, but . . ."

A knock on the front door silenced her. By the second, she'd reached the hall. The third rap, she'd turned the lock and knob. An old man with white, unruly hair dressed in a tattered wool coat nodded a greeting then stuck out his hand.

"Mister Nash told me you'd surely give a reward for information about his situation."

"Yes, of course! Come in. Where is he?"

"Oh, that isn't necessary, Miss. I'll wait here."

She whirled. "Ma, bring my pocketbook. Quickly!" Facing the old gentleman again, her heart pounded against her ribs. "What's happened? Is he alright?"

"Oh, yes, ma'am. Quite alright."

At last, she could swallow again and gasped. Thank Heaven above.

"He's in detention, ma'am."

"Detention?" Whatever could be detaining him? "Do you mean . . . in jail?"

"Yes, ma'am, precisely."

"For what?"

"Drunk and disorderly conduct they said, but those coppers . . . well . . ." The old man laughed, exposing pearly white, perfect teeth. Now how could that be? He touched his hatless forehead, then turned and took the steps like a man half his age.

"Wait! Where exactly is he, sir?"

Without a glance back, he threw an answer over his shoulder. "Brooklyn, across the river."

She stepped out, but the man had practically skipped halfway down the street. She wrapped her housecoat tighter and hurried back inside.

Her mother stood in the entryway, holding a wad of greenbacks with her mouth gaping open. She stared after the fellow as if she'd just seen a ghost.

"Mother, what's wrong?"

Chapter Nineteen

After she dressed—and at her mother's insistence— Charlotte marched to her lawyer's office with Honey in tow, and found a rather junior associate. Apparently, the more senior men didn't come in at that early hour.

Business handled, she, her partner-assistant, and the attorney headed south toward the Brooklyn Bridge in a rented coach.

"Yes, sir." The desk sergeant informed her barrister they indeed had a Nash Moran in their holding cell. It only took one double eagle to secure his release.

Relief flooded her soul.

The man dropped onto the hired hackney's bench next to her. Honey and the handsome lawyer took the seat opposite. Seemed her partner sat a bit close to the young man.

Then she'd caught her making eyes at him at each turn on the way to the jail. Oh well, so long as it wasn't Nash. Mister Moran offered no excuse nor did she ask for one until she found herself alone with him back in her office. She sat what used to be her brother's desk and nodded toward the guard chair.

"Sir, I do believe . . . no . . . I am certain that I deserve an explanation. And a heartfelt apology."

He smiled. "I would like an answer first, dear lady, on my proposal."

"Oh, you would? Well, you can forget that. Right now your interest should be focused on convincing me that you are not some disorderly drunken fool!"

"I'm not! You know I'm not. Did you talk to the old man at all? I thought you'd be pleased."

"Pleased? Excuse me? Why should it please me that you went and got yourself incarcerated? And on the most important night—up until this time—of our relationship? Indeed if we are to have any serious liaison."

"Of course we are."

"I hope you know I considered kicking you out this very morning. Not only my building, but from my life as well! Do you even know how disappointed I was? I am?"

"But . . . didn't he tell you?"

"That old geezer? He told me you'd been arrested!"

Nash shook his head. "The gentleman said he knew your mother. That he'd fallen into the same trap that snared me."

Was he still drunk? "Nash! Calling that old reprobate a gentleman is a stretch. What trap?"

"Charlotte, Mister Dithers is the epitome of a man's man, and a gentleman is exactly what he is. Or rather a gentleman's gentleman. Didn't you love his British accent?"

His breath did not reek of liquor, and he didn't smell as though he'd spent the night in the same clothes as expected. Then again, she hadn't gotten that close either.

"You've lost it, Moran. The old guy who came to the brownstone looked at best a longshoreman who'd been rode hard and put up wet too many times . . . if not a downright bum."

"He came to the brownstone? I'd asked him to stop by the building once he was released."

"Forget the old man. What trap? And why were you in Brooklyn in the first place?"

Up north on the Knik River, Deidra Graves helped her sister-in-law with the laundry but kept one eye and both ears peeled. The Texan was overdue. She and Becca feared the worst, though neither admitted it to anyone but each other.

As if saying it openly would give it credence and make it so.

Once upon a time, the man's older brother might have been able to stand up to Joel, but she didn't think so now. The Ranger—pushing decrepit, bless his heart—acted so goofy over his new wife.

To hear him tell it, Crockett would be along any day and there was no reason at all for him to go looking.

Why had Randal promised her to Joel?

"No, no, no." The baby tugged on her shirt then pointed outside. "Noooo."

"What is it, Bubba?" She scooped the boy up as Becca opened the door. An icy blast chilled her cheeks.

"It's them! They're back!" Becca didn't even bother with her coat. She scooped the baby up and hurried toward the trading post.

Closing the door, Deidra stepped to the window. At the perfect angle, she could see her reflection in its glass.

Why had she worn that dress for such a day? She fluffed her hair, threw on her jacket, then stepped out as though only another trapper had shown to barter his furs.

Where was Joel?

Who was the other man who'd come with Crockett?

While her brother saw to the sled dogs, she slipped inside and took a seat in the far corner. The men warmed themselves by the fire. Between hot mugs of spiced ale, multiple bowls of caribou stew, and extra-large hunks of black bread, the story got told. Must have been a beautiful coat for Joel to react so violently.

But then why had Crockett even got involved? That part didn't make any sense.

Kind of on the sly, gold coins changed hands between Levi Baylor and the man called Tuck. She couldn't see how much and never heard exactly what the payment was for.

The most important thing was that Crockett survived and returned.

And Joel . . . well, he wasn't there yet, and if he never . . .

She couldn't rightly bring herself to wish the man ill, but perhaps he'd decide to winter elsewhere. And if Becca had her way, they'd all be gone south at breakup.

Wasn't even all that dark yet, but far as she was concerned, the thaw couldn't come soon enough. What she'd seen once as a grand adventure had turned into a frozen nightmare. She wanted to go anywhere warm and civilized. Texas sounded perfect.

Once warm and half full of stew, Crockett used his bowl as cover to steal glances at the young lady. He liked it that she quietly sat the corner, not calling any attention to herself.

If only she'd reacted like Bubba and ran to him, throwing her arms around him then begging to sit his lap. He could stand a lot of that.

Perhaps one day that would be the case. One day soon he prayed. Should he ask his nephew for her hand? Would Randal consent to his sister marrying at seventeen?

And could she even be interested in him, be willing to accept a proposal? If her brother said yes, would Deidra? What would his mother think?

He humphed aloud, but never meant to. She glanced his way and returned his smile. He sure was full of questions. Hadn't pondered so much since he couldn't remember when.

Oh well, if he got back to Texas with a little bubba of his own, his mother would forgive him marrying before he got home.

Why, she'd give him and his new wife a party the likes of which Llano had never seen.

'Mercy, Son, you're hitching the horse, and you don't even own the wagon.' His father's words echoed across the soul. What would the old man think of her if he hadn't of gone and got himself bucked off that stud colt?

Then if he hadn't, Crockett would be in New York that very minute and never enjoyed the pleasure of meeting his beautiful Deidra.

The conversation turned back to the coat. Old Tuck elbowed him. "Best show them, Son. I speculate there's a lot of disbelief about exactly how pretty that fur be."

Crockett had wanted to wait until the right moment, but that might be it. "Of a fact, the proof is right outside." He faced Deidra. "Would you be so kind as to model it for me?"

Though she shrugged, the smile and twinkle in her eye bore witness to her true enthusiasm. "Sure, I'd be happy to." He liked that; liked about everything she said or did, and couldn't wait to see her in it.

He made himself not hurry out to the sled, retrieved the bundle the garment was wrapped in, then strode back inside. Deidra still sat the far corner. He joined her with his back to the room and handed her the bundle.

With his own coat spread, he formed a screen. "Might want to shed your jacket. I think it'll fit better without it."

Grinning ear to ear, she shucked her coat without putting the package down then slowly unwrapped the rabbit skin pouch that encased the mink and fox. Her eyes widened as she beheld it, and she gasped. "Oh, Crockett." She slipped into the garment. "It's . . . it's perfectly gorgeous." She rubbed the mink with her eyes closed. "And so soft."

"Pull the hood up."

She complied, then he stepped aside, offering his arm toward the young lady who gently rested her hand atop his.

"What did we tell you?"

Becca gasped. Sophia covered her mouth with both hands then went to oohing and ahhing to beat the nines. The men grunted their approval, but he loved the ladies' reactions . . . like they couldn't say enough.

He leaned in close to Deidra. "I bought it for you."

She spun around. "What? Oh no. I couldn't. It's much too valuable. I mean, it's absolutely the most beautiful thing I've ever had on in all my life, but really . . ."

The room silenced as one then the other realized what Deidra was saying, but he didn't care.

"It isn't as beautiful as you, and it wouldn't look as perfect on anyone else. It's got to be yours. I bought it for you."

The beauty looked at her brother, her eyes questioning, begging for his approval. "What about Joel? He'll—"

"Forget about him. The coat's yours, or would you prefer I burn it?"

"No! You can't do that! Why would you?"

"I couldn't stand the thought of anyone else wearing it."

"Oh, Crockett. It's fabulous! Butter on bacon!" She flung her arms around his neck like he was the only one in the room. Yes, sir. That was more like it. "Thank you! But . . . are you thinking that—"

"No conditions. Pure and simple: a beautiful coat for a beautiful woman."

She hugged herself. "I love it. I've never loved anything more!"

"Good, then. Walk around some, I want to see it on you."

She blushed, but complied to his every whim, waltzing around the room, twirling as she went, keeping her eyes on him.

What a knockout. Could she be any more perfect?

Perfection was the farthest thing from Charlotte's mind. If Nash Moran hadn't gotten under her skin, and if he wasn't squatting in her building, she might forget all about the good-looking galoot.

To keep busy, she helped Honey decorate the shop and unpack inventory until mid-afternoon. Bammie even came to help with the ironing.

Her partner found a stopping point, and before she could start another project, Charlotte insisted the time to go back to the brownstone had arrived. The girl didn't much want to stop, but what could she say?

It wasn't like she didn't have three more days before her grand opening. The boutique looked wonderful.

What a stroke of brilliance on Nash's part to hang sheets in the front window with only one dressed razzle dazzle mannequin holding a sign with the opening date.

Or had that been her idea? She definitely loved her partner's genius in changing its name. The Razzmatazz Boutique! So much better than boring Honey's.

She allowed herself a smile. The sign's lettering had at least been her contribution.

Around the two of them, a person might think Charlotte never had a clever creative thought, but she certainly surrounded herself with the right people to root for.

Once home, she marched straight to her mother's office. Ma sat behind her big desk scribbling on a page. Too many to be a letter rested next to the one her feather danced over. Was she working on a new novel?

No, she hadn't said anything about it, and surely she would have. She raised her feather pen.

Humph, why wasn't she using her new fountain pen? How could she ever get comfortable with it, if she didn't use the thing?

The grand lady looked up. "Is Nash fine?"

"No, he is not. The man is infuriating."

She laughed. "Well, what happened? How'd he get in the soup?"

"Didn't you get my note?"

"I did, but I couldn't believe he'd really gotten smashed. Wasn't there some mistake?"

"I don't think so, but he still refuses to tell me why he was in Brooklyn. Plus he's claiming that old bum who told me—"

"Hold it, dear. That old man is no bum. He's top brass. Actually, not a man at all."

"What? Gee whiz, Ma, have you been imbibing all morning?"

"Never you mind, young lady. I take it the two of you had a fuss."

"To say the least. When he refused to tell why he went across the river." She threw her hands into the air. "Suffice it to say he's coming tonight at seven. Sharp, he said. But . . . well . . ."

Charlotte wanted to cry or laugh or jump on the first train back to Texas. Even better, maybe she'd go north and find her brother then slap him dotty for sending her to New York.

"Are we feeding him?"

"Yes, I didn't intend to, but I let him wrangle an invitation. He promised to tell all tonight."

Her mother smiled. "You love him, don't you?"

"How could you say such a thing? The man is almost as pigheaded as Pa was. Why do you think I do?"

"Just now . . . the range of emotions you went through. It seems to me the man's gotten hold of your heart. Otherwise, why would you agree to let him come for supper?"

"Well, that's no reason. After all, we are still partners. But I may boot him tonight, depending on his story."

"Actually, he's your brother's associate."

"Humph, I'm so invested in everything Crockett's done up here, I'm the brass. He and Nash Moran are the peon partners. And my brother has no part in the fountain pen. That's you, me, and Nash."

She laughed. "That's right."

"Crockett's cut smooth out of that deal."

"But still, being in business with the man shouldn't give him leave to encroach on your evenings. Then stand you up."

"What if he really does have a good reason? Don't you want to hear it?"

Her mother's lips thinned like she had to try real hard to keep from laughing. Charlotte hated that expression.

"I've been meaning to ask. Did he say anything about your hair?"

"No! Not a word! Can you believe that? Men are so unobservant. They drive me mad."

"Maybe he took the sage old advice that if you can't say something nice, then don't—"

"Mother! It's high-toned; the spanking latest of fashion! Don't you read the papers at all?" She went to flip her curls—her habit when upset—but flipped only air. The tresses were gone. Why did she keep forgetting? She smoothed her neckline and sideburns instead. "Way to kick a girl when she's down."

"No, darling. Never. I was only offering a . . . But he probably did notice. It'd be hard not to." Ma always knew just what to say. "Hey, want to hear the first chapter of my new book?" Ha, the change-the-subject route.

Suited Charlotte just fine.

Though she didn't really want to hear it—not right then—it'd be so rude to say no. How could she deny her mother? "Another pirate book?"

"No, ma'am. I'm done with Red Rooster. Killed him off. Evie's still got that manuscript. That child is amazing. Her instincts flabbergast me again and again. Definitely my little prodigy. Anyway, this one's different. I'm thinking of calling this new one *Angels Unaware*."

"Is it a sequel to the Lone Star Loves trilogy?"

"No. Sit back and let me read you some. I want your honest opinion."

Why would she say such a thing? Honest would be the only opinion Charlotte would give. How many times had Pa said that? Angels, huh? Very different indeed. She obeyed and sat herself across the desk.

From the first, she'd loved her mother reading to her, especially her own work. And anyone else's worthwhile, too. The only thing she loved more was when both her parents took turns with her father reading the men's parts. Getting into a new story might be just what she needed to get her mind off that man.

Abel balled his fist, but resisted the urge to hit his brother. "Put that rock down, Cain. We still have time to select a lamb and get back to the altar."

"No."

Blinding pain . . . then he sank to the earth. Strong hands grabbed his arms. He floated through solid rock. How was that possible? He touched his head then looked at his hand. No blood, not even a bump.

"Wait." Charlotte scooted to the edge of her chair. "You're writing a story about the Cain and Abel? The Bible brothers?"

"I am. Well, it isn't about them, but they're in it."

"What brought this on?"

"Oh, your father had a pet theory about them being twins, and—"

"I never heard him say anything about Cain and Abel being twins."

"Sweetheart, you were not privy to all of your father's and my conversations. Now do you want to hear this or not?"

"Yes, I do, but let me run tell Bammie about Nash coming tonight." She stood then remembered. "What was that 'and'?"

"What 'and'?"

"A minute ago . . . about them being twins, and . . . Isn't that what you said? I interrupted you. Sorry."

"Go on and hurry back. I'll tell you later."

Chapter Twenty

Dear Evelyn,

I'm so sorry your parents nixed the idea of coming to Kansas City. The stock yards are amazing. We didn't lose one head on the drive, got the herd here all safe and sound, then Pa negotiated top dollar for them.

We did right nice for ourselves. More than a year's provision Pa said.

For a celebration, he took us to a la-di-dah restaurant for a T-bone steak dinner. And we stayed one night in a fancy hotel, too. Crystal chandeliers and gold gilding everywhere.

You would love the architecture here. It's so obvious that there's so much money flying around the whole area. They're building Queen Ann houses everywhere; the streets around the square are full of them, and I know you'd love the style.

Pa and I looked at one. He's suck a corker, acted like he was thinking seriously about buying one.

All he wanted to do was to get ideas though for building Ma one. She fancies a new house back at the Red River Ranch. Maybe I'll build one someday, too. I know you would love them.

Anyone would. With all their original woodwork—everything's one of a kind and made by a master-crafter. We'll have to import that.

And inside the house, from room to room, they have doors that disappear into the walls. To open them, you slide the things right into the wall, I promise. They call them pocket doors.

There are balconies everywhere, off almost every bedroom, and stained glass to beat the band.

Big old wide, wrap around porches and even fancy porte-cocheres—that's where there's a roof coming off the home's entrance, and their buggies can drive right thru them.

If it's raining, the people don't get wet! And butler's pantries . . . I wish you could have been here to seen them, too. No doubt your parents would have enjoyed the trip.

Maybe next year. Pa's already planning another drive.

How's Twink and Queenie doing? Did Sally ever learn to ride her pony without holding on to the horn?

That's great that MayMee put your name on the book as an author. You're a good storyteller, and I think you should have quite a future as a famous author.

Why, you can do anything you set your mind to being so smart as you are, and be a great success at it, too, no matter what you chose.

Well, the sun is almost overhead, and Pa said not let him nap too long he wants to make Clarksville before supper. The coming back was so much faster and easier than the going, but still plenty to do keeping the horses on the move.

Sure could have used an experienced horselady. Anyway, I better sing off if we do make town this evening I intend to post this.

Keep writing. I love getting your letters. It's hard for me to remember you're only seven, but you'll be eight before too long. I'll have to think of something special for your birthday.

Oh, and speaking of surprises, be watching for a package. Got you a little something in KC, but I can't send it yet. You'll understand when you get it.

    Be good and mind your mama,
    Yours always, Nathaniel

He folded the letter, stuck it back in its envelope before stowing it in his saddlebag. "Pa, it's time."

His father removed his hat, glanced upward, then nodded. "You get any rest?"

"No, sir. I spent my siesta composing a letter. I was one behind."

"Evie?"

"Yes, sir."

Once Nathaniel had that day's mount saddled up, only took two whistled notes, and his dogs had the herd on the move. Man, he would have loved seeing and knowing Blue Dog. Everyone bragged on his mutts.

Those who were around in the day say he should have seen their greatest great-great-great-great-great-great grandsire—however many greats it was.

Couldn't imagine how any dog would ever be any smarter or better than his two. Or Evie's Queenie either, from the way she boasted on her pup.

His thoughts turned from the animals to his dream after a bit. He resisted the urge to spill his guts, but not telling . . .

And the way his Ma acted every time his Pa got back from being gone so long, no telling when he might have him alone again. For a mile or so, he hunted for the right words, but finally decided there simply weren't any.

Reining his gelding in close, he opened his mouth. "Pa, we're keeping each other's secrets, right?" That came out pretty good.

"I sure hope so, Son."

"Well . . . uh . . . I've been having this dream, and well . . ."

"Spit it out, boy. Whatever you tell me, I'll not repeat."

"Yes, sir. In my dream, Evelyn and I are married."

"You and Evie?"

"No, sir. Not the little girl. All grown up Evelyn. And in my dream, there's all these folks standing on and all around this big porch, like trying to see inside the house."

"Like a mob?"

"They're all being respectful. No one pushing or shoving. You're there, too, tugging on one of my arms, and Evelyn is pulling my other hand. You're hollering, 'The Lord is mighty to save!' And . . . well . . . I've got my heels dug in.

"Then Evelyn starts to cry, and you go to crying. Ma comes out of the house, and she's blubbering, too. A little like when the General died, but the other folks . . . I don't know, but . . ."

"What house is it?"

"I'm not sure. I've never seen it before, but I've had the same dream a lot. Over and over, and well . . . the part about me and Evelyn being married . . . well . . . That night back in Kansas City, when . . . uh . . . those ladies were wanting . . . uh . . . Anyway, a part of me wanted to. Uh . . . but more than anything, I was worried about doing anything to hurt her."

For the longest, his father didn't say anything. Then he turned sideways in the saddle. "Son, I do love your mother, but . . ." He shrugged. "Guess you could say that I love women. All of them. The whole gender in general."

"They are soft."

He winked. "And they seem to love me pretty well, too." With another shrug, he sat back. "What your mother don't know won't hurt her."

There it was. And he best tell the rest, get it out, seeing as how they were keeping each other's secrets. "Evelyn asked me to wait for her, and I plan to."

"She's what, Son? Six?"

"Seven."

"Eleven years is a long time."

He laughed. "She's figuring on ten. Aunt CeCe has claimed plenty of times that at seventeen, she was ready to marry Uncle Elijah, if only the General hadn't of been so pigheaded."

"Either way, that's a long time."

"I know." He smiled.

The Evelyn of his dreams would prove worth any wait.

In New York, Charlotte hadn't been having any dreams about Nash or anyone else that she remembered.

Bammie seemed thrilled that Mister Moran was coming for supper again that evening, but the dear needed help if there was to be anything on the table for the man but cut-backs, which would never do to hear her tell it.

So instead of returning to her mother's office and hearing her Bible story . . . had the woman lost her mind? Everyone wanted more Red Rooster stories.

Who didn't have a Good Book if they wanted to read about Cain killing Abel? And that title *Angels Unaware* . . . the brothers weren't angels.

And Pa thought they were twins? Why in the world?

A full fifteen minutes before the hall's grandfather clock struck seven, knuckles rapped the front door. She nodded permission at Honey who'd already jumped to her feet. Charlotte fluffed her hair, what there was left of it, then plastered on a smile.

He better say something nice about her new haircut.

"Escort him into the parlor. I'll fetch MayMee." Why had she called her mother that? Could it be because everyone else used the moniker?

She cold-trailed the young lady then ducked into the office and closed the door before Honey let in the visitor who'd better be Nash. She listened. Moran's baritone brought her a bit of comfort, but he best have all his pockets full of good excuses on why he got himself detained across the river in Brooklyn's pokey.

Humph. That he wanted an answer to his proposal before he explained himself still stung.

As if she would engage herself to a man who was a drunk, guilty of disorderly conduct in public. At least their clients hadn't seen or heard of the arrest—she hoped!

"What was that, dear?"

"Oh, I was simply thinking out loud. Nash is here. Bammie's almost ready, and I told Honey to put the man in the parlor."

Her mother grinned. "You've got it bad . . . or should I say good?"

"What are you talking about?"

"Nash, of course. You're talking to yourself about him. Plus, all day there's been this sadness hovering over you like a dark cloud, but now—"

"What are you saying? That I'm in love with the big lug? How could he be the right man for me?"

"Only saying what it looks like to me. But sweetie, you are the only one who can really make that assessment. Oh, did you hear they're changing baseball's rules? A runner can now steal the next base. Imagine, stealing legal in America's game! Isn't that something? I read it in the paper today."

"Mother. What has that got to do with anything?"

"Darling daughter, it's an interesting bit of information. Men really like it when a lady knows things about the games they love. Why do you think your father and I taught you how to play them all?"

"Pa . . ."

Oh, how she loved all the memories he'd left her. Never thought that was the reason he always made certain she played right along with the boys.

And it had come in handy over the years. Instead of sitting on the sidelines with the wallflowers, she was right there in the big middle of whatever game her brothers and cousins played.

"We did have a lot of fun, didn't we?"

"Your father liked to work hard then play even harder."

"He sure did."

"One of the things I loved about him." The grand old lady stood, a picture of femininity although she'd hit the winning run in the last baseball game they'd all played. "Shall we? I for one am anxious to hear all about exactly why my future son-in-law was arrested. I cannot imagine him being drunk or disorderly."

"Oh, Ma."

Nash sat on the chair's edge. His hand kept wandering to his chest, feeling the bump, reassuring himself it remained stashed, properly hidden, but at the ready for the exact right moment. Movement pulled him to his feet.

If his love aged as gracefully as her mother, he'd be in for a lifetime of beauty.

"Good to see you, Mrs. Buckmeyer."

"I seemed to remember telling you to call me MayMee."

"Yes, ma'am. Forgive me, MayMee."

"That's better. Now I want to hear all about yesterday."

His love strode in and stood next to her mother. "Yes, indeed. Please tell us. Why were you in Brooklyn?"

He grinned, pulled the little box from his coat pocket, stepped closer. Kneeling on one knee, he opened the lid and extended the ring. "Marry me, Charlotte."

She stared at his offering. "Nash. It's beautiful." She backed up a step and stared right into his eyes. "Why were you across the bridge?"

He scooted closer on his knee. "That's where my jeweler's shop is. He's been working on your ring for weeks now, and . . ." Might as well tell her all of it. "It took all of the money I had on me to pay him off, or I would have had enough to get myself out of jail. Then you'd never have known that I fell into their trap."

Charlotte freed the ring from its encasement and slipped it on her finger. She held it out. The diamond sparkled in the light of the chandelier. Definitely an exquisite stone and in an even more superb and unusual setting.

So beautiful. And a perfect fit. "How'd you know my size?"

"I asked MayMee."

She glanced at her mother, who only grinned. "You knew? You sly old woman. You could have said something."

"And ruined his surprise? Really, young lady. You know better than that. I would never have spoiled Nash's plan."

Her eyes found his again. "So you weren't drunk?"

"No, ma'am. Please now, don't keep me waiting any longer. Will you make me the happiest man in New York or shatter my heart?"

She glanced at Ma then right back. He was so handsome, and she'd never intentionally hurt him. Her heart screamed she better or she'd regret it for the rest of her life. But could she trust . . . "Yes! Yes! I will marry you, Mister Moran."

He jumped to his feet and grasped her shoulders. "What do you think, MayMee? Is a kiss in order?"

"One short one, but don't be taking any liberties. Nothing is settled yet."

What? Nothing's settled? Hadn't she heard her say yes? Charlotte glanced at her mother. "What are you talking about? He proposed. I accepted. What isn't settled? Are you against the marriage now?"

"No, of course not. I'm delighted that everything has worked out for you two. But darling, in the absence of your father, I would expect Mister Moran to secure your brother's and Levi Baylor's blessings. Without their consent, you don't have mine."

"What?"

Chapter Twenty-One

The baby jumped up, scattering his blocks, then ran toward his mother. His uncle reached for him. He dodged. "No!" Deidra got a piece of his shirt, but he wiggled free. "No!" Then the scalawag raced to the table where his mother sat.

Becca ignored him as she stared at her cards. "Two hearts."

"No! No, no!" Bubba tugged on her shirt, then let loose with the loudest and shrillest exclamation yet. "NumMEES!"

The boy's nursemaid folded her hand and set it face down on the table. "Sorry, folks. Looks like I'm needed. Tuck, want to play my cards?"

The old trapper sat beside the fire, his nose in one of the pirate books Becca's Aunt May had written.

"No, ma'am. Not me. Red Rooster is about to fight old Black Bull, and if he don't win, Madam Merciful has to marry the Bull, and Rooster loses the Lone Star Maid. Can't quit the story now. 'Sides, don't care much for Whist."

"I'll get you his blanket." Deidra picked up Bubba. "Maybe you'll be able to do both."

Soon Becca had the baby satisfied, all the while preserving her modesty with the blanket draped over her shoulder and right to the edge of the baby's face. Deidre liked that about her sister-in-law.

Some of the Russian wives didn't think a whit about nursing their babies anytime anywhere, breasts fully exposed. She'd seen the men gawk. How could they help but?

Rejoining Crockett at the corner table, she lowered her voice.

"Are you sure about this? They're playing for money, and you've never played Biritch."

"It just a variation of Whist though, right? Didn't you say some called it Russian Whist?"

"Indeed I did. But still, what if we lose? I'm not a very good player. I couldn't stand it. You already had to borrow money from Levi to pay Tuck for getting you back here safe."

Worse, though she didn't give it voice, would be if he needed her to sell her coat. She'd hate it, but would if he needed the money. What else could she do?

"My big brother will loan me whatever I need. We both have plenty of coin in the bank."

How many times had she heard that before? Every man Jack who made his way to the Knik River always had a poke hid out, overflowing with dust or a fur cache worth its weight in gold.

But some part of her wanted to believe Crockett. Becca claimed her Texas PawPaw was wealthy, and that her parents were plenty well-to-do also.

Still, so far she hadn't seen any evidence of it. Randal and Joel had been supporting the house by trading. "Show me again what you've figured out."

Smiling, he turned toward the table. She loved the way he grinned almost all the time. Seemed to be such a happy fellow; plenty handsome, too. Kind and generous. Almost an exact opposite of that brutish Joel. "We'll play the winners."

The whole time he talked and explained his plan, she tried to concentrate on his every word and understand what he showed her. But the thought of losing his money wore hard on her. It'd be almost more than she could bear.

How in the world did Becca and Randal stand it? They were the big losers at the table, already better than ten dollars in the hole.

Crockett put his hand over hers. "Calm down. Money is not that important. I own a building in New York City, and my family has over twenty thousand acres of prime timber and cattle land in Red River and Llano Counties.

Playing Biritch for a tenth of a cent a point . . . it's nothing."

"What kind of building?"

"Brick, three stories tall. My sister and partner are overseeing the remodel as I speak. Hopefully by now, they've found some renters and have at least the ground floor full. It's truly prime real estate. Already turned down several cash offers, but we're holding out for a percentage of the gross sales."

Plenty of big talkers had been by and bragged to the men. She shook her head. On occasion, she'd seen trappers who flashed some color, big-dogging is what her brother called it. But this man . . .even his tone sounded different than all of them.

Her best friend's uncle had risked life and limb, buying her that most gorgeous of fur coats away from Joel. He couldn't have known Crockett meant to give it to her, or . . . or . . .

Why, that crazy man would have killed him for certain. And yet, the gentle Texan hadn't asked for any favors or acted in any way like she owed him something.

Sure seemed to love little Bubba, too. Almost as much as if the boy was his own. "Tell me about your sister."

He chuckled.

"Why did you laugh?"

"Oh, I figure by now, she has killed my partner. Either that or they're engaged."

"Why would you think that?"

"Because she's a spoiled rotten, headstrong spitfire. Very pretty, but nowhere as beautiful as you."

"Crockett!"

"Oh, she still has a certain amount of good looks though. I figured Nash—he's my partner—would be exactly what she needs.

The man is a hard working go-getter, sometimes too reckless, but easy going, and fair looking . . ."

"Is he as handsome as . . ."

"Me? Nope."

"Actually I was going to say Randal." She laughed. "Or a younger Levi Baylor."

He grinned that little crooked smile. "Anyway, I'd been wanting to get the two of them together for a while. When Pa asked me to come north to bring Becca home, I saw a perfect opportunity. Asked her to go take care of my interests there, and she couldn't very well turn me down."

"Do you do a lot of matchmaking?"

"No, ma'am. This is my first and maybe last attempt."

"And have you ever been married?"

"No, ma'am."

"You don't have to call me ma'am, Crockett Buckmeyer, I'm only seventeen. Ever been engaged before?"

"Don't care how old you are. You deserve respect. Ma and Pa both drummed manners into me, and no. I was about to ask a young lady awhile back. Before I caught her making eyes at another man, that is."

"So you're the jealous type?"

"It wasn't that I minded her making eyes, it was that her making eyes didn't bother me at all. I figured if I loved her, it should have. Wouldn't you think? Anyway, it relieved me more than anything else. The guy did me a favor."

Her brother stood. "Crockett, you and Deidra are up. Maybe you two can restore the family honor and do better than Becca and I did."

Jumping to his feet, he extended his hand. She let him pull her to her feet, but then he didn't let go. She liked that. She more than liked it. Would he still be so nice though if she bid wrong or played the wrong card and lost some of his money?

While her brothers were playing card sharps in the frozen North, Charlotte had bigger chickens she wanted to come home to roost. If only her pigheaded mother hadn't reared up to stand in the way of her happiness.

After all the angst of figuring out that Nash Moran was the man she wanted to spend her life with, Charlotte needed the show on the road!

She hadn't tried her whining beg in years, but it might come to that if Ma refused to withdraw her ludicrous suggestion that her brother's and Uncle's blessings were necessary.

Ridiculous! She finished her ceiling gazing, rolled over, propped herself up on her elbow, and looked at the grand old lady. "How about—"

"No." Her mother set her book on the quilt. "Scoot over a bit. I need to stretch my legs."

The least she could do was hear her out. Charlotte scooched closer to the side. She certainly liked that bed. "You didn't even hear what I was going to say."

"Doesn't matter. You and Nash will have to wait. Levi and Crockett will be back when they're back, and not a minute before. True love can wait."

"But, Mother!" She wanted to say more, find a different tactic. Ah ha! "How many times have I heard the story of how quickly you and Pa tied the knot after you got saved? You waited? What? Fifteen minutes?"

"We had your Uncle Chester's blessing. God rest his soul."

A gust of all the air in her lungs rode out on an exasperated ugh. Why did she have to have the most stubborn mother in the whole world?

No other argument came to mind right that minute, so she elected a change of subject until she could think of one. "Did I tell you we leased another shop?"

"No, which one?"

"The second one, next door to Razzmatazz. Two brothers took it. They're both tailors and make fantastic suits." A little chuckle escaped. "Honey wasn't too happy at first, but she soon saw the error of her thinking."

"What error are you talking about?"

"Well, they negotiated, as a condition of their lease, the placement of one male mannequin in the boutique's front window."

"Oh. Then I can see why she'd be unhappy with the arrangement. How'd you convince her otherwise?"

"Didn't really have to since I'm the majority partner until my initial investment is paid off—even though it never came to mentioning that."

"I see."

"We lowered her rent by the amount we added to the tailor brothers' so how could she refuse. Plus, once my partner understood that a haberdashery next door would only increase her business, she relented."

"Who are the brothers? Anyone I know?"

"I can't remember their name. It starts with a 'B' I think. Nash knows. Ask him."

"Speaking of the man, did he speak with his mother? And has William accepted your invitation?"

"Yes and no. We're all set for Sunday-next for you to meet Mother Moran. That's what Nash said she wants me to call her, and so far, Mister Vanderbilt has not responded."

"Hmmm, I wonder why."

"We think he must be out of town and hasn't received his invitation yet. I mean, as taken with you as he was, he's bound to attend, don't you think?"

"We can hope. Are you going to have the time to travel on to Glen Falls with me?"

"Will Harold Junior be there?"

"I believe so. He's supposed to be. Why? Does that pose a problem?"

"No, but it is a consideration. If he'd gone back to Texas, I'd be less inclined to accompany you. As it is, I'll give you a strong maybe."

"Best decide. I need to make arrangements if you aren't going."

"Will tomorrow be soon enough?"

"Yes, dear, that will be fine. Now how about you get out of here and let me finish reading this chapter so I can go to sleep?"

Charlotte sat up then scooted to the edge, but instead of vacating her mother's room, she tucked her feet under her. "Ma, how much is the Llano ranch worth?"

"Mercy, girl. Who knows? It's over twenty thousand acres. But I can't see what difference it makes. I'm not planning on selling it. Hopefully, you and Crockett won't either."

"Well, what about the brownstone? What's it worth?"

"What have you got up your sleeve, young lady?"

"Oh, I've been thinking. I truly love New York, and I've concluded that I want full ownership of the building, and the orchard, and the brownstone."

"And?"

"And I'm thinking my share of Llano would offset Crockett's part here. What do you think? Does that sound fair?"

"I don't know. But the ranch is all mine as long as I'm still alive."

"Of course; I know that. But other than the timber business, we didn't inherit any of the Red River property, right?

"That's correct. We split our share of that—Levi and Rebecca owned a part outright from their fathers—between Houston and the girls. Why?"

"Because I can't stand the thought of Crockett waltzing in here and thinking he can just take everything back over. He isn't exactly . . ." She shouldn't say what she was thinking, even if it was true.

"Controllable? Is that what you were going to say? That Nash will be prone to do whatever you want, and your brother will go against you for spite?"

"Maybe I wouldn't use those exact words, but yes, ma'am. Something like that. And if you must know, Mister Moran is not a total pushover. He does want to please me, though."

"Who doesn't, my darling girl?"

"Isn't he the most wonderful man? Just think. Wouldn't it be heavenly if we could get on with planning our wedding without having to wait on—"

"No! Now get out of here."

Exactly two thousand five hundred and seventy-two miles across the country, another member of the clan was being told no.

Evie glared at her mother. "Why not?"

"Baby, we've been over this before. Uncle Levi is more than capable of taking care of himself and Crockett and Becca than all of us put together. We will not be going North."

"Oh, Mother. I haven't heard a word in over a month! If Uncle Crockett was fine, he'd write. Something's wrong. I know it. We could be in Victoria in a matter of a few days, and I found out where they went from there, and—"

"Evelyn May. Your mother said no. Now drop it. Your uncles are fine, and most likely busy. Besides, once things get cold and icy, the ships stop sailing. A letter couldn't get to you even if he did write."

How she hated that tone of his! Like that was final, and he always knew best. She jumped to her feet, glared first at her father then his stubborn wife. They both disregarded her as though she didn't have a brain to know a thing. "May I be excused?"

"Can we have a smile first?" Her mother! Why would Evie want to smile?

With much effort, she spread her lips into what probably looked like a sick one, but a smile nonetheless. It had to be pretty clear that her heart wasn't happy. Her eyes surely conveyed as much. "Now may I be excused?"

"That isn't very pretty, but yes. You may. Why don't you take Queenie out before you go up."

"Yes, ma'am."

The cool night air helped calm her some, but she still hankered to go find her uncles something awful. Not soon enough, she and the best dog ever lounged in her loft.

Maybe reading about one of her other uncles might put some wind in her sails . . . so to speak. Isn't that what MayMee said to do? Use metaphors and similes?

A pat on her leg told Queenie to snug in tight, then Evie picked up the last page she'd read.

"Remember? The *Gray Lady* just dropped anchor in Sidney, Australia. That's south of the equator, on the other side of the world. Do you remember? I showed you on the globe."

An extra strong tail whacked her leg twice as though Queenie knew exactly where the *Gray Lady* docked on the hook . . . down under!

"Good." She cleared her throat then began to read from the manuscript. She loved that part.

Houston found the first mate in the pilot house. "Mister Savage, the captain desires a word. He's in his cabin."

The first mate appeared none too pleased that a lowly second mate had been entrusted with an order from the captain, especially on that day.

The surprise the man had coming almost brought a smile to Houston's lips, but he needed Savage. Hopefully, he'd be able to handle the new order.

Tapping the cabin's door, Savage entered when ordered to do so. Houston waited in the hall, his head in the doorway, for his own invitation.

That minute the captain remained the master of the *Gray Lady*, as was only right.

"Ah, there you are, Mister Buckmeyer. Please do come in."

The old man had everything in order. The log books out on the desk, his bunk stripped of all bedding, and his carpetbag packed.

"Did the first watch get off without any problems?"

"Yes, sir. The skiff should be back within the half hour."

The captain nodded. "I've got a bit of bad news, Mister Savage. The new owner has decided not to give you the *Lady*."

"What? When was this? I thought you held the majority. Now there's a new man to deal with, and he doesn't want me?"

"Didn't say that." The older man looked right at Houston. "Mister Buckmeyer and I talked it over last night and decided he's ready."

Savage spun, glaring, then turned back. "What has this boy to do about anything? Ready for what? He's been to sea for six months; now you're not . . ."

"Because..." Houston waited until the first mate turned back around and faced him again. "I've exercised my option, going from minority to majority owner of the *Gray Lady*.

"In a few minutes, I'll be her new captain. Now, if you cannot abide taking orders from a boy like me, then perhaps you need to find yourself a new berth, but I do rather hope you'll see your way clear to stay.

"I need you, Mister Savage."

The man's eyes steamed but quickly cooled. That calm under pressure, Houston appreciated. Exactly the kind of first mate essential for his purposes and experience.

"I know you and trust you, Savage. There's no one I'd rather have, but I understand if . . ." He let his words trail off to give the man a few more minutes for consideration.

If he was unable to submit to his new authority, he'd be no good to have aboard.

"No, sir. I like my berth well enough." He clicked his heels then brought his right hand to his forehead. "Any orders, Captain Buckmeyer?"

"At ease."

Chapter Twenty-Two

The next morning, like most, Evie spent her first three hours downstairs with her parents. Chores before breakfast, as though her father didn't have oodles and ahs of money! He could hire all the help necessary, but made her do regular and odd jobs all the same.

She didn't need any more character built.

Liked herself real good exactly like she was, but they were her parents—sort of co-captains, and no one could claim Elijah Eversole didn't run a tight ship. She really loved reading *Gray Lady Down* and hoped upon hopes one day, Uncle Houston would agree to it being published.

The world should read his wonderful story!

Finally, morning lessons were complete. Would she ever use math beyond making change at the store? And history! What difference did it make that Columbus had red hair.

At least she had two whole hours to herself before dinner. Then her afternoon session in the library reciting the stupid multiplication tables.

Her best friend could barely add two and six, and her parents never said a word about it. But no . . . Evie's pigheaded, too-brilliant mother claimed that she manipulated numbers in all sorts of directions when she was six!

Hogwash that she thought at seven Evie shouldn't have any trouble with mathematics. Numbers were so boring. She loved English best.

Bet MayMee wouldn't make her spend her time on tedious lessons, not when so much high adventure needed to be written and read. Why couldn't Mama understand?

Once in her loft, she wanted to get back to the *Lady*, but first, opened her cigar box and pulled out Nathaniel's last letter.

Absentmindedly scratching Queenie's ear, she imagined being on the cattle drive to Kansas City with him.

As always, it tickled her funny bone thinking of him singing off, raising his voice to the sky, belting out—she sang it loud— "Evelyn, dear Evelyn, now your letter's through! I hope that one day soon, I'll be stepping out with you!"

She wavered her voice and held out the high-pitched yooooou, and Queenie raised her nose toward the ceiling and sang a little with her. Evie giggled, and her pup looked up with those big brown, expressive eyes.

"Don't you just love him, Queenie? But we need to do something about his spelling. If only he could live here, he could help me with my numbers, and I could drill him on his letters." She sighed. If only.

The dog nodded as though she understood perfectly. Maybe she did. After all, she was the smartest dog in the whole world—of that, Evie was convinced. "Ready to hear some more *Gray Lady*?"

Queenie barked once then rested her head on Evie's leg.

"Good. Let's see . . . where were we? Oh yes, the clipper is Captain Buckmeyer's now."

Australia's wool delivered to Hong Kong, the *Lady* took on barrels of tea, bolts of silk, and kegs of spices. The one-pound bags of opium produced the highest profits.

Houston loaded as many aboard as he could procure then closed the triangle to San Francisco where he enjoyed a nice layover, visiting family.

His crew loaded bags of wheat, barley, beans, and oats. Waving goodbye at the docks to siblings and all those nieces and nephews, he set sail for Sidney again.

The almost nineteen thousand miles of his triangle route cost the *Lady* less than three months, depending on how long it took to offload then take on more cargo for his next stop.

At various and sundry times, he lost or added a seaman looking to make his fortune.

Each leg grossed the *Gray Lady* over a hundred thousand dollars, with expenses less than twenty-five percent of that.

Even with Mary Rachel's and Jethro's bonus, Houston paid off the note he'd taken out at the Miners' Bank two years before its due date.

January 1867 found the *Gray Lady* anchored in Hong Kong's bustling bay. Once his men offloaded the three thousand tons of wool, and with the first watch at liberty, Houston sent his steward to fetch Mister Savage. Shortly, a light tap on his door announced the arrival of his first mate.

"Enter."

The older man stepped in, saluted, and gave a slight nod. "You wanted me, sir?"

"I did. I've decided we won't take on anyone else's cargo this leg."

"But sir." Savage's expression of bewilderment came as expected.

"I prefer to transport my own merchandise. Buy whatever bargains are to be had here. We know what sells, and there's a lot more money to be made hauling our own trade goods."

"Or lost. Have you considered the downside?"

"I considered them indeed, but my father didn't get rich worrying about the negatives. Timing has a lot to do with the outcome of a rain dance. Besides." He smiled. "I'd love to buy another ship, and you, sir, would make a right nice captain."

"I see . . . it is a decent plan . . . double your profits . . . use the extra for a second clipper. I like the way you think, Captain Buckmeyer."

All bafflement flitted away, and the idea of having his own boat blossomed into a gleam in Mister Savage's eyes, maybe even a sparkle.

"Good, then it's settled."

"And I agree, sir. I'll make you a great captain, sir. Believe you me! Want me to go ashore first, digging around for deals? Or would you rather have the honors?"

"No, you go ahead. See what's out there. Find anything we can make a good return on. The brokers will take your marker."

As expected, his first mate proved too timid and didn't buy nearly enough. He did make a good deal on a hundred short bolts of silk though.

Houston figured he could triple his money at the least.

The last afternoon right before he took on paying cargo, he found enough tea to almost fill his hold at two cents below market.

Also made the acquaintance of two brothers with fifty crates full of caged mongooses in need of a berth for themselves and their animals.

The elder—in decent English with a bit of an Indian accent—made the offer. "We pay double tonnage and work for our passage to Hawaii."

"But I'm bound for San Francisco."

The younger brother stepped forward. "That tea." The man nodded toward the barrels. "You sell for big profit in Hawaii, take on cane molasses. Good market in San Francisco. See Bay Sugar Refinery for sweet deal."

He laughed at his pun.

Hmmm, had an idea though . . .

The older one joined the merriment over the joke then piped up himself with an interesting proposition.

"Ever been to paradise, Captain? The islands worth extra miles. Plus, more money for you."

Houston eyed the men. Neither looked away. "Ever shipped out before?"

"Aye, sir, two journeys. Both able body, work hard."

Glancing over at the caged animals, Houston's curiosity got the best of him. "Why mongeese?"

"Eat rats. Cane farmers in Maui pay big dollars."

"I've never heard of the place. Where is it?"

"Second big island to Hawaii. Lots cane farmers there. Too many rats." The almond-eyed man grinned ear to ear.

"I take it you don't have the tonnage cash now."

The older brother nodded. "True. Why offer double."

"What if they don't buy your critters?"

"No problem to sell. But we stay on board if no good. Work off what owed."

Houston stuck out his hand. "Deal." He'd been hearing about Cook's Islands.

A loud, long whistle sounded, followed by her little sister's scream. "A ship!"

Leilani grabbed her bag and raced to the beach, reaching their canoe half a step ahead of Keliona. "Ha! Beat you again."

"So? You're three summers older. When I'm sixteen, and you're an old woman, I'll run circles around you."

Instead of responding, Leilani tossed in her bag and pushed the vessel into the surf. "Get in or be left behind!"

Her sister did as told; not a total baby, but three of the boys' outriggers beat her off the beach and out to the ship.

They were already halfway up the big rope ladders the sailors always threw overboard when they dropped anchor.

Steering her canoe to the side, Leilani draped her bag of trade goods over her shoulder and grabbed the rope.

Facing her sister, she glared. "Stay here."

"Where are you going?"

"Same place as the boys! On board."

"Please wait. They'll drop a line, and we can trade without getting out of the canoe. What if something happens to you?"

"You forget I speak their tongue. I can make better deals for us. Give me your bag."

"No, father will be outraged. You should not go up there."

Standing, she sighed at the scared baby. "He'll never know unless someone tells him!" She pulled herself onto the knotted rope, climbed up, then worked her way over the rail."

Like she was ready-roasted pig, two dozen sailors crowded around, but instead of her trade goods that she held out, they only leered at her.

One older man stuck his hand out and touched her cheek. "Ain't you a pretty one now?"

The sailor next to him reached for her chest. She backed away.

"Hawkins!"

Her would-be accoster froze and turned around. "Captain. Yes, sir."

Her attention moved toward the one who stopped the sailor. Dressed in a fancy suit—had to be hot clothes—he must be their chief. He stared right at her.

She locked her eyes onto his, but instead of averting his gaze, he peered even deeper into her soul. Her heart boomed. Her breath caught in her throat. Who was this . . . this . . . Captain?

She willed her eyes to look away, but they refused and drank him in. He was too handsome, too powerful, too . . .

Dropping her bag, she turned and ran to the rail. Glancing back once, she balanced on it then dove over the side. She hit the water a few feet from where her sister remained seated in the canoe.

Never in all his days had Houston laid eyes on a more desirable female. So exotic. Big, almond eyes, full lips, black-as-a-moonless-night hair that hung to her waist.

Suddenly, he owed the mongoose brothers his undying gratitude for steering him to the islands. Were all the women there as beautiful? Why had she run away?

The whole time on Maui, he searched each face for the young lady, but while the folks in general were a good looking lot, none of the females matched his mystery girl's beauty.

Why had he thought they could? He'd seen her for two, no more than three minutes before she climbed the rail and dove into the surf.

But he could not erase her from his thoughts . . . not that he wanted to.

What he desired more than anything was to see her again, speak with her, know her name, and everything about her.

Hating to leave Maui without even another glance of her, he sailed to the big island, trading the last of his tea for more molasses and a few crates of almost-ripe pineapples.

The whole of that day, he continued to look for the young lady, hoping she either lived there or had made her way over from Maui.

For sure and for certain she harbored no fear of the ocean.

With a full hold and his water tanks and larder stocked to the brim, he found no other reason to stay in what truly was one of the Lord's wondrous paradises.

"Mister Savage, have the lads unfurl our sail. San Francisco awaits."

"Aye aye, sir. You heard the captain! Let's set the *Lady* on course for our home port."

Immediately, the men went to work, their song more lively than Houston had ever heard. Four days in utopia had worked wonders. He walked toward the rail and cast his eyes toward the beach.

A woman ran to the water's edge. Through his spy glass, he determined it was her. Where had she been? Why then, after he'd set sail?

Raising his hand high into the air, he moved it back and forth.

How had that white man gotten so deep into Leilani's soul with only his gaze? What kind of power did Captain Buckmeyer have that even the highest ranking ali'i deferred to him?

Was he a chief amongst his people, too? The missionaries spoke of a great leader that lived in Washington. Could he be that man? Was that why he'd captured her heart in an instant?

"Sister, we have to go! Father will sacrifice us both."

Had he waved to her? How could he have seen she'd come out of hiding? She shook her head, trying to clear it of his hold. The *Gray Lady* turned away as it caught the trade wind. With it, she took Leilani's heart. She spun and glared at her younger sister.

"You worry too much about what our father will or will not do, Keliona."

"And you don't worry enough about it! Come on. I can't believe I let you talk me into coming over here. I'm so stupid. I should've known better."

Houston continued to watch even after the other girl came out of the palms. A friend or younger sister perhaps. What mattered was that she'd come.

Did she think of him as he did her? But why hadn't she at least asked his name? Looked him in the eye?

Maybe someone detained her until the last minute.

Or had she been watching him the whole time he searched the Polynesian faces?

Idiot. Put her out of your mind. There're hundreds . . . if not thousands more suitable . . .

The part of him that chided his heart didn't know what it spoke of. Suitable indeed, forget that. He wanted—no, needed—to see the young lady again. Talk with her. Could she even speak English?

How hard could the Hawaiian's language be to learn?

Mama spoke three. Charlie two. He could learn and teach her. What fun would that be!

Collapsing the spy glass, he slipped it into its holder on his hip and turned his attention to his crew. Mister Savage spoiled him.

While he'd learned the basics, his first mate chartered the routes and mastered the ship. Shortly the man joined him.

Without looking at Houston, he held his hands behind his back. "How'd we do, sir?"

"Excellent. With Hawaii in the mix, we can have that second ship sooner than I expected."

Chapter Twenty-Three

Houston glanced at the piece of paper, folded the draft, then stuck it in his inside coat pocket. "Pleasure doing business with you, Mister Spreckels."

"Call me Claus. And I assure you, Captain Buckmeyer, the pleasure is all mine. We'll take all the molasses you can deliver at that price."

"Good." Houston touched his hat-less forehead. "I'll see you in three months or so."

"I'd like it better if you'd cut that time in half . . . or less."

Definitely a thought to consider, but Hawaii wasn't paying what he could get for grain in Melbourne or Sydney. "I'll think about it. Been considering another ship, but don't look for me until you see the *Gray Lady* drop anchor."

The man extended his hand and smiled. "I'll be watching."

From the Bay Sugar Refinery's office, Houston hurried to the warehouse he'd sent Savage to earlier that morning. Found his first mate haggling with a broker over half a cent. He hung back listening. Finally, the two split the difference. Something Houston would have suggested fifty words ago.

"Ah, Captain Buckmeyer. Your mate here drives a hard bargain."

Nodding, he faced Savage. "How much room do we have left after the wheat you just bought is loaded?"

"Fifteen tons. Maybe a half more."

"Any ideas?"

"Maybe. You?"

"No."

The broker handed Savage the bill of laden. The mate signed it then looked back. "How about some timber? I know where we can get fifteen tons of redwood."

Houston nodded. "Do it. Think we can sail on the morning tide?"

"Aye aye, sir."

"Good. I'll see you then."

From the wharf, Houston hired a carriage to take him to the Lone Star Mercantile. Mary Rachel had practically doubled it in size since his last visit . . . what that been? Four months?

After a hug and a good bit of fat chewing with his second oldest sister—he'd been taller than all of them forever and had stopped calling the four 'big' sisters a long time ago—he strolled across the street to the Miner's Bank.

Jethro Risen must have seen him coming off the sidewalk. He met him in the lobby. The building smelled like money. His brother-in-law stuck out his hand. "Heard the *Lady* dropped anchor last night. How long you in town for this time?"

"Sailing on the morning tide. You got a minute?"

"Always for my little brother." His banker grinned then nodded toward his office. "Come on back. I think we still have coffee, want a cup?"

"No thanks." He followed his elder, but not that much bigger, man then sat the right hand guard chair. He slid the draft from Bay Sugar Refinery across Jethro's desk. "With that, I'm half way to another ship. Want to partner with me on her?"

"Mary Rachel and I'll definitely take a share. Want to make it public? The bank could oversee the offering. The papers might even trade ad space for a few points."

"That's an idea."

"Never hurts to spread the risk and reward around. With yours and the *Gray Lady*'s growing fame, we shouldn't have any problem raising the cash."

"Those rags making up stories about me again?"

"Nope, only reporting the facts. No one your age has ever done more on the high seas than you, Brother."

A small part of Houston liked seeing his and the *Lady*'s name in the papers, but the whole truth? He'd rather be able to slip around unnoticed.

Letting the public in sounded right nice. Who knew? Might raise enough for two more ships. With two he could deliver molasses for Claus every month.

That time next year, he might even be buying his forth cutter. Didn't bother him a bit that the Miner's Bank would get a cut for ramrodding the offering either.

The way things were going, there'd be plenty of greenbacks for everyone with him taking in the lion's share. He stood.

"Mary Rachel invited me for supper, but I'd rather take everyone out. I've been hankering after an egg roll."

Words of acceptance died on Jethro Risen's tongue. The nightmare that had woken him early and drove him to his knees suddenly came to mind. For a heartbeat, he relived the water crashing in on the *Gray Lady*.

"Jethro. What's wrong?"

He focused. "This morning, I woke in a cold sweat, but could only remember the night vision had been bad. Just now, I saw it again."

"Saw what?"

"A giant wave like no one I've never seen crashed into your ship. The mast was almost even with the water when I woke up with the sweats. Went straight to prayer. Beware,

Brother, it was the seventh of seven if that makes any sense."

"Did we survive it?"

He shook his head. "I don't know. Could be symbolic, but I'll keep you in my prayers as always."

"I've heard about rogue waves. The old salts say the seventh is always the worse, but who knows for sure? Any advice?"

A chill washed over Jethro. "Trust in the Lord, lean not to your own understanding."

The younger man looked rather perplexed. "Could you be more specific?"

"Sorry, no. But if the time comes, I'd listen to the still, small voice and not what the old salts say. Past that, I don't know."

Houston seemed to be absorbing what he'd been told then smiled. "So how does Chinese sound?"

Not good food, nor even better company could shake the foreboding his brother-in-law's words brought on. That night, instead of staying in one of his sister's many spare rooms, Houston returned to his berth . . . almost like he needed to be on board to protect the old girl.

For sure and for certain, he'd spend more time on his knees than had been his habit of late.

Like all the voyages before, the *Gray Lady* got him and his cargo safely to

Australia forthwith, but nowhere near the record—too broad of beam and goodly weight for that nonsense.

He loved the sea, especially the sunrises and sunsets out on the water. Beat any he'd ever seen in Texas or anywhere else on land.

Though blessed with fair winds and following seas, he suffered the nagging that still refused to leave.

That giant wave Jethro spoke of from his night vision.

It was out there . . . somewhere. Houston was sure of it.

So far, he'd not spoken to anyone about the seventh of seven. No reason to give his crew pause. He hated the knowing of it, and that he couldn't get away from or forget it. The thing disquieted his soul day and night.

Scouring his right nice collection of books on sailing and the sea, he discovered sure enough that others had experienced colossal, one-of-a-kind, killer waves. A few lived to tell a harrowing story.

Most didn't. Ships sank, and only a few of the crew survived. Would that happen to the *Gray Lady* because of his stubbornness?

The scriptures haunted him.

Had he cursed himself and his crew because he hadn't honored his father? Running off to sea when he'd been expected home with no word except what he'd passed by Bart?

The next leg of his voyage, from Australia to China, laden with five-hundred-pound bales of cotton passed without incident.

A few squalls but nothing of real note or that warranted any concern. The *Lady* hardly noticed.

Hong Kong harbor proved a welcomed sight, too protected for any killer wave.

Early the second morning in Chinese waters, Houston watched the crew from the foredeck. The men worked well together. Offloading the lint onto the barge Savage had hired, they kept a rhythm to a lively song.

Loyal and steady . . . a good bunch.

The first mate materialized at his side. "That's the last of it, sir. The skiff's ready."

Houston faced the man. "Who are we leaving on board?"

"Wilkerson."

"Good choice. Shall we then?"

"Yes, sir."

With a nod toward the new third mate who rode the barge. "Seems like Mister Franklin is working out well. Good hire, Mister Savage."

"Thank you, sir. I sailed with him when he was a boy."

"Right. I remember now."

While the crew helped the stevedores and coolies get the cotton warehoused, he inspected the tea samples his first mate had located.

The price quoted, considerably more than the last, had climbed higher than Houston wanted to pay, but the quality might be worth the extra coin.

An older gentleman dressed in a tailored waistcoat strolled along the bales, fingering a bit of lint here and there. Flyaway white hair making a bit of halo beneath his top hat's brim.

The odd fellow stopped right in front of Houston. "They speak vanity—every one with his neighbor. With flattering lips and with a double heart, do they speak."

"What did you say, sir?"

The guy tapped his gold-tipped cane on the board floor. "Good day, Captain Buckmeyer." Without another word, the old boy sauntered off.

The words echoed in Houston's soul. Was that a quote from the Bible? Sounded like it. He should know it better.

Though he wanted to follow, in the middle of negotiating the deal on the tea, he simply could not.

Though he tried to forget the encounter, each time he tucked the incident away, a remembrance of first one and then another of the crew speaking to Savage.

Hadn't thought much of the hushed tones at the time . . . but after the strange message . . .

He didn't know.

Payment made and arrangements to load the baled tea leaves, he ventured deeper into the city accompanied by his first mate and five of the crew.

The building housing the opium sellers didn't need to be on the wharf. Their product—light in weight and highly prized by both addicts and healers—could be easily carried.

What would dentists and doctors do without the drug?

Once the pound packages proved true in weight and purity, Houston and his men—loaded with the harvest product of the poppy fields—headed back.

The same old man Houston encountered fingering his lint at the warehouse walked toward him again.

Was the guy following him?

He stopped right in front of Houston and tapped his cane on the boardwalk.

"Distress not the Moabites, neither contend with them in battle." He smiled exposing perfect teeth. "Cast thy bread upon the waters, for thou shalt find it after many days."

"Are you crazy, old man?"

"Your father didn't think so. If only your mother would have taken his advice." The man tipped his hat with his cane then turned and hurried away.

A chill washed over Houston.

Was that . . . How could it be?

How many years ago had that been?

But the stranger knew his name . . . not so unusual. His photo had been plastered in the newspapers plenty of times. Probably had read his mother's books, too.

So what if he knew all about the Cuthand Trading Post . . . and his mother getting her wagon stuck in the creek . . . after being warned by a strange old . . .

Deep down, a part of him wanted it to be true, but his more logical side refused to believe the ludicrous thought for one minute.

Evie reached for the first page of the next chapter. Queenie whined then licked her hand.

"Fine, sugar dog, I'll take you out since you're such a good girl." She put the page back on the stack. Sure did love her uncle's story!

How many times had she read it? Yet, she could hardly stand not picking up the next page . . . one of the most exciting parts. But when the best dog ever already indicated twice she needed to go outside . . . well . . . it'd be mean to make her wait.

Besides, Evie hated cleaning up accidents.

She scooted down the slide. "Come on, girl."

As always, the dog beat her to the back door. For all her whining, the silly pup took a good five minutes to find the perfect spot. Back inside, Evie located her father in his office, reading a stupid, forget-about-your-daughter newspaper.

His ignoring her might be more understandable if the thing wasn't so boring.

She cleared her throat.

The page lowered and he peeked over it. "Hey, baby girl. Was that you running through the house?"

"Queenie was." She smiled. "Isn't telling on myself against my constitutional rights?"

Folding then laying the paper down, he gave her a grin. "It is, except here, I'm king. And in my castle, polite and mannered young ladies don't run through."

Putting on her best contrite face, she hiked both eyebrows. "Yes, sir."

Like he saw right through her, he nodded once. "How did it go at the stable today?"

"I finally got Sally to let go of the saddle horn."

"Good for you. And her."

"And Twinkle Toes let Queenie ride him bareback! You should have seen them, Daddy."

A hearty chuckle filled the room. "That'd be a sight, I'm sure." He patted his knee then held out an arm. Her invitation to sit in his lap and garner his undivided attention. "Did Mama tell you we're planning a trip to Texas this spring?"

"No. Why?"

"From what we hear, there's going to be a big wedding. The whole family will be there."

"Can we take Twinkle Toes? And can Sally go this time? I'm certain Queenie will love going back to visit her mother. She can go, right, Daddy? Because if she can't, then I'll have to stay here with her. She'd be too sad without me."

"No, I don't think so, and of course Queenie can go."

"Hey, you made a rhyme. Why don't you think Sally can go? She's dying to see Texas."

"I'm sure her parents would miss her too much."

"Who's getting married?" She closed her eyes.

Wouldn't it be wonderful if she and Nathaniel were the bride and groom? Then he could come to California and they could live together so he could teach her how to ride even better. If only she could grow up quicker! At only seven, she probably had at least another eight years, ten at most. According to her mother, there'd be time enough for all that later.

Chapter Twenty-Four

Wetness, too much.

Her eyes popped open. Queenie whined. Evie pushed her away, looking around. "Aw, come on! Why are you licking me? I just took you out."

The next whine sounded more urgent.

"Oh, alright. You can go again." She stood. The manuscript slid off her lap. "How'd we get up here, girl?"

Of course, the best dog ever didn't answer. She already slid down and waited at the door, wagging her tail.

Evie rode the banister then ran through the kitchen. Once Queenie took care of business, Evie marched to her daddy's office. Was he memorizing that stupid newspaper?

He looked up. "How'd it go at the stable this afternoon?

Huh? She tilted her head. What was going on? That was so off kilter. Didn't he just ask her that same question? "Good . . ." She spoke tentatively, unsure of the deja vu. "Sally finally let go of the saddle horn."

"Excellent."

"Who's getting married?"

His brows furrowed, and his eyes squinted. He folded his old paper and laid it down, patting his knee and holding out his arm. "Haven't heard of any pending nuptials. Who are you talking about?"

"Well, Daddy, Mama must have told you because you're the one who told me we're going to Texas in the Spring for a big wedding, and you already said I could take Queenie, and Twinkle Toes wants to come, too. But you said Sally probably couldn't."

She walked toward him. "This is very strange. Don't you remember all that?"

Helping her up, he shook his head. "Not me, little girl. Either some other guy was masquerading as your dear old dad, or you've been dreaming."

Had she dreamed it? Was that why Queenie needed to go twice so close together? Had she fallen asleep reading? "So why can't Sally go with us? She really wants to see Texas."

"First of all, far as I know, no one's getting married, and your mother and I haven't talked about going at all. I can't imagine me saying you could take your horse. There's no reason in the world to haul him back and forth even if we were going."

"Why not?" With a half grin—only one corner of her mouth lifting—she kept at it using the tactics PawPaw had taught her. Always ask for more than you really want. She'd even pulled it on him a couple of times.

Crockett took the steaming mug from Deidra. "Thank you, pretty lady. Sit a while. I've got an idea."

The beauty glanced at Levi and Sophia, sitting next to each other on the far side of the hearth. She looked back. "Is this about the Whisk game?"

He nodded then eyed the chair that would put her back to Levi. "Yes, ma'am."

She eased down then leaned in too close. Mercy. How could he even think with her so near?

"I'll sit, but I don't want to play anymore. We're thirty-one dollars and fifty-two cents in the hole, and I can't stand the thought of having to sell my coat."

"No one is selling your furs."

"But, I can't stand the thought of—"

"Forget about the money. It's the losing I can't stand. But I think I've got it figured out."

"You promise?"

"Listen to this, and see what you think." He glanced over her shoulder. Levi remained engrossed with his bride. Crockett looked back. "You play great. It's the bidding that keeps getting us in trouble."

She nodded. "Yes, so what's your idea?"

"Well, there's forty total points, so ten per hand is average. Don't be the first one to bid if you don't have better than average count."

"Yes, sir."

"If one of us opens, then the other one knows they have better than ten. Let's agree that the one who didn't open will not respond without at least ten points in his or her hand."

"That's easy enough. You sure about the money?"

"Positive. Now tell it back to me."

Oh, how he loved listening to her talk; her voice enriched his ears like cream on peaches. So intelligent was his marvel of a lady that she quoted the plan back exactly.

If she looked any more gorgeous, his eyes couldn't stand gazing on her. He couldn't abide the thought of being anywhere without her.

Proposing brightened his future as nothing ever had, but he first needed to ask her brother for her hand, get his blessing. That Joel! What a terrible match. How could Randal Graves promise his sister to such an awful man? Surely he would see his error and rectify the bad choice, especially once he knew Crockett loved her.

"Are you going?"

He focused on her words, rehearsed them to grasp the meaning and what she was talking about, then shrugged. "Haven't decided."

"Randal said I could go so long as you'd watch over me."

"You want to go moose hunting?"

"Not unless you're going."

Pride in her swelled his heart; a weird chortle escaped. It sounded surprised and confused and pleased all at the same time. She wanted to go because he'd be there. Glory bumps rose and covered his extremities. Was that love?

"Then it's settled. We best get ready. Levi said he wanted to leave right after breakfast."

Riding in the sled thrilled Deidra, trailing out had always been a joy, but with the Texan riding the footboards behind her, her elation grew into pure bliss.

Was he really that rich?

Miss Sophia and Becca claimed the brothers inherited thousands of acres with cattle herds grazing and enough gold to salt a dozen mines and not miss an ounce.

But did it matter?

Would Joel let her go without a fight? She'd only seen lust in the man's eyes, while only pure love swam in Crockett's.

With the determination of her brother's partner, was she apt to get the Texan killed? Tuck claimed he'd heard Joel had cut a miner from can-to-cain't over a sporting lady. But the trapper said a lot in a long day.

Balderdash. What was the man doing with a whore if he loved her as he claimed? Every discussion she'd opened with her brother ended in an argument. Him and his integrity! He should have never given his word in the first place. Randal loved her, but he let Joel manipulate him.

The hunt went great, except a cow went down, and she had a calf, but the yearling was big; hopefully, it could survive without her. While she would've preferred a bull, the meat would feed them and the dogs until breakup.

Oh, Lord. Bring that about before Joel returned.

Early in March, the first sled from the interior showed up at the trading post. Though it wasn't the man whose return she dreaded, the fact that the pass was navigable concerned Deidra.

If it had opened enough to cross the Alaskan Range, Joel might show any day, and that knowledge set her on edge.

Crockett refused to worry or make any preparations to leave at all. That in itself drove her to distraction. And his brother seemed even worse . . . as if there was nothing to be troubled about.

Becca and Miss Sophia understood, but what could the ladies do?

Each morning, she trudged through the mud and slush to the ridge where she could see the harbor, praying along the way the steamer that would carry her south out of the cursed cold for once and for all would be sitting there.

If she ever got out of Alaska, she'd never return. Was Texas really as hot as they all claimed?

She hated it all to blue blazes and back that she had to wait.

Of course, the scriptures were true.

Her worst fear came upon her on the very morning the steamer dropped anchor in the harbor.

As if her brother's partner had been camping on the outskirts of town, watching her daily trek to the harbor ridge and waiting for that exact moment the ship arrived to sled his team in and ruin her hopes.

Keep Mister Buckmeyer safe, Lord. Choose between him and the evil man. The dear Texan is truly the desire of my heart, and didn't you promise . . . And change my brother's heart, too, Lord, regarding his word and giving me to that horrible Joel to wed.

Because she never would.

She'd rather be dead.

Out the front window, Crockett had spotted the sled running along the river a good two miles before Joel stopped his dogs. Like Randal had been watching, too, he strolled outside.

Shortly—not near enough time to unhook his team and get them settled—the man strolled in and walked straight to the table where Crockett sat with Deidra.

"So. You made it back. I never figured you could." He glanced to the far corner where Tuck leaned back in his chair, looking rather amused like he figured the idiot was about to provide a bit of entertainment.

The man snorted. "Randal says he's going with you and your brother when the steamer sails."

Crockett nodded.

The man looked over his shoulder at the young woman. "Deidra stays."

"No. She's going with me."

"Indeed. I'm ready to get out of this freezing place. I hate the cold." Her voice cracked, sounded nervous, like she was trying to make light of her decision, but Crockett didn't take his eyes off Joel.

The man turned sideways then spun. Steel flashed. Crockett threw himself sideways, kicking with his boot as he fell toward the floor.

A boom blasted. The blade fell to the floor. Joel grabbed his bleeding knife hand.

Levi stood half in the room, half in the hall. "Pull another weapon and I'll put the next one behind your ear."

Crockett found his feet, stepped toward the intruder, and brought his right fist up square on Joel's chin. The man reeled back, righted himself, then charged.

Two, three, then four blows were exchanged. Deidra hollered something, but Crockett's ears rang too loud to make it out. Joel kicked at him, but Crockett danced out of the way then landed a solid blow to the man's temple.

Joel's eyes glazed over. He stumbled back then crumpled to the floor.

It seemed Deidra was instantly by Crockett's side. "You're bleeding. Come sit down." She tugged on his arm. Crockett let her pull him to the chair, but he never took his eyes off his attacker. The man didn't move.

Had he killed him? Or did he miss another shot? Maybe the idiot pulled another weapon.

No blood pooled beneath either ear though.

He'd promised himself he'd never take another man's life, but if that's what it took to win his love, then so be it.

Evie tried to read the *Gray Lady* at least once a month, but March had proven difficult.

For one thing, the new Mark Twain novel had debuted, and she loved the author, reading his story three times in three weeks, but instead of a fourth, she made herself go back to the manuscript. After all, one day she would complete the novel.

Finish Uncle Houston and Aunt Leilani's story. Then she would be a bona fide author, walking in her grandmother's footsteps.

With each read through, she'd make more notes in the margins on new ideas or better words to choose than the ones MayMee had used. Evie could hardly wait to talk face-to-face with her about her edits.

On the third afternoon of page turning, she reached that place where she'd fallen asleep and dreamed about going to Texas. She held that page out and tried to see the future again. Was there going to be a wedding?

And a trip waiting for her?

If only she could have seen the bride and groom. But she hadn't. Oh well . . . she let her eyes feast on the words again.

From Hong Kong, the *Gray Lady* sailed straight and true to Hawaii. Every morning there, Houston scanned the shores, but no beauty—or even her little sister—came into sight.

Though a storm blew hard and steady the night before, the wind never reached gale force, and his *Lady* rode heavy into the harbor laden with barrels of molasses and crates of pineapples.

No enormous wave. Not that he'd expect one right there in the island's bay.

Maybe the wave was symbolic.

The evening came when the Lady would sail on the morn following and he hadn't seen the exotic young woman as he'd so hoped.

Where could she be?

Would he ever lay eyes on her again?

Chapter Twenty-Five

Leilani hated not kissing her little sister goodbye or trying once again to explain why she had to leave.

Her father had been deceived, and she was not marrying that horrible old man. She couldn't believe he would even think to give her to such a fat, angry pig.

Twice her eyes tried to betray her and close, but she sat up straighter, shook her hands, then splashed water on her face and breathed deeply.

No. She could not sleep through that night. If she waited for Captain Buckmeyer's and his *Gray Lady*'s next visit, it would be too late. She'd be the property of her new husband.

Except she would kill herself before that happened.

With each pull of her paddle, her heart beat faster. Everything in her wanted to look back, but she couldn't, wouldn't. That might taint her resolve.

Her canoe glided closer to the *Lady*, looking much like a leviathan in the new moonlight. She'd hoped the man on watch wasn't watching too well.

Why would he though? There was no danger in the islands' waters. The ship and its crew brought tea and grains in exchange for their molasses.

The much welcomed guests caused them no harm, only good. Her people preferred trade, not thievery.

At the anchor's chain, she slung her pack over her shoulder, grabbed the iron links with both hands, then pushed her canoe away with a foot.

It was done.

Slowly and surely, she climbed toward the ship's deck. She waited at the rail, but the watchman only sat there, facing the open sea.

Was he asleep?

Why wasn't her booming heart waking him?

Was the sailor deaf?

She could hardly hear herself think it was so loud.

Holding her breath, she eased over the side and moved as silently as a stalking cat. She tip toed to the closest dingy and climbed in.

Scooting down under the sail's canvas, her foot kicked something metal that rattled loud as rolling thunder. She held her breath.

The watchman cleared his throat, his boots banging slowly toward her hiding place. Then he stopped.

No, no, no! She couldn't be found now! Not now!

Opening her mouth wide, she sucked her lungs full as quietly as she could, lying still as one dead. The man walked past her little boat.

Finally, she heard him no more.

Her need for air lessened, and the pounding in her chest eased. Her heavy lids covered their eyes and sleep descended on her like a monsoon on the beach.

Shouts followed by countless footfalls signaled the new day, though her hard bed remained semi-dark.

Soon, a chorus of male voices sang in unison. She'd heard the sailors' music before as they worked, but never close enough to hear the words.

Fun that they sang as they worked.

Rhythmic metal scraped wood, then a big thump sounded. The anchor? Canvas popped, and the song changed. Were they hoisting the sails?

Movement! She peeked. Half the sails billowed in the morning winds, and the *Gray Lady* stirred on the waters.

She'd done it!

A tinge of regret nipped at her heart. Would she ever see the islands again? Or her family? Poor Mother and Keliona; they'd miss her so much.

What would she find out in the other lands across the waters? She hated leaving, but it fell fully on her father's shoulder,

all his fault; his and those missionaries'
condemnation of her people's ways.

If only they'd stayed in their own land
and not come to Hawaii, everything would
have been so different. She'd be marrying
her brother as generations of royalty
before. She loved Acuna.

He would make a good husband. With a
long, stifled exhale, she lay back and
rested her eyes again. Let herself relax.

None of that mattered anymore.

All she had to do was be still and quiet.

The *Lady* would carry her to a new land
and a new life.

Houston laid the book on his desk and
tilted his head toward the ruckus. Didn't
sound like a fight—only the first day out—
who would be stealing water?

Had some idiot got into the rum? A
multitude of excited voices neared then
quieted all together as the footfalls
proclaimed a mob nearing his cabin.

A light respectable tap sounded.
"Captain?"

Houston stood. "Enter."

The door swung inward. Savage filled its
opening, backed by at least half the crew.
"Sir, we've got a stowaway."

Houston flipped his hand. Why was the
mate bothering him? "Put him to work. He can
pay for his keep."

"Sir." The man stepped in then turned sideways. "He's a she." The second and third mates behind Savage each held an arm. Her eyes glared as she tried to jerk free of her captors.

"Leilani?" He looked to the oafs. "Let go of her." So beautiful, her eyes and lips stirred his insides as none before. He cleared his throat and steadied himself to steel.

How in God's green earth had his dream come true?

At his mention of her name, the young lady settled herself. She grinned sheepishly and rubbed the red handprints still on her arms. "Captain Buckmeyer."

"You know her, sir?"

He nodded. "How far have we sailed, Mister Savage?"

"A hundred knots, no more than one ten."

"Plot a course to Maui."

"No!" She stomped her foot at his first mate. "I will not go back. If you turn your ship around, I'll jump into the sea."

Turning those deep pools of obsidian on him, she searched his for any mercy to be had. Her tone changed from defiant to a soft imploration.

"Don't take me back. Please."

"Why not? Tell me why you boarded my clipper."

Her lips tightened. She glanced around then back, pleading with her eyes.

"Mister Savage, if you would be so kind as to get our crew back to work."

"About the course, sir?"

"Steady as we go. Let me see what our guest has to say for herself."

"Aye aye, sir." The mate spun around and shooed the mob with a slight wave, closing the door behind him.

"Thank you, Captain."

"Where'd you learn English?"

"The Missionaries. My father insisted, so . . ." She shrugged. "Do you have any water? I'm so thirsty. Didn't bring enough."

He retrieved his pitcher and poured her a mug full.

She wet her whistle, then downed the rest. "Thank you."

"What are you running away from?"

"The pig of a man my father has arranged for me to marry." She held out the mug.

"Want more?"

"No, thank you."

He set the metal cup on his desk. "How'd you get on my ship?"

She told him a rather detailed yarn that took twice as many words as his mother would have used writing one of her stories, but he loved the telling.

The missionaries had schooled her well. He found her command of the English language quite impressive. The sound of her voice, the wonderful way she acted out her tale, her eyes . . . Too soon, she finished. "So, here I am."

"Wasn't the *Sea Hawk* in your harbor a week ago?"

She nodded.

"Why not board her? What happened that made you pick the *Gray Lady*?"

One of her shoulders hiked a smidgen. "Can I stay? I'm a good worker. Everyone says so. And I know my numbers, too. I could . . ."

She stood straighter, stretched up all the way to what? Five feet? No taller than Charlotte at twelve.

"Whatever needs to be done, I will do. Help in the kitchen, swab the deck, anything. So can I stay? Please?"

"Did anyone hurt you when you were found out?"

Glancing sideways, she studied the floor, but looked him in the eye again before speaking.

"A couple of the men put their hands where they didn't belong, but the one called Savage made them stand back. Is he a high ranking chief?"

"Of sorts, I suppose. My first mate. That means he's right under me."

"You haven't answered my question. Can I stay? Only until your next port, then you can put me off. I promise not to be any trouble."

"I . . . I'm thinking about it. You being aboard presents a multitude of problems."

"Why? I promise to be good, work hard as any sailor."

Houston nodded toward his chair and walked out from his desk. She eased into it without taking her eyes from him.

"I don't have a private room for you, unless I put Mister Savage out of his berth, and . . ."

"I can stay here with you. I'll sleep on the floor."

His heart beat wildly at the thought. He couldn't make it stop. Truth be known, didn't want to. The woman's eyes captivated his. "What would your father say about that?"

"Does it matter?" She shook her head. "He was going to give me to that swine."

Did he dare? Could he resist the temptation of her?

But could he really take her back? He'd been so disappointed over not seeing her that trip, and now . . . she sat there begging to stay in his cabin, sleep on his floor.

"I suppose we could spread a pallet. Couldn't trust my men if you slept anywhere else."

"Keliona and I sleep on grass matts. Your floor will be fine."

"Who's Keliona?"

"My sister."

Leilani leaned back in the man's chair. Things were working out better than she hoped. "What do you want me to do first? I'd love to steer the ship. May I?"

"No, ma'am." He chuckled. She loved the sound of his mirth. "Only the officers and a few of the able-bodied sailors man the helm."

Lowering her chin, she gave him her pouty face. The one that once upon a time worked wonders with her father.

Not when it came to her betrothal though. She liked how uncomfortable the captain seemed. Even better, how the man couldn't take his eyes off her.

What she'd seen the last time the *Gray Lady* had been in port . . . His admiration of her still remained.

How many nights had she lain awake, picturing the handsome captain?

If only her sister had kept her mouth shut, then . . . She put that thought away. Right there was where she wanted to be. Her father and the pig could . . .

What? She'd loved him all her life and could barely believe he would give her to such a . . . a . . .

If only he would have listened to reason and been logical. Why had he stopped loving her?

The captain eased down on the edge of his bunk. "So what made you pick my ship to stow away on?"

First, she filled her lungs then exhaled slowly. Was he stupid? "How old are you, Captain Buckmeyer?"

"Twenty-two. And you?"

"All the other captains I see are old. How did you become the leader at such a young age? Is it because you're so smart?"

"Well, hopefully that's at least partly true. I'm also the owner."

"Don't the ships belong to someone else? A man far away. A person other than its captain. The one he answers to?"

"Most, yes. My brother-in-law and I plan on buying a second clipper when I get to San Francisco. She's in the harbor there now.

We'll make Mister Savage master of that vessel."

The ship swayed to the right then seemed to pick up speed. The man jumped to his feet. "I'll be back. You stay here."

Offering a salute, hand to her forehead like she saw the seaman do, she grinned. "Aye aye, sir." She raised her eyebrows. He didn't return the salute, but did smile. Then he disappeared through the door.

Searching the rather large room, she found it to reflect the captain's masculinity, from the rich teakwood paneling to the art on his walls.

One painting, obviously the *Gray Lady,* took her breath with its beauty. Poking around, she discovered the water closet. She fingered the mirror and the coolness of the granite basin.

She sat in the man's desk and rummaged his drawers. A good stash of jerky and hardtack hidden in the back of the middle one, provided her a nibble.

Digging deeper into the desk's contents, she came across a book wrapped in oilcloth. Across its front, Ledger. She opened it, fascinated.

Buckmeyer was rich. How had he gathered so much wealth in only twenty-two years?

Where was his gold?

One double eagle and a few silver dollars was the most money she'd ever held in her hands at one time. Could the numbers be right? But then . . . Why wouldn't they be?

The swaying increased, but the ship seemed to be slowing down.

Was something wrong?

Her heart quickened. Awful thoughts raced through her head. Would the consequences of her not honoring her father be meted out on the ship and her whole crew? Was she to become fish food?

Maybe she should go see.

Except he told her to stay in the cabin.

But what if the *Gray Lady* was in trouble? What if he needed her? No, he said stay. She rewrapped the book then put it back where she'd found it. She stood.

The rocking got worse. Her stomach rolled and set her back down in the captain's chair.

If the ship sank to the bottom of the ocean, she didn't want that room to be her tomb. She'd rather be free.

Should she go? Ignore Buckmeyer's order as she had her father's?

Everything would be fine. Big boats sailed all over the ocean. And the captain, obviously smart and capable, would keep his ship and all his men—and her—safe.

The door opened. He stepped inside.

She ran to him. He smelled of sweat and seawater.

"You're all wet." She reached for his top button, undid them all down his chest, then stepped in close and removed the soaked shirt.

"Where's a dry one?"

Houston pointed to the middle drawer below his bunk.

Not trusting his mouth to speak of anything but her beauty, her fingers on his bare chest . . . so intoxicating. He should turn around and run, but his heart wouldn't consent to that action.

So, he stood there, bare chested, and drank in her loveliness.

Her graceful movements—bending, retrieving his dry blouse, then standing with a twirl toward him—mesmerized him. He wanted only to take her into his arms. She helped him into the garment and hooked every button.

"Uh . . . my . . . uh . . . slicker." He nodded toward the drawer to the left of the open one.

Thanking God for her presence aboard his ship, he stood there, waiting, enjoying her every service to him.

The Polynesian beauty retrieved his raincoat then held it out. He stuck in one arm then again, let her help him put it on.

"Your trousers are wet, too. Take them off."

For a heartbeat, he weighed her suggestion, but he didn't dare. His duty was on the quarterdeck. "They're not that bad. I've got to get back. The storm and . . ."

She smiled, stepped in close. "Can I help?"

"No, You stay here where I know you're safe."

She slipped her hand beneath his, lifted it, then covered it with her other. "If that's what you want. I'll wait right here for you."

What he wanted . . . He cast the thought away.

The giant wave was out there, somewhere. He could feel it in his bones.

If he wasn't on the bridge when it came, Savage would certainly rely on his experience and not trust in the Lord's still, small voice.

For too many breaths, he stood there drinking in her beauty, then forced himself to turn and walk out the door. He joined Mister Savage in the quarterdeck's pilot house. "The glass still dropping?"

"No, sir. Looks like we might outrun her after all."

"Good call on taking us south."

"Only going by the book, but thank you, sir."

Houston stayed with his first mate through the biggest part of the night. When his steward brought coffee and hardtack, he decided he could retire.

The second mate was on hand, and two able bodies manned the helm. "Fetch me if there's a change."

"Aye aye, sir."

Both mates gave him a leering smile, but he didn't take their bait. He stopped at his cabin's door. "Give me strength, Lord."

He slipped inside, found the matches, and lit the oil lamp. She lay on the floor in the far corner from his cabin, covered in a blanket and all curled up nice and tidy.

With a glance heavenward, he mouthed a thank you, shed his wet clothes, snuffed the lamp, then put himself to bed.

Even with her only a few feet away, he closed his eyes.

Weight on his feet pulled him to consciousness. He hated abandoning his dream. Though the new day had broken, the storm still roared.

Thank God not with the same fury as the night before though. He pulled his feet and sat up.

The woman of his night vision lifted her head and smiled, curled in the place his feet had vacated. "Good morning."

"What are you doing in my bed?"

Chapter Twenty-Six

Leilani grinned, sat up, and stretched. "Don't you know the story of Ruth and Naomi? You have a Bible there on your shelf." She crawled toward the head of the bed.

The man oozed strength and integrity. His aura drew her from the first time her eyes feasted on him, so handsome with his dark hair and wide eyes.

"Do you read it?"

For a few moments, he appeared to be lost in a fog cloud then realization dawned in his eyes. "I do . . . So . . . I'm Boaz then?"

She nodded and held her hands out, palms up, surrendering. He didn't reach for them though. For such an intelligent man, he acted dense. She moved closer.

"What are you doing? You don't know me."

"I know enough."

"Marriage is forever."

She fixed her gaze on the windows of his soul.

He stared right back.

Without breaking the longing gaze passing between them, she marveled at him, amazed that he mentioned matrimony.

That, she'd never expected.

She'd been willing to . . . He would take her for his wife?

"I . . . agree . . . forever. You're a good man, Captain Buckmeyer. I knew it. Why do you think I chose the *Gray Lady* to stow away on?"

"Get up. I need to find Mister Savage."

What? Savage? Why? What was he thinking?

Scenarios swirled in her mind, one after another, but none of them made sense—none that she could accept as a logical explanation.

She studied him. "You . . . need his permission?"

"No, beautiful lady." His smile practically split his face in two. He chuckled. "Not at all. The only permission I need is yours. If I make my first mate temporary captain, he can marry us. Legally."

"The missionaries taught from your Bible that when a man lies with a woman, they are married."

"I know, but I prefer more formality."

She scooted off the bed. "If you desire to be so legal and fancy, then I will need cloth for my ceremony dress." She drank him in and loved the taste.

Acutely aware of his smell, manly and of the sea . . . of his eyes, more blue than the sky or the ocean and as deep, full of truth . . . of his skin, though tanned by the sun, pale and lovely . . .

She moved closer still. Of his breath on her face. She glanced to the portal.

"Listen." Eyes closed, she lifted her chin exposing her neck to him in case he wanted to kiss it. "The storm is dying."

With no white material to be found except for sail canvas, the steward and sailmaker helped her turn a bolt of multicolored cotton into a flowing muumuu.

One of the sailors made paper flowers for her hair, and with her instruction, strung a traditional lei.

One for her and one for her groom to exchange during the ceremony.

While the storm quieted to a steady shower, all the preparations were completed.

Shame the man had no pig to roast, but Cookie prepared a decent luau feast. As captain, Savage asked a few questions of her.

Did she take Samuel Houston Buckmeyer to be her lawful husband? And did he take her? The first mate pronounced them husband and wife, and the men cheered.

The best part proved getting him back to her new cabin. So gentle and sweet he treated her, nothing like the swine her father would have given her to. What would he think of her choice?

She loved being married; loved her man's tenderness.

If only her father . . .

Evie set the page on the stack then closed her eyes. She loved the story. They'd both fallen in love at first sight.

Then three months later, Aunt Leilani sailed away with him and they married. What a wonderful love story. And best of all, it was true. She looked at the top of the manuscript. She hated the next part though.

Queenie nudged her leg then let out a low whimper as if she, too, knew what was coming.

"What? You want me to read more?"

The best dog ever sat on her haunches and looked toward the slide.

The faint clomp of horse hoofs on cobblestone announced his arrival. She jumped to her feet. "Daddy's home."

As usual, Queenie beat her to the front door. Evie never had any chance of beating her, especially not since she'd promised her father not to slide on the banister anymore.

A hard vow to keep, but her pawpaw had taught her a girl's word was her bond, and once she gave it, never to welch. Actually, she'd told both her parents she would stop, even though she didn't think it was that unladylike.

With hugs and kisses for her and puppy pats aplenty—she loved alliteration almost as much as big words—Daddy returned home from a day of work. He worked very hard, not with his muscles, with his brain, but that tired a body for sure and for certain.

She appreciated him and how smart he was . . . especially since he passed his intellect on to her.

Once in his office, with her settled on his lap, he unfolded his stupid newspaper. Except of late, she'd actually enjoyed reading some of the stories, but most of them were just boring, and she wanted to talk with him.

"Oh, I almost forgot." He pulled a letter from his inside coat pocket. "This came for you today."

"Daddy." She snatched the missive from his hand. Had he really forgotten to give it to her? Or was he only teasing? She examined the post mark. "Victoria, British Columbia. Think it's from Uncle Crockett?"

"That'd be my guess, but you'll have to open it to know."

She kissed his cheek then slipped down and sat the wingback that guarded his desk, tapped the letter to one end, then carefully tore open the other.

"Yes, it is. I was right."

"Want to read it to me?"

She really didn't, but he was her father and probably got one of his own—or at least one written to Mama. "I can do that."

She smoothed the single page. "It's dated one week and two days ago."

Sweet Evelyn,

What an adventure we've been on. We're on our way to Llano, and I wanted to drop this line to let you know we're safe and sound.

I will not attempt to tell you all that has happened here, but hopefully, your parents will bring you to the big ranch in a month. Love you a bushel and a peck, and wish I could hug your neck.

Uncle Crockett

"It's so short, and he didn't tell me anything. No stories at all." She looked over the page. "Can we go to Texas?"

"Your Aunt Mary Rachel got one even shorter, but yes. We've already started making the plans."

With pursed lips, she stared at him for a moment. "So you didn't forget after all. Just teasing me. I see how you are."

One shoulder hiked, and he grinned. "I love you, baby girl."

"I love you, too, Daddy, even if you are a terrible teaser. But oh well, We're going to Texas! Can we take Twink? And Queenie has to go, of course. She hasn't seen her sister since she came home with us. And please say Sally can go this time."

"Haven't we already had this conversation?"

Standing on Dallas' train station platform, Deidra waited with Becca and Miss Sophia. While the men helped the driver load everything into the coach's boot, she contemplated Texas's lovely warmth.

Even though Crockett claimed it only got hotter, she loved it. Most of her life, she'd been cold and the heat felt great.

If only she could relax and enjoy the trip. But the 'what ifs' shrouded her, no matter how many times he told her his mother would love her, she still couldn't put the nag away that the woman would hate her.

Think she was too young, or not pretty enough for her wealthy son. She couldn't stand it if Mis'ess Buckmeyer thought she was a gold digger.

Would she send her packing?

What man could defy his newly widowed Ma? She hoped the woman wouldn't be too sad and depressed still.

Once the driver stowed the last carpet bag, her intended strolled to her side and extended his arm. "They're going on to the hotel, but there's a store along the way I particularly enjoy. Want to ride with them, or walk with me?"

"That's an easy choice." She took his arm. "I'll walk with you, of course. What kind of store is it?"

With a wave, he sent the others off then gave her one of his remarkable grins. "Haberdashery, but right next to it, there's a dress shop that specializes in wedding gowns."

The thought of spending money on a store-bought dress she would only wear once—if at all—distressed her.

Being too extravagant would only fuel the fire in his mother, thinking she only loved the money and not her son, but one thing the man had convinced her of was that he had plenty of gold coin.

"You spoil me. But what if . . ."

"No 'what ifs'. I've told you a hundred times, she's going to love you as much as I do. If that's possible."

After a few more steps, she stopped. "Why do you?"

"Why do I what?"

"Love me."

Stepping past her, he spun and faced her. "Right there! That's perhaps the biggest reason. For sure and for certain, you do not know how beautiful and desirable and smart and . . ."

"But . . ."

He held his arms out. "How could anyone not love you, Deidra? Why, you're perfect. Ma is going to think you hung the moon, especially when she sees how happy you make me. I'm her favorite son."

"No one's perfect, Davey Crockett Buckmeyer." Still, she loved him saying it. If only it could be true. "What if she doesn't?"

"That'd be David whenever there's anyone else around. Can't have any of them picking up on it. I've already fought those fights."

"Oh, is that right? Still, I never hung a moon, dearest. Not even a star."

He turned back around and offered his arm. "Quit your worrying. Ma will, but if some crazy disease has robbed her of common sense, then . . ." He patted her hand on his arm and looked into her beautiful green eyes. "I cannot and will not live the rest of my life without you. So with or without her blessing, we will be married."

She nodded then leaned her head against his shoulder. He stopped again and wrapped her into his arms and squeezed. If only he could hug her tight enough and long enough that all the doubt went away.

Two hours and fifteen minutes later, according to Crocket's gold pocket watch, he bought himself a fancy suit and paid for the most beautiful dress she'd ever laid eyes on.

The nice lady who'd helped her in and out of so many had bagged the one Deidra decided would be the most practical.

"Was this your favorite one?"

Though she never meant to hesitate, she couldn't think of how to answer without a lie, but the dear woman opened her trap and spilled the beans, and she didn't have to say a thing.

While she stammered, the sales lady smiled demurely. "No, sir. It isn't, there's another that made her feel like a princess." She glanced at Deidra. "And she looked like it on, but it's twice the price."

"Could you wrap that one for us, ma'am. Don't mean to cause you any trouble, but I want my lady to have her favorite dress. She'll only get married once, and I want her to feel like a queen."

"Oh, yes, sir. No trouble at all, sir." The lady smiled and gave her a wink.

"Crockett . . . it's too much."

"Nonsense. You'll be the most beautiful bride in all of the world. It's truly probably prideful on my part because every other man in the room will be wishing they were me when you come down those stairs."

"I love you so much. Thank you for saying the sweetest things . . . and for the dress." She grinned. "But your mother—the great and gifted May Meriwether—is the queen. Please don't think for one minute I want to take her place."

He laughed and paid the woman.

How could he spend so much money like that without even giving it a second thought?

Oh, but the dress! The kind dreams were made of! She considered her mink and fox coat extravagant . . . but . . . but . . . At least she could wear the fur some during the winter. According to all the Texans she'd spoken with, Llano had a few cold days.

The fewer the better as far as she was concerned.

Her own prince . . . Who would have ever thought . . .?

Chapter Twenty-Seven

"Mercy! Are you sure?"

Charlotte rolled over but didn't open her eyes. "What did you say?"

No response, save a light snore. Charlotte pried one eye open. The renowned May Meriwether talking in her sleep? How cute and quaint.

Had her father known about that? He must have. They'd not slept apart—except for during the war—the whole of their married life . . . that she knew of anyway.

"What a surprise." The old lady giggled like a school girl.

"Ma. Wake up. You're talking in your sleep."

"What?" Her eyes opened, but she still seemed far away. "Where did he go?" She looked around. He was just here. Right here."

"Who, Ma?"

"Mister Dithers." Her mother finally met her eyes. "Except that isn't his real name." She laughed. "He was telling me that your brother . . ."

She lost her again. "Mother? What about Crockett? Did you get your tongue wrapped around your eye teeth and couldn't see what to say? What did the man allow?"

"Don't be quoting your father, young lady. He said that your brother is . . ." She faced Charlotte again. "Getting married. Imagine that. And to a young lady almost half his age."

"Oh, Mother, that's nothing but silly." She sat up and stretched her arms above her head. "You were dreaming. Nash and I are the ones getting married. Remember? Not my brother."

"But—"

"Honestly, I don't know if he will ever find a woman who'll put up with his immaturity." She replayed her mother's words. "Well, he might fool a girl into it. Half his age, you say?"

"Mister Dithers—the real man, at least—was a strange old bird. Lacey Rose swore he foretold when the war was going to end . . . and where. Plus, a man who looked strangely familiar to the one Rose described told your father about the only path across White Oak Creek back in '32."

"Oh, mother, please don't tell me you—"

Then—I know you think this sounds just foolish—but there was another time . . . when Charley was only a boy, and Levi had rescued him and his mother from the Comanche in '44."

"Mother."

"I know. But you weren't there. This old man with wild hair knew about Charley . . . and Houston."

"Oh, please." She flopped back on her pillow.

How could such an intelligent woman get snookered into believing in angels unaware?

"Don't start with the angel business again. I know what the scripture says about entertaining angels. But you weren't entertaining that old geezer. He was only a weirdo, pure and simple."

"Fine, if you don't want to believe. Why would he come to my dreams if not to tell me the future?" She shrugged then reached toward her housecoat. "Hand me my wrap, baby, and find us some coffee. Don't forget the cream, please."

After three cups of coffee, Charlotte stared out the window and watched the landscape rush by. The train rumbled west, chugging along at the breakneck speed of thirty miles an hour or more.

If her brother really was getting married, it wouldn't be fair. How could he be in love after only a few months?

And cradle robbing at that.

Probably some girl's mother figured out he was well off and plastered dollar signs in her daughter's eyes. Oh, how ridiculous could she be? There was no way Crockett would ever propose!

But still. What if . . .

He would simply have to listen to reason. Mother would have to throw the brakes on and nip it before infatuation could bloom. The girl could ruin all her plans to trade the Llano ranch for the brownstone and his New York holdings.

What gold digger ever wanted to live in the boondocks?

"What's wrong, sweetheart? Decided my dream might have been prophetic after all?"

Prophetic, her eye! If anything, it was an evil old fortune teller visiting her mother's dreams. Tearing her eyes from the passing fields and trees, she faced her.

"How could you believe Crockett's in love? It's . . . ludicrous. Even if it were true, he couldn't have known this child more than a few months. And you're willing to accept he'd want to marry her?"

"Sweetheart, it's bound to happen sometime."

"Are you saying—if he had met someone—that you'd be fine with it? Because I most certainly would not! We don't need another partner . . . especially not a fortune hunter."

"Oh my. Being somewhat judgmental, my darling daughter?" Ma leaned forward and took her hand. "Consider this, baby girl. He's most likely known the young lady about as long as you've known Nash Moran."

"That's preposterous."

"You seem sure enough about marrying him. We have to trust your brother's ability to know his own heart."

"But he's so immature. He never uses his head, and you know it. You've spoiled him rotten."

"No more than your father spoiled you. Besides, he's too smart for some young woman to hornswoggle him. You don't think for a moment Nash is after your wealth, do you?"

Humph. That wasn't the same, not at all. Her brother knew Nash well. Plus, she'd worked side by side with the man for all that time her brother had been traveling all over who knows where hunting a goose named Becca.

"Well, it still isn't fair. You insisted we had to wait to get his and Levi's blessings. Whose permission does he have to get?"

She only smiled.

"Well? Are you going to tell him he can't get married if this . . . this . . . child is only out for his money?"

The smiled vanished. "Daughter, he's a grown man. Besides, Levi is with him, and I trust his judgement impeccably."

"Oh, Mother. That's simply wrong. Pa said it a million times how badly you spoiled my brother."

"And I suppose you're going to say your father didn't give you every one of your heart's desires? You and Crockett were both loved very dearly, that's all."

"He was loved a little too dearly if you ask me. And Pa most certainly did not give me everything I asked for either. Remember that palomino stallion? I wanted that horse bad."

"Wasn't his name Jessie? The animal was too much for you. My goodness, you were only seven."

"Still, he didn't get me everything. What has Crockett ever gone without?" She shut her mouth.

Jessie might have been the only thing she'd wanted with her whole heart that Pa had put his foot down. She hated it when the horse got sold to someone in Tennessee.

Never any doubt, though, who Henry Buckmeyer's true favorite was. No matter what he told all the others.

Besides, for sure and for certain—and only right, too—that he should give her whatever she needed . . . and wanted. What was money for after all?

"Cat got your tongue? Or is it that you simply can't think of anything?"

"Oh, Charlotte; sometimes I can't believe you."

"Well, hopefully, your dream was simply that. Only a night vision."

Her mother smiled, but said nothing else, as if time would tell the tale. As if no more words on the subject were required.

However, the more Charlotte thought on it, the more Crockett's cryptic letter requesting her and Nash's presences at the Llano ranch made sense.

If he had fallen in with some young woman with loose morals, was infatuated . . .

It made sense, and she hated it.

Unlike her and Nash, he'd gone straight ahead and made his wedding plans. It couldn't be true.

"Oh, I almost forgot, Ma. Nash wanted me to thank you again for inviting Mother Moran to come with us."

"Mercy. He's already told me twice himself. What time is it? Maybe you should check on your intended and his mother. We don't want to eat without them."

Two days later, shining around the high life in Dallas had been replaced with the necessities of the grind. Crockett extended his hand. "Thanks again, Tuck. I—"

"No thanks needed, Sonny. You would have made it back without me." He grinned. "I like Texas and working for Levi."

"He's a good man."

"Yes, he is. Leastwise, I suspect working with him will be a good life once we actually get to it." He spread his lips, exposing missing teeth. "Thank you for the introduction to your big brother."

The man winked, spun, and climbed aboard the stage.

Levi stuck his head out of the window. "Sophia and me and the rest of the clan will see you at the wedding. Wire us the time, we'll be there."

Strange. Him leaving choked Crockett up . . . like he might come to tears. He nodded then mouthed a thank-you, not trusting his voice.

The driver slapped leather over the horses' rumps. He never got to know the famed Texas Ranger as well as on the trip, and his insides hated seeing him go. He indeed was a great man.

As a boy, he'd been jealous of his father's love for the man who wasn't even kin.

The big wheels began turning, and he found the words. "Take care, Brother."

The older man nodded. "You, too."

Crockett stood there in the road, watching the stage rumble east on Main Street until it disappeared in a cloud of dust. He turned around. Deidra, Becca, and Randal—who held the baby— waited on the sidewalk.

"We've got time for dinner before our train."

Bubba held his arms toward him. "Unk. Unk!"

Living life as Deidra Buckmeyer would be far beyond any dream she'd ever dreamed, far beyond her nut. Only a few months ago, she'd resigned herself to being married to Joel on her eighteenth birthday.

But even if his mother hated her and disapproved vehemently, Crockett claimed he would still take her as his wife . . . that nothing could stop him from it.

How could he love her that much? Like her own knight in gleaming armor, he'd charged into that bitterly cold tundra and rescued her from all that was evil, swooped her off her feet and into his arms.

What had she done to deserve such a man? Such love? Nothing, that was what. Not one thing. God had blessed her beyond measure.

And Levi. Why, he acted like the knot had already been tied, no matter what the famed May Meriwether thought.

Surely the woman would see a sliver of value in her. That Crockett loved Deidra so much . . . that alone should be enough to win her over; especially if he was her favorite like he claimed.

But would he truly choose her over his mother?

Please, let her like me, Lord.

Trying her best to eat the steak he'd insisted on her ordering, she chewed the second bite but could barely bring herself to swallow again. The first settled like a brick in her stomach.

If only he would marry her there in Dallas, forget going south to introduce her to his mother. Then Mis'ess Buckmeyer would have to accept her.

When the meal was done, the train would travel on to Austin. If only . . . but she might as well face the fact. She'd be going exactly where she didn't want to be, facing the last woman on earth she wanted to be judged by.

If only she could crawl under a rock until her wedding day. Or even better, the day after.

What if she hated her?

Then what could Deidra do? She wanted Crockett, had from the moment she'd first seen him, but . . .

"Sweetheart." Crockett slipped his hand into hers and squeezed. "Stop fretting. It'll be fine. You're going to love Ma, and she's going to love you."

Filling her lungs, she dabbed her mouth with her napkin, found a smile for him—though from where, she had no idea—then nodded. "Do we have to go today?"

His eyes softened, and he glanced around the table before leaning in close. "Bubba loves train rides, and we've already told him we're going today."

"Fine, but . . ." Oh, how she longed for an argument to win the postponement of the inevitable.

He shook his head. "She will love you. Trust me."

Being a ninny! That's what she was doing. May Meriwether Buckmeyer was an older lady, and Deidra had always gotten along with her elders. Still, she could lose everything . . .

The whole way south, that word plagued her. Ninny indeed. Dallas to Austin took less time than the wagon ride from the train station to what her intended called the big ranch.

Did he really have a small, medium, and large one like some merchant selling shirts in all sizes? She couldn't even imagine over twenty thousand acres.

Crockett put the mules' reins in one hand then pointed. "See that pile of stones?"

"I do. What about them?"

"Levi and Uncle Wallace gathered those in '44 if I've got the story right. Anyway, that's the northeast boundary of our property."

Our property. She loved him calling it part hers, like the wedding was a done deal, and she was already his wife. An hour passed, but nothing changed. The rolling hills, one after another, revealed no house or barn or any sign of the thousands of cows he claimed he owned. All of the land around her that he'd traveled over since those rocks . . . so beautiful dotted with . . ."

"What kind of trees are those?"

His gaze followed her pointed finger. "Live oaks."

"And the bushy ones?"

"Cedar. They make great fence posts."

"It's lovely here, Crockett. How much farther to the house?"

"Another hour or so."

"Really? And all this is . . . your land?"

"Yes, ma'am. It's all mine, or rather ours. I'm glad you like it."

Her brother spoke up. "What's not to like? Answer me that."

"The heat?"

"Oh, no! I love the heat!" A hearty laugh from the others did little to ease her uneasiness. But her beloved had asked her to trust him, and she guessed she should.

The sun's warmth beating down on Texas, she loved. She even loved the perspiration beading on her forehead and trickling down her back. At last, she was warm, truly warm.

After crossing two nice-sized creeks and a passing smattering of cows, the wagon rounded another corner, nearing the top of yet another hill. A monstrous roof came into view.

A railed porch around both visible sides pushed her back. Why would anyone build a banister across the front of a house?

The wagon topped the rise and revealed that she'd been seeing the second story. The balcony must have an exquisite view. Across the front of the house, six enormous columns held it up, four more rounding the corner. It was a castle.

The mansion sat on the top of the hill, the expanses stretching out to the horizon.

The setting sun painted the enormous breadth of sky in beautiful hues of gold and pink and purples, bathing the rolling acres in a surreal portrait for her to behold. She tore her gaze away long enough for a glance at Crockett then had to look back.

"You grew up here?"

"Well, I was twelve when we moved. Levi lives in our old house, the one I was born in. You'll get to see it someday. But this is home."

"I love it. It's . . . it's . . . amazing. I truly love it."

"So do I."

The front door flew open as they neared, and a whole host of folks poured out.

"Is that your mother and sister?"

"Yes, ma'am. Ma's in the lavender. See? She isn't so scary. And that's Nash Moran by Charlotte, my business partner in New York."

"You told me about him."

"And I'm guessing that's his mother in the blue. I think I've only met her once. Wonder why she's here."

The look in her dearest's eyes as he scanned the sight overwhelmed her. She looked again. The place was . . . it was home. She finally found her home in Crockett's eyes, his love, and his big Texas ranch.

Her heart swelled.

It had to work out. No matter what the grand lady said. The magnificent estate was home.

They were all smiling. That was good.

Oh, Lord, work it all out. Please don't let anyone ever cast me away from this place.

A hand on her shoulder pulled her from her prayer.

Becca grinned. "They're all going to love you, Sis."

Hopefully, her sister-in-law knew what she was talking about.

On the porch while everyone hugged and kissed each other, May waited, then finally caught her son's eye. She gave him a wink then called him to her with a nod.

He extracted himself from his sister's embrace, grabbed his young lady's hand, and the two of them took the porch steps together. "Mother, this is Deidra Graves, my fiancé. Sweetheart, this is Ma, May Buckmeyer."

His face, how she'd longed to see it. She hadn't realized how much she'd missed it. God bless his heart. He hadn't forgotten his manners. Extending both arms toward the young woman—was she old enough to marry?—she studied the girl's eyes. "If you're going to be my daughter, come give me a hug, sugar."

The child embraced her, but without much conviction. If what May had seen in her eyes proved true, the girl might be terrified of her, but why?

What had Crockett told her? Or Becca. Had her granddaughter painted an ugly picture? Why would she though?

"Let's get inside. We've been waiting supper."

Though May tried to focus on the young lady, little Bubba stole her heart. What a doll angel! From the first, the youngster took her breath away then sealed the deal with a long sloppy kiss as if he'd been knowing her for the whole of his sweet, young life.

Then, of course, he insisted on sitting by his MayMee at the table. Such a shame Henry couldn't have met his first great-grandson.

That notion rambled around in her thoughts as she invited her son and his intended into her office for a private parlay after the meal. She slipped into her dead husband's chair—except he wasn't dead.

He still lived; in Heaven...with Sue. Would he be waiting for her? If only she knew how that would all work there.

His chair once fit her so well, but of late, seemed much too big for her. The old goat had to get himself bucked off that colt. He should be the one sitting there having the conversation with his son, with her balanced on the chair's arm.

That's how it should be, but he'd left it for her to do. She must weigh the young lady against the scales and render a verdict.

Not that her pigheaded boy would ever do what she wanted.

Yes, she'd spoiled him, but not rotten. David Crockett Buckmeyer not only looked like his father, he also had a lot of his old man's horse sense. She faced the young lady. "It's such a pleasure to meet you, Deidra. Are you a believer, dear?"

"Oh, yes, ma'am. I love Jesus. Got saved when I was nine, and loved Him ever since."

"Please, call me Ma, or MayMee if you're uncomfortable with that."

Bless her heart. She looked like a frightened fox trapped by the hounds, her eyes as big as saucers. The girl nodded a bit too vigorously. "Yes, ma'am. Uh, Ma."

"Relax, darlin'. I'm not the big bad wolf. I promise not to eat you or anything." She turned to her son. "What have you told this girl to frighten her so?"

"Nothing, Ma. She's only afraid you won't like her."

The girl hung her head, obviously embarrassed.

"Oh, mercy, dear, please don't be concerned about that. If my son loves you enough to spend the rest of his life with you, then I'm predisposed to love you, too."

With tentative eyes, she peeked up under lush, dark eyelashes, bobbing her head even more. "Yes, ma'am. Thank you."

Crockett patted her hand then faced May. "We love each other, Ma, and would like your blessing."

For a couple of heartbeats, probably too many, she stared at her only son, wanting to ask what if she refused to give it.

But as much as she wished she could get to know the girl a little better before rendering such an important pronouncement, could she deny him this young lady? Would he stand for it?

So much like his father.

If Deidra proved only half as sweet as she was pretty . . . and the love in Crockett's eyes was certainly obvious. Or was it infatuation?

"How long have you two known each other?"

One shoulder hiked a bit, almost unperceivably, then his lips thinned. "Over four months." He eyed her hard, as though daring her to insist they wait. "Longer than you and Pa when you married."

"I see. But remember, my love, I was forty-one and your father fifty-three. A bit different, wouldn't you say?" She smiled at the girl. "How old are you, dear?"

"Seventeen, almost eighteen though . . . in June."

"So he's almost twice your age."

Lifting her chin, the young woman met her eyes squarely and smiled. "I love Crockett. I have from the first time I saw him, even though my brother had promised me to another man."

"What does Levi think? And Randal and Becca?"

"We have their blessings. All of them. My brother loves Crockett almost as much as I do."

Glancing at her son, she noted his confirmation. "Who's this other man? Do you have any affection for him at all?"

"Oh no, ma'am. Joel used to be my brother's partner. But no, I never had any desire to marry him, only dread. Then when he tried to kill Crockett, I wanted to shoot him myself."

"What?" She faced her son. "Someone tried to kill you? When? Why? Where was Levi?"

Chapter Twenty-Eight

For sure and for certain, May's only son was every bit the storyteller his father had been. Shame he had no interest in prose and couldn't spell his way out of a tow sack. But thankfully, like his father, the boy could evidently defend himself if needed.

Definitely Henry's son whether he matched up to Levi Baylor or not.

May studied hard on Crockett. "So this Joel guy tried to kill you? Twice?"

"Yes, Ma."

The mere thought of her firstborn and only son being in danger of losing his life weighted her stomach. Resettling in her chair, she swallowed, forcing down bile, then smiled. "Well, praise the Lord he didn't get a third opportunity."

"Amen to that. So what's your pleasure, Ma? Want to throw us a big wedding? Or should we elope?"

"Those are my only choices?"

Nodding, he turned puppy dog eyes on the young girl. Seventeen. Could one so young actually know her heart? Cecelia had chosen well at the same age, and she and Elijah remained blissfully happy to that day.

But that was different. CeCe had Henry as a father and was so mature for her age then.

Seemed like the poor little girl had practically been reared by her big brother, and what would a boy know—

"Mother." He called her back to the situation at hand. "The way I see it, life isn't worth living without Deidra."

The girl's smile grew even bigger. "Amen to that. I feel the same way about him, Ma."

Hearing her call May 'Ma' tickled her ear in an odd way. "You'd throw it away for this . . ." What should she call the girl? " . . . young lady?"

The child's big smile vanished to level lips as water finds its own. Her eyes fell to the floor.

"Pa left me plenty, and from the little Nash managed to get in sideways between my baby sister's constant chatter, my New York investments are doing well. If you're referring to your estate . . ."

"No need to be crass, Son."

"Actually, if we leave this house naked and penniless, then so be it, long as we're together. If we do that, I guarantee we'll be married as soon as I can find a minister."

Sounded like true love. But young men so easily fall into lust. Either way, only time would tell.

Except, he wasn't giving her any. What could be wrong with letting her get to know the girl? Or was there a reason for all the rush? She offered her best smile. "Son, would you be so kind as to make your mother a hot toddy?"

He shook his head. "You love having me run errands for you, don't you?"

"Of course. Your father spoiled me so, waiting on me hand and foot . . . but now . . ." She grinned. "I take two spoonfuls of honey."

"I know how you like your nightcaps." He stood and patted Deidra's shoulder. "I'll be right back."

Once he cleared the door, May turned her attention to the young woman. "Well now, sweetheart, is all the hurry because you're in the family way?"

"Oh, no, ma'am." She blushed bright red. "I've never ever even . . . Besides, Crockett is such a gentleman. He'd never . . . We've only hugged the one time, and that was in front of everyone. I thought . . . he might kiss me then, but he only stared into my eyes, and . . ."

"I see."

The girl's gaze locked onto May, and she never faltered. "But I want you to know. If it weren't for your son, I'd be willing to wait for however long it takes to get your blessing."

"That's reassuring."

"The very thought of being married to the most wonderful man in the world . . . well, it takes my breath away. Before he walked into the trading post, I had no future. Only misery to fill all my days married to a horrible man."

"I'm sorry for that. Truly, I am."

"But now? Oh, Ma, he's like my most wonderful dream come true. I love him with my whole heart. I do. If it is only a dream, I don't ever want to wake up."

The girl certainly said all the right things, and who knew anyone else's heart? She offered the starry-eyed coquette a teasing little grin. "May I ask about grandbabies?"

"I'd love a whole house full of children, but . . ." She closed her eyes, dipped her head, and sighed.

"What, baby girl?"

Her green eyes peered from beneath those long lashes again, so demure and beautiful. "I never knew my mother. She passed giving birth to me, and . . ." She hiked one shoulder. "My granny, God rest her soul, told me she'd almost bled to death when she birthed Mama and that my mother almost passed when Randal was born."

"Oh, dear . . ."

"The midwife told her she could never risk having another child. Our womenfolk have had trouble birthing for generations."

Sounded like a curse. That could be dealt with, but . . . May smiled. "You're for sure and for certain about Crockett, dear? Marriage is forever, you know."

"Oh, yes, ma'am. I love him so much, and I swear to you I'll spend all the days of my life doing everything in my power to please him and make him happy."

Movement pulled her eyes from the child.

Her oldest stood in the door, holding a steaming cup. A lone tear ran down his cheek. He swiped his face with his sleeve and extended the toddy toward her.

"See? Can you see why I love her so? Now what's your pleasure, Ma? You've stalled long enough, and we need to know."

"Have you talked with your sister?" She took his offering.

"Not yet. Why would I? She has nothing to say about me getting hitched."

"No, of course not, but I know she wants to speak with you."

"She mentioned that she and Nash needed a private moment with me, but didn't say about what." He sat again, taking Deidra's hand.

A chuckle escaped. "I told them they needed your and Levi's permission to wed, seeing as how your father went and got himself bucked off that colt." She wanted to spit every time she even thought of why he left her alone.

But mercy, he was in a far better place, especially with the promise of the annual scorch upon them.

"Married? I knew he'd be perfect for her. That's why Nash's mother is here, isn't it?"

"Yes, darling, but don't let on that I spoiled Charlotte's surprise. So then . . . if you're approving of your sister's union . . . How would you two feel about a double ceremony?"

Evie stomped her foot, balled her fist, then forcefully jammed them on her hips. "You're so mean! Twink wants to go! He told me."

Her mother glared. "No, Evelyn May! We are not taking your horse. Period. Now I don't want to hear one more word about it. And if I do, you'll have to cut a switch."

She pursed her lips. Her father was about to bust a gut, trying so hard not to laugh, but leaving Twinkle Toes was not a laughing matter. She wanted her pony to go, and hated the thought of leaving him there all alone.

Still, the look in her mother's eyes told the tale. For sure and for certain, she didn't want another spanking, The one she'd gotten last year was enough.

She plastered on her best fake smile. "May I be excused? I want to finish packing my bag."

Her mother nodded. "We leave in an hour. Be ready."

"Yes, ma'am." She turned, marched out, then tippy-toed three quick steps back to the door's edge.

"Why didn't you back me up?"

A muffled haw sounded, then a couple of her father's funny chuckles. "I couldn't say anything. How'd you keep a straight face?"

If only she could have talked him into it and got him on her side. They'd be loading her horse on the train right then. She covered her mouth to stifle her own humor and soft-shoed all the way to the stairs, flying up two at a time.

She'd promised not to slide the banister, but no one ever said a word about how she went up.

Going to Texas! She loved it!

If only her pigheaded parents would have let Twink go, too, it would be perfect. Nathaniel had written about there being plenty of mounts at the Llano Ranch she could ride, but . . . well . . . she'd never been on a full-sized horse.

They were so big, and . . . and . . . she might be afraid. She never wanted him to know how scared it would make her.

Maybe when she was ten or fourteen, she could . . . would . . . She put that thought away. Why borrow trouble? PawPaw always said not to. Besides, it would be fine because Nathaniel would be there to catch her if she fell. Right?

At the last minute, she decided to take her copy of the *Gray Lady*.

Surely Uncle Houston would be there if the whole family was coming, and maybe she might have a chance to talk to him about letting all the people in the world read his wonderful and exciting story. He just had to agree, or it wouldn't be fair.

It'd been weeks since she last read it anyway.

Hopefully, she and MayMee would have some time to go over the changes she wanted, then her grandmother could help present her case to him . . .

Maybe, she should talk to Aunt Leilani first. She'd see what MayMee thought about who'd be best—or easiest—to convince.

The whole clan boarded the train this trip. All her family filled up the three whole special cars that Daddy and Uncle Jethro hired, but not a one of them wanted to do anything with her.

They were all too busy talking to each other or playing cards—she didn't like cards or dominoes—or reading stupid newspapers. Well, mostly stupid, especially compared to books.

Still, it would have been so much more fun if Sally came. Her best friend wouldn't ignore her like everyone else did. Her big cousins were so mean.

And why did parents have to get mean, too, in their old age?

Mercy, it wasn't Evie's fault they waited so long to have her.

That night after supper, the conductors came and set up the beds. At least she had her own berth with an oil lamp she could read by.

Her mother stood in her little door. "You all set?"

She pulled Queenie in tight. "Yes, ma'am. We're fine."

"I'm right outside if you need anything."

Smiling, she patted her stack of tattered pages. "I'm fixing to read some of *Gray Lady Down* before I go to sleep."

"Fine, sweetheart. Don't forget your prayers."

"I won't."

"Sweet dreams then.

"Thank you, Mama. You, too."

The door shut, and she picked up the very first page. Halfway down, a flash of lightning brightened her little room. Right after, a boom of thunder, so loud and close, startled her then rumbled across the sky.

Big drops of rain pelted the window.

Where had the train gotten to? It never rained that hard at home.

Maybe the conductor had to drive through bad storms like the one that drove the *Gray Lady* south.

But the tracks would keep him on course. She thumbed through the manuscript, about three-quarters of the pages down, searched a couple more pages then found the spot she wanted to re-read.

Leilani lay on his chest with one ear to the storm and the other listening to his heartbeat. She loved him so much and could not remember how she had lived before.

Her head rose and fell with his breaths. The man could sleep through anything. For the longest, she relished being his wife, enjoying the rain and thunder.

The sounds of the gale suddenly quieted, and the ship slowed. Maybe it had finally played itself out.

Then the *Lady* stopped . . .

Completely . . . even the rocking. She sat up. That never happened before.

Why wasn't she moving?

Houston raised his head. "What is it?"

"From the sounds, it seems the storm is over, but . . . We're not moving." She gazed down into his eyes. "Are we?"

"Maybe not, but that's good." He pulled himself up and kissed her good morning. "Let's get coffee."

"Not me. I hate your hot black drink." She puckered her face. "So bitter!"

On the bridge, she stood beside him and watched the *Lady* come awake, her crew on deck, working like ants. She especially liked the songs they sang doing their jobs.

All the sails, struck during the storm, were soon hoisted back up, but no breeze unfurled them. Becalmed, the men whispered across the deck.

What did that mean? Maybe it referred to the winds, but where could they have gone?

Mister Savage *claimed* it not unusual after a big storm, especially with the glass rising.

What that meant...also a mystery. But she didn't much care. She knew she loved being married, loved the big ship, and most of all, loved her captain.

A week came and went, but hardly any winds blew. What little breeze did blow didn't move the ship more than a few furlongs, the *Lady* stopped dead in the water again.

On the eighth day, much to the men's chagrin, the captain halved their food and water rations. Some of the men glared at her.

But why? She only got the same half portions. The thirteenth day of being in the doldrums, he cut them in half again, and the crew murmured and complained.

Houston didn't respond to the crew's displeasure or say anything to her, but she could see the concern in his eyes.

Day fifteen broke hot, and the temperature rose faster than her sister climbing a coconut tree. The men gathered in little groups and threw glances her way, angry menacing looks.

That evening, the men mobbed together and marched toward the fly deck where she and Houston searched the horizon for any sign.

Savage carried a pistol and led what appeared to be all the crew behind him. He stopped short.

"Captain, sir, to a man, we have decided the *Gray Lady* has been cursed, and this woman here . . ." He nodded right at Leilani. "She's the reason."

"That's ludicrous."

"No, sir. The storm began right after she stowed away, and now we're becalmed."

"Don't be stupid, man. My wife hasn't cursed us. Why would she?

"Not saying she put a curse on us, but it's her presence here . . . where she don't belong . . . it's vexed the *Lady*."

"A curse doesn't come without a cause, Mister Savage. Now stop this nonsense."

"Call it whatever you will, sir, but we mean to put her off."

"Are you crazy? Leilani isn't going anywhere."

What were they saying? Put her off the ship? She scooted in behind Houston and pressed close. Her heart tried to beat out of her chest.

Did they mean to murder her? Throw her overboard? How could Houston stop them all?

"Yes. She is, sir. No matter what you say. Her being here is the reason we're stuck. Now step aside."

"I will not. Now you men disperse, and I'll forget this incident."

"We will not. It's decided. Now, sir, step aside, or we'll have to lock you in your cabin."

What would he do? What could he do but give them their way?

Her bright future dimmed. A tear rolled down.

He couldn't save her.

She was doomed.

Houston studied Savage's eyes. The man showed no weakness. Were they all crazy? But he couldn't fight them all. A chill washed over his soul. The old man's words sounded in his heart.

Distress not the Moabites, neither contend with them in battle: Cast thy bread upon the waters: for thou shalt find it after many days.

"Give us the long boat and our food and water ration for a week."

"Us? You planning on going with her?"

"You thought I would leave her?" He raised his voice above the jeers. "She's my wife."

Fear never took hold. He had the Word, knew the end from the beginning. He shook his head. "Give us time to pack, and I'll not prefer charges when I get to San Francisco."

The first mate guffawed.

Once he caught a breath, he agreed in spurts of laughter. "Sure. Take however long . . . you need, so long as you're on board by the time the men get the boat readied."

Of course, the mate sent two armed men with him with orders to impound any weapons.

In mere minutes, he and Leilani stowed the belongings and water and food rations onto the longboat.

Waving his pistol, Savage issued the order. "Get in, Captain."

"Last chance, Savage. Do this, and you're dooming yourself and the crew."

"Get in, boy. Your days as captain are over. But we'll see you in San Francisco!" Laughter erupted from all the men. "Remember, no charges!"

Houston held out his hand and helped his wife step over the gunwale, then followed her. He wrapped his arm around her.

The men raised the boat, swung it over the ship's side, then lowered it into the still, glassy water of the Pacific.

Praise the Lord they hadn't physically attacked his wife and thrown him and Leilani overboard.

Hoisting a paddle, he pushed off a few feet. He fitted the oars into the outriggers and rowed away from the *Lady*, pulling with all his strength.

Knowing without him his ship wouldn't survive hurt his heart. But now it made sense. Without Jethro's dream and the words of the old man in Hong Kong, he might have done something stupid.

Got himself killed then Leilani taken advantage of then thrown overboard.

She didn't say a word until he'd rowed a good hundred yards from the ship, then she stood and spit toward the *Lady*, shouting something in her native tongue.

"Sweetheart. Sit down. We need to save our strength."

"Why? We'd be better off if they killed us! We'll starve if we don't first die of thirst. A slow, hard death."

"Wrong. We've got food and water. I've got my books." He patted his satchel then pulled out his compass. "And this. We'll survive. God will provide and protect us."

"Your God should have protected us from the mutiny." She sat back down with a thump then crossed her arms over her chest.

He rowed until the *Lady* was out of sight, found east by northeast, and put the boat's nose in that direction. He then went back to pulling on the oars.

"Wait. You're going the wrong direction! Hawaii is behind us."

"I know, but North America is a bigger target."

"You can't row all the way there."

"I'm not planning on it." He nodded toward the mast with the sail wrapped around it. "Once I get us out of the doldrums, we can catch a breeze and sail there."

She looked away like she wanted to protest, but didn't know what to say. Or perhaps didn't want to argue against him getting her to shore.

Finding a rhythm, he rowed until the sun touched the western horizon then stowed the oars. "Care for a sip of water and some hard tack?"

She nodded then handed him the jar. "Want me to row a while?"

He took a little chug, nowhere near what he wanted. "Not now. Figure we'll rest until I can see the North Star."

"You really think we can make it?"

"I do." A chill washed over him. "The Lord warned me about this day. Instead of getting myself killed and you raped then thrown overboard, here we are.

"Safe in the long boat with water, food, and a canvas to sail with and that will trap water for us when it rains. Think about it. But for God, why would those mutineers give us any rations at all? It makes no sense."

"I think if we do make land, my husband, it is because you are intelligent and strong. I love you, and I'm happy I am your wife. Even if we die, we'll die together." She held her arms out.

He scooted into her embrace. "I love you too, darling. We will get there, and it will be by God's grace and mercy."

Taking turns, he figured he and his wife rowed the long boat at least three nautical miles, maybe more.

From the last sextant sighting Savage had shot, he calculated he needed another thirty miles to get away enough from the equator to find some wind.

Well before dawn, Houston stowed the oars, unfurled the sail, and doubled it into a pallet; Leilani took her place on his right arm.

Like always, he found sleep quick and easily. After a few blissful minutes of dreaming, he'd returned to the *Lady* with his bride.

Then everything changed.

Chapter Twenty-Nine

"Wake up!"

Houston sat up, but didn't open his eyes. The pleasantry of the dream clung to his consciousness, and wetness covered his face. How had Blue Dog's pup gotten on the *Lady*?

Then realization wrangled him completely awake. Clouds stretched to the horizon painting the sky the color of the ocean.

Rain, but not big drops; more of a shower dampened his clothes, but not his spirit. He lifted his face to the sky, mouth wide opened and his tongue out.

A steady mist drizzled water into his mouth and down his parched throat.

Leilani smiled and nodded past him. "Look."

He spun. A bank of dark clouds promised more falling water, much more. "Quick, let's get the sail ready to trap as much as we can."

The storm brought enough rain to fill the jug plus give him and her a gullet full, as much as he could hold.

But even better, once he captured all the water he could store, he hoisted the sail and caught the wind in it. The longboat raced along ahead of the storm.

Definitely proved somewhat tricky, translating what he'd learned aboard the *Lady*. He'd mostly only read about skippering a skiff.

However, with his wife's help—she obviously had way more small boat experience —he soon had the vessel coursing forward on a path east by northeast, heading for Mexico's coast.

Tending the sail with one hand and with his other, holding an oar on the rear outrigger as a rudder, about wore him out.

"Houston." She shook her head. "You're fighting it. Let the wind and the sea do the work."

The desire to raise both hands and let her see what would happen boiled, but no good could come of that. He shot her a smirk. "Do you want to man the helm, Mis'ess Buckmeyer?"

"Not right now. I'm busy. But you need to relax." She raised her hands, exposing what looked to be a bunch of small cords.

"Where'd you get that?"

"Found it stowed under the back seat. It's perfect."

"For what?"

"A net."

The ramifications were evident, but . . . could he eat uncooked flesh? "Have you ever eaten raw fish?"

With an expression that teased his reluctance, she grinned. "Of course I have. But we can dry it if you'd prefer. With no salt though, it won't last long."

Cecelia cracked the door. Her baby girl lay with her face toward the window. The pup looked up, thumped her tail twice, then snuggled in tighter, her chin over her mistress' leg.

With practiced care, she eased Evie into a more comfortable sleeping position. She picked up the last page her daughter had been reading.

Of their own accord, her eyes skimmed the page, translating the letters into words. In a heartbeat, they transformed her back to the most horrific time of her life.

In her mind's eye, once again she sat Mary Rachel's kitchen table, listening to her brother-in-law retell the story he'd just heard from the wharf.

Jethro finished but offered no opinion.

The *Gray Lady*? Down?

Cecelia looked from him to her sister then back. "She's lost at sea? And there are . . . no survivors? Is that what you're telling us? Our brother . . . Houston . . . is dead?"

Shrugging, he shook his head. "The night before he sailed— the last time I saw him—I had a dream. I couldn't remember it until I saw him that next morning. But the Lord showed me this monster wave."

"Oh no."

"I watched it approach and capsize the *Lady*. Why would God show me that vision if not to warn Houston? If not to preserve his life."

"Did you tell him? What did he say? Why did he sail then, if you told him what you saw?"

"CeCe, I . . ."

"Jethro, why didn't you tell us about your dream before? We could have been praying, or better, help you convince our pigheaded brother not to go." Mary Rachel seemed to want to say more, but only glared at her husband.

Though he looked contrite, the man offered no apology. How could he have let Houston go like that?

Praise God it hadn't been true. Well, not the vision, but the reports of her brother's demise.

Couldn't prove it by the tears streaming fresh down Cecelia's cheeks. Her throat always formed a rock whenever that terrible memory reared its head, but she'd learned not to linger in the past.

She swiped away the wetness then set the stack of papers on the little table beside her daughter's berth.

Back at the diner car where those still awake sat, she took her seat between her husband and her oldest sister—not counting Rebecca, of course.

Her half-sister was always so much older, and she hated that she did that all the time. But in her brain, Mary Rachel would always be the oldest, and Gwendolyn, the closest.

Jethro sat across from her, shaking his head. "Something wrong? You've been crying."

"Tears?" Elijah tiled her chin toward him. "What is it, my love?"

"Oh." She waved them off and chuckled. For sure and for certain, no mirth lived in her heart. Not after that reminder of such a horrid day. "It's Evie's pages. She's been reading MayMee's manuscript about Houston and Leilani again . . . for the hundredth time. That child . . . Anyway, sucker that I am, I read a few lines. They took me straight back to that afternoon around your kitchen table." She turned to her sister.

"When Jethro told us about the Sea Hawk's captain reporting that the *Lady* left Hawaii right before that big typhoon blew in?"

"That would be the exact day."

"Ah . . ." Jethro raised his chin a bit then brought it back to its normal position. "And worse than that was when those two seamen showed up claiming to be the *Lady*'s only survivors. That all other lives were lost."

Elijah laughed. "If only those two had told the truth, but when Houston arrived with Leilani on his arm, the mutiny was forgotten. What a miracle . . . those two surviving on open seas for over a month in that little boat."

Jethro nodded. "To me, the bigger marvel was the first mate and crew gave them the long boat in first place."

"That had to be the Lord." Mary Rachel stretched. "No one could say differently. Praise God everything turned out well."

Who could argue with that?

For Cecelia, though, the matter of her sister-in-love's soul remained an unsatisfactory, unsettled issue. But what could she do about it? Other than pray, of course. She faced her sister. "Have I told you that MayMee has put Evie's name on the manuscript?"

"No!"

"Right under hers? It's true."

"When?"

"A while back. She seems to think our baby girl has a gift for writing and wants to encourage it."

For the next few miles, her one and only child's talents were extoled. Still, for all the pride resting in her heart, Cecelia also harbored concern.

Not that she would give it voice. It bothered her somewhat that it seemed her precious Evelyn May was reading right through her childhood. She remembered playing with her sisters and baby brother on the Clarksville prairie and in the woods along the creeks.

Evelyn never played.

Even with the orphans, she always wanted to read to them. Not a bad thing, but . . .

If only the Lord would have seen fit to bless her and Elijah with more children.

Then on the other side of the street, could she have handled a houseful if they were like her baby girl?

With great care, Nathaniel folded her latest letter, opened the cigar box's lid, and placed it on the top of the stack. He secured the container with a strap then wrapped it with the oil cloth, and put it back in its place safe beneath the board.

Second thoughts had him retrieve his pint from the hidey hole. He swigged a taste then another.

Wouldn't want his mother to find either. For sure, she wouldn't understand. How could he explain his vision or promise to wait for Evie? Much less the booze. After one more burning swallow, he capped it tight and returned the floor plank.

Strolling out of the barn, he headed to the back corral. The Black's great-great-granddaughter raised her head and walked toward him, leaving the other two-year-olds in the far corner.

Shame he couldn't take the filly with him to Llano, or even better, ship her to San Francisco. Evie had surely outgrown her pony.

But, plenty of time for that. The lady of his dreams was at the least still years away. The dream she wrote about—of him, her, and the pup dog racing across the Texas prairie sounded great, but Twinkle Toes wouldn't be able to keep up.

The beauty nuzzled his shoulder and he dug a sugar cube out of his jean pocket. The filly took his offering with her lip then nodded. He laughed, opened the gate, then walked around until behind the small herd. He took his hat off and waved. "Go on, now. Get." He slapped his hat against his leg and whistled.

All but the filly broke into a run. She stood there looking at him, like she expected another treat. He walked to her and gave her a good rub behind her ears then one more cube. She tossed her head and trotted out the gate. If ever two young ladies deserved each other, it'd be this gal and Evelyn.

An idea smacked him right between the eyes. What if . . .

A two-tone whistle pulled him around.

"Sweetheart, you ready? We don't want to be late and miss everyone." His mother stood on the back porch, decked out in one of the new dresses Pa had brought her. Good thing she didn't know they were guilt offerings.

He waved. "Yes, ma'am, I'll be right there."

During the buggy right to Clarksville, he held his peace mulling over his idea until he looked it right in its belly. Riding the rails from there to Dallas didn't give him much of an opportunity to talk with his father out of Ma's earshot.

Once the clan boarded the train for Austin though, she clutched up with the other ladies and he had a chance for a private moment.

"You know that filly I've been telling you about? The one I call Beauty."

His father, who'd been looking past him over his head—probably at some strange lady—eyeballed him. "What of her, Son?"

"I want us to take her and the other two-year-olds to San Francisco."

"Why would we want to do that?"

"You, money. Me, I'd like to give the filly to Evelyn."

"Explain yourself."

"Well, I hear tell that horse flesh, especially the way we train them, brings double, maybe even more, in California."

"Interesting, but sounds to me like you want to give all our profits to that little cousin of yours."

"Thought maybe Aunt Cecelia and Uncle Elijah might want to pay the shipping, and maybe even what we could get for the filly here. That way, we all win."

The Briggs boys roughhousing caught his attention, but he looked right back to his father.

"I'll think on it." Nodding, a good sign. "Might even run it by Eli and CeCe." He smiled, looking past Nathaniel again.

Leaning in close, he spoke under his breath. "Best watch yourself. Mama's fuse sure has been short of late."

His pa nodded and winked, whispering in Nathaniel's ear. "There's a bottle in my grip if you're interested, but best watch your own self. She'll tan your hide if she catches you . . . and I'd have to let her."

May's youngest's tirade mutated to a coherent argument, but her son, as usual, wasn't moved by his sister's logic. How many times had she or Henry moderated a similar exchange with only a different subject under debate?

In the way of her husband, she held her hands out over the desk. "Enough."

Silence ensued. She loved it. They were good children...or rather young adults. Still ready to obey, at least in some matters.

"Now listen, you two. They'll be here any second. Let's get this settled before you two go on your honeymoons."

Crockett shrugged. "It's a bottom fact Deidra and I want the ranch, but . . ." He looked to his sister with disdain then back. "She's wanting too much for her half."

"Oh, I am not!"

"My share of the building alone is worth your interest here. No way am I giving up the brownstone and orchard, too." He glared. "You're being unreasonable."

"Unreasonable? The value of the building has doubled because of my work. Why shouldn't I be compensated? You're crazy if you think this ranch isn't worth a small fortune. Look at all the cattle! They even out the brownstone!"

"And I can't believe you cut me completely out of the pen deal. Nash is my partner, or at least he was. I ought to . . ." He made a fist and threatened her as he had so many times in the past. But of course, he'd never laid a hand on her.

"Mercy, Brother!" she resettled herself in the wingback. "Here's my final offer, but unclench your fingers right now. You know perfectly well Pa would rise from his grave and whip you proper if you ever hit me."

Crockett laughed. "Fine, I'll have Nash take care of you once you two are hitched, which all depends on if my big brothers and I decide that's appropriate."

Charlotte flashed red and glared. "You cannot threaten me with that, you . . . you . . ." She mouthed *mother* at May, but she refused to take that bait.

That stinking fish had been hashed quite enough. "You two are going to be the death of me. Now, baby girl, did you have a new offer?"

"Number one, he keeps his room in the brownstone, though it goes into our name. We can all stay partners in the orchard, but for that, I get half of the ranch's calf crop for the next five years."

"Three years, and we have a deal, Sis."

"Four." She struck her hand out. And I get all of the Blue Moon profits, too."

Shaking his head with obvious disdain, he took his sister's hand and gave one quick pump. He stood, meeting May's eyes across the desk.

"We're letting Becca and Randal pick out a home site on whatever five hundred acres they want. They're going to stay on and help with the ranch. She said you could make it a part of her inheritance from Pa."

"That's wonderful." May resisted hugging herself. Having Bubba around was going to be so much fun and would surely keep her young!

Mary Rachel might not love the plan, but at least her daughter would be in Texas and not gallivanting in the frozen north, exact location unknown. She must appreciate that.

Levi stared across the general's desk at his youngest sibling and her beau. How had it come to this? He ought to abstain and leave the onus on May, but then, he'd hate to face Henry in the next life and explain why.

He looked to Crockett then Houston. Neither of the young men seemed to want the lead.

With extra arced eyebrows, he nodded toward his youngest sister though they shared not a drop of blood. "I got your letter, Charlotte."

"Good. So what do you think?"

"I'd like a few moments alone with Mister Moran."

The young lady flashed red then pressed into the wingback. "Is that really necessary? I mean, we are about to be one, so ask away. I am not a child who needs protection from adult topics, dear brother. We have no secrets from one another either. Isn't that right, sweetheart?"

Sitting straighter in his chair, the man cleared his throat. "Yes, of course." He glanced at Levi . . . "We've been honest with each other, sir." . . . then quickly looked away.

Being honest and being open might be two different things. Keeping secrets, completely another. But as to her maturity . . . well . . .

Debatable in his estimation, but he'd hang onto that one for another day. He cleared his own throat, calling the man's attention back, then bore into the windows of Nash's soul.

"You ever been married or engaged before?"

"No, sir."

"The sir isn't necessary, Nash. You're wanting to be my brother."

"Yes, sir. I mean—"

"Any children?"

"None."

"Possibility of any?"

"Levi Baylor, what kind of question is that?"

"Sweetheart." Moran put his hand on Charlotte's forearm. "Let him ask me anything he wants. And to answer your question, no. I've never known a woman in the Biblical sense if that's what you're asking."

Charlotte glared at him, but her lips betrayed the pleasure her betrothed's answer brought.

"You a believer, Son?"

"Yes, sir." Well, he had called him son, so he deserved that he supposed.

"Been baptized?"

"Sprinkled. I grew up in the Catholic church."

"If your and Crockett's investments go south, how can you support my sister? Have a trade?"

"Not really, sir. Worked some as a carpenter, but mostly, I've bought and sold. But short of the East Coast falling into the Atlantic, our investments are paying well, and there's no reason to think that would end."

"Marriage is for life. Are you prepared for the duration, no matter what?"

"Yes, sir."

"She's got a temper and can be stubborn as a mule at times."

Charlotte scooted to the edge of her chair, her eyes flashing. "How dare you compare me to a mule!" She glanced toward Nash. "I'll readily admit Pa spoiled me . . . a little." Her glare turned back toward Levi. "But I'll have you know, I'm a grown woman now and can certainly exhibit a modicum of self-control!"

"I did ask for a private moment with Mister Moran."

"Still. A mule? An apology is definitely in order."

Crockett tapped the desk. "Sis, hush. We need to hear from Nash."

The girl glared at her only full-blood brother then crossed her arms over her chest and turned away from him.

Levi redirected his dialogue to the young man. "You'll have your hands full."

"Yes, sir, I'm fully aware of that. But I love her. My whole heart is invested, belongs to her. And I'm convinced she loves me. Neither of us is perfect, but together, side by side, we are a perfect match."

Good answer. He looked to his left and right; both of his honorary brothers shrugged. "What about you, Charlotte? You sure about Mister Moran? Until death alone parts you?"

Her leg, crossed over the one connected to the floor, bounced even higher, swinging with great gusto. "Of course I am, or we wouldn't be here, would we?"

Her tone made him want to laugh, but then she'd probably come across the desk and try to claw his eyes out, so he kept his mirth at bay. "You love him?"

"Oh mercy! Yes, I love him. Of course I do. Really. Your questions are insulting! I wouldn't have accepted his proposal if I didn't love the man. And he loves me! For the sake of matrimony, can we get this over with?"

"You two take a walk and calm down. Give us a couple of minutes."

Nash stood then offered his hand to Charlotte. "Thank you, sir." He glanced at his partner, obviously searching for an advocate. "Crockett. Houston."

Once the love birds were out, and the office door closed. "What do you men think?"

"Well, I know him best, and from the first, I thought Nash would be perfect for Charlotte."

He faced Houston. "And you? You've been pretty quiet. Any reservations?"

"She's a handful, that's for sure. But what woman isn't? I say yes."

Levi nodded, but he had one more question. "Call them back in then."

Chapter Thirty

That didn't take long. Good, right? Charlotte strolled back into her father's office—it would always be his as far as she was concerned—and took the wingback that had always been her chair. She smiled at Levi and gave him a little nod.

Fine.

The silly men had their confab, so she could get on with her wedding planning.

Crockett could not get married before she did. It wouldn't be fair.

"What if I say no?"

"What? No? Why on earth would you do that?"

Nash's hand on her forearm silenced her. "If you do, sir. Then I will do everything in my power to change your mind."

She spun in her chair. "What are you saying, Nash? He can't stop us!"

"Sweetheart, we can't go forward without your family's blessing."

Her eldest brother's words replayed in her mind's ear. She pursed her lips and turned toward Levi. "You said what if . . . so, what is your answer?"

He hiked one shoulder. "I asked a question. Mister Moran told me what he'd do. What about you?"

Was his inquiry some kind of dumb test? Had her father put him up to it? It sounded like something Henry Buckmeyer would do . . . issue an idiotic deathbed request.

Surely not though. He loved her and would never want her tormented or . . . "Why are you doing this, Levi? Why are you being so mean to me?"

"Why aren't you answering my question?"

What a pigheaded turkey buzzard. She hated the whole familial philosophy that someone else should have any say on whom she chose to marry! Hated it that men had any power over her future, but then that's the way it had been her whole life.

Ugh! She plastered her best smile on then sat back in her chair.

"What choice would I have, Levi? You heard Nash, and like my fiancé said . . . We will . . ." She flashed a real smile. "Have to tie you down and tickle you until you change your mind! Same as how you used to count my ribs when I was little to get me to do what you wanted."

"I wondered if you remembered that. I do love you, you know, and only have your best interest at heart. So you'd wait?"

"Yes, sir. Nash and I are about to become one. How could I get married with him dead set on earning your blessing? How can we do anything if we're not in agreement?"

He smiled. "Good answer. Both of you. So then, yes. We are all in agreement."

Flying to her feet, she glared. "You're saying we have to wait?"

"No, little sister. I'm saying that..." He glanced at Crockett and Houston. "We're in agreement to give you two our blessing to marry."

"Hip hip hooray!" She turned and hugged Nash's neck then ran to her oldest honorary brother and flung her arms around his neck. "Good, that's wonderful. I though . . . nevermind what I thought!"

She hugged her half-brother next, saving Crockett for last. She whispered in his ear, "You're such a brat. You could've told them how perfect Nash is for me. You know good and well he is!"

"Sister, sister, sister. I'm happy for you both." He threw a grin toward Nash. "You, my friend, are getting a handful here, but I'm sure you know that."

"I love a passionate woman."

The men all laughed as her face heated. But who had time to be upset? They'd said yes! She was getting married!

"I have so much to do! Come on, Nash. You can help." She stuck her hand out. He took it, and she leaned back, pulling him to his feet before facing her full-blood brother one more time. "You best come, too."

"Me? What do you think I'm going to do? Get Deidra instead."

"I need you! Your child bride won't do. Now come on."

Shaking his head, he looked at his partner. "See what I mean?"

A part of Becca only wanted her to get there; another part dreaded her arrival. The strangest part proved to be that she couldn't decide which desire was stronger.

Still, no matter the what or when, they were coming. MayMee received word of their leaving Austin, so they'd be there that day.

Marveling at Zach's features, she forgot the debate momentarily. She loved it when he suckled drinks in minutes. Truly a wonder that all her fretting hadn't soured her milk. Although with all the new family members making over him, her son might not have let on.

With all the extra help in the kitchen getting ready for the hordes, her services weren't needed there.

Her only focus as Diedra's matron of honor could go to her best friend and bride-to-be, making certain her wedding day—only two more nights' sleep away—turned out perfectly. She laid the napping boy down then went to the closet.

Quietly turning the door's lock, she tiptoed in and extracted the bridal veil.

Her Randal, such a dear, had obliged her and bought the little bag of seed pearls she added to the delicate lace as a surprise for sweet Deidra. She spread the veil to where she'd left off and went to tacking on the intricate ocean bobbles.

A two-toned whistle sounded—the one the entire family had used her whole life long before if the stories were true—broke her concentration and interrupted her malaise.

With no idea of how long she'd been sitting there engrossed with her labor of love, she quickly pulled the strings to close the little velvet pouch of pearls and gently folded the veil.

From out front, a male voice shouted, "I can see their dust cloud! They'll be here shortly!"

Running to the full-length mirror, she straightened her dress and tucked an errant curl back into her bun. She hurried out of her and Randal's room, heading straightaway to Deidra's. She needed reinforcement, but no best friend napped there.

The lace curtains blew into the room on the breeze, drawing her to the window. She glanced out.

The procession came into view.

Bubba! Where was Bubba?

Oh yes, taking his nap. She raced back to her room. No baby-sized lump in the bed. If he'd awoken, why hadn't he come for her like always? Little Rascal. Perhaps his daddy—or uncle—had scooped him up.

Searching the chifforobe, she located the outfit bought in Austin for him to wear on the occasion of meeting his grandparents for the first time ever.

But where was the boy to fill the suit of clothes?

Finally, she located him in the barn with his daddy, uncles, and cousins. Her baby sat atop a horse; bareback, no less! "What are you men doing? Give me my baby!" She glared at Randal.

Crockett snatched Bubba up and turned away. "No! You can't have him. He's our boy."

"Horsee! Horsee!" The toddler stretched his arms out toward the huge animal, arching his back as if trying to escape his uncle's embrace. His eyes met hers, and his fighting to get back on the horse stopped. He wrapped both arms around his hero's neck. "No, Mama. Unk!"

"I do not have time for this. Give him to me right now or I'll . . ." She let her voice trail off since she didn't know what she'd do. Hopefully, the steel in her tone would motivate compliance. "Come on now, Zachary."

Her favorite uncle handed him over. "Sorry, Bubba."

Apparently, her son got the message, too, with no protesting over being passed off. He did whisper, "Horsee," in her ear.

"Hurry, precious! We need to get you dressed." She flew back to the house. With less struggle than usual, she got him ready. The boy even allowed her to run a comb through his hair.

Before totally satisfied with her efforts, she lost any chance of finishing. The dogs went to yapping, and Bubba broke and ran from the room.

His daddy scooped him up as she reached the entry hall. He hefted him onto one shoulder—her son's favorite high place—then held out his other arm toward her. "Come on, sweetheart. I'm ready to meet my in-laws."

Cuddling into the safety of his right side, she and her husband and son joined the family out on the columned porch just as the first carriage rounded the last corner.

Her throat dry as though someone had filled it with cotton, she needed to swallow so bad. What would her mother say? Her beating heart threatened to explode. Would she hate her for running away?

And what about Daddy?

A second carriage came into view followed by a wagon loaded with luggage. The first coach's door flew open even before it came to a complete stop.

Her mother jumped out. "Becca! My Becca!"

Her heart surely stopped beating and time stood still. Mam's tone carried no hate, not even a hint of anger. She left her husband's haven and ran down the steps into her mother's embrace.

"Mama!"

Tears streamed down her cheeks. Oh, how she'd missed those hugs that confirmed unconditional love. Other hands touched and patted her, pulled at her.

Her name sounded again and again, but she couldn't let go of Mama or lift her head from her mother's shoulder and neck. Sobs barely held at bay choked her.

She'd missed her so much.

How could she ever have left?

How foolish she'd been.

Only a familiar tug on her skirt broke the reunion. Reaching down, she lifted Bubba. "Mama, this is Zachary, your grandson." She caught Randal's hand. "And this is Randal Graves, my husband."

Oh, how Evie loved it!

Reunions were so sweet. If only someone would tell her why Becca ever ran away! She hated everyone treating her like a child. But one thing she knew for sure and for certain. She would never run away from her parents, not ever.

It definitely appeared that Aunt Mary Rachel and her cousin had forgotten about whatever it had been.

That baby boy would sure be fun getting to know, and she liked his name. She didn't know anyone named Zachary.

First things first, though . . . where was her pen pal? She spotted Nathaniel over near the end of the porch, headed toward the wagon with several other boys. Just like him.

Always ready to help. Mama pointed out what a good quality that was in a young man. Another reason to marry him when she grew up. Shouldn't he at least come to say hi? Couldn't all the others get the luggage?

Or it wouldn't hurt it to wait. All the bags could sit there lots better than her.

He probably figured he was in for a scolding. His last letter arrived almost seven weeks ago, so his promise to write once a month was in jeopardy. He laughed with the boys and acted like she hadn't even ridden the train halfway across the country.

"Evelyn May Eversole. You get yourself over here and give your grandmother a hug!"

The rest of that day and the next, she saw him plenty, and she always joined in the games and conversations of all the cousins, but she never could catch him all by himself . . . almost like he avoided her on purpose.

Could it be the lack of his timely letter? Or was it something else?

Playing blocks with Bubba and reading him stories offered some distraction and solace. She adored the little guy, the cutest baby she'd ever known.

And he sure seemed to love her, too. But she wanted to talk with Nathaniel, and him dodging any alone time upset her to no end.

The wedding day finally dawned. Everyone stayed so busy right up until the time. Everyone in the whole state must have showed up because there were about a thousand people.

Mama helped her get into her new Alice blue gown. Looking into the mirror, she could easily see that Mama told her the truth. She'd said Evie would look even more beautiful than the brides.

The whole time during the preacher marrying the two couples, the big party afterwards when everyone danced and ate and talked until dark, then the newlyweds leaving—soon followed by all the guests who weren't family—Mama insisted she stay right near on account of all the strangers about.

Nathaniel barely spoke to her.

That night, lying in her MayMee's bed listening to the crickets singing and frogs' croaking and her grandmother's funny little sleep puffs, she replayed the wedding vows the couples said to the preacher.

Her and Nathaniel's life would always richer and better, and she hoped he'd never get sick. She wouldn't know what to do.

Next thing she knew, that rooster crowed at the sun. She sat up and for only a minute, couldn't remember where she was, but then figured it out. MayMee must have already gone downstairs.

Maybe now that the big day was done, she could get to visit with Nathaniel.

Later in the day—she hadn't even seen him yet—her mother got her to read Bubba to sleep. Leaning forward, Evie stopped.

Just as she suspected, the sandman claimed another victim. She rocked a couple more times for insurance—that's what Aunt Deidra called it—then carefully rose, hefting the little booger into bed.

Though tempted to read more, she headed toward the barn. Nathaniel might be done with his chores or close to it. Mercy. A body would think with all of PawPaw's money, MayMee could hire enough help that Evie's beau wouldn't have any chores when he came for a visit.

It didn't seem a bit fair.

Uncle Charley sat in the parlor playing cards . . . Whisk, if she remembered right. She didn't know why they liked the game. And Uncle Crockett taught anyone who'd sit still long enough how to play Russian Whisk. She'd so much rather be reading.

Hmmm . . . the barn could wait a few minutes.

Standing quietly beside the table, she watched. Wouldn't do to interrupt; that'd be rude. She for sure and for certain did not want to give her mother any reason to switch her legs.

Finally, the last card hit the table. Uncle Charley gave her a big grin. "You hunting Nathaniel?"

"Yes, sir. I figured he might be in the barn doing chores, then I saw you."

"No, ma'am. He isn't there. Trailed out a couple of hours ago with a few of MayMee's men."

Trying her best to keep her disappointment from showing, she twirled the toe of her new cowboy boots over a rose on the rug. "Do you know when he'll be back?"

"Dark, maybe dark-thirty."

"Oh." She turned.

"Wait."

Making a full circle, she faced him again. "Yes, sir?"

"I need a favor if you're so inclined."

"A favor? Of course, I'd certainly be inclined to oblige you, Uncle. If I can."

"My boy's been training a filly, and we've talked to your pa about you riding her for us when you and your family come up to Clarksville. He says the plan is to spend a few days there at your Uncle Levi's."

"Oh, I'd love to do that! But I don't think I could saddle one of those great big horses. I'm too short as you can plainly see." She giggled. "But I'm growing. Maybe Daddy would let me ride her bareback. Did you happen to ask about that?"

"No, but no need. We'll saddle her for you. Nathaniel could bring her over after a day or three, once we're back."

"Oh, yes, that'd be wonderful. What's her name?"

"Nathaniel's been calling her Beauty, but a new owner . . . would call her whatever they want."

"Oh, like Black Beauty! I love that book. Have you read it, Uncle Charley? It's so good. Beauty is a perfect name, especially if she's black. What color is Beauty? Is she black like PawPaw's famous stallion?"

"I'd call it midnight, black as the ace of spades. And she's actually a granddaughter of The Black. 'Cept she does have one tiny spot of white on her belly."

Evie loved it. However, if the filly belonged to her and she got to choose, she'd name her something special . . . like . . . Oh, Starless Night's Beauty or Beautiful Ebony Midnight or . . .

"I can't wait, Uncle!" She skipped out of the card parlor then spotted the clutch of aunts and older girl cousins with her mother. They sat at the big supper table, each holding a needle of some sort.

What were they sewing? It didn't look like a quilt. Seemed they were doing more visiting then actual sewing. Maybe they were knitting.

Stopping beside Aunt Leilani, she waited. Mama sat across the table, reminding her about her manners with that look. But Evie knew better than to speak before being spoken to.

Not practicing perfect etiquette would embarrass her mother in front of all the other ladies and be the quickest way to get into hot water.

Finally, the Hawaiian princess held her hand up and turned toward Evie. "You sure are polite." She glanced across the table then back. "Your parents must be so proud of you, Evelyn."

"I hope so. Auntie, may I ask a boon?" She loved that word almost as much as she loved the slight hint of tropics in her aunt's voice.

The pretty lady smiled. "Ask away, sweetheart."

"Well, you see, Mama has one old newspaper from when you and Uncle Houston returned from the dead when you were lost at sea, but just the one article. I'm wondering if you have more, and if you do, I would love to see them. Do you?"

"Oh my, yes, child. I've saved a whole box of old newspapers, and we can look at them any time. Your mother says you're coming to Clarksville before going back to San Francisco. Let's set a date to go up into the attic and find it while you're there."

Oh joy! She resisted jumping up and down or shouting or showing out at all.

Instead, she rose onto tippy toes and kissed Aunt Leilani's cheek. "That's wonderful! It is a date then. I'm so glad we're coming to Clarksville. Uncle Charlie wants me to ride his filly, too.

Nathaniel's been training her with him, and they want to see if she would make a good mount for a little girl—not that I'm little anymore."

"How old are you, Evie?"

"I'll be ten in only three years." She nodded. "I'll come to your house one day then. If that's acceptable with everyone." She smiled at her mother, who seemed to be trying not to laugh. She'd joked plenty about Evie saying she'd be ten in three years, so that couldn't be it. Plus, some of the others appeared to be stifling themselves.

Hmmm.

"Excuse me, did I say something funny? Why is everyone laughing at me?"

Aunt Leilani leaned over and put her mouth close to her ear. "They aren't laughing at you, dear. But believe me . . . it's a good thing. I promise you'll like the surprise, so run along now, and be happy for yourself."

A surprise! For her? She loved unexpected good things, but not so much knowing one waited around the corner, especially when no one gave her any kind of hint.

That was just so wrong.

Did Nathaniel know about it? If he did, wouldn't he tell her? Could knowing it have something to do with him acting mad at her?

For sure and for certain, he avoided being alone with her at all cost.

The trip from Llano to Clarksville took too long, and instead of having loads of fun and the miles whizzing by, time crawled. Way too many opportunities to wonder about that good thing every single body—except her—knew about.

It wasn't fair.

If not such a lady-in-the-making, she'd spit.

Chapter Thirty-One

Leilani set the box on the hall's sideboard then twirled around, but he was nowhere to be seen. "Samuel Houston Buckmeyer, what are you doing? We need to go."

Sauntering through the bedroom door, he worked at buttoning his shirt. "Relax, my love. We've got plenty of time. Charley said the boy wouldn't get there until well after dinner."

With her head cocked, she stepped toward him and drilled a stare into him in the same fashion she'd seen his father do a dozen times.

"But my darling, I don't want to be rushed. Come on, now. Tuck in your shirttails, and let's get gone. We're burning daylight, you know."

"Mercy, woman. You need more steel in your voice if you're going to quote the old man." He flashed his little boy grin—the one that melted her into a silly little girl most days, but not that one. She could hardly wait to get there and see Evelyn's face.

That young lady sure had won a sweet spot in her heart. Such a doll, and so smart!

She nodded toward the news clippings. "Bring that and please come on. That new fellow you hired brought up the team fifteen minutes ago."

"Good man." He grabbed the box then held the door for her.

The ride to the old home place took its normal hour and half, though it seemed more like five for some reason.

A strange urging to be in the company of her little niece almost overwhelmed her; she loved it that Evelyn wanted to see the newspaper stories and could hardly wait to show her the old clippings and enjoy them again through the girl's eyes.

But it was more than just that.

Almost as if the child held the key to a longing that lived deep in her soul. A hunger she had no way of reaching or even knowing its name or what it looked like.

Houston set the brake, jumped down, then held his hand out.

Accepting his support, she let him help her to the ground. "Don't forget my box."

"How could I?" He chuckled and climbed back aboard.

That man thought he was so funny. She ignored him and hurried up the steps. After a bevy of hugs and hellos, Leilani found her niece in the parlor . . . reading a book, of course.

"Hello, Evie dear! I brought the newspapers. Your Uncle Houston is carrying the box in from the barn."

The girl jumped to her feet and beamed. "Oh, Auntie, thank you for remembering! Can we look at them now?"

"Well, sure we can. I'd love nothing more. Since you first mentioned going through them, I've been excited at the prospect. They take me back to when I first fell in love with your uncle almost twenty years ago. He was so handsome and brave."

With Levi's blessing, she and Evelyn retired to his library, except he still called it the General's as if Henry Buckmeyer had only loaned it to him. But then, why not? Even from the grave, the old man cast a long shadow.

After better than an hour of reading headlines and ogling over the vast array that chronicled her and Houston's phenomenal story—she especially liked her copy of the London paper—Evelyn leaned back in her chair. Her pretty little face appeared somber.

"Auntie, I've been thinking about you and Uncle a lot of late."

Leilani turned in her chair, studied on the child a moment, then nodded. "You've been on my mind, too. Perhaps it's your interest in the *Gray Lady*, but . . ." Both shoulders rose. How could she articulate what was in her heart?

"Could be." The girl's eyes widened and sparkled. "Was sailing on her wonderful?"

"Oh, yes, I loved it. Especially with Houston."

"I can't believe you were so brave to leave your home and family when you stowed away." She grinned ear to ear and winked. "But I'm so glad you did."

"Hmmm, brave or coward? My father would call me rebellious. If only the missionaries had never come . . . who knows?"

"But those men brought God to your people, didn't they? And if it hadn't been for them coming . . ." Evie shook her head. "Well, you wouldn't be here now."

"No, they were mean, hateful people whose God ruined my life."

"Oh, Auntie. God would never ruin your life or do anything to hurt you. Daddy says the Lord only wants to help us and bless us. Think about this. If they hadn't come, then your daddy would have married your aunt. Isn't that right?"

"Yes, and I would have been . . ." She stopped herself. What would she have been? A princess, even queen perhaps. But could she ever have been happy without Houston in her life? The one her heart beat for, her hero and king and savior.

"But then, wouldn't you have had to marry your brother?"

The truth hit hard like a falling coconut landing right on her hard head. How had this child become so wise? "Yes, that's true. It was our way. Until those men changed everything."

Tears filled Evie's eyes then overflowed. "But Auntie, they were Christians, and your people didn't even know about God or how much He loves you. I never knew you were mad at God. You just can't miss out on Heaven though. Won't you please ask Jesus to save you now?"

The missionary's hellfire and damnation hadn't pierced her heart, but the child's tears certainly did. How could the faith of one so little be so pure? She wanted what Evelyn had. "How? He would never want to save me. Not after I've hated Him so long."

"That's not true. Not true at all. He loves you no matter what, and He always forgives anyone who asks." Tears rolled down her cheeks and dripped off her chin. She sniffed then put her hands together fingertips up. "Do this. Then just ask Him. He's very easy to talk to. The Bible says that all those who call upon the name of the Lord will be saved."

Leilani placed her hands exactly so and closed her eyes. A part of her screamed not to do it! Hold fast to her hate! But the longing in her heart proved too strong to listen to such nonsense. More than anything else, she wanted to be free.

"Jesus, I want you to save me. Will You, please? Can You forgive me for not believing in You until now? If so, please save me."

A wave of liquid love washed over her, cleansing her soul, filling every void. The sweetest peace she'd ever known settled over her.

It'd been so easy. Why had she waited so long?

Joyful tears filled her eyes. "Oh, sweet Evelyn! Thank you!" She held out both arms to the child. "Thank you for telling me the truth."

The child jumped to her feet and threw herself into Leilani's embrace. "I'm so happy! Now you'll be with all of us in Heaven forever! I love you, Auntie."

Evie hugged and kissed then hugged some more on her new sister in Christ, but her feet wanted to dance. She pushed away and twirled and leapt around PawPaw's old library. Was he dancing, too, up on those Golden Streets?

Surely the Lord would let him know his daughter-in-law just got saved.

Leilani joined her. Holding hands, she and her aunt danced and jumped then took to whooping and hollering praise to the

Lord, like at camp meetings. Uncle Houston came running in, found out what had happened, and he danced, too!

Tears streamed down his face. Evie's heart filled to the brim with joy!

Soon the whole house was abuzz with Leilani's conversion; caused dinner to be half an hour late, but no one seemed to mind. Well past dishes, when resetting the table for supper, Nathaniel burst through the door.

"Evelyn? You here? Come see! I brought my filly."

"In here." Evie put the silver down in a pile. She could finish that chore later. She'd been waiting so long to see his horse. "Where is Beauty? Where is she?"

"Right outside. Come on."

Slipping her hand into his—she forgot all about caring over him being mean to her in Llano—she stopped at the door. The most beautiful horse she'd ever seen in the world stood outside, staring right at her.

"Is that her? Is that Beauty?"

Nathaniel held the screen door open. "Yes, ma'am. Go on out and meet her. She's sweet as she is pretty."

With each step down off the porch, the horse got bigger. She stood at least twice as tall as Twinkle Toes. Evie stopped and held out her hand toward the shining black filly. How could she have grown so big in only two years?

And standing there with no halter or saddle. Nothing. Evie glanced at Nathaniel then back at the filly. "Why isn't she running off?"

One giant leap off the porch landed him on the ground almost beside her. He took his hat in hand. "Watch this."

His Stetson went flying right at Beauty's front hooves, but she didn't flinch or anything. The animal only stood there, all calm and nice and easy. He picked the hat up then walked toward the south end of the house, and the filly followed right behind.

He hollered over his shoulder. "Hurry up and go put on your riding gear. Meet me in the barn."

"Yes, sir. I'll be there in a minute!"

If anyone had bothered to time her, for sure and for certain, she beat anyone's record for changing clothes and getting to the barn. She slipped in the side door. The filly rested patiently, all saddled and ready, in the barn's big hall.

Nathaniel stood with his back to her, stuffing something in-between two grain sacks. He turned around. "That was fast."

"What were you hiding?"

"What?"

"I saw you, Nathaniel Nightingale. You were hiding something in those feed sacks."

"Not really hiding." He shrugged then pulled an envelope from his shirt pocket. "I've got you a letter."

She hurried to him. "Don't try to sidetrack me. What were you hiding?"

He shook his head.

"Nathaniel, you promised not ever to lie to me."

"I ain't lying about nothing."

She leaned out, looking at the grain sacks. "Well, you're not telling me the whole truth. And that's the same thing."

"No, it surely is not."

"Just tell me. Or better, show me."

He ducked his head, retrieved his hideaway, then held out a brown bottle.

She took it, pulled the cork, and sniffed, wrinkling her nose. "Is this whiskey? You shouldn't have hard liquor, should you? No, you should not. That's why you were hiding it. Even I know you're too young. Why are you drinking it? The stuff smells nasty!"

"Are you going to tell?"

"No. Why would I? Daddy says love covers a multitude of sins." She tilted the bottle, spilling the contents onto the dirt. "But I want a promise. Alcohol makes you drunk. Promise me that you'll never touch another drop. Not for the rest of my natural-born days."

He filled his lungs then exhaled softly. "What about beer? Or wine?"

Wasn't it just last month the preacher quoted the Apostle Paul writing a letter to Timothy? "You can take a little wine for your stomach's sake—or communion—but no more hard liquor. Agreed?

"Will you promise? Because if you don't . . ."

He seemed to be teetering then finally sighed out all his air and closed his eyes, nodding. "I agree. I promise you, Evelyn."

"Good. Now tell me all about your other brother."

"How'd you know about him?"

A funny sound escaped, almost like a huff but with a voice that sort of choked her. "Mama and the aunts, silly! It's all they've been talking about. They discuss all kinds of stuff when they think I'm asleep. Why haven't I met him? He's my cousin, too, right?"

"Well, sort of, but how about we save the whole story for when you're older."

"How old? Ten?"

"I was thinking sixteen."

"Twelve."

"Fine then. Fifteen."

"Let's shake on it." She stuck her hand out. "When I turn thirteen."

He took it. "Deal." She shook one firm, crisp pump. "So are we ready for me to ride your gorgeous filly? You named her just perfect. I've never seen a horse more beautiful than her."

"Yes, ma'am. Glad you like her." He nodded toward the south double doors. "Come on. You'll love her gait. Why, she's smooth as . . ."

"As what?"

"I was going to say fifty-year-old bourbon, but seeing how you've never tasted such nectar—and I'm a teetotaler now—let's say smooth as silk instead."

"That sounds great. I like silky smooth."

With the bravest expression she could muster, she followed him toward the corral. A part of her wanted to run away.

The filly stood so tall and probably could jump right over the fence easy as pie. She might run off to who knew where, and Evie would never be able to pull hard enough to stop her.

But the horse seemed so gentle and well-mannered . . .

And Nathaniel would be right there if . . .

He stopped and turned toward her, holding his hands out. "Come on, I'll lift you into the saddle."

Her heart boomed. Air came hard. She sucked her lungs full then closed her eyes as his hands neared her sides.

Plop.

Nothing.

One eye peeked. She sat so high, like on top of the world, but it wasn't too bad.

"Give her a little nudge."

"Silly, I know how to ride. Remember? You taught me."

"Well, ride then."

She picked up the reins, gently touched the filly's flank, and clucked, pressing in with her knees. Silky smooth couldn't describe how easily Beauty walked.

Nothing at all like Twink. She clucked again and the horse broke into a trot. Maybe not as smooth, but not that bumpy either. What horse didn't jar you a bit, jogging? The third time around, she eased the black into a canter.

Goosebumps rose all over Evie. She loved the horse. Twinkle Toes would surely hate her if she . . .

Movement caught her eye. Her parents, uncles and aunts, and most all of the cousins stood outside the corral's fence. What were they doing? Why had they all come to watch her ride?

She reined the filly to stop by her mama. "Is something wrong?"

"No, darling. How do you like her?"

"Oh, she's perfect, Mama. She's awesome. I don't like her, I love her." She looked over at Nathaniel. "But she belongs to him."

"Well, your daddy and I were thinking if you liked her, we'd agree to let Nathaniel give her to you."

Had she heard right? She whirled toward Nathaniel again. "Give me Beauty?" Then turned back to Mama. "Is that what you said?"

"Yes, ma'am. Him and Uncle Charley are coming to San Francisco in the spring. They can bring her to California then."

Grabbing the saddle horn, she slid off, ducked between the rails, then hugged her mama's waist. Her father wrapped his arms into a giant family hug around her and her mother.

She loved that day!

If only she could be old enough to marry Nathaniel, it would be perfect.

Epilogue

Nathaniel and Charley freighted the filly with ten other long-twos to San Francisco that next spring. Made so much coin, they came back each year for the next eleven. As promised, the spring after Evelyn turned thirteen, Nathaniel told her all about his other brother Tex and the trouble Marah, his mother, and his visit had caused.

He also kept his promise to abstain from imbibing hard liquor as Evelyn asked, but . . . Oh well . . . why mention that now?

Evelyn and Nathaniel's love story is well told in the next installment of the beloved Texas Romance Family Saga series.

But then, if you have to know a bit of it, please enjoy the following first chapter of book nine, MIGHTY TO SAVE—just after . . .

Caryl's Titles' Five-Star Reviews

Historical Texas Romances

...for Vow Unbroken

With an intriguing plot line and well-developed characters, McAdoo, who's written nonfiction and children's fiction, delivers an engaging read for her first adult historical romance.   --*Publishers Weekly*

After reading Caryl McAdoo's story of Henry and Susannah in "VOW UNBROKEN," I felt like I'd had another adventure with Tom Sawyer and Becky, this time as young adults.
--Alan Daugherty: columnist *The News-Banner*

...for Hearts Stolen

Get ready for a wild, uplifting, heart-tugging, page-turning ride. *Hearts Stolen* grabbed me at the start. Sassy's feisty, fighting spirit...I couldn't set it down. Burnt dinner, but forget eating, I ate this book up. This master storyteller weaves Texas history into a well-crafted plot with unforgettable and totally loved characters.
--Holly Michael, author, *Crooked Lines*

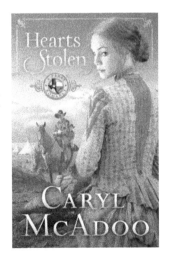

...for _Hope Reborn_

With memorable characters, Caryl's signature humor, and plenty of adventure, drama, and romance, "Hope Reborn" is anything but fluff. A strong message of salvation runs through, but well within the storyline. Enjoyed a unique twist with May writing the stories of the previous characters – clever and fun!
--Pam Morrison, Tennessee reader

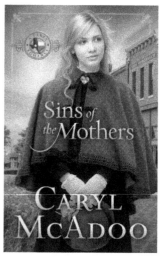

...for _Sins of the Mothers_

I tell you what, folks, this girl can write! I do love this series, and maybe most especially this book. Mary Rachel Buckmeyer can out-negotiate the experts, out-guess marketing trends, and out-stubborn a mule. Trouble is, she tends to follow her heart into disaster. The guy she marries has meandering eye, lies like a braided rug, and has all the loyalty of a new-born pup. Mary hops from one frying pan to another until one man shows up who could steady her and get her out of the fixes she gets herself into. Such a great story! I know you'll love.
--Anne Baxter Campbell, author _The Truth Trilogy: The Roman's Quest, Marcus Varitor, Centurion,_ and _The Truth Doesn't Die_

...*for* <u>*Daughters of the Heart*</u>

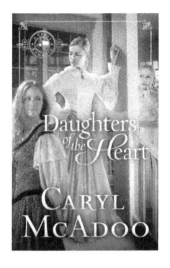

A fun packed Christian romance novel with plenty of action, heartbreak, tears, deception, twists, and turns. [The three sisters] made a pact never to break their father's heart, but when suitors show up, it's hard for them to stay determined. Will they find true love? Will Dad accept a suitor for them and give his blessings?

--Joy Gibson, a Tennessee reader and pastor's wife

...*for* <u>*Just Kin*</u>

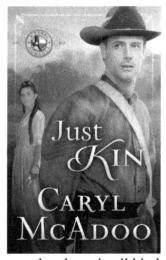

I have followed this historical romance series from the beginning and they just keep getting better. Lacey Rose loves Charley and is devastated when he leaves to fight for Texas with the Confederate army. Charley doesn't realize Lacey Rose is in love with him but is both surprised and pleased with the goodbye kiss she gives him. After Charley sends a hurtful letter trying to discourage her from waiting for him, Lacey Rose runs away and ends up in all kinds of trouble. Charley also stirs up some trouble of his own when he begins looking for her. Don't miss out on this book. I loved it!

--Louise Koiner, Texas beta reader

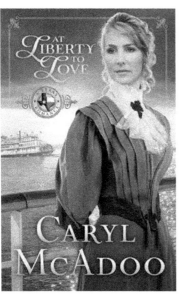

...for _At Liberty to Love_

This was one of the best books I have ever read. The characters got so close to your heart you wish they were your family. From the beginning till the end you fell in love with each of them. The two adopted baby boys brought laughs and joy. The love story has strong Christian threads throughout. Highly recommend this book. You will love it.
--Jane Moody, reader

...for _The Bedwarmer's Son_

I really loved this book...didn't want to put it down. I love the way it's different than most historical romance novels, and I read many. I loved the way the author used the old man to tell Jasmine's story. I also loved both Will's stories. Being a Christian novel just made it better. I enjoyed it so much I hated to see it end. This is the first novel I've ever read by this author, but I doubt it will be my last. --Author BJ Robinson, Author of River Oaks Plantation, Siege of Azalea Plantation, Azalea Plantation and others

Contemporary Red River Romances

...for <u>The Preacher's Faith</u>

This was my first book to read by Caryl McAdoo and I absolutely loved it. I will be reading more. I love the way she prays that her story gives God Glory and dedicates The Preacher's Faith to Him and His Kingdom...a good clean book to read. I was drawn into this story right from the start. I loved this book and can't wait for book two.

   --Elizabeth 'Liz' Dent, Alabama reader

...for <u>Sing a New Song</u>

   Sing a New Song is a delightful breath of air. Caryl eloquently brings her audience nearer to God [with] fresh ways of viewing Christian life and all it offers. The characters are loveable and humorous. Illuminating, the story shares the Gospel beautifully. Samuel's sermons as well as the gorgeous lyrics of Mary Esther's songs fill our hearts with newfound worship. Truly an inspiring tale. Christian fiction in its best; a romantic love story that brings its readers closer to God. A treasure for sure.

   --Christine Barber, author of *Broken to Pieces*

...for <u>One and Done</u>

Faster than a major league outfielder pulling down a popup fly ball, this romance is guaranteed to snag baseball lovers and romance readers alike. The Christian story is written with wit, verve and Caryl's usual flare for dialect and spicy dialogue. Be warned. Those readers searching for a saccharine, man-meets-woman story will soon discover this is no sanitized romantic fairy tale. From the beginning, the reader will identify with real people who live clearly in the mind, so much so, that a person can almost smell locker room sweat or the mouthwatering scent of spicy Mexican food. Identification with the hero and heroine is nearly immediate. With so much to rave about, this reviewer cannot begin to cover all the delightful surprises, so the reader simply must buy "One and Done" to see for themselves.

–Cass Wessel, multi-devotion author

Contemporary Apple Orchard Romance

...for <u>Lady Luck's a Loser</u>

A very unique, witty plot. I couldn't put it down. I love that my favorite characters are still active at the end of the book, only their relationships have changed. What a way for Dub to fulfill his promises to his deceased wife. Love, trust, forgiveness, and many emotions make for a well written book.   --Joy Gibson, Tennessee

The Generations Biblical fiction

...*for* <u>A Little Lower Than the Angels</u>

Caryl McAdoo used her research and knowledge of biblical scripture combined with an incredible imagination as a foundation to fill in the gaps of the story of Adam and Eve and their children. I was caught up in the story from page one to the ending. I particularly appreciated the "Search the Scriptures" section at the end which explains some of the Biblical clues for this work of fiction. I loved it and highly recommend it.

--Judy Levine, reader, Arizona

...*for* <u>Then the Deluge Comes</u>

Deluge is the second book in The Generations Series, and if the books still to follow are as good as this one and the first one in the series are it is going to be an incredible series. The author has a way of breathing life and emotions into the characters that made me feel like I was on the sidelines watching their stories unfold. This is some of the best Biblical fiction that I have read and I look forward to the rest of the series. I was furnished with an e-copy of the book in return for an honest review.   --Ann Ellis, reader, Texas

...*for* <u>Replenish the Earth</u>

Caryl tells the story of the flood in such a unique way.. I like how she makes the characters so real. This Bible story just comes to life. Noah's family on the Ark taking care of the animals and then when they come to a stop, starting all over on a barren earth. I found that the family conversations, their actions and the descriptions just made this more real to me. I like that Caryl gives scripture references and her thoughts at the end of the book.

--Deanna Stevens, reader, Nebraska

...*for* <u>Children of Eber</u>

So much of the tale remains faithful to the Scriptural account, but where there is silence, Caryl's author voice sings through in delicious detail. For the reader familiar with the Biblical account, she fleshes out a mere paragraph or two until the narrative vibrates with life. As if transported through a time machine, the reader reenters the world of the Ancients experiencing their lives and seeing their surroundings afresh. Those who know the Biblical account will delight in following the ancient pair into Egypt, then back to Canaan again.

--Cass Wessel, multi-published devotional author

Mid-Grade that Grandparents love

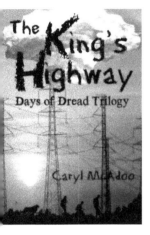

...*for* The King's Highway

I can't remember when I have enjoyed reading a book as much as this one. If I really like a book, I can read it in a day. I read this twice in two days. I couldn't quit reading. It has to be right up there with my all-time favorites. If anyone thinks they won't read it because it's for mid-grade, I encourage you to reconsider. You'll miss a blessing. Anyone reading age from the mid grades to senior citizens (that's me) will love this book. The characters in the book are delightful.
--Louise Koiner, reader, Texas

Non-Fiction

...*for* Story & Style, The Craft of Writing Creative Fiction

This is a wonderful book for those wanting to learn more about writing. I know from experience. The content helped me tremendously!! It especially helped me gain a clear picture of POV and the use of action versus attribution to strengthen my writing and make my debut book the best it can be. Thank you, Caryl, your continued helping hands are a blessing to many of us rookie writers!!   --Andy Skrzynski, author of
The New World, A Step Backward

So, Coming Soon...

Texas Romances
Mighty to Save   debuts May, 2017
Chief of Sinners   debuts September, 2017

Companion stories *to the Texas Romance series*
Son of Promise debuts January 2018

Days of Dread Trilogy *Mid-grade and Young Adult, but Grandparents love them, too!*

The Sixth Trumpet

Compelled by a vision, Jackson Allison leaves the safety of Red River County on a quest to free his mother from the clutches of a traitorous double agent. Accompanied by Albert Einstein Hawking, his personal nerd, and the Great Pyrenees guardian, Boggs, the high school freshman must elude Communist patrols, slavers, and bangers.

The Kidron Valley

By day, Jackson Allison fights alongside his grandfather, uncles, and other red-neck defenders of the cattle and grain rich Red River County. Plagued by dreams of his dad by night, he somehow joins his father's Marine unit that's fighting the last great battle between good and evil in the Kidron Valley. It seems so real, but how can it be?

The Texas Romance Family Sagas

Characters…alphabetically

<u>Warning !</u>   <u>Reader beware !</u>   <u>Spoiler warning !</u>

If you aren't up to date on reading the series, you might find facts you'd rather wait to know.

The Baylors

1823 – Andrew Baylor married Susannah Abbott in 1822, then he and brother Jacob are killed in a logging accident, leaving five-year-old Levi Baylor an orphan. Aunt Sue rears him, and later that year, delivers daughter Rebecca Baylor who never knew her daddy.

~ **Baylor, LEVI Bartholomew** – born November 2, 1817 orphaned at age five; was reared by Aunt Sue Baylor until fourteen, then Uncle Henry Buckmeyer, too, after he married Aunt Sue. Levi became husband to Rosaleen 'Sassy' or 'Rose' Fogelsong Nightingale Baylor and step-father to Charley Nightingale and Bart Baylor (Comanche Chief Bold Eagle's blood son); then Pa to Stephen Austin, Daniel Boone, Wallace Rusk, and Rachel Rose. Widowed then marries Sophia in 1885
HIS TITLE: HEARTS STOLEN
On Scene in: VOW UNBROKEN, HOPE REBORN, and JUST KIN, COVERING LOVE
Mention in: SINS OF THE MOTHERS, DAUGHTERS OF THE HEART, JUST KIN, AT LIBERTY TO LOVE, and mentioned in contemporary Red River Romance SING A NEW SONG

~ Baylor, Rosaleen 'ROSE' (SASSY) Summer Fogelsong Nightingale – born August 24, 1823, married at fifteen in the fall of '38 to Charles Nightingale, then stolen by the Comanche in the summer of '39. She lived with the tribe five years as the captive third wife of the chief—birthing Nightingale's son in February, 1840—until being rescued in October of 1844 by the Texas Rangers. She married Levi mid-December of that same year. She gave birth to Bartholomew, the Comanche chief's blood son in 1845, followed by Stephen Austin in April, 1846, Daniel Boone in '49, and Wallace Rusk in '53. She finally had a baby girl, Rachel Rose.
HER TITLE: HEARTS STOLEN
On Scene in: HOPE REBORN, JUST KIN, AT LIBERTY TO LOVE

Mention in: VOW UNBROKEN, SINS OF THE MOTHERS, DAUGHTERS OF THE HEART

~ Baylor, Bartholomew 'BART' – born July 20, 1845 to Rose and Levi, but blood son of Comanche chief Bold Eagle
On Scene in: HOPE REBORN, DAUGHTERS OF THE HEART, and JUST KIN
Mention in: HEARTS STOLEN

~ Briggs, Clayton 'CLAY' Butterfield – born October 13, 1827 to J.T. and Maud Briggs. He courts and marries Gwendolyn Buckmeyer.
HIS TITLE: DAUGHTERS OF THE HEART

~ Briggs, Jake – born in 1812 to J.T and Maud, married to Clover, father of Jedidiah
On Scene in: DAUGHTERS OF THE HEART

~ Briggs, Jasper – born in 1837 to J.T. and Maud, marries Bonnie Claire Buckmeyer in 1866
On Scene in: DAUGHTERS OF THE HEART, JUST KIN, AT LIBERTY TO LOVE

~ Briggs, Jedidiah – born in October 1845 to Jake and Clover
On Scene in: DAUGHTERS OF THE HEART, JUST KIN

~ Boyd, Francine 'FRANCY' – born October 28, 1842, a California orphan God sends to Jethro to take to Mary Rachel. She quickly becomes a part of the family.
On Scene in: SINS OF THE MOTHER, AT LIBERTY TO LOVE

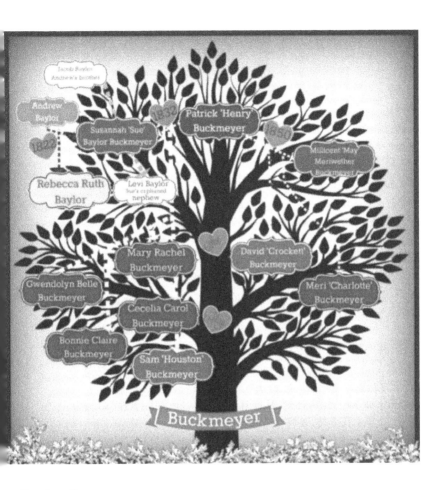

The Buckmeyers

1832 – Sue meets and marries Henry Buckmeyer.
1833-1844 – Sue gives Henry four daughters, Mary Rachel, Gwendolyn Belle, Cecelia Carol, and Bonnie Claire, and a son, Samuel Houston, then leaves him a widower.
1850 – Henry marries May Meriwether.
1851-1854 – May gives Henry a son, David Crockett, and a daughter, Meri Charlotte.

~ Buckmeyer, BONNIE Claire – born December 2, 1840. Henry and Sue's fourth child.
HER TITLE: DAUGHTERS OF THE HEART
On Scene in: HEARTS STOLEN, HOPE REBORN, and JUST KIN, AT LIBERTY TO LOVE
Mention in: SINS OF THE MOTHERS, COVERING LOVE

~ **Buckmeyer, CECELIA Carol 'CeCe'** – born April 10, 1836. Henry and Sue's third child. Marries Elijah Eversole in 1854.
HER TITLE: DAUGHTERS OF THE HEART
On Scene in: HEARTS STOLEN, HOPE REBORN, and JUST KIN, AT LIBERTY TO LOVE, COVERING LOVE
Mention in: SINS OF THE MOTHERS

~ **Buckmeyer, David Crockett** – born October 4, 1851 firstborn of Henry and May. Marries Deidra Graves in 1886
HIS TITLE: COVERING LOVE
On Scene in: DAUGHTERS OF THE HEART, JUST KIN

~ Buckmeyer, GWENDOLYN Belle or 'Gwen' – born Nov. 29, 1834. Henry and Sue's second child. Marries Clay Briggs in 1854.
HER TITLE: DAUGHTERS OF THE HEART
On Scene in: HEARTS STOLEN, HOPE REBORN, and JUST KIN, AT LIBERTY TO LOVE
Mention in: SINS OF THE MOTHERS, COVERING LOVE

~ **Buckmeyer, Millicent MAY Meriwether** born August 23, 1808 to the Commodore and her mother. A successful New York dime novelist, May heads to Texas to interview a couple of Texas Rangers for new inspiration after seeing a newspaper article about Levi Baylor and Wallace Rusk. She marries Henry Buckmeyer there and gives birth to David Crockett in 1851 and Charlotte in 1854. MayMee to her grandsugars.
HER TITLE: HOPE REBORN
On Scene in: SINS OF THE MOTHERS, DAUGHTERS OF THE HEART, JUST KIN, AT LIBERTY TO LOVE, COVERING LOVE

~ **Buckmeyer, Patrick HENRY** - born March 6, 1798; killed a man at fifteen, fought in the Battle of New Orleans at sixteen. At thirty-four, he married Susannah 'Sue' Baylor in 1832, and became stepfather to her Rebecca—also honorary pa to Levi Baylor—and daddy to Mary Rachel, Gwendolyn Belle, Cecelia Carol, and Bonnie Claire before becoming a widower in Dec '44 at his son Houston's birth. Finding love again, he married May Meriwether in 1850 and fathered Crockett and Charlotte. He's Grandpa to a slew of grandsugars with many more to come!
HIS TITLE: VOW UNBROKEN, HOPE REBORN
On Scene in: HEARTS STOLEN, HOPE REBORN, SINS OF THE MOTHERS, DAUGHTERS OF THE HEART, JUST KIN, AT LIBERTY TO LOVE, COVERING LOVE

~ **Buckmeyer, Sam HOUSTON** – born December 11, 1844. Henry and Sue's fifth child, first son. His mother passes at his birth, so he was motherless until six years old when his pa married May.
HIS TITLE: GRAY LADY DOWN, COVERING LOVE
On Scene in: HOPE REBORN, DAUGHTERS OF THE HEART, JUST KIN, AT LIBERTY TO LOVE
Mention in: HEARTS STOLEN, SINS OF THE MOTHERS, DAUGHTERS OF THE HEART

~ Buckmeyer, Susannah 'SUE' Alicia Abbott Baylor – born May 15, 1803, married Andrew Baylor at eighteen in 1821, widowed at nineteen and became guardian aunt to orphaned Levi Baylor, birthed Rebecca in the next year. At twenty-nine, she married Henry Buckmeyer in 1832. Mother to Mary Rachel, Gwendolyn, Cecelia, Bonnie Claire, and Samuel Houston.
HER TITLE: VOW UNBROKEN
On Scene in: HEARTS STOLEN
Mention in: HOPE REBORN, SINS OF THE MOTHERS, DAUGHTERS OF THE HEART, AT LIBERTY TO LOVE

~ Dempsey, Frederica 'FREDDIE' May's publisher who Charley turns to for help in New York City on his search for Lacey Rose.

She has a widowed daughter, Marah O'Connor, and grandson—Charley's son with Marah—Leland Charles O'Connor Nightingale

~ Dithers a strange old man who spouts prophesy and seemingly never dies . . . an angel unaware . . . Namrel

~ **Eversole, ELIJAH** – born January 2, 1826, moved to California in the gold rush days where his parents abandoned him as a teen. He followed in his father's blacksmith trade and loves inventing and building new helpful machines. Jethro Risen and Moses Jones make him a partner in a gold mine. He marries Cecelia Buckmeyer in 1854.
HIS TITLE: DAUGHTERS OF THE HEART
On Scene in: SINS OF THE MOTHERS, AT LIBERTY TO LOVE, COVERING LOVE
~ Ford, Julia and Michele, Marcus' first wife and daughter, died on the yellow fever epidemic in New Orleans
Mention in: AT LIBERTY TO LOVE

~ Ford, MARCUS Aurelius, Major in the Civil War with Levi Baylor and Wallace Rusk under General Buckmeyer. Lost his first wife Julia and baby Michele to yellow fever epidemic in New Orleans. Meets the Widow Rusk in 1865; marries her in 1866 and adopts her two adopted sons, becoming father to Michael and Gabriel Ford.
HIS TITLE: AT LIBERTY TO LOVE

~ Ford, MICHAEL - exact day of birth unknown, about four years old in November 1865. He and brother Gabriel were adopted by Rebecca Rusk then by her husband Marcus Ford.
On Scene in: AT LIBERTY TO LOVE

~ **Ford, REBECCA Ruth Baylor Rusk** – born June 12, 1823; Sue's daughter by 1st husband Andrew (who died before Rebecca's birth). The nine-year-old on the Jefferson Trace in 1832 (book 1) turns twenty-one in 1844 (book 2) before finally meeting Wallace Rusk. Marries him at age twenty-seven in 1850, then is

widowed in 1864. Adopted two boys, Michael and Gabriel in 1866 then married Marcus Ford when she's forty-two.
HER TITLE: AT LIBERTY TO LOVE
On Scene in: VOW UNBROKEN, HEARTS STOLEN, HOPE REBORN, COVERING LOVE
Mention in: SINS OF THE MOTHERS, DAUGHTERS OF THE HEART

~ **Eversole, EVELYN "EVIE" May** – born June 28, 1878 to Elijah and Cecelia Eversole
HER TITLE: , COVERING LOVE, MIGHTY TO SAVE
On Scene in:

~ **Graves, BECCA Joy Risen** – born to Mary Rachel Buckmeyer Risen and Jethro (blood daughter of Clinton) April 10, 1853, ran off and went North, met and married Randal Ramsey Graves in 1880, Mother to Zacharias "Bubba" in March 1884
On Scene in: COVERING LOVE

~ **Graves, DIEDRA** – born in September 29, 1868, orphaned at the age of eight and reared by her brother Randal
HER TITLE: COVERING LOVE

~ **Graves, RANDAL Ramsey,** born in 1850, took in orphaned eight-year-old sister at twenty-six, Marries Recca Risen in 1880, Father to Zacharias 'Bubba' Graves born March 1884
On Scene in: COVERING LOVE

~ **Graves, Zacharias 'ZACH' or 'BUBBA' Randal** – born to Randal and Becca Risen Graves March 6, 1884
On Scene in: COVERING LOVE

~ **Jeffcoat, CLAUDIA,** a wealthy married woman and avid reader of dime romances who befriended and helped Charley on his search for Lacey Rose. Pauleen Shriver's sister.
Mention in: JUST KIN

~ Jones, LANELLE Wheeler – born February 26, 1831, Caleb's cousin, John's sister, marries Moses Jones in early fall 1851.
On scene in: SINS OF THE MOTHERS
Mention in: AT LIBERTY TO LOVE

~ Jones, MOSES – born October 13, 1816, a Scot partnered with Jethro Risen in a gold mine, marries Lanelle Wheeler in 1854.
On scene in: SINS OF THE MOTHERS
Mention in: DAUGHTERS OF THE HEART, AT LIBERTY TO LOVE

~ Jones, 'JOSH'ua Jethro, also 'JONESY' – born January 19, 1852 to Moses and Lanelle, but the blood son of Caleb Wheeler

~ Meriwether, CHESTER born a slave on October 7, 1803 to Commodore Meriwether's field hands Silas and Honey Pie. He was 5, about to be 6, when his half-sister Millicent May was born. He marries JEWEL (formerly Mammy, the Buckmeyers' cook) in 1851.
On Scene in: HOPE REBORN, DAUGHTERS OF THE HEART
Mention in: SINS OF THE MOTHERS, JUST KIN, AT LIBERTY TO LOVE

~ Meriwether, JEWEL (formerly Mammy) Rozier the Buckmeyers' cook after Henry rescued her and her son Jean Paul Rozier who also works for the Buckmeyers.
On Scene in: HEARTS STOLEN, HOPE REBORN, DAUGHTERS OF THE HEART
Mention in: SINS OF THE MOTHERS, JUST KIN, AT LIBERTY TO LOVE

~ Meriwether, Silas born a slave in 1808 on the Meriwethers' Sea Side plantation, father of Chester and also blood father of May
Mention in: HOPE REBORN

~ **Moran, Meri 'CHARLOTTE' Buckmeyer** born in December 2, 1854 to Henry and May. Marries Nash Moran in 1886

HER TITLE: COVERING LOVE
On Scene in: JUST KIN

~ **Moran, NASH** – New York business partner of Crockett Buckmeyer, marries Charlotte Buckmeyer in 1886
HIS TITLE: COVERING LOVE

~ Nightingale, CHARLES Nathaniel, Senior - born 1805, married Rosaleen Fogelsong and fathered Charley, though was never around him. Lives in St. Louis with his first wife and two daughters.
On Scene in: HEARTS STOLEN

~ **Nightingale, Charles 'CHARLEY' Nathaniel** - born son to a Comanche chief Feb 27 '40 to the captive third wife Rosaleen, but Charles Nightingale was his mother's husband and Charley's blood father. He's rescued in 1844 with his mother by Texas Rangers Levi Baylor and Wallace Rusk. He killed a man at ten when Comancheros came to steal him and his mother to return them to Bold Eagle. He marries Lacey Rose Langley in November, 1865.
HIS TITLE: JUST KIN
On Scene in: HEARTS STOLEN, HOPE REBORN, COVERING LOVE
Mention in: SINS OF THE MOTHERS, DAUGHTERS OF THE HEART, AT LIBERTY TO LOVE, COVERING LOVE

~ Nightingale, LACEY Rose Langley born November 16, 1844 in Nacogdoches to Laura, only fourteen when Lacey's father, a Comanche brave, had captured her. Lacey marries Charley in November, 1865
HER TITLE: JUST KIN
On Scene in: HEARTS STOLEN, DAUGHTERS OF THE HEART, JUST KIN

~ Nightingale, LELAND Charles O'Connor illegitimate son of Charley and Marah O'Connor, conceived while on his search for Lacey, born unknown to Charley, in the fall of 1866

~ O'Connor, Curry CYLE, Junior Marah' fourteen year old son
Mention in: JUST KIN

~ O'Connor, CURRY Cyle, Senior Marah's dead husband
Mention in: JUST KIN

~ O'Connor, MARAH A beautiful older woman (twenty-nine) who almost wins Charley's heart. She breeds thoroughbreds in Conneticutt and is the daughter of Freddie – May's publisher who helped Charley in New York

~ **Risen, JETHRO** – born September 22, 1830 partner of Moses Jones in a gold mine. Married Mary Rachel Buckmeyer Wheeler in 1853 and later that year, reconnected with his estranged father, Boaz. Founds the Mercy House Orphanage and Miners' Bank in San Francisco.
HIS TITLE: SINS OF THE MOTHERS
On Scene in: AT LIBERTY TO LOVE, Covering Love
Mention in: DAUGHTERS OF THE HEART

~ **Risen, MARY RACHEL Buckmeyer Wheeler** – born August 3, 1833. Henry and Sue's firstborn eloped with Caleb Wheeler in 1951 without Daddy's blessing and moved to San Francisco where she took over the renamed Lone Star Mercantile. Her husband soon murdered, she becomes the widowed mother of Susannah "SUSIE" Wheeler. Remarries Jethro Risen in 1853, adopted an orphan, Francine "FRANCY" and birthed baby girl Rebecca "BECCA" in April, 1853 (blood daughter of Clinton) and Boaz Reuel, Jethro's firstborn son, in December, 1854.
HER TITLE: SINS OF THE MOTHERS
On Scene in: HEARTS STOLEN, HOPE REBORN DAUGHTERS OF THE HEART, AT LIBERTY TO LOVE, COVERING LOVE

~ Rozier, JEAN PAUL son of the Buckmeyer's cook, Mammy or later, Jewel. He and his mother were freed by their former owner when he died and both went to work for Henry. Her in the kitchen,

him supervising the cotton fields. He marries Laura Langley, another soul Henry took in.
On Scene in: HEARTS STOLEN, HOPE REBORN, JUST KIN
Mention in: DAUGHTERS OF THE HEART, DAUGHTERS OF THE HEART

~ Rozier, LAURA Langley was rescued at fifteen in 1844 along with Sassy. Pregnant at the time, she delivered the next month—a baby girl, Lacey Rose on the way to the Buckmeyers' for Thanksgiving that same year. She stays on there as teacher and marries Jean Paul Rozier.
On Scene in: HEARTS STOLEN, HOPE REBORN, JUST KIN
Mention in: DAUGHTERS OF THE HEART, DAUGHTERS OF THE HEART

~ Rusk, WALLACE – born August 15, 1819, a sixteen-year-old orphan picked up by Henry Buckmeyer and young Levi Baylor on the way to the Battle of San Jacinto, served with Levi Texas Rangering, fell in love with his sister Rebecca sight-unseen. After six years of proposing, marries her in 1850. Fatally wounded in the Civil War, he dies from stubbornness. No children, but Lacey Rose Langley Nightingale was named after him.
On Scene in: HEARTS STOLEN, HOPE REBORN, JUST KIN
Mention in: SINS OF THE MOTHERS, DAUGHTERS OF THE HEART, AT LIBERTY TO LOVE

~ Shriver, PAULEEN a Wealthy married woman and avid reader of dime romances, befriended Charley on his search for Lacey
Mention in: JUST KIN

~ Wheeler, Caleb – born August 29, 1828, cousin to John and Lanelle, partners in the Mercantile in San Francisco after eloping with Mary Rachel Buckmeyer in 1851, father of Susannah.
On Scene in: HOPE REBORN, SINS OF THE MOTHER
~ Wheeler, John – born April 17, 1825, Lanelle's brother, Caleb's cousin, partner in San Francisco Mercantile.
On Scene in: SINS OF THE MOTHER

~ Wheeler, Susannah "SUSIE" – born October, 1851 in San Francisco to Mary Rachel (father Caleb deceased)
On Scene in: SINS OF THE MOTHERS
Mention in: DAUGHTERS OF THE HEART, AT LIBERTY TO LOVE, COVERING LOVE

Mighty to Save

Chapter One

Short of the door, Evelyn paused. "Dear Lord, could she be a little bit better? For sure and for certain, please don't let her die." Filling her lungs, she marched into the hospital room then stopped cold.

An elderly black woman sipped from a steaming porcelain cup, sitting next to a freshly made, crisp, empty bed. "Oh, I'm sorry, ma'am. I must have the wrong room."

The lady glanced over and smiled. "You Evelyn Nightingale, dear?"

How could she know her name? "Why, yes, ma'am. I am. I'm here to visit Miss Ann. Where is she? I hope she didn't . . ."

"Why, Ann Lacy's gone home, dear."

But Evelyn had never doubted, not once. She'd had such faith, been so certain. Her heart sank. "Home . . . as in Heaven?"

"No, no, not at all, sugar. The world wouldn't be as bright without Ann Lacy Ellison in it. I meant home to her house." Sitting her cup into its saucer, the lady extended her hand. "I'm Pearl, dear. Pearl Harris, and it is my blessed pleasure to meet you, Evelyn. I've heard so much about you, honey."

The sweet, faint fragrance of rosewater wafted with the woman's movement. Evelyn took Pearl's hand in her left then covered it with her right. "So what happened, Miss Pearl? Miss Ann was still so sick just yesterday."

"A miracle, that's what." The elder lady laughed. "Why, that precious sister-in-the-Lord left this place healthy as a horse. Practically skipped out."

"Praise the Lord!"

"Can't do much anymore, but I can mind the sick of an evening. Ann Lacy and I've been friends more than forty years, and she told me all about you praying for her and anointing those nasty ol' boils with oil."

"I couldn't imagine having something so horrible."

"Yes, ma'am, I hear you. Ann shared with me how you asked the Lord to heal her, same way He healed King Hezekiah when Isaiah prayed for him."

"Yes, ma'am. It was my honor. I had the faith He would heal her, but even that is a gift from God."

"Well, He sure did! Dried up all those sores. All that poison is gone, little Sister! The doctor called it unorthodox. Far as I'm concerned though, nothing short of a miracle."

A warmth swept over Evelyn then seeped deep into her soul. "The Lord is mighty to save." Tears welled, ushering in a sob that almost choked her. She sniffed, wiping her cheeks. "He's so good. Mercy! Mis'ess Ellison was so sick and . . ." She laughed. "I thought . . . Why me, Lord? It's Nathaniel—my husband's the Reverend Nathaniel Nightingale, you may have heard of him—anyway; God's definitely given him the gift of healing."

"Course I've heard of your husband. Been in several of his meetings."

With her chin tilted up and her eyes closed, Evelyn spoke directly to her Father. "But then You put it in his heart to sign up for the war, so . . . I only want Your will. Keep my beloved safe in the name of Your Son, Jesus."

Miss Pearl's stirring opened her eyes. The lady stared into the windows of her soul. "Join me, please, Evelyn. I've a favor to ask."

Retrieving the room's other straight-backed visitor's chair, she set it across from her new friend. God was indeed good! "A favor? If I can, of course."

"It's my grandson, John Harris. He's serving in Captain Carpenter's 'A' Company. I'm hoping you'll agree to write your husband and ask him to look in on my boy some. John Robert—well, his mama was a Cambleite, and we Harrises always worshipped with the Methodist, but . . . Denominations aside—"

"Cambleite?"

"Church of Christ. You've never heard that?"

"No, ma'am." She grinned. She'd heard of the staunch beliefs of the Church of Christ folks, but never heard them called that.

"Well, you see dear, I'm not sure about the well-being of John's soul. And with him being so far off . . . way over there in France and all..."

"Consider it done, Miss Pearl! I'll write him this evening and post it tomorrow."

"Wonderful. That's just wonderful. And Ann tells me you're May Meriwether's granddaughter, too? She must have been such a blessing to you growing up."

"Yes, ma'am. MayMee was a wonderful grandma; the only one I ever had, so I loved her extra special."

"She helped you write *Gray Lady Down*, didn't she?"

"Well, she wrote the first half or more, and I helped her, then it ended up that I finished it after she passed on to glory."

"You don't say. Well, I couldn't tell you where she stopped and you started for the life of me. You've definitely got her way with words. Always thought my life would make an interesting story for folks to read . . . how a slave girl became a queen."

Of their own, Evelyn's writer's juices heightened and flowed with an innate interest. She smiled. "A queen?"

"Oh, yes, ma'am. My Julius was a king, all right. That made me his queen. I started life as a slave. He was my young master, except he never treated me that way. Now, his granddaddy? That mean ol' buzzard sold me off for spite. Course, he loved the gold, too. But he hated Julius treating me like a friend, that's what it was all about."

"How awful. How old were you when you got sold?"

"Fourteen—it was right before the war."

Intriguing. Evelyn had four works in progress, but wasn't in love with any of them. A shadow passed and ended her contemplation. She turned her attention toward the door.

A nurse stopped inside the room, grinning. "Isn't it wonderful about Mis'ess Ellison? We were thinking maybe you might pray for some of our other patients."

"Of course." Evelyn stood then extended her hand. "Care to join me, Miss Pearl?"

Pearl prayed with the young lady for those who the nurse said requested a visit, but no miracles ensued—at least not any instant ones. Maybe by the next morning . . . like Ann. Poor Evelyn. Apparent disappointment stole the sparkle from her eyes.

Perhaps the girl's even equaled her own.

In the hall after the last supplicant, Pearl slipped her hand into her new friend's. "Coffee? The café across the street makes a delicious buttermilk pie."

Glancing at the big clock hanging in the hall, the young woman nodded. "Sure, I've still got time; and especially yes if you promise to tell me about getting sold. I can't even begin to imagine such a horror."

"I'd love nothing better. Truly was a horrible day."

Took her half a piece of lemon meringue pie and two cups of black coffee to get to that heinous day, but to her credit, Evelyn didn't try to rush the story, like most.

"So anyway, I'm helping boil the wash. I stirred the clothes with a big paddle. That's when old man Harris came around the mansion with a rough-looking white trash of a man. Two giant slaves flanked him. My Julius was upstairs reading. I know, on account that's what he always did until my chores were finished."

A muffled scream wove itself into the Latin text that passed before Jules' eyes on the stage of his mind. The Roman General, in his scarlet cloak, galloped into the breach.

A naked wail shattered the morning. Putting the great man's narrative aside, he rushed to the balcony's rail, shielding his eyes from the sun's brightness.

Two Negroes, both bigger than any his grandfather owned, dragged his Pearl toward a wagon full of manacled darkies.

He flew from his room and down the stairs. His mother stood in the doorway with her arms folded across her bosom. Her eyes, set hard as granite, stopped him cold.

"Mother, get out of my way."

"Go back to your room, Jules."

Tears formed. She was worse than her father, but there was no time to argue. Without another word, he pushed past her and sprinted toward the side yard.

His maternal grandfather and a man he'd never seen before stood by the wagon's team and chatted while the larger of the Negroes lifted his love toward the waiting hands of a catcher in the wagon. She kicked and struggled like he'd never seen her fight.

Fifteen paces from his goal, the old man turned toward him. "Jules, no." He held up a hand as if that'd be ample to stop him. Jules swerved out of his reach and launched himself toward Pearl's abductor.

His shoulder caught the giant in the back and knocked him against the sideboard. The man dropped her, and she scrambled under the wagon. Jules righted himself, raised both fists, then faced his grandfather.

No one moved.

The old man pulled out his pocket watch and studied it a moment. "Well, boy, you've got more spunk than I figured, but you're a fool if you think you can keep me from selling that nigger."

Maybe he was a fool, but what did it matter? He loved her, loved her with everything in him. Right or wrong, whatever anyone said, he loved her. "Then sell her to me. I've got money."

A haughty chuckle boiled Jules' blood.

"No, boy, I own you and the few dollars your worthless pappy left. Now quit your foolishness and get back to the house."

The tears returned and trickled down his cheeks. "You best kill me then. I'll not let her go." He moved his fists in tight, daring circles.

His grandfather threw a nod over Jules shoulder. Vice-like hands grabbed him from above, lifted him into the wagon, then pinned both his arms with a bear hug.

Quick as a cat, the giant dropped to one knee and yanked Pearl from under the buckboard. Amidst her wails, he herded her around toward the back of the wagon.

Jules stomped the heel of his boot onto the bare foot of the black man holding him, then wiggled a hand free. He spun around and flailed at his captor.

The fieldhands already in the wagon shied back. Their chains clanged against the wooden floorboard. Ignoring what had to be broken bones in his foot, the slavetrader's man grabbed his hand mid-air then turned him toward the back of the wagon.

"She be bought and paid for. Ussins aim to take her, so best stop your fighting 'fore I's hurts ya." The words—whispered into Jules' ear—chilled him to the bone. Not because he feared the man, but because he spoke the truth.

Pearl swung her outstretched arms and legs wildly and screamed like she'd been burnt with a whiskey rod, but the giant chained each ankle as though her blows and bellowing were an everyday affair.

The man holding Jules picked him up then jumped off the wagon. He landed on his feet like he did that every day, too, and twice on Sundays. Then without word or warning, he rolled Jules to the ground face down and held him there with his bare foot.

"Don't you dare hurt him." His mother came storming out into the yard.

Pearl's wails turned to resigned sobs. The old man's leather sole replaced the bare foot and pressed hard against Jules' back. Too soon, wood creaked and leather slapped horse hide. He raised his head as much as he could.

The wagon pulled away with Pearl flanked by field hands and house niggers.

She strained against her shackles and held out her arms. "Jules! Don't let them take me! Help me, Jules."

Oh, Pearl. His sweet Pearl. He pushed against the weight on his back.

"Hold still, boy." The old man's voice held no compassion.

"Let me up." Jules struggled more and, pushed harder, but the pressure only increased. Rustling petticoats grew nearer, then his mother's small hands on his cheek drained some of his fight.

"For goodness sake, let him up, Father."

The boot lifted. Jules struggled to his knees. She wrapped her arms around his shoulder and bent to his ear. "Don't do anything stupid, Son. That girl is not worth it."

He glared. "Not worth it? How can you say that? Pearl's worth everything to me. I love her, Mother."

She reeled back, obviously cut by his words. "Good heaven's above, Son. Don't you ever say a thing like that! Why . . . Why . . . you couldn't. You can't. Even though her skin is light, she's still a Nigra." She moved toward him, but Jules stood and stepped backwards.

"Son, you're only seventeen. I know you've known little Pearl long as you can remember, and it's wholly understandable to . . . to . . . care for her. Yes, you may certainly care for the girl. There's nothing wrong with caring. Why, just take my Pal. I cared so very much for that dog that when he died, I thought I would cry myself dry. But love? Son, you don't know what that is."

How could Jules respond? How could she compare Pearl to a dog? She was the one who didn't know about love. Only married his father for his cattle to save the plantation and keep it in the family.

The old man, now surrounded by his overseer and a trio of Live Oaks' field hands, shook his head. "Enough of this nonsense, boy. Get to your room 'fore we put you there."

The wagon made the corner at the bottom of the hill where the big house sat. Jules could barely make out her ivory skin in the sea of ebony.

At least there seemed no further struggle. She must be so scared, but smart enough to have realized, there was nothing more to do. At least for the moment.

"Curse you, old man. If my father was still alive—"

The back of his grandfather's hand smashed into Jules' mouth. He reeled.

"Well, he ain't, and you will do what I say. Now get to your room and stay there."

Jules' fists clinched, but a physical contest with the heartless brute, even if he got in the first lick, would be like a fight between a mountain lion and a house cat. He stepped away then turned and ran to his room like a whipped piccaninny.

Evelyn waited for more of the story, but the old woman looked off like she had lost herself in her past. "Miss Pearl?"

The ex-slave focused then smiled. "Where was I?"

"For sure and for certain, I want to hear the rest of this story. And I'd love to write it—if you'll let me, that is. But I've got to go right now. When can we get together again?"

The lady's lips spread wide, erasing half the wrinkles of her cream-colored skin. "Child, I'd love nothing better than to see my and Jules' story in print. Let's visit next when it's best for you. Other than sitting with the sick, I'm free."

She stood and extended her hand. "Tomorrow then. Is noon good? We can talk over dinner—my treat."

"Yes, ma'am. Noon it is."

Evelyn paid the check then hurried out. Bless the Lord! What a well-named gem the Lord sent her in Miss Pearl.

Could tomorrow come soon enough?

Be watching for the debut of *Mighty to Save,* coming in May, 2017.

Reach out to the author!...

Website   http://www.CarylMcAdoo.com

Newsletter   http://tinyurl.com/TheCaryler
                 (Get FREE books for subscribing!)
Reviewers   http://carylmcadoo.com/christian-evaluaters
                 (Join Caryl's Street Team!)
YouTube   *(Hear Caryl sing her New Songs!)*
https://www.youtube.com/channel/UC_1hQx6UZbWi3OYwmKK
xh6Q
Blog   http://www.CarylMcAdoo.blogspot.com
                 Heart"wings" Blog

Facebook   www.facebook.com/CarylMcAdoo.author

Twitter   http://www.twitter.com/CarylMcAdoo

GoodReads   http://tinyurl.com/GoodReadsCaryl

Google+   http://tinyurl.com/CarylsGooglePlus

Pinterest   http://www.pinterest.com/CarylMcAdoo

LinkedIn   www.linkedIn.com/CarylMcAdoo

Author Pages : *(please follow)*
Amazon   http://tinyurl.com/CarylsAmazonAuthorPage

BookBub   https://www.bookbub.com/authors/caryl-mcadoo

Simon & Schuster   http://tinyurl.com/S-SCarylsPage

Email   ComeVisit@CarylMcAdoo.com

Author reaching out to you!

Hey dear Reader!

I am thankful for you? My career is blooming thanks to the Lord and YOU! I always pray my story gives God glory and hope you enjoy everyone! My desire is that each novel brings you closer to Him and gives you scriptural principles and issues to ponder, asking for God's perspective.

I need your help. You can help me spread the word of these Kingdom books! First, if you want to stay on top of all my book news (debuts, sales, awards), please subscribe *The Caryler*, my quarterly newsletter. I try to make it fun with a Scripture and lyric and a few of my favorite things.

And speaking of lyrics, I'm so blessed that God gives me new songs! There's nothing I love more than praising and worshiping Him in song which lends to being called the Singing Pray-er. Now you can hear the new songs! Listen at my YouTube channel! And please subscribe while you're there! Don't miss any new songs!

If you enjoy my story, it'll be a big boon if you could take the time to review it at Amazon, Goodreads, your blog, and anywhere you enjoy reading about books. And click "Follow" under my picture while you're at Amazon and GoodReads. ☺ Of course, tell your friends, too. Word of mouth is invaluable! Follw me at BookBub, too!

I love hearing from and visiting with my readers, and have a group of special readers who help me even a little more than most. Let me know if you'd like to join my Christian eVALUaters, my review crew and top fans.

Stop by my Facebook page, too! Just search Caryl McAdoo. And last but never least, I pray that God will bless you as you have blessed me, that He will give you favor in everything you do!

Love in Christ and many blessings,

Caryl

A few links Others might find helpful:

Needing help with your online presence? Go to <u>Rocksteady</u> <u>Resolutions</u> for websites, email lists, and all social media assistance. CEO Janis McAdoo (my daughter-in-love) will be the best virtual assistant you could have. Knowledgeable, energetic, brim full of integrity, I promise, she'll be a God-sent blessing to you!

Have a Book you want to Publish? Contact <u>Celebrate Lit</u> <u>Publishing</u>

Subscribe to receive free and low-cost Christian books in your Inbox! <u>The Celebration Reading Room</u>

Facebook groups I love:
<u>Christian Indie Books</u> a great place to find books from new authors posting releases, special sales, and sometimes, even free books!

<u>Christian Indie Authors Readers Group</u> is a great place to visit to meet new authors who post deals and often even free books!

<u>5-Star Reviews of Christian Fiction</u>: Find all the favorites of readers here! Join and post your own reviews of books you love!

Blogs:
<u>Heart"wings" Blog</u> with wonderful daily devotionals that amazingly seem to be exactly what readers need to hear that very day!

<u>Stitches Thru Time</u>

<u>Sweet American Sweethearts</u>

CPSIA information can be obtained
at www.ICGtesting.com
Printed in the USA
LVHW03s1209091018
592959LV00001B/264/P